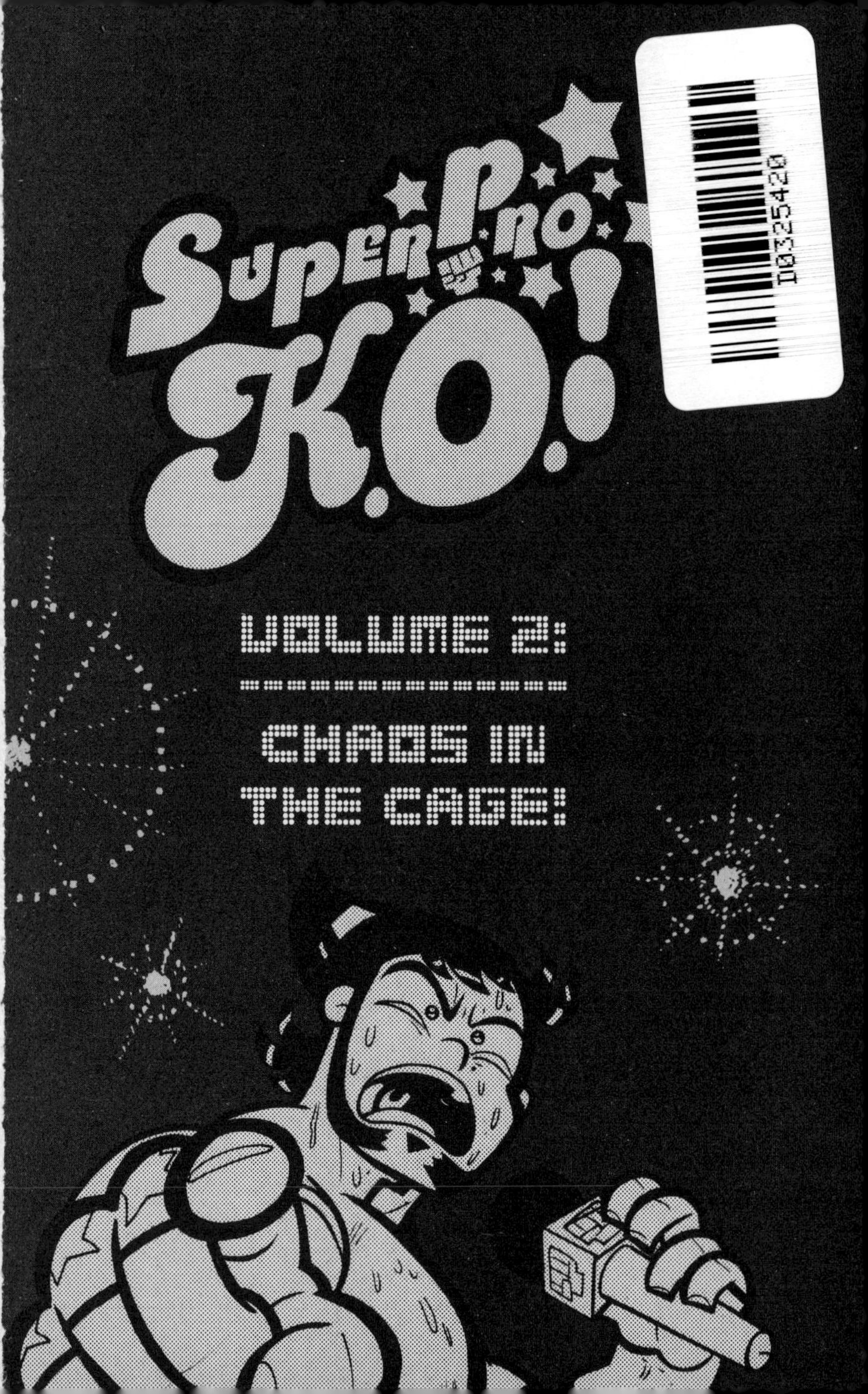
SUPER PRO K.O.!
VOLUME 2:
CHAOS IN THE CAGE!

Published by
Oni Press, Inc.

publisher **Joe Nozemack** ∗ editor in chief **James Lucas Jones**
marketing director **Cory Casoni** ∗ art director **Keith Wood**
operations director **George Rohac** ∗ editor **Jill Beaton**
editor **Charlie Chu** ∗ digital prepress lead **Troy Look**

onipress.com lunarboyland.com

ONI PRESS, INC.
1305 SE Martin Luther King Jr. Blvd.
Suite A
Portland, OR 97214
USA

First edition: November 2011

ISBN: 978-1-934964-51-4

Library of Congress Control Number: 2011906140

1 3 5 7 9 10 8 6 4 2

Printed in the U.S.A.

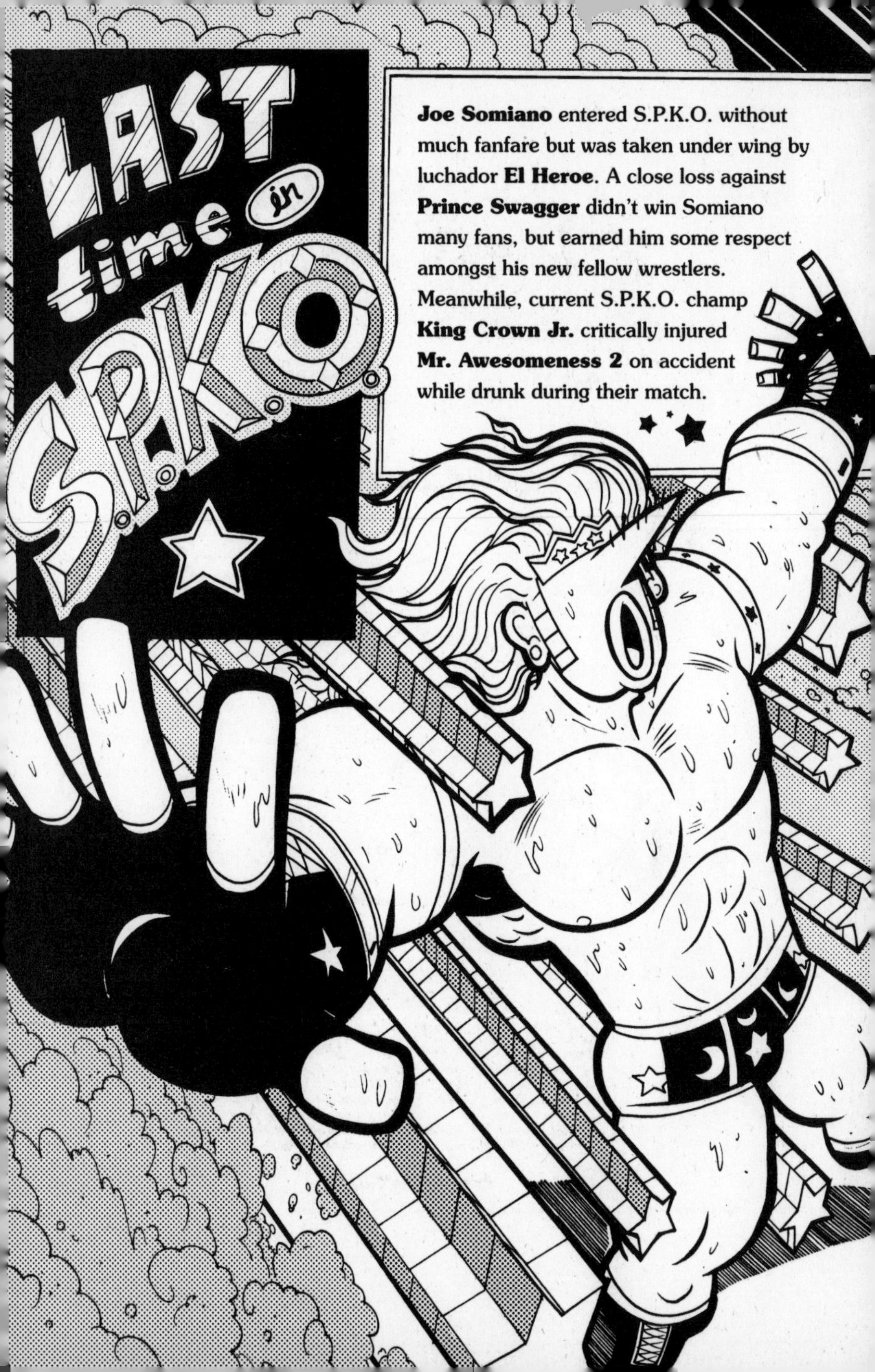
LAST time in S.P.K.O.
Joe Somiano entered S.P.K.O. without much fanfare but was taken under wing by luchador **El Heroe**. A close loss against **Prince Swagger** didn't win Somiano many fans, but earned him some respect amongst his new fellow wrestlers. Meanwhile, current S.P.K.O. champ **King Crown Jr.** critically injured **Mr. Awesomeness 2** on accident while drunk during their match.

SUPER PRO K.O. VOLUME 2: CHAOS IN THE CAGE!

By *Jarrett Williams*

Tones by *Matthew Razzano*

Cover colors by *Dan Jackson*

Design by *Keith Wood*

edited by *Charlie Chu*

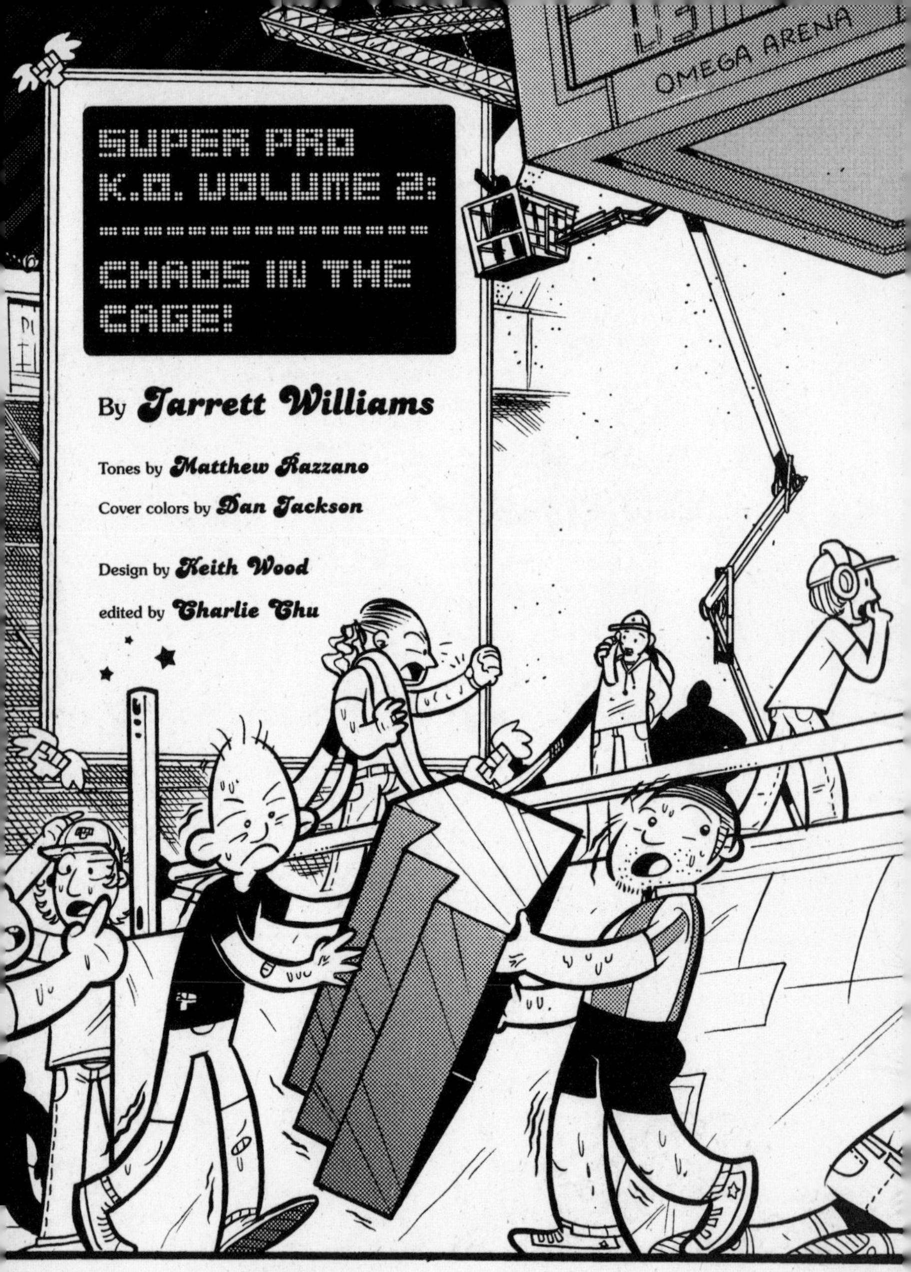
OMEGA ARENA

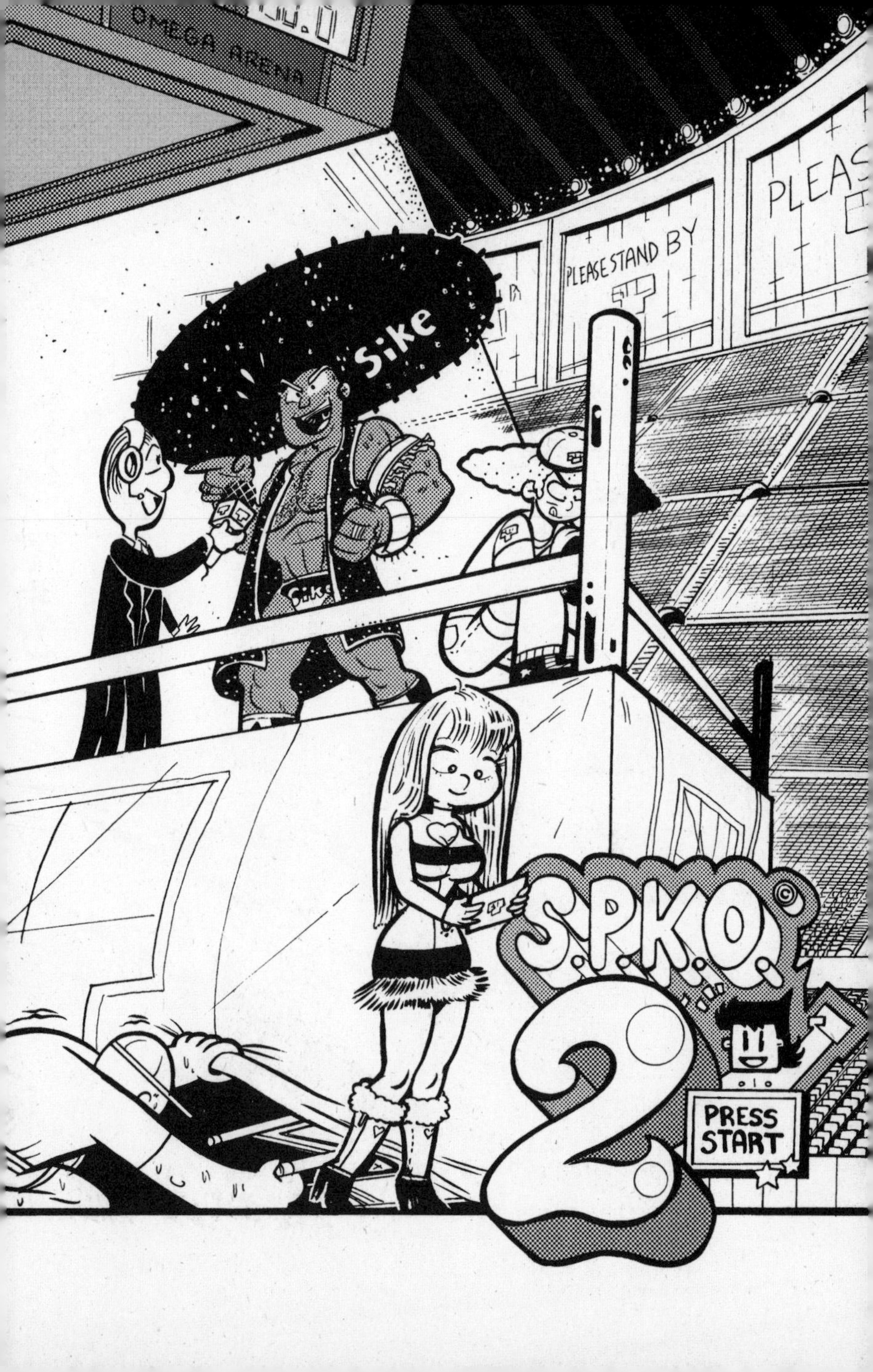
OMEGA ARENA
PLEASE STAND BY
Sike
S.P.K.O.
2
PRESS START

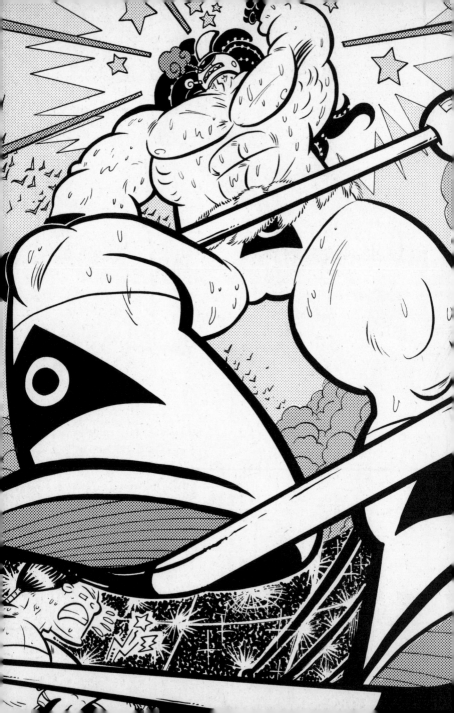

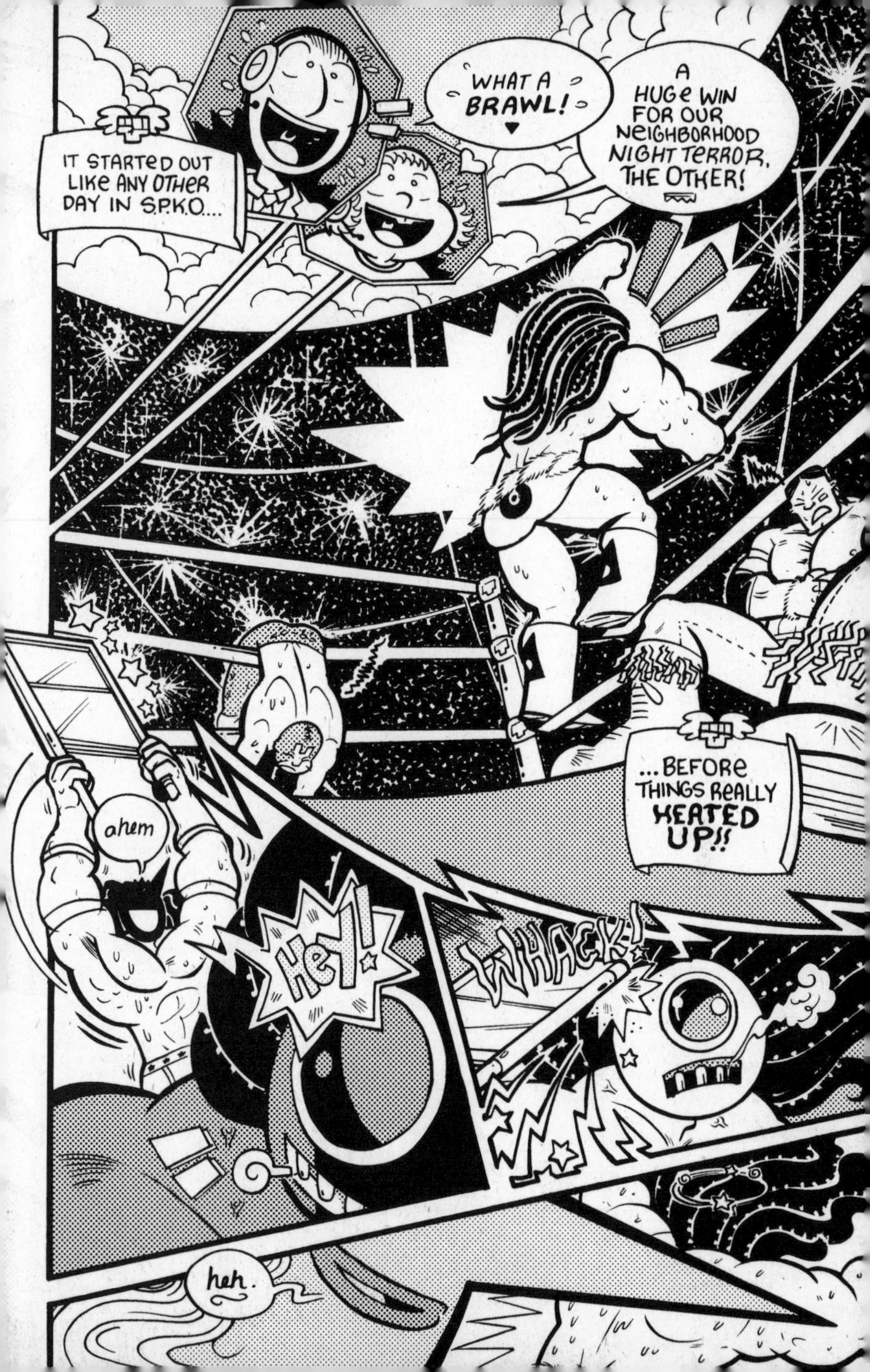
IT STARTED OUT LIKE ANY OTHER DAY IN S.P.K.O....
WHAT A BRAWL!
A HUGE WIN FOR OUR NEIGHBORHOOD NIGHT TERROR, THE OTHER!
...BEFORE THINGS REALLY HEATED UP!!
ahem
HEY!
WHACK!
heh.

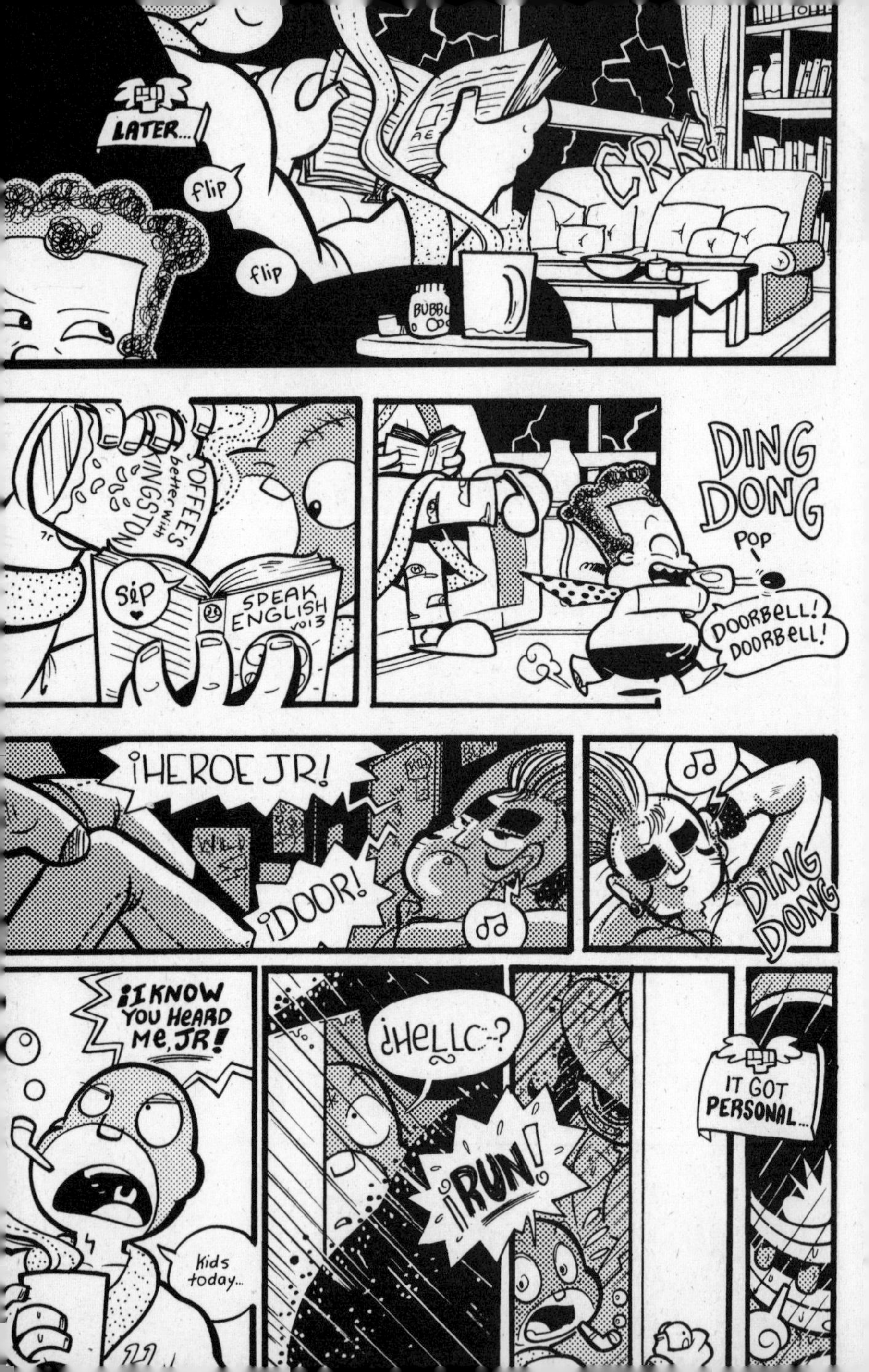
LATER...
flip
flip
CRK!
BUBBL
AE
COFFEE'S better with KINGSTON
SIP
SPEAK ENGLISH vol 3
DING DONG
POP
DOORBELL! DOORBELL!
¡HEROE JR!
¡DOOR!
DING DONG
¡I KNOW YOU HEARD ME, JR!
Kids today...
¿HELLO--?
¡RUN!
IT GOT PERSONAL...

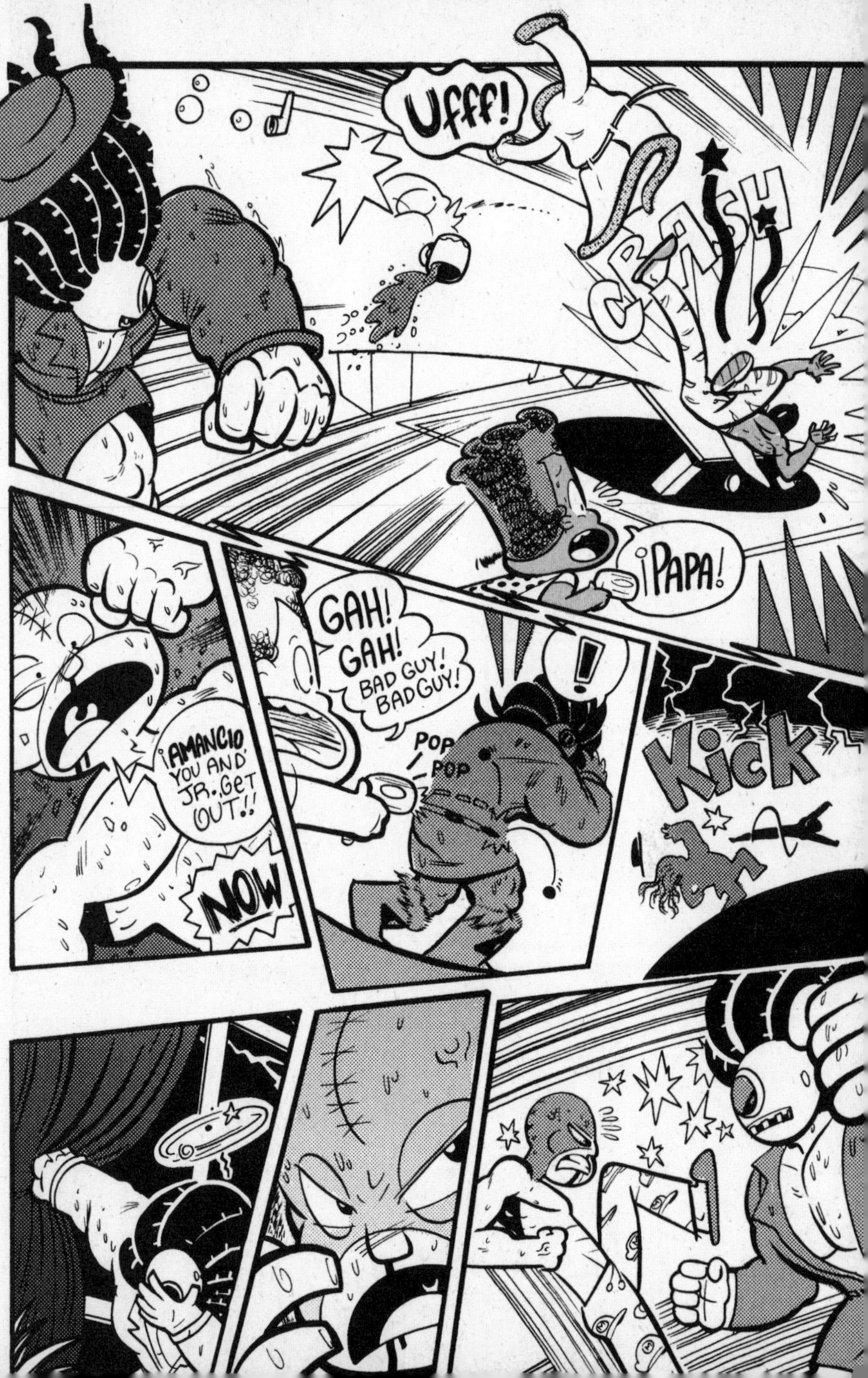

Ufff!
CRASH
¡PAPA!
GAH!
GAH!
BAD GUY!
BAD GUY!
!
¡AMANCIO
YOU AND
JR., GET
OUT!!
NOW
POP
POP
KICK

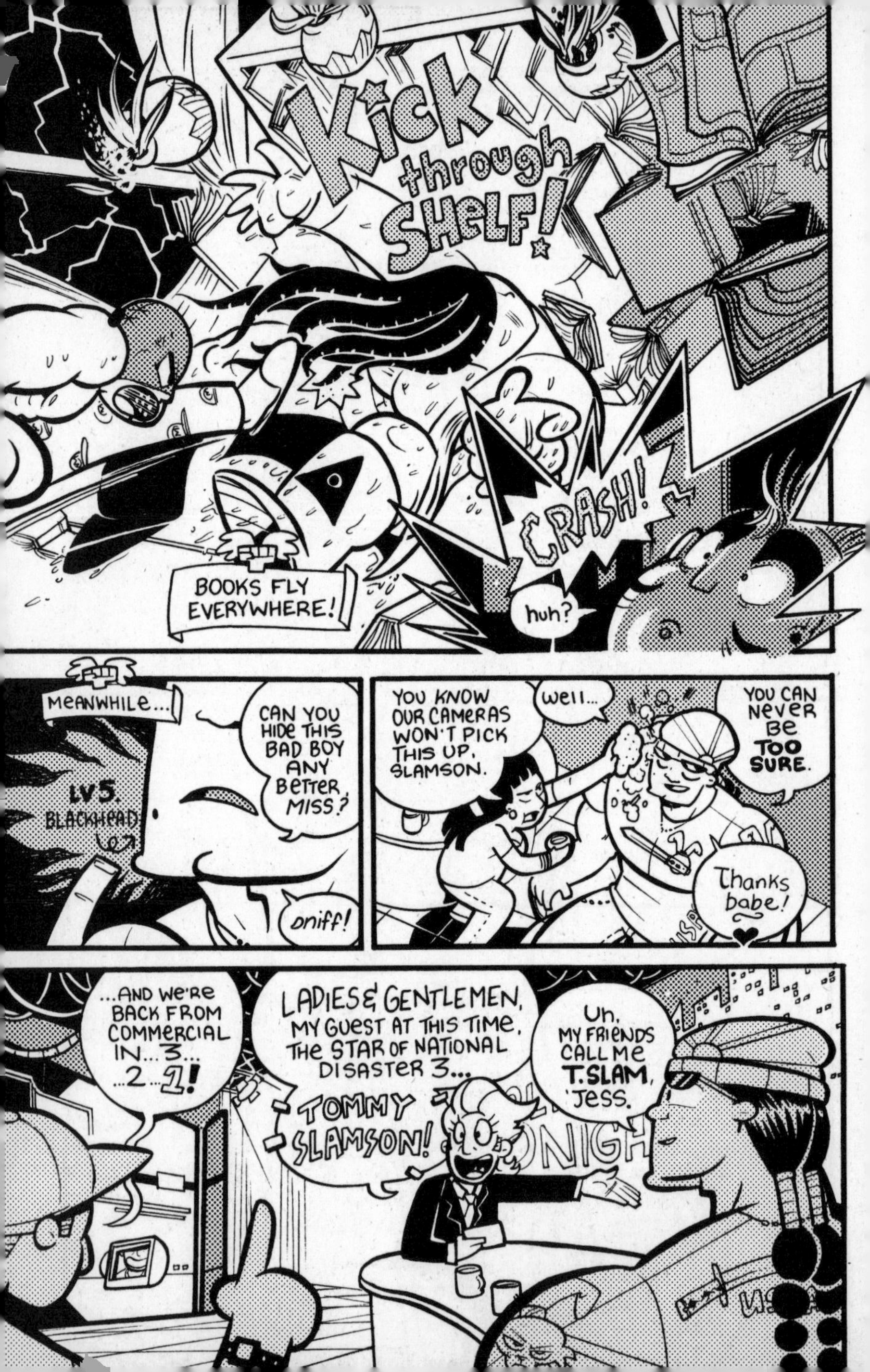
KICK through SHELF!
BOOKS FLY EVERYWHERE!
CRASH!
huh?
MEANWHILE...
LV5. BLACKHEAD
CAN YOU HIDE THIS BAD BOY ANY BETTER, MISS?
sniff!
YOU KNOW OUR CAMERAS WON'T PICK THIS UP, SLAMSON.
well...
YOU CAN NEVER BE TOO SURE.
Thanks babe!
...AND WE'RE BACK FROM COMMERCIAL IN...3... ...2...1!
LADIES & GENTLEMEN, MY GUEST AT THIS TIME, THE STAR OF NATIONAL DISASTER 3... TOMMY SLAMSON!
Uh, MY FRIENDS CALL ME T.SLAM, JESS.

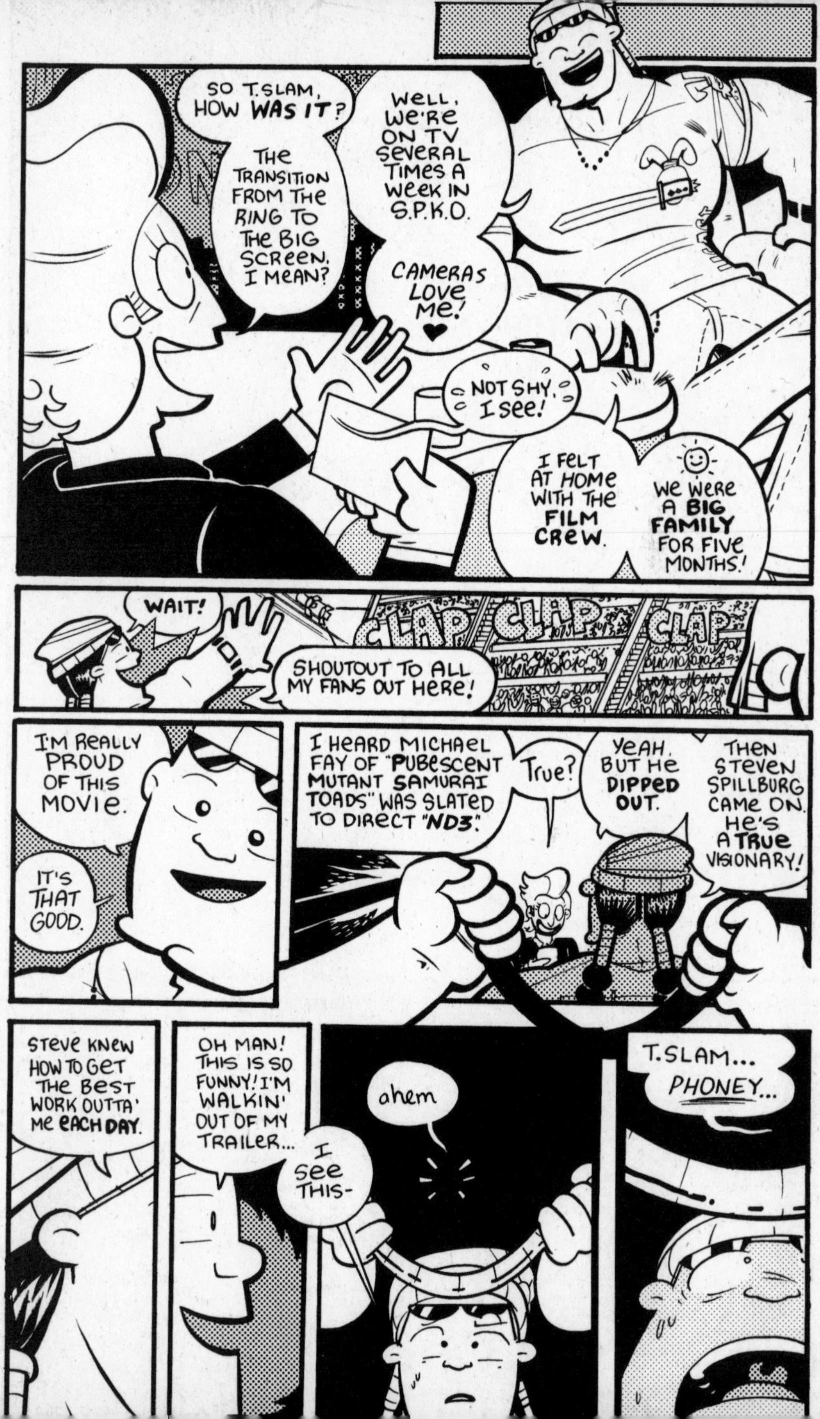
SO T.SLAM, HOW WAS IT?
THE TRANSITION FROM THE RING TO THE BIG SCREEN, I MEAN?
WELL, WE'RE ON TV SEVERAL TIMES A WEEK IN S.P.K.O.
CAMERAS LOVE ME!
NOT SHY, I SEE!
I FELT AT HOME WITH THE FILM CREW.
WE WERE A BIG FAMILY FOR FIVE MONTHS!
WAIT!
CLAP CLAP CLAP
SHOUTOUT TO ALL MY FANS OUT HERE!
I'M REALLY PROUD OF THIS MOVIE.
IT'S THAT GOOD.
I HEARD MICHAEL FAY OF "PUBESCENT MUTANT SAMURAI TOADS" WAS SLATED TO DIRECT "ND3".
True?
YEAH, BUT HE DIPPED OUT.
THEN STEVEN SPILLBURG CAME ON. HE'S A TRUE VISIONARY!
STEVE KNEW HOW TO GET THE BEST WORK OUTTA' ME EACH DAY.
OH MAN! THIS IS SO FUNNY! I'M WALKIN' OUT OF MY TRAILER...
I SEE THIS-
ahem
T.SLAM... PHONEY...

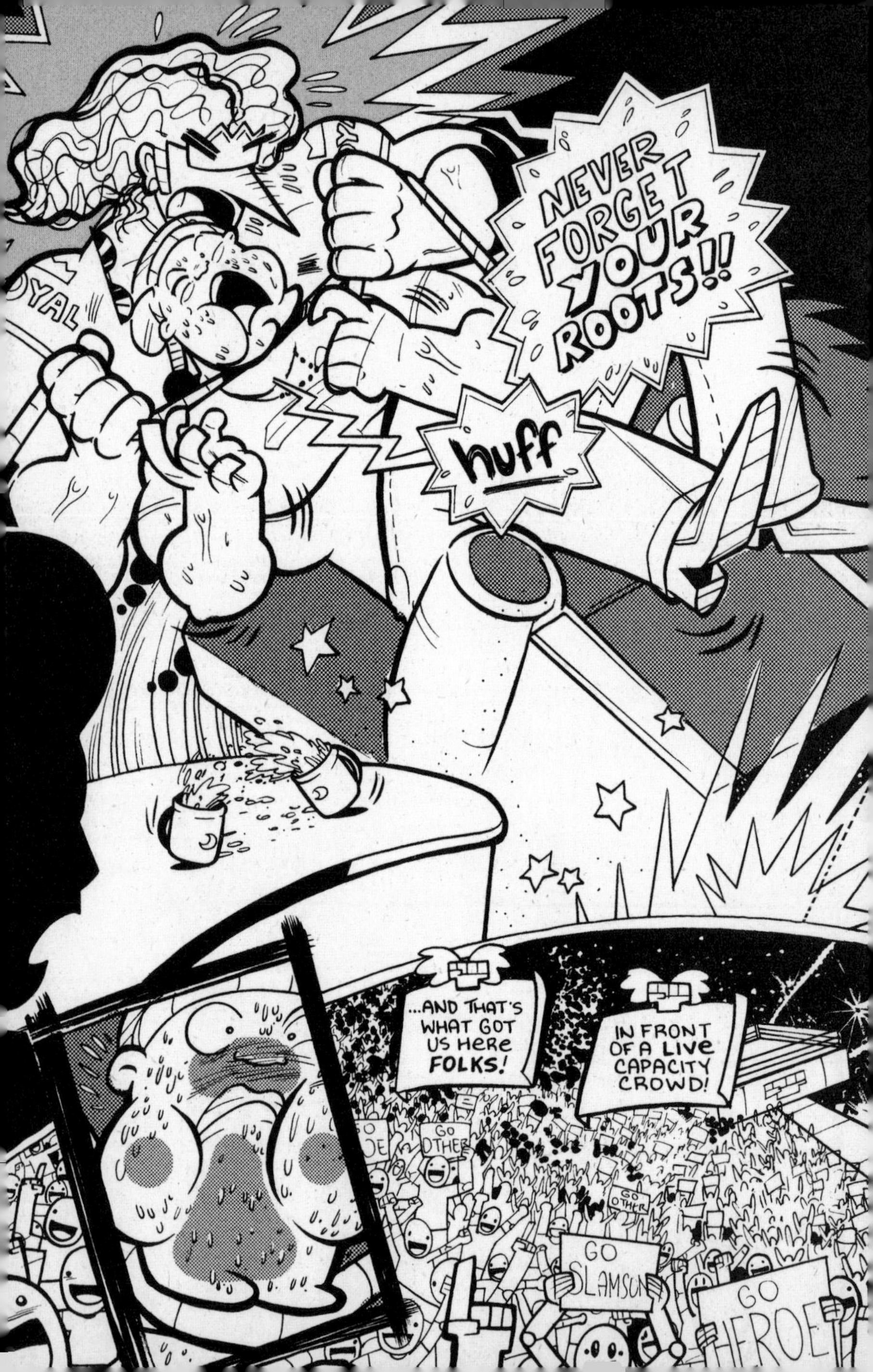
NEVER FORGET YOUR ROOTS!!
huff
...AND THAT'S WHAT GOT US HERE FOLKS!
IN FRONT OF A LIVE CAPACITY CROWD!
GO OTHER
GO OTHER
GO SLAMSON
GO HEROE

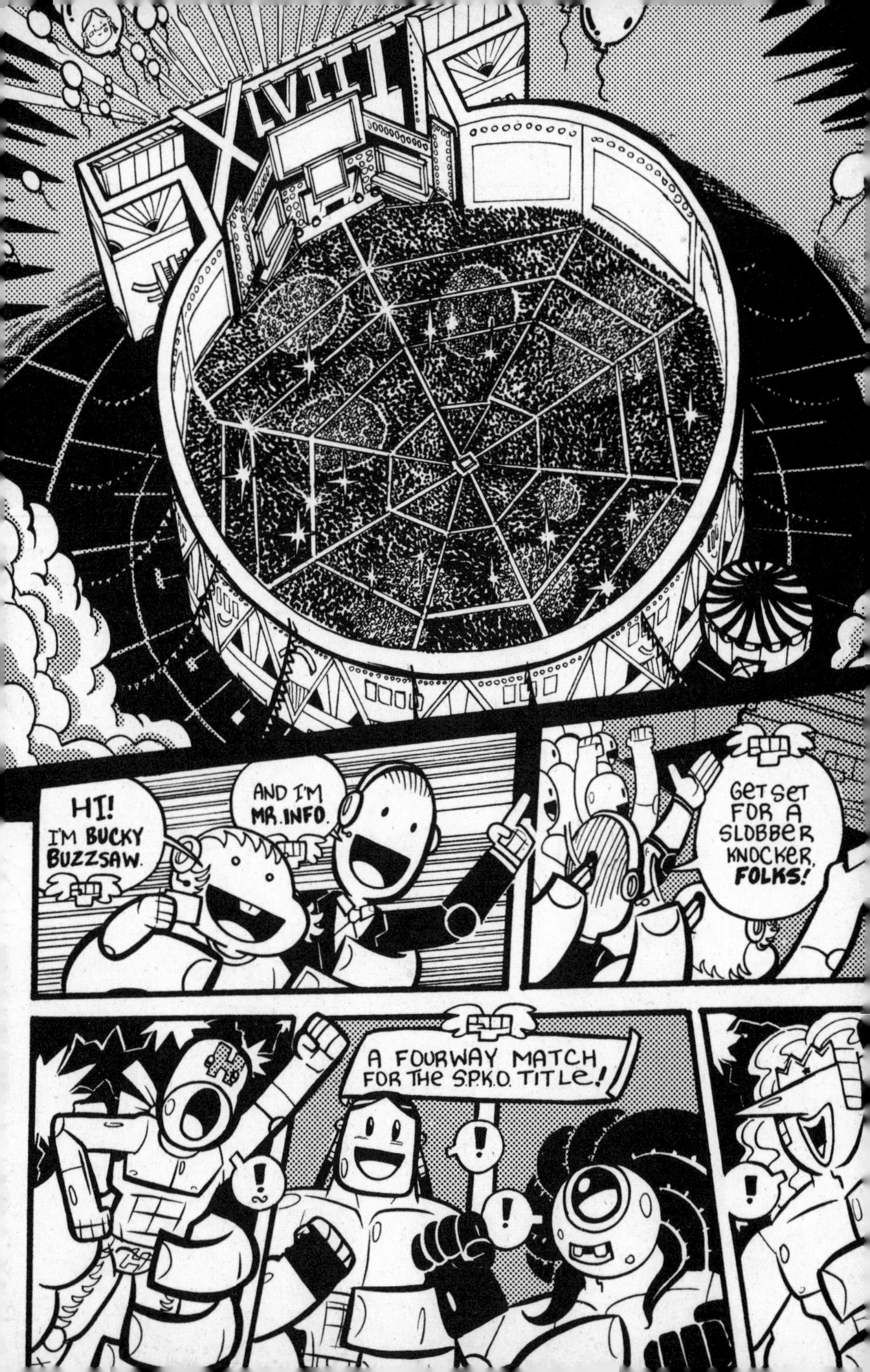
XLVIII
HI! I'M BUCKY BUZZSAW.
AND I'M MR. INFO.
GET SET FOR A SLOBBER KNOCKER, FOLKS!
A FOURWAY MATCH FOR THE S.P.K.O. TITLE!

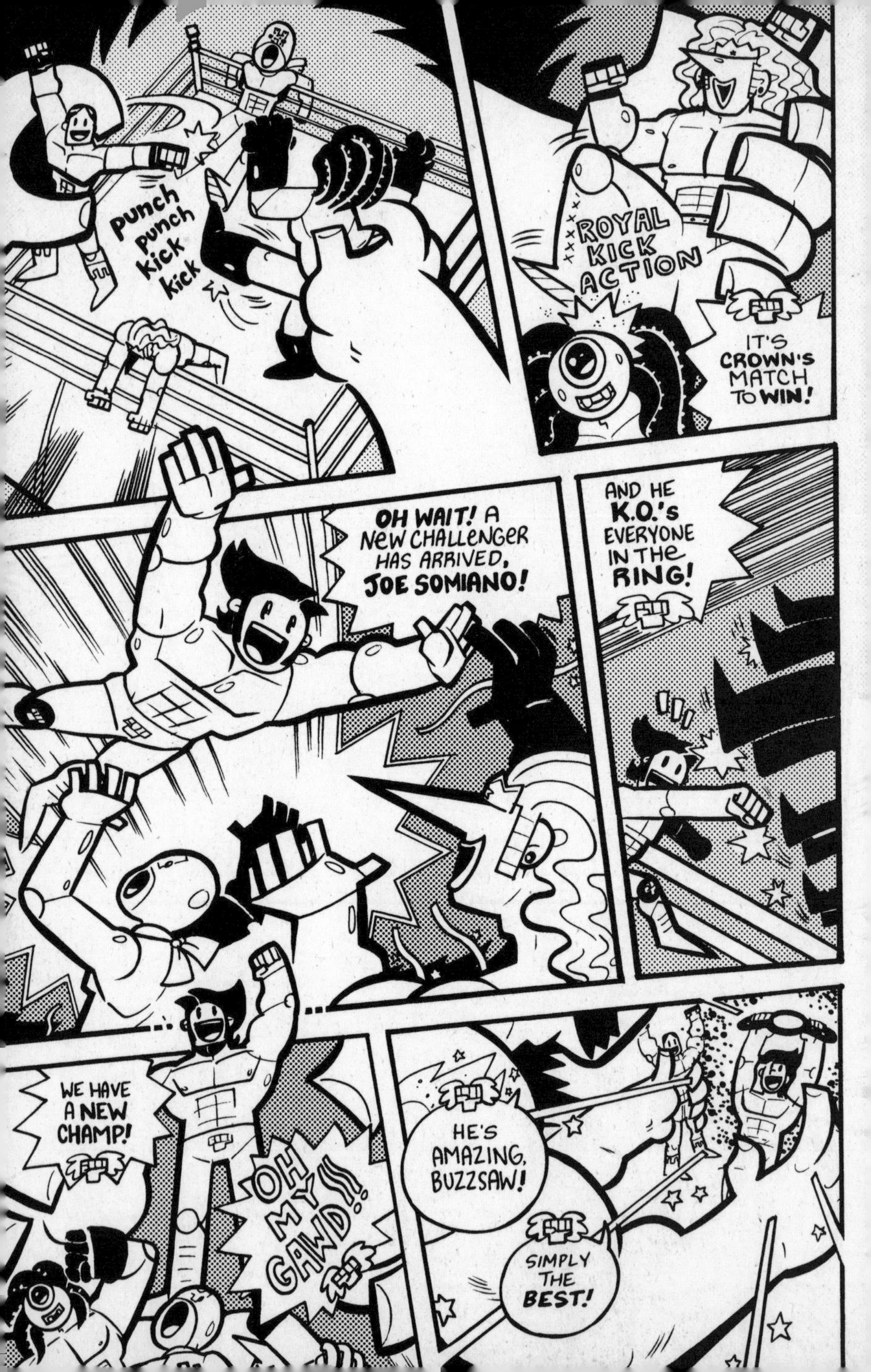
punch punch kick kick
ROYAL KICK ACTION
IT'S CROWN'S MATCH TO WIN!
OH WAIT! A NEW CHALLENGER HAS ARRIVED, JOE SOMIANO!
AND HE K.O.'s EVERYONE IN THE RING!
WE HAVE A NEW CHAMP!
OH MY GAWD!!!
HE'S AMAZING, BUZZSAW!
SIMPLY THE BEST!

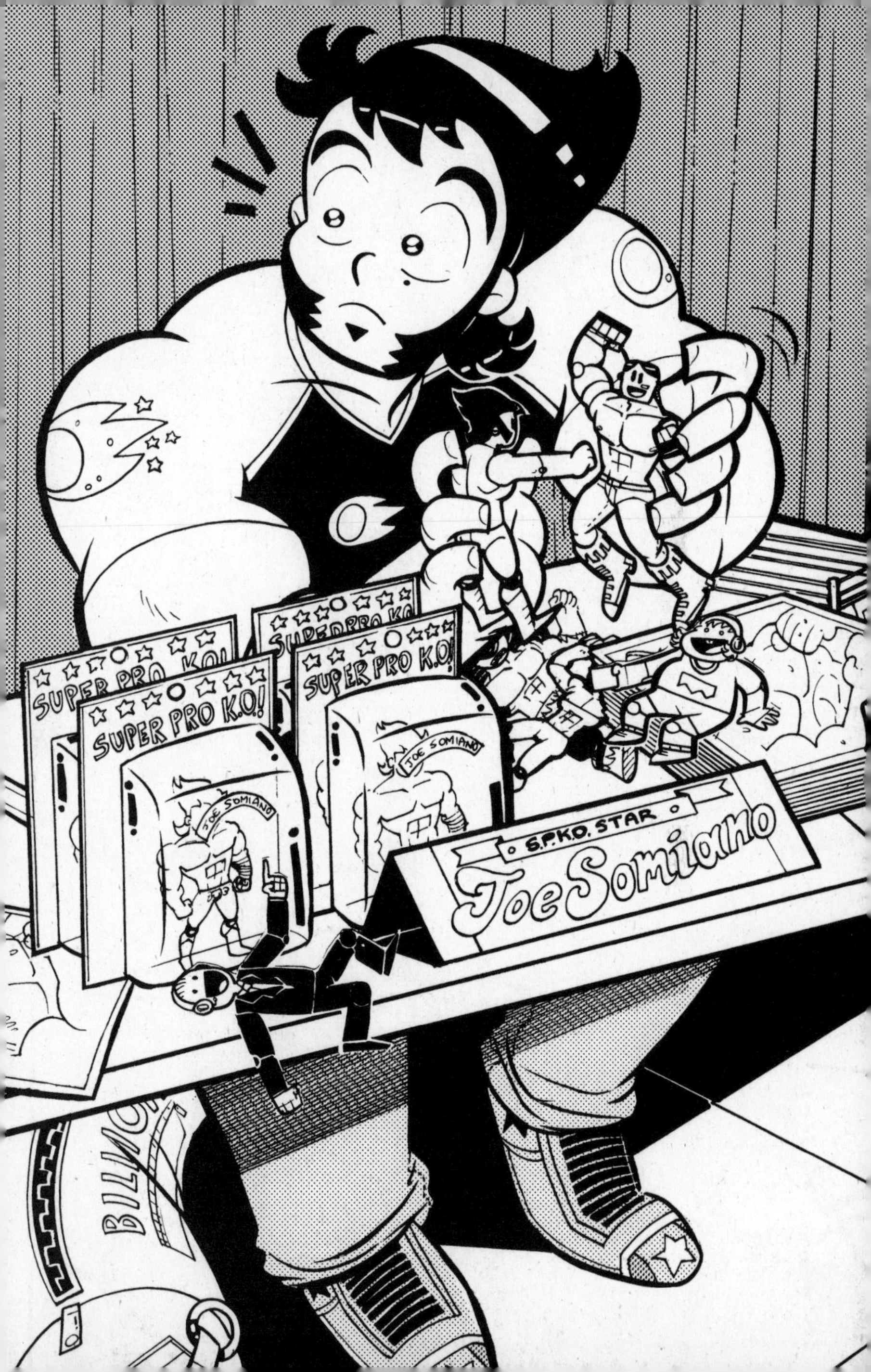
SUPER PRO K.O!
SUPER PRO K.O!
SUPER PRO K.O!
SUPER PRO K.O!
JOE SOMIANO
JOE SOMIANO
JOE SOMIANO
S.P.K.O. STAR
Joe Somiano

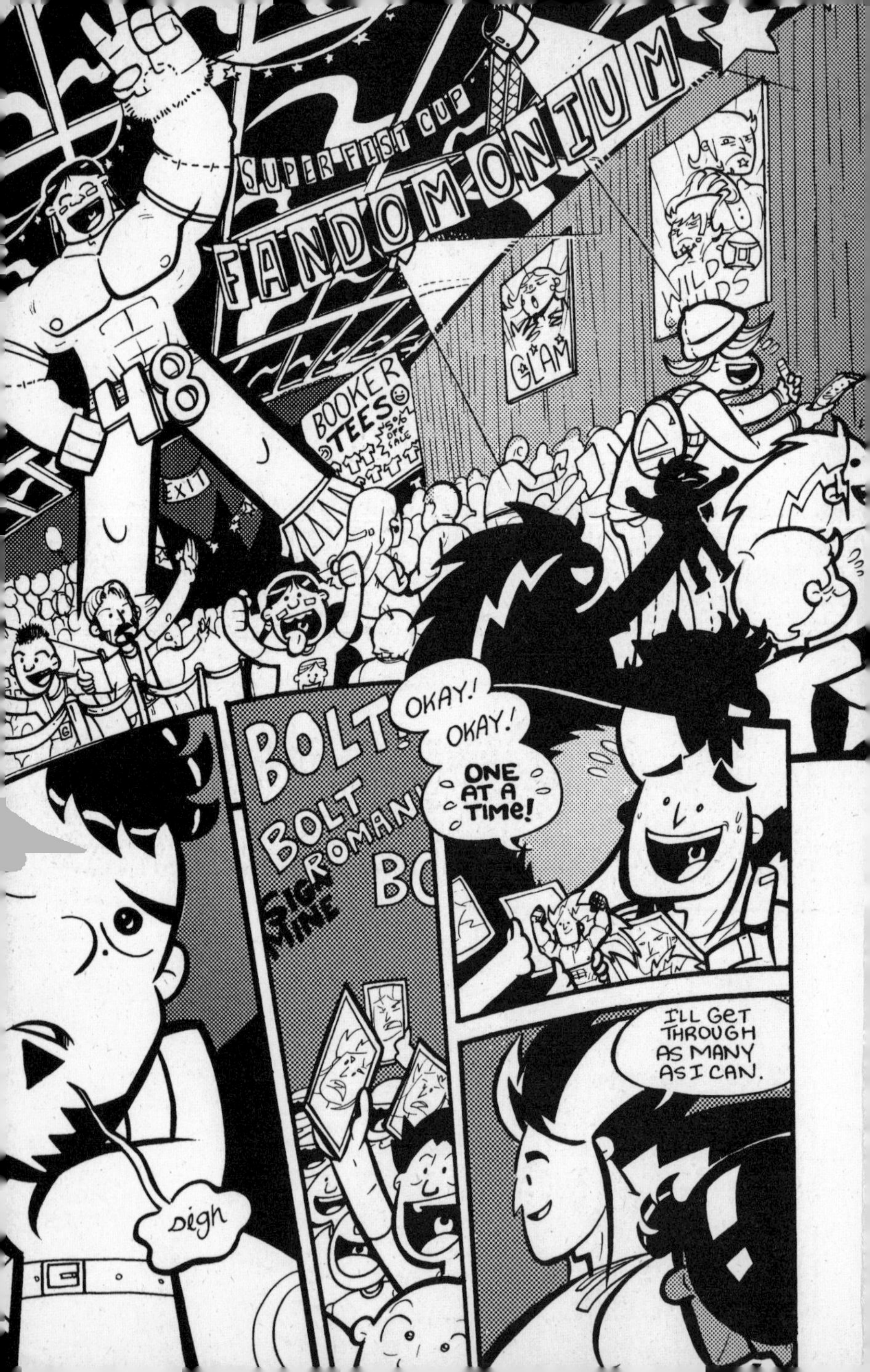
SUPER FIST CUP
FANDOMONIUM
48
BOOKER TEES
5% OFF SALE
EXIT
GLAM
WILD WILDS
BOLT
BOLT ROMAN
BO
SIGN MINE
OKAY! OKAY!
ONE AT A TIME!
I'LL GET THROUGH AS MANY AS I CAN.
sigh

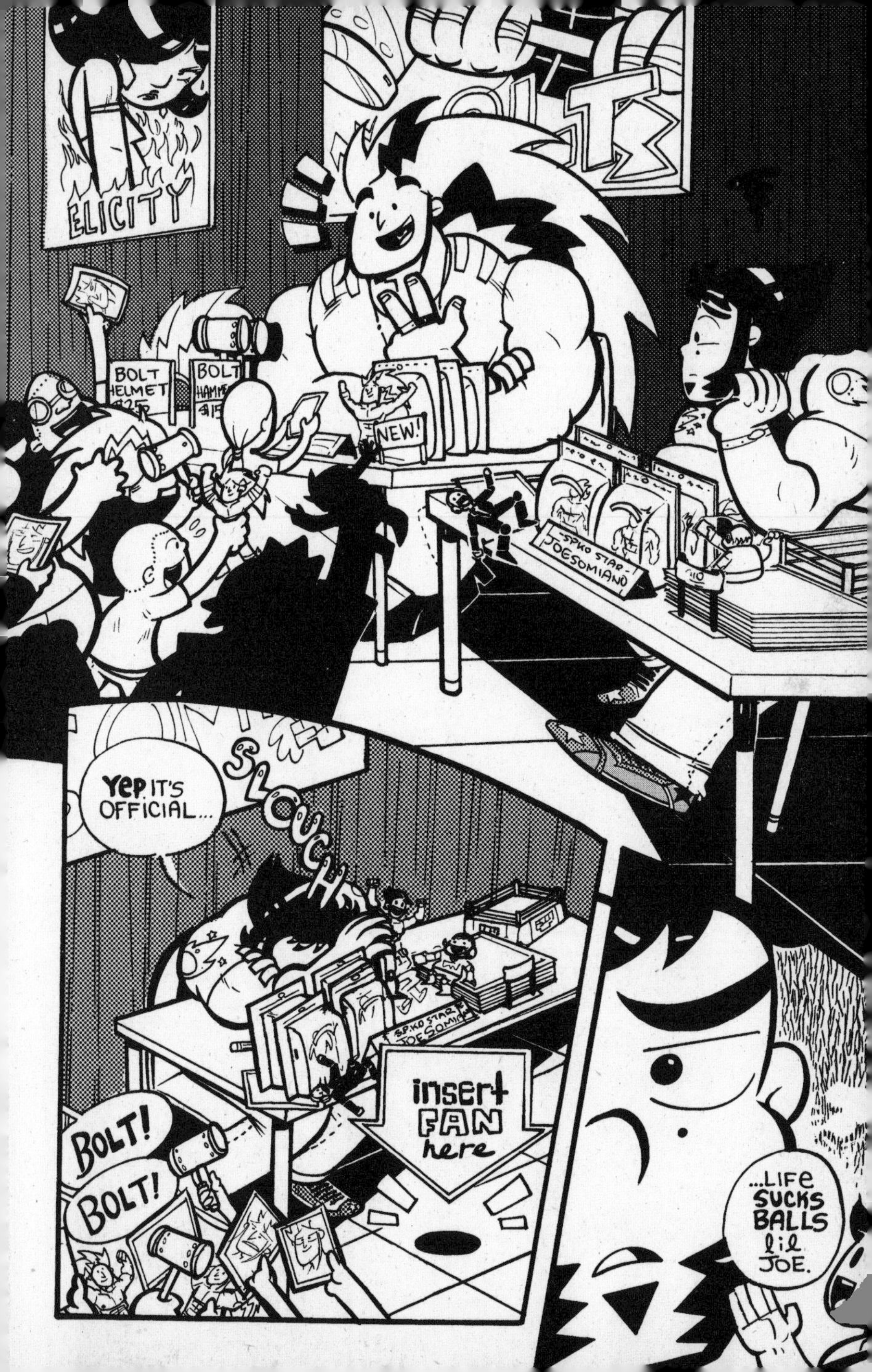
ELICITY
BOLT HELMET $25
BOLT HAMMER $15
NEW!
SPKO STAR JOESOMIANO
YEP IT'S OFFICIAL...
SLOUCH
BOLT!
BOLT!
insert FAN here
...LIFE SUCKS BALLS lil JOE.

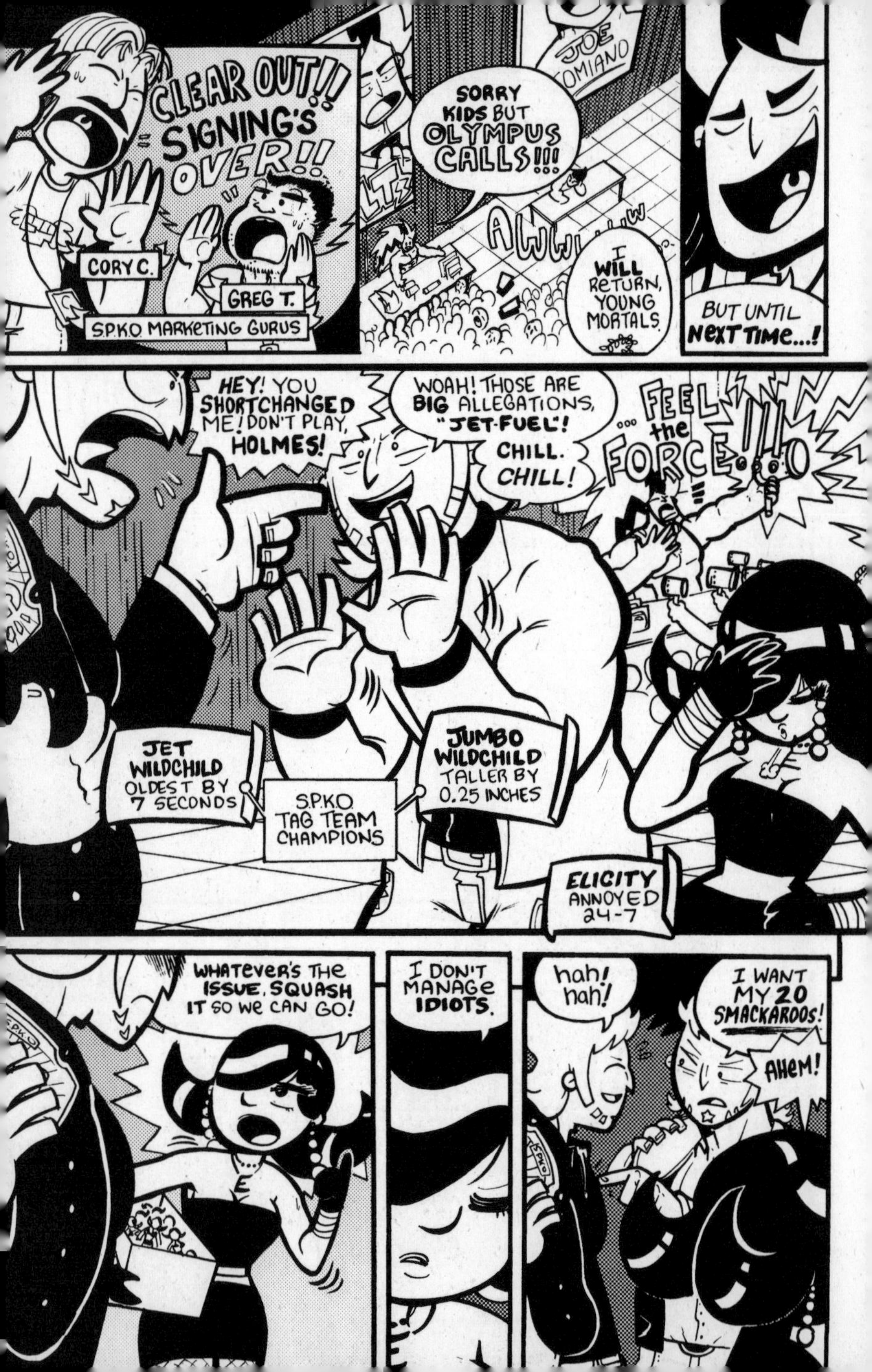
CLEAR OUT!! SIGNING'S OVER!!
CORY C.
GREG T.
S.P.K.O. MARKETING GURUS
JOE ZOMIANO
SORRY KIDS BUT OLYMPUS CALLS!!!
AWWWWW
I WILL RETURN, YOUNG MORTALS.
BUT UNTIL NEXT TIME...!
HEY! YOU SHORTCHANGED ME! DON'T PLAY, HOLMES!
WOAH! THOSE ARE BIG ALLEGATIONS, "JET-FUEL"!
CHILL. CHILL!
... FEEL the FORCE!!!
JET WILDCHILD OLDEST BY 7 SECONDS
S.P.K.O. TAG TEAM CHAMPIONS
JUMBO WILDCHILD TALLER BY 0.25 INCHES
ELICITY ANNOYED 24-7
WHATEVER'S THE ISSUE, SQUASH IT SO WE CAN GO!
I DON'T MANAGE IDIOTS.
hah! hah!
I WANT MY 20 SMACKAROOS!
AHEM!

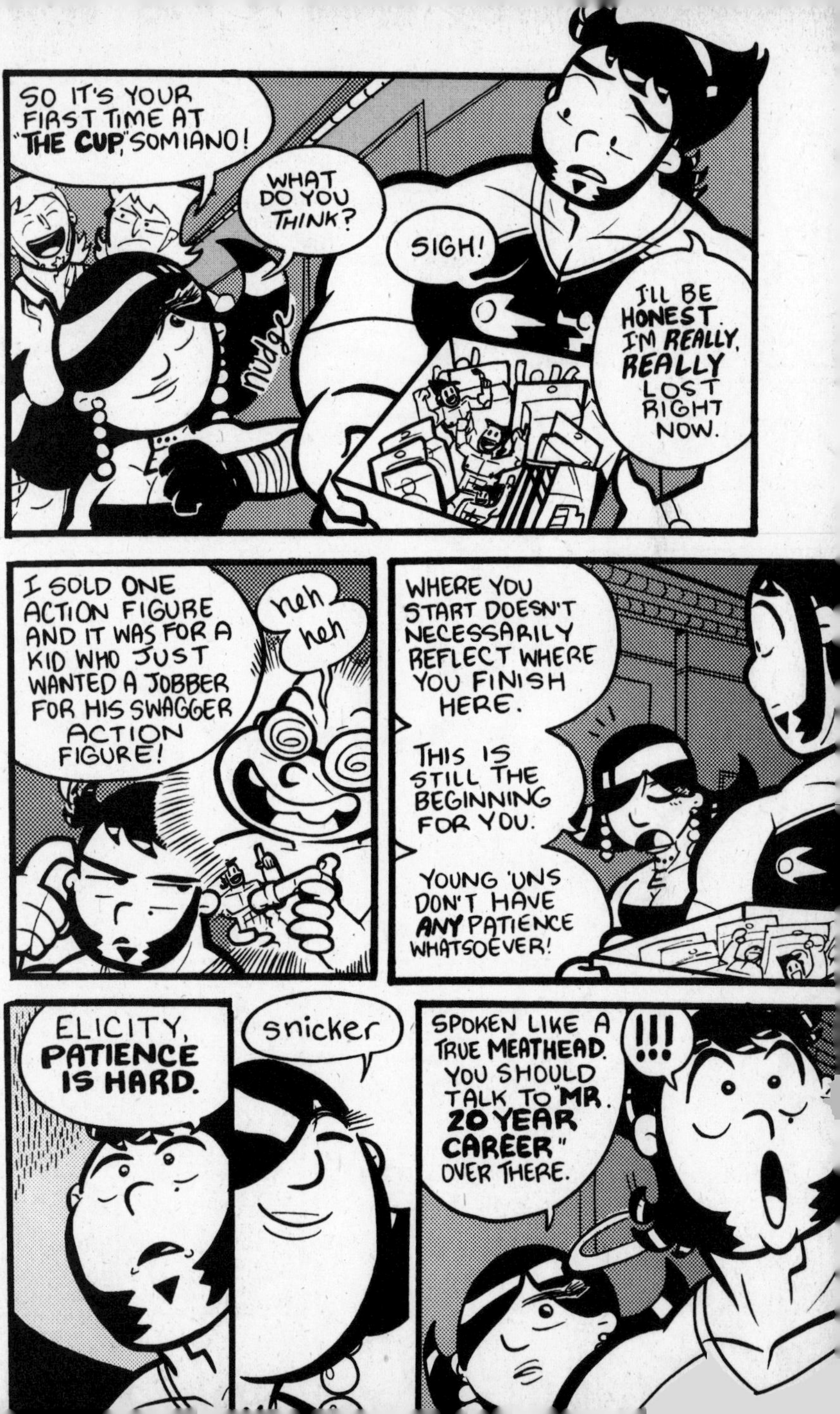
SO IT'S YOUR FIRST TIME AT "THE CUP," SOMIANO!
WHAT DO YOU THINK?
nudge
SIGH!
I'LL BE HONEST. I'M REALLY, REALLY LOST RIGHT NOW.
I SOLD ONE ACTION FIGURE AND IT WAS FOR A KID WHO JUST WANTED A JOBBER FOR HIS SWAGGER ACTION FIGURE!
heh heh
WHERE YOU START DOESN'T NECESSARILY REFLECT WHERE YOU FINISH HERE.
THIS IS STILL THE BEGINNING FOR YOU.
YOUNG 'UNS DON'T HAVE ANY PATIENCE WHATSOEVER!
ELICITY, PATIENCE IS HARD.
snicker
SPOKEN LIKE A TRUE MEATHEAD. YOU SHOULD TALK TO "MR. 20 YEAR CAREER" OVER THERE.
!!!

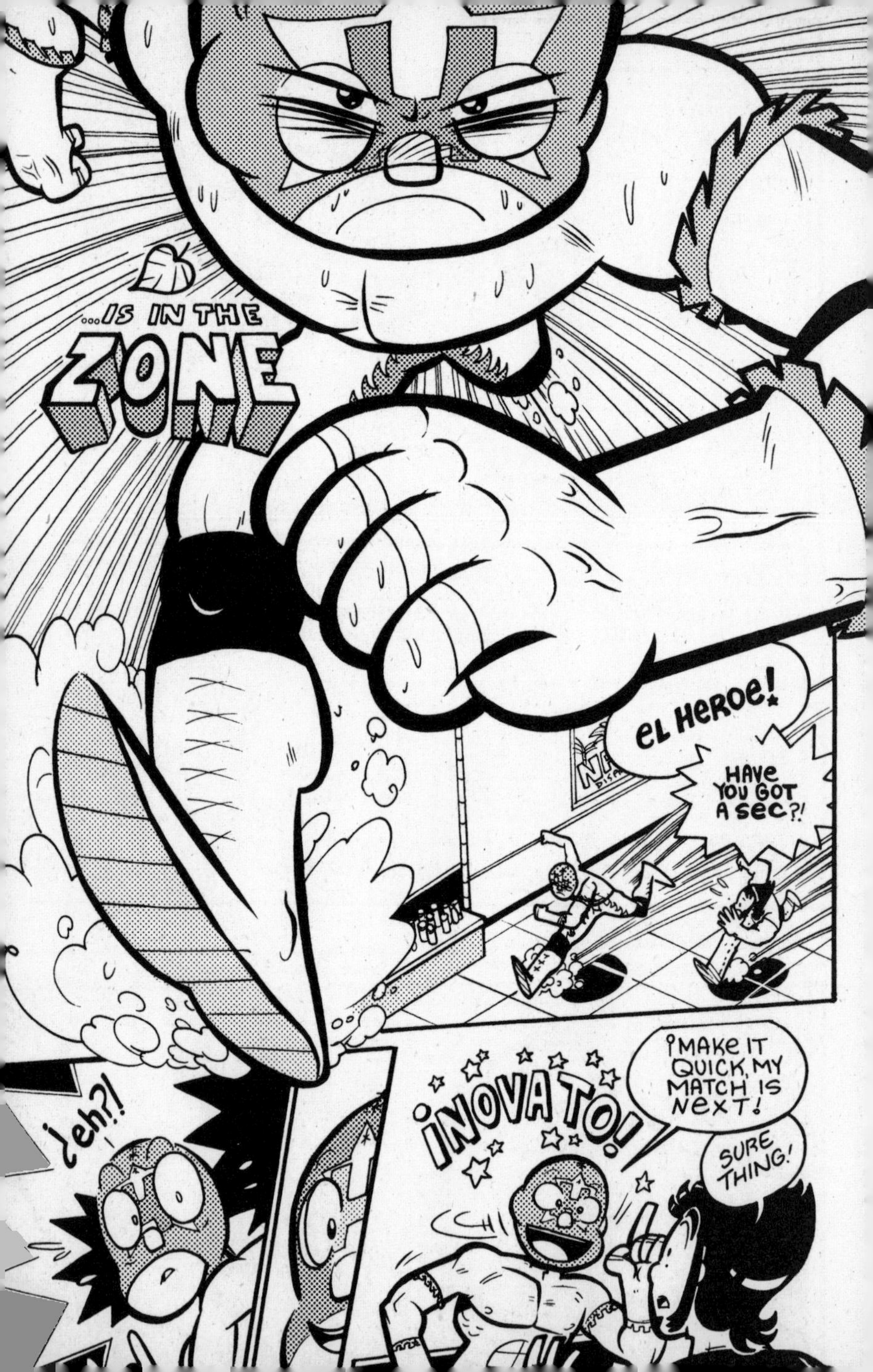
...IS IN THE
ZONE
EL HEROE!
HAVE YOU GOT A SEC?!
¿eh?!
¡NOVATO!
¡MAKE IT QUICK, MY MATCH IS NEXT!
SURE THING!

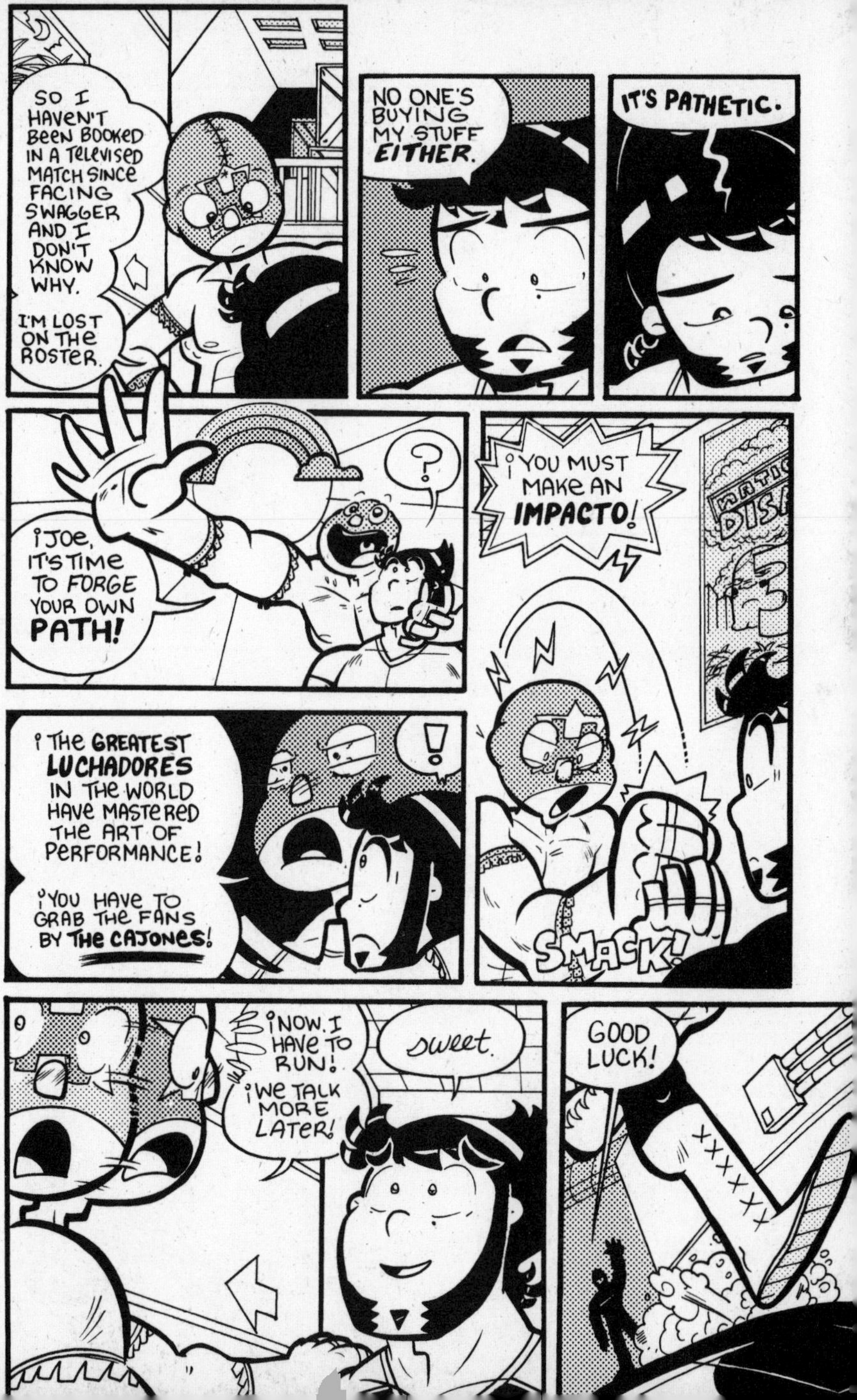
SO I HAVEN'T BEEN BOOKED IN A TELEVISED MATCH SINCE FACING SWAGGER AND I DON'T KNOW WHY.
I'M LOST ON THE ROSTER.
NO ONE'S BUYING MY STUFF EITHER.
IT'S PATHETIC.
¡JOE, IT'S TIME TO FORGE YOUR OWN PATH!
?
¡YOU MUST MAKE AN IMPACTO!
¡THE GREATEST LUCHADORES IN THE WORLD HAVE MASTERED THE ART OF PERFORMANCE!
¡YOU HAVE TO GRAB THE FANS BY THE CAJONES!
!
SMACK!
¡NOW. I HAVE TO RUN!
¡WE TALK MORE LATER!
sweet.
GOOD LUCK!

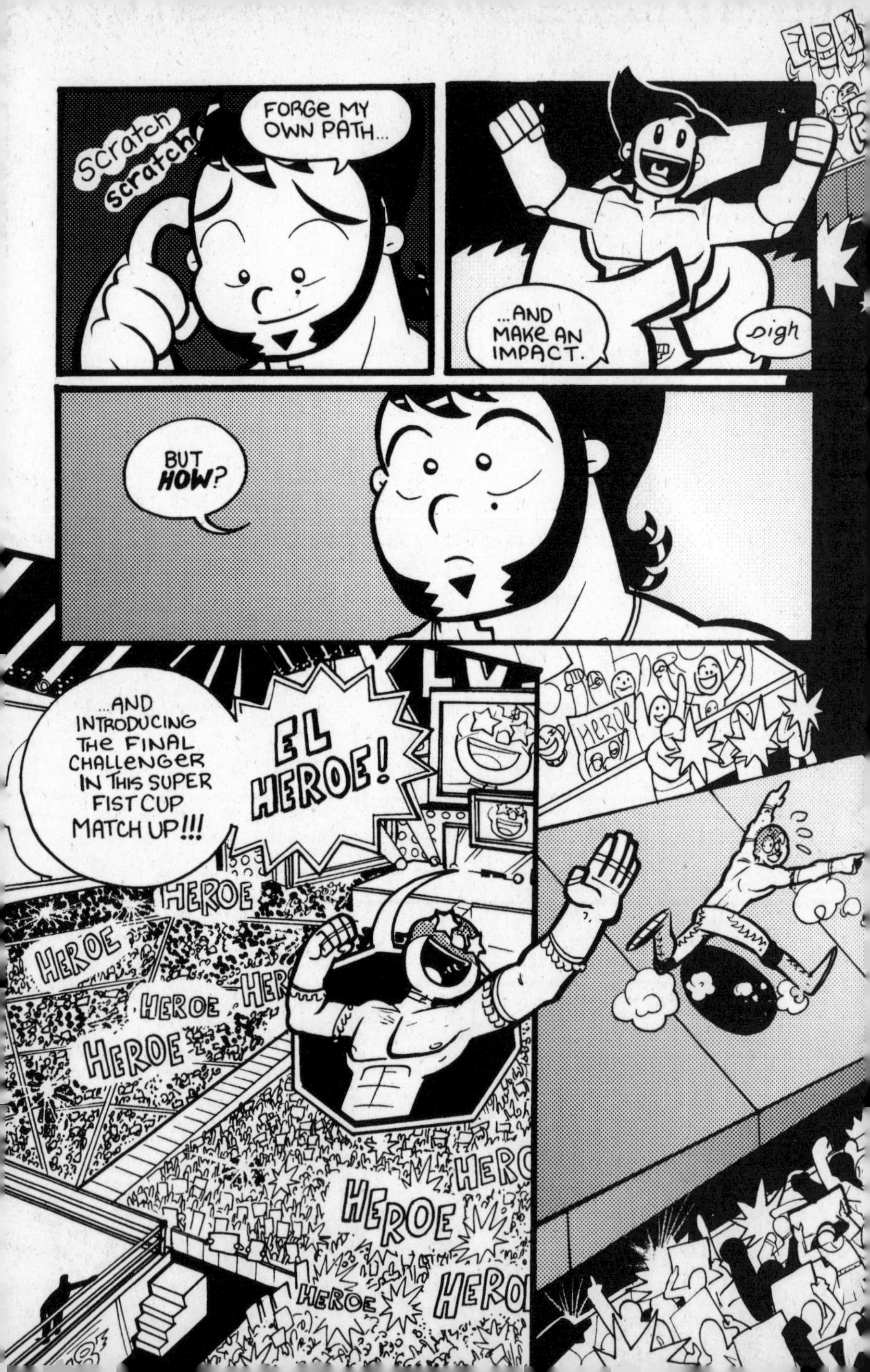

FORGE MY OWN PATH...
Scratch scratch
...AND MAKE AN IMPACT.
sigh
BUT HOW?
...AND INTRODUCING THE FINAL CHALLENGER IN THIS SUPER FIST CUP MATCH UP!!!
EL HEROE!
HEROE
HEROE
HEROE
HEROE
HEROE
HEROE

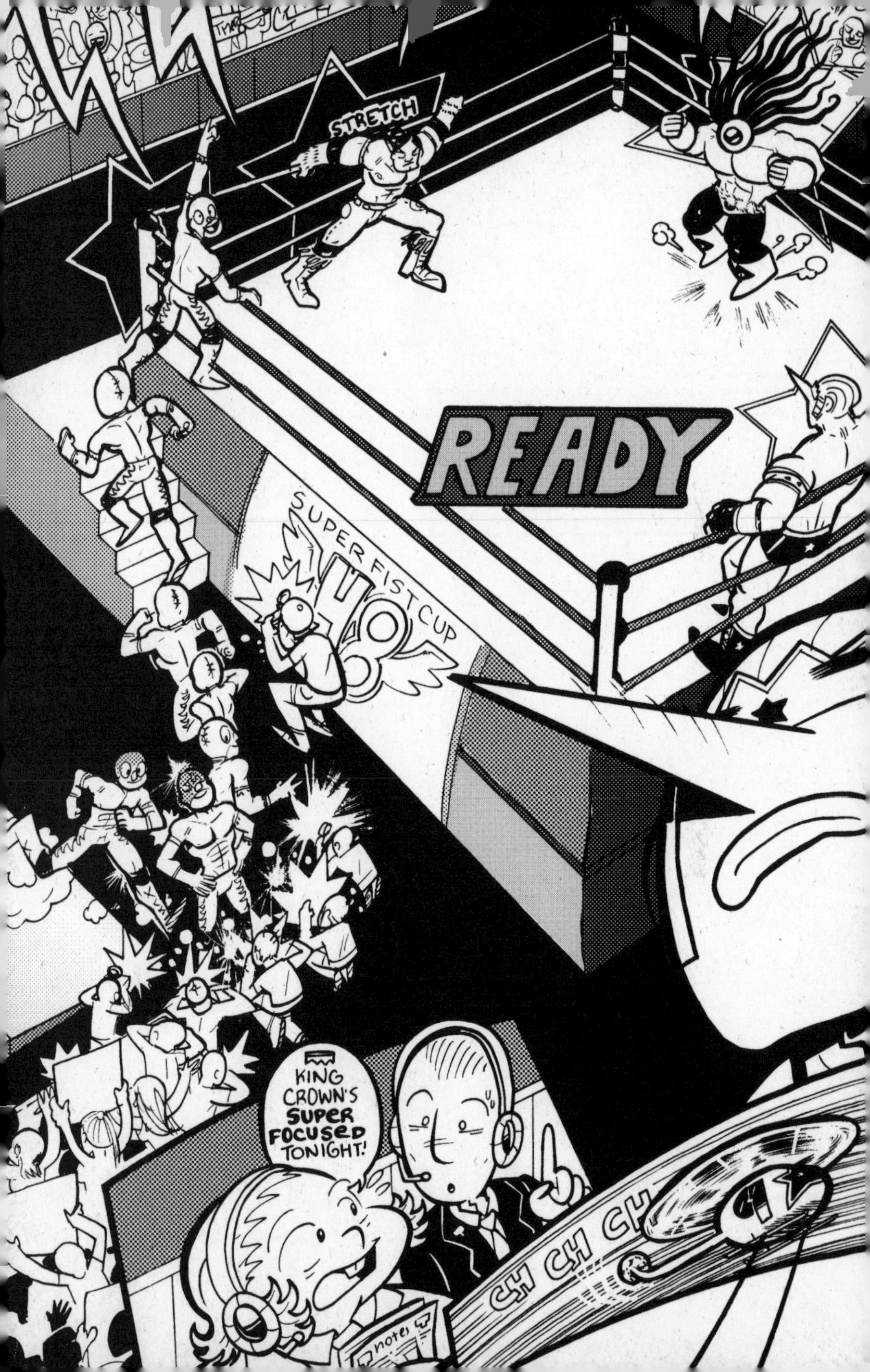
STRETCH
READY
SUPER FIST CUP
KING CROWN'S SUPER FOCUSED TONIGHT!
CH CH CH
notes

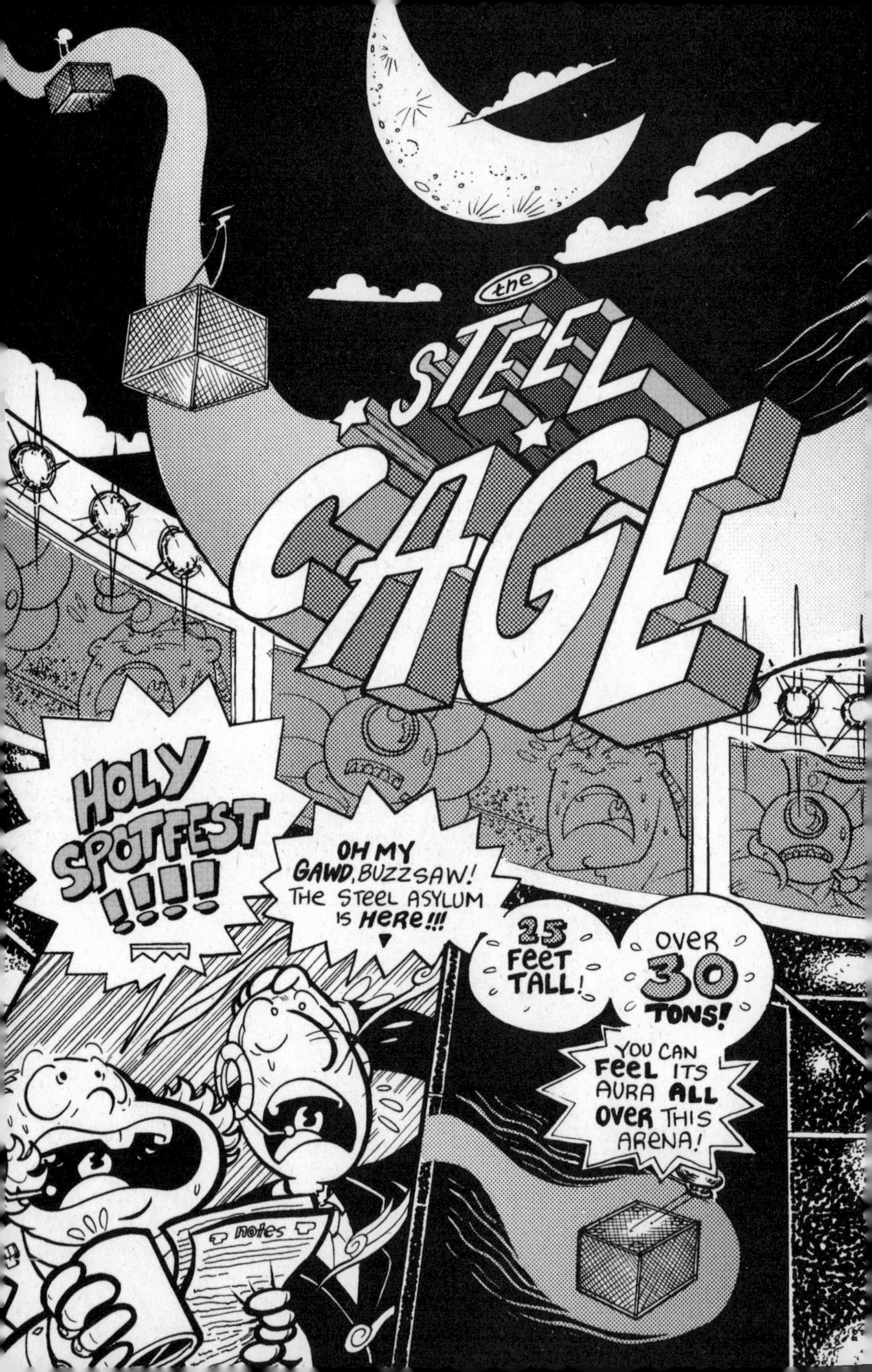
the STEEL CAGE
HOLY SPOTFEST !!!!!
OH MY GAWD, BUZZSAW! THE STEEL ASYLUM IS HERE!!!
25 FEET TALL!
OVER 30 TONS!
YOU CAN FEEL ITS AURA ALL OVER THIS ARENA!
notes

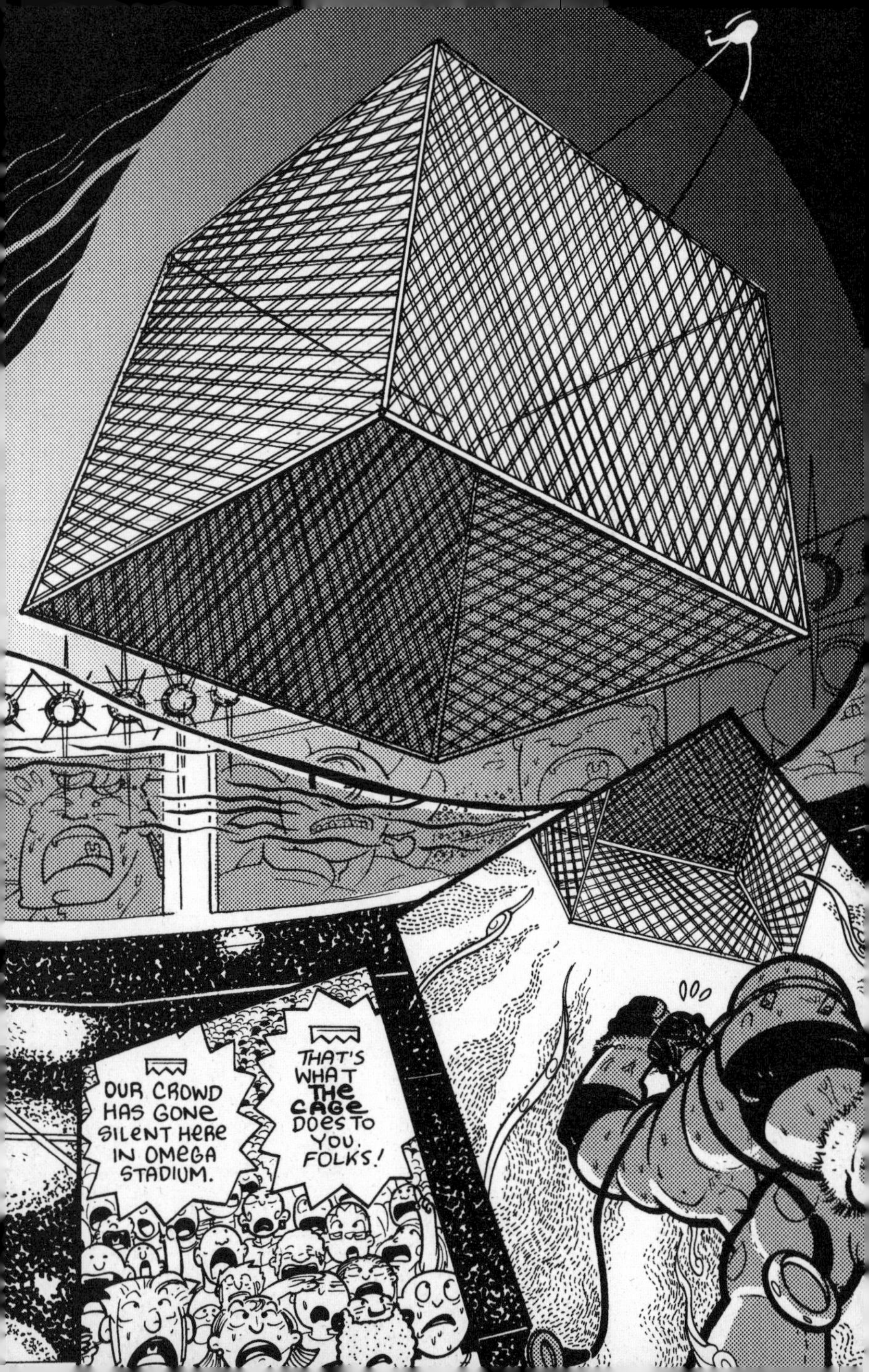
OUR CROWD HAS GONE SILENT HERE IN OMEGA STADIUM.
THAT'S WHAT THE CAGE DOES TO YOU, FOLKS!

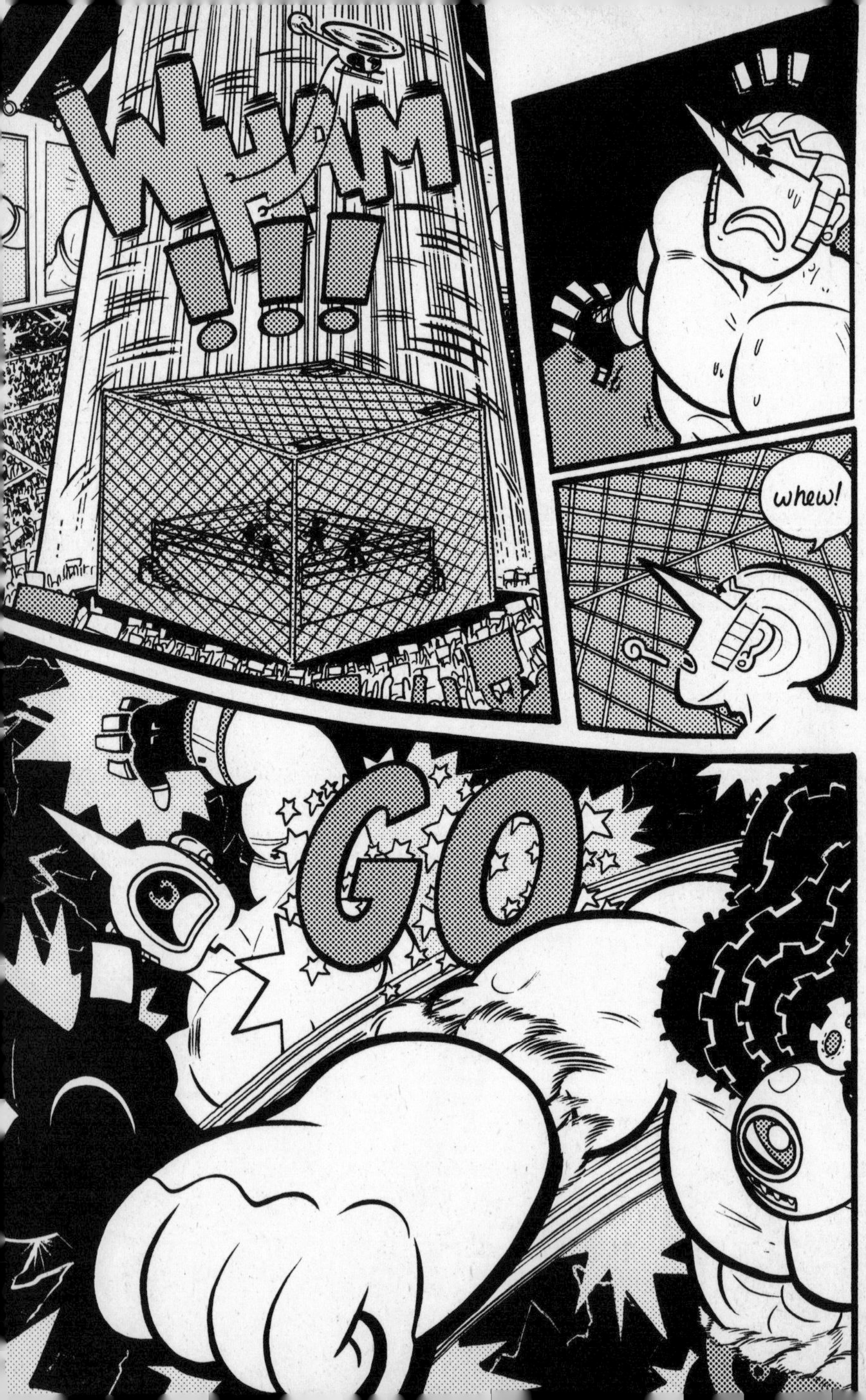
WHAM!!!
!!!
whew!
GO

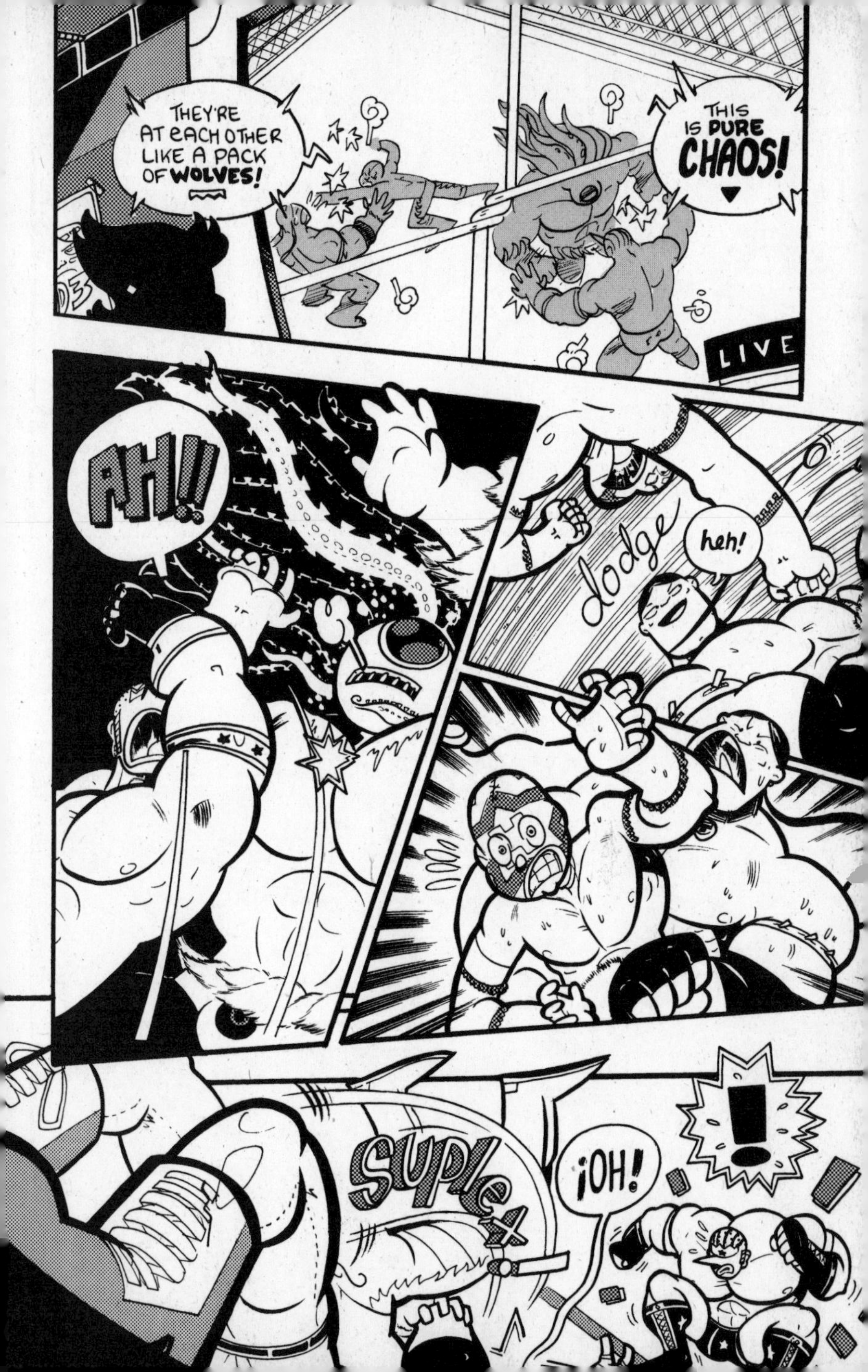

THEY'RE AT EACH OTHER LIKE A PACK OF WOLVES!
THIS IS PURE CHAOS!
LIVE
AH!!
dodge
heh!
SUPLEX
¡OH!
!

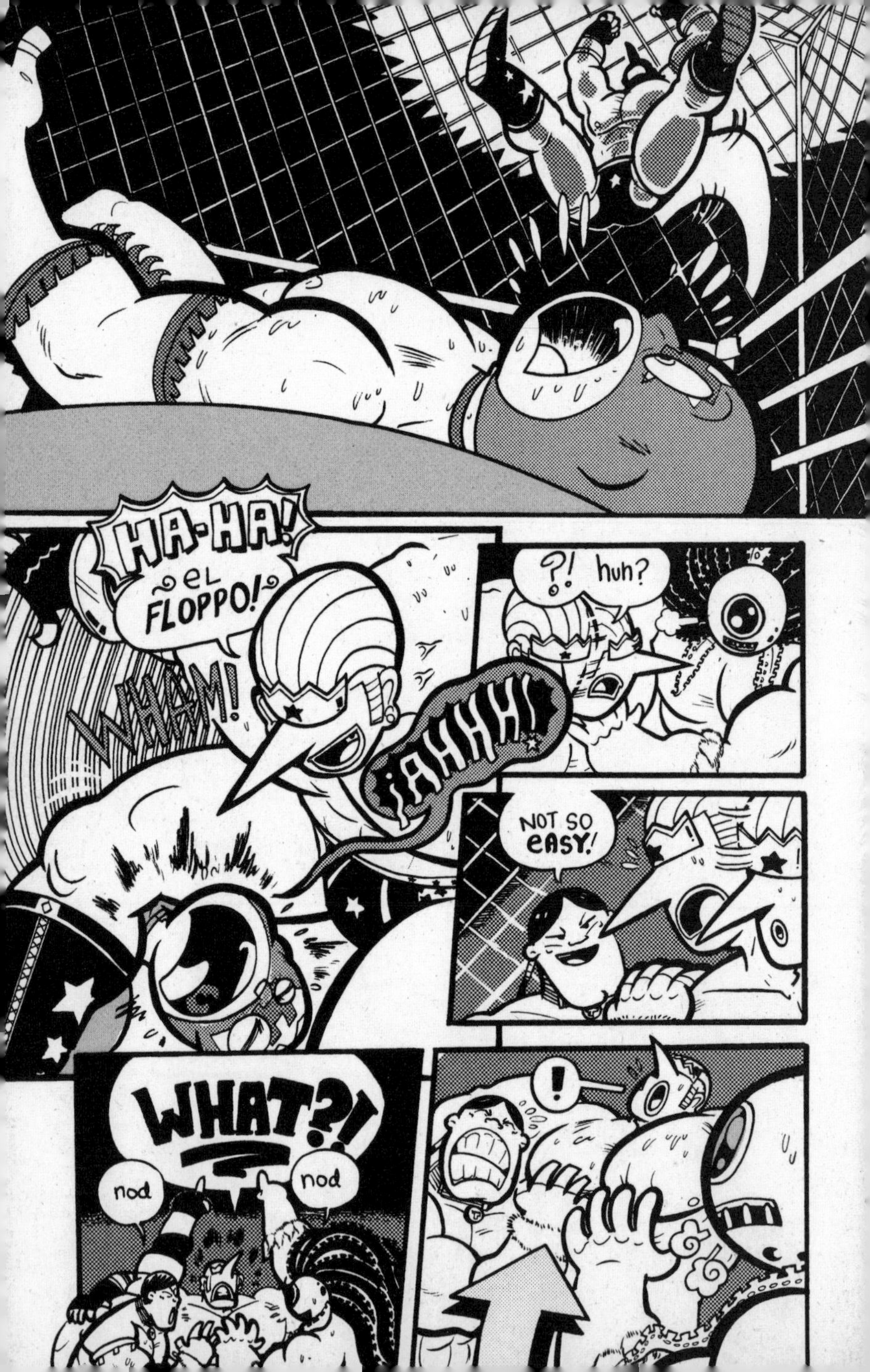
HA-HA! EL FLOPPO!
WHAM!
AHHHH!
?!
huh?
NOT SO EASY!
WHAT?!
nod
nod
!

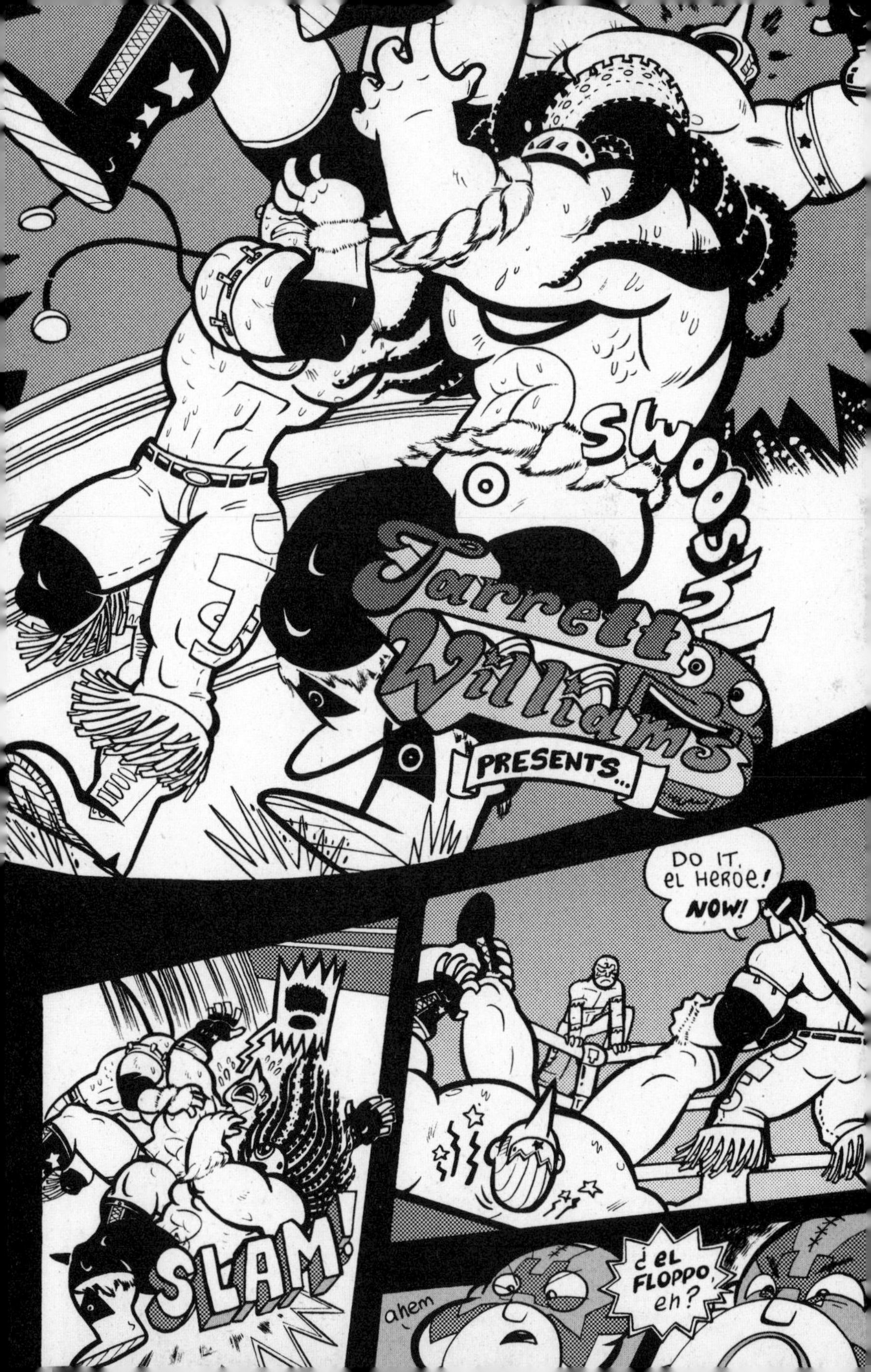
SWOOSH
Jarrett Williams
PRESENTS...
DO IT, EL HEROE! NOW!
SLAM!
ahem
¿EL FLOPPO, eh?

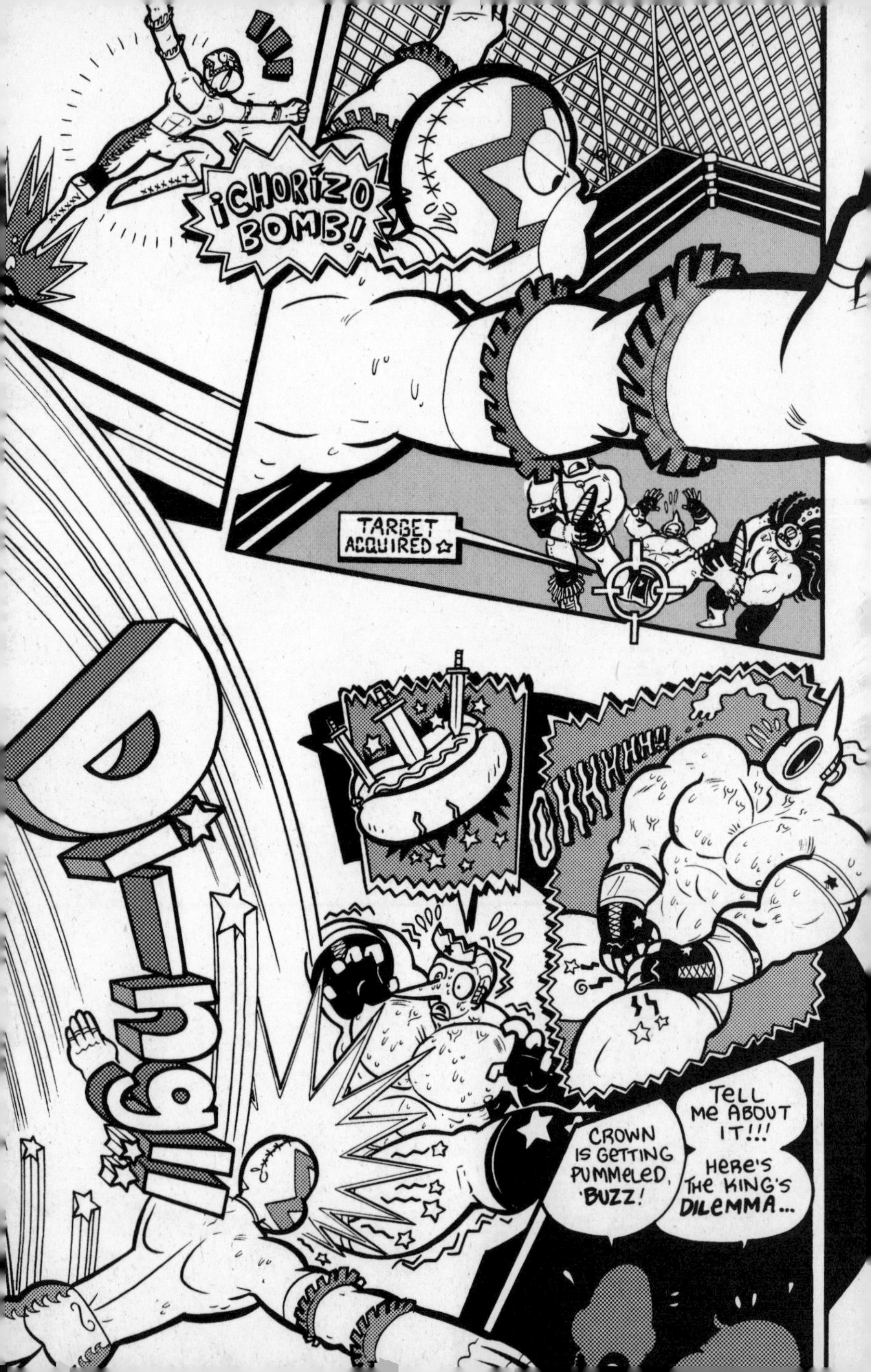
¡CHORIZO BOMB!
TARGET ACQUIRED
OHHHHHH!!
Dingy!
CROWN IS GETTING PUMMELED, 'BUZZ!
TELL ME ABOUT IT!!!
HERE'S THE KING'S DILEMMA...

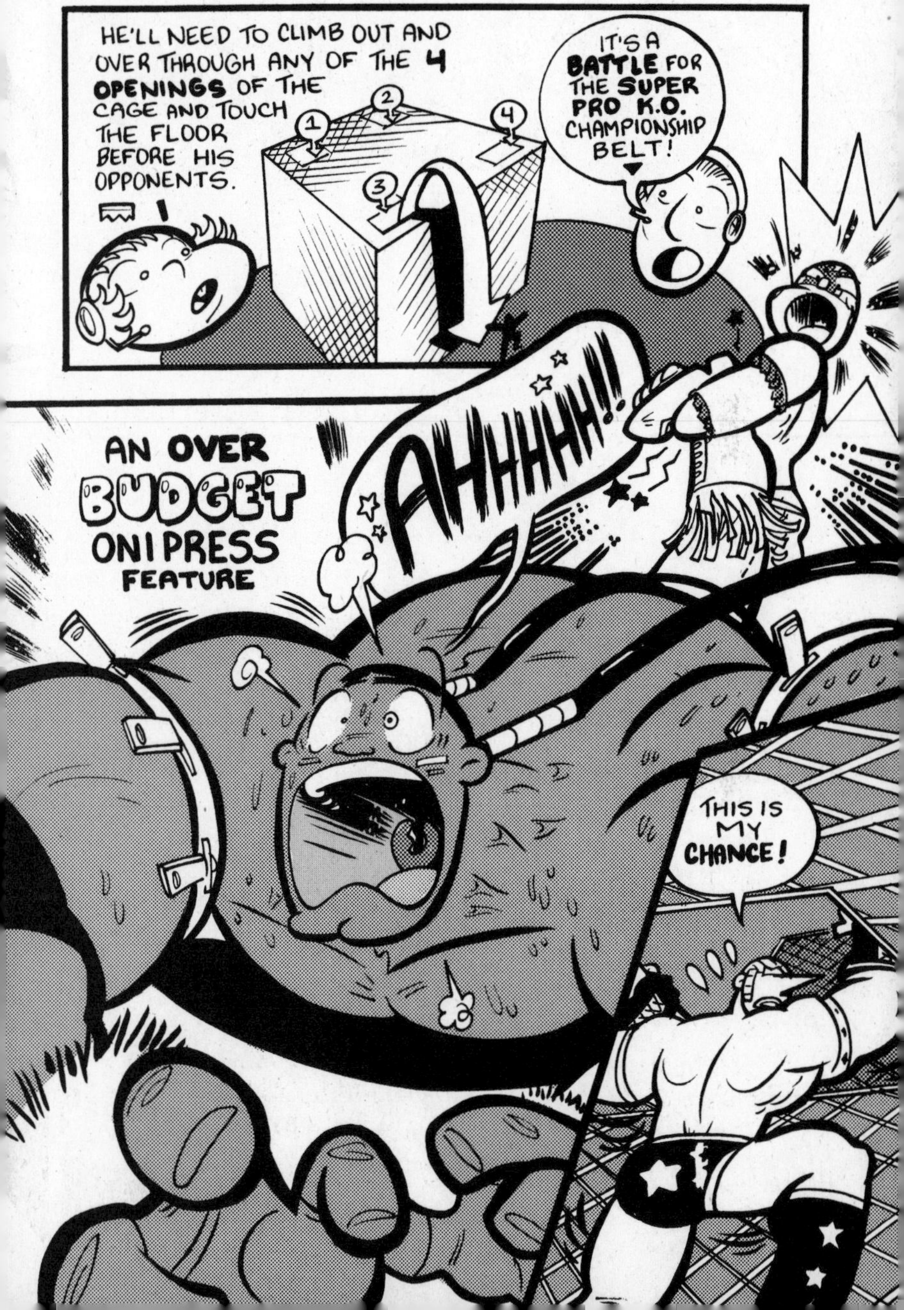
HE'LL NEED TO CLIMB OUT AND OVER THROUGH ANY OF THE 4 OPENINGS OF THE CAGE AND TOUCH THE FLOOR BEFORE HIS OPPONENTS.
1
2
3
4
IT'S A BATTLE FOR THE SUPER PRO K.O. CHAMPIONSHIP BELT!
AN OVER BUDGET ONI PRESS FEATURE
AHHHHH!!
THIS IS MY CHANCE!

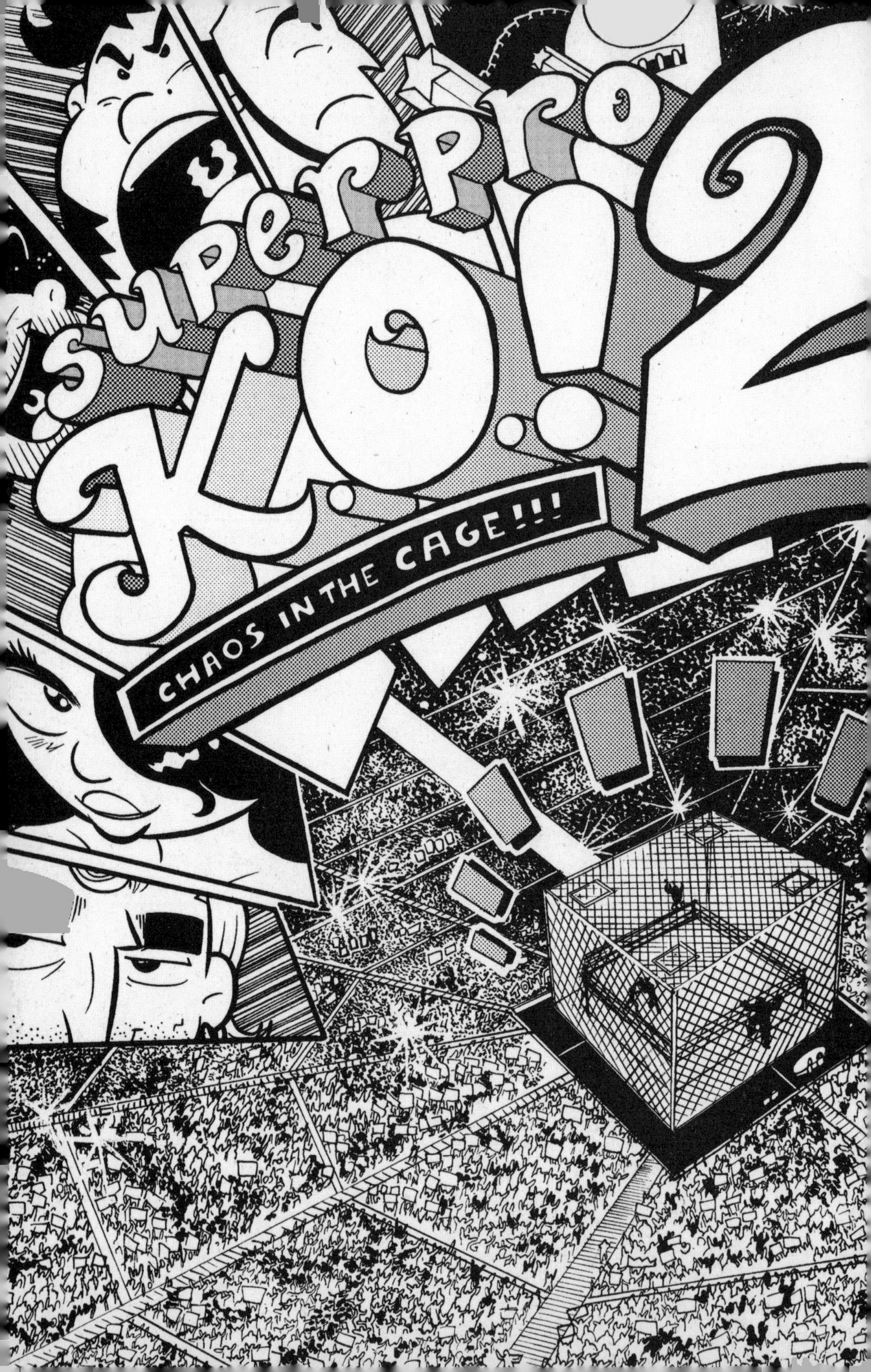
super pro K.O.!! 2
CHAOS IN THE CAGE!!!

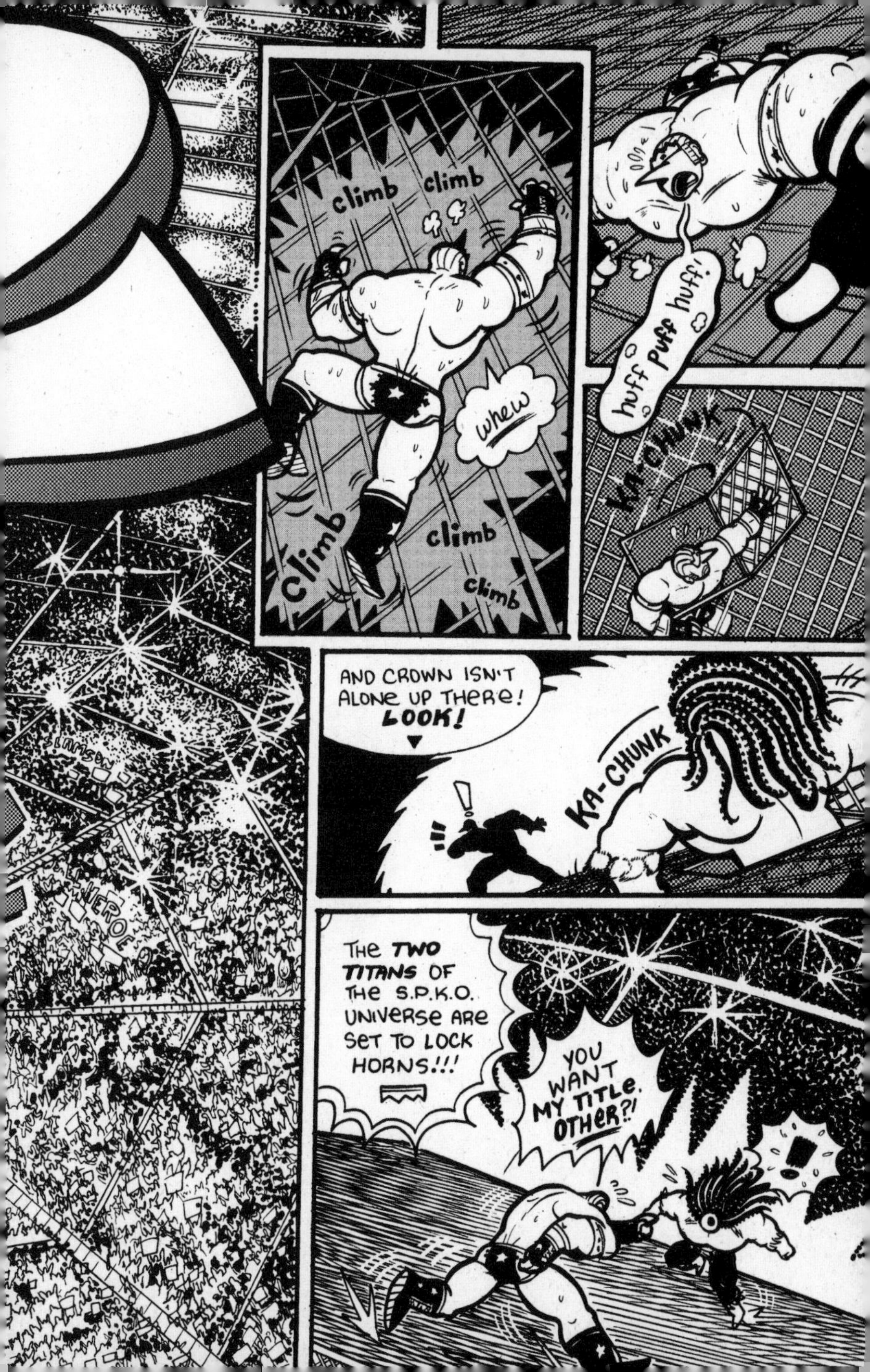

climb climb
whew
climb
climb
climb
huff puff huff!
KA-CHUNK
AND CROWN ISN'T ALONE UP THERE! LOOK!
KA-CHUNK
!
THE TWO TITANS OF THE S.P.K.O. UNIVERSE ARE SET TO LOCK HORNS!!!
YOU WANT MY TITLE, OTHER?!
!

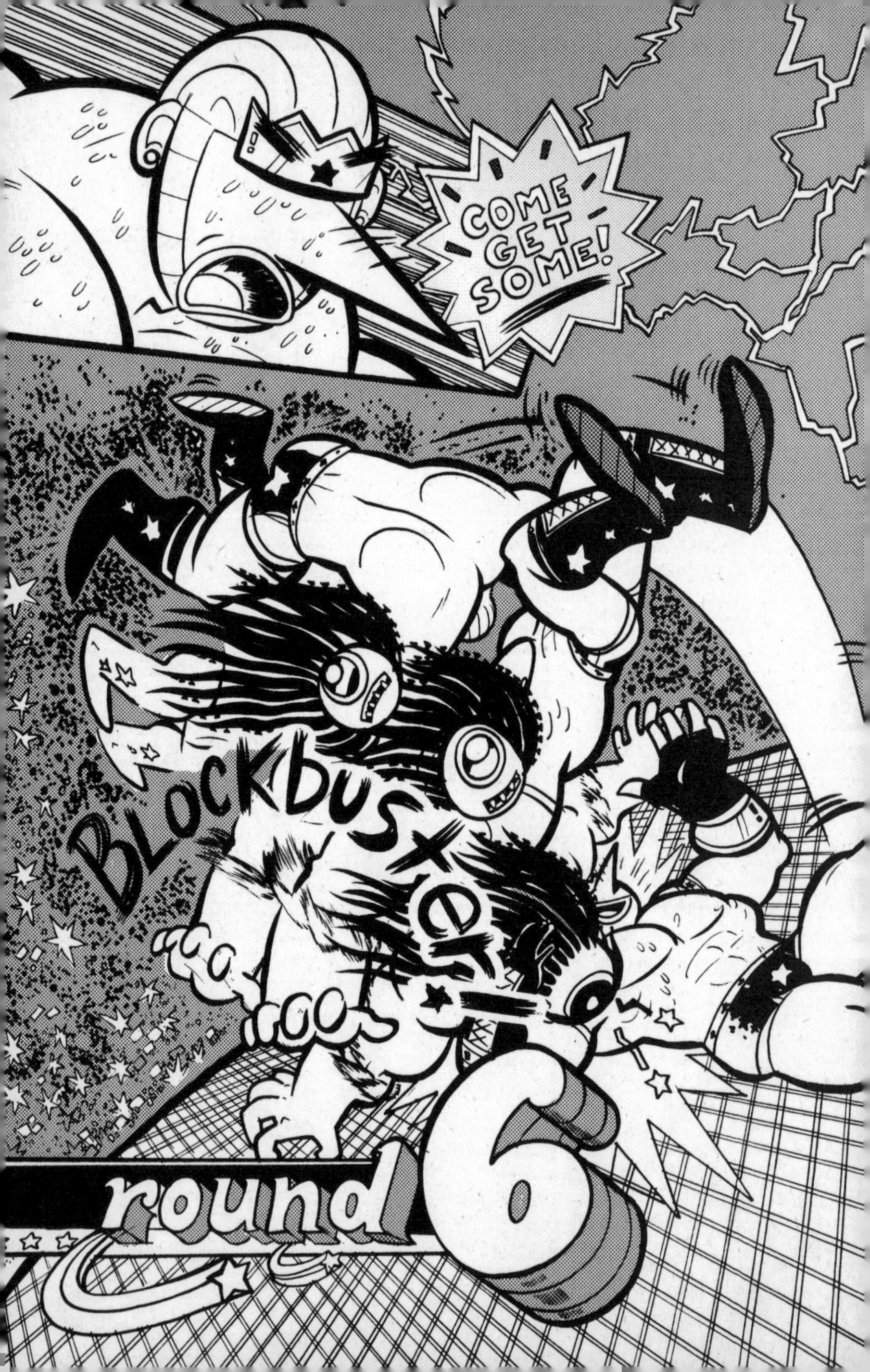
COME GET SOME!
BLOCKBUSTER
round 6

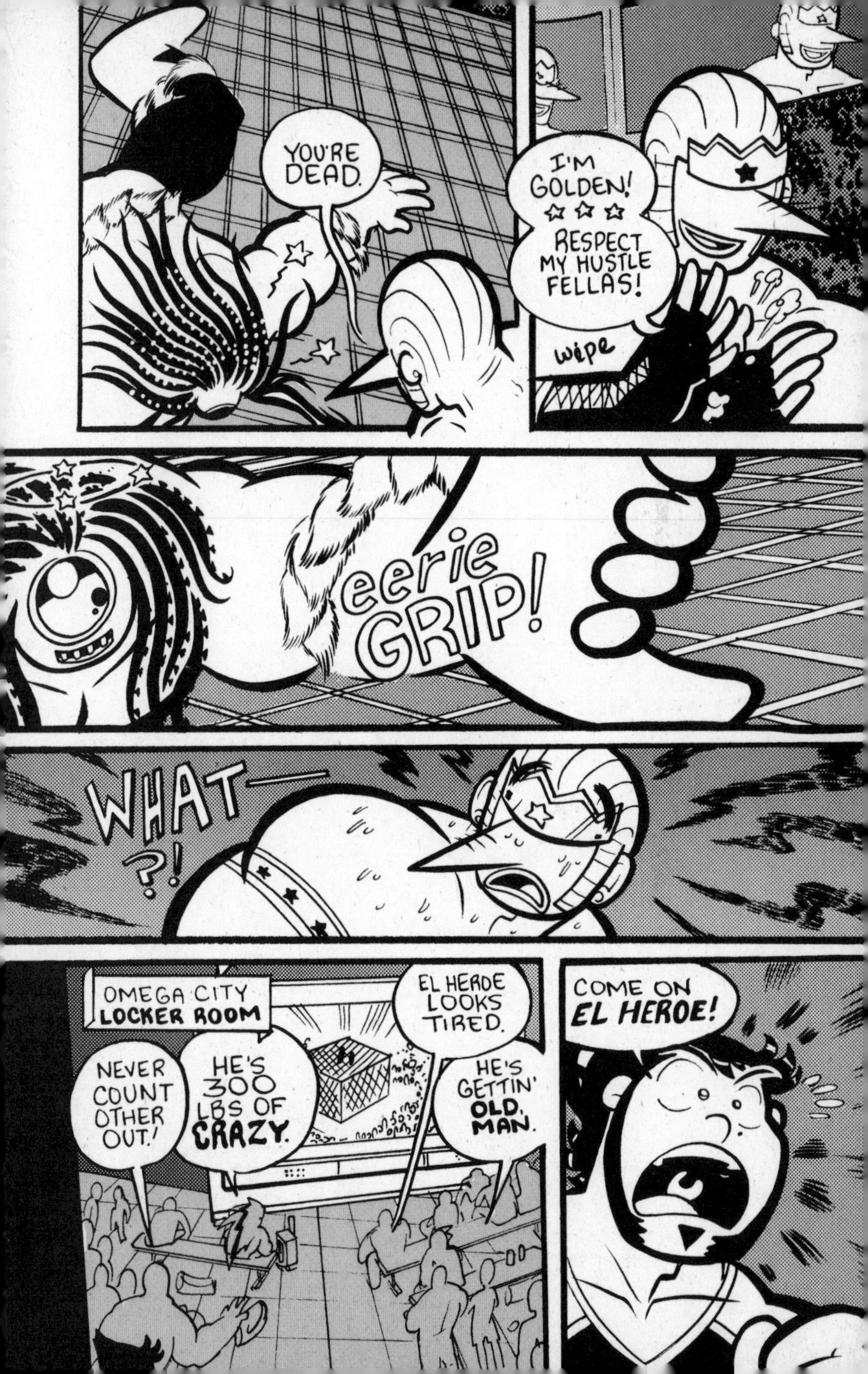

YOU'RE DEAD.
I'M GOLDEN! ☆☆☆ RESPECT MY HUSTLE FELLAS!
wipe
eerie GRIP!
WHAT— ?!
OMEGA CITY LOCKER ROOM
EL HEROE LOOKS TIRED.
HE'S 300 LBS OF CRAZY.
NEVER COUNT OTHER OUT!
HE'S GETTIN' OLD, MAN.
COME ON EL HEROE!

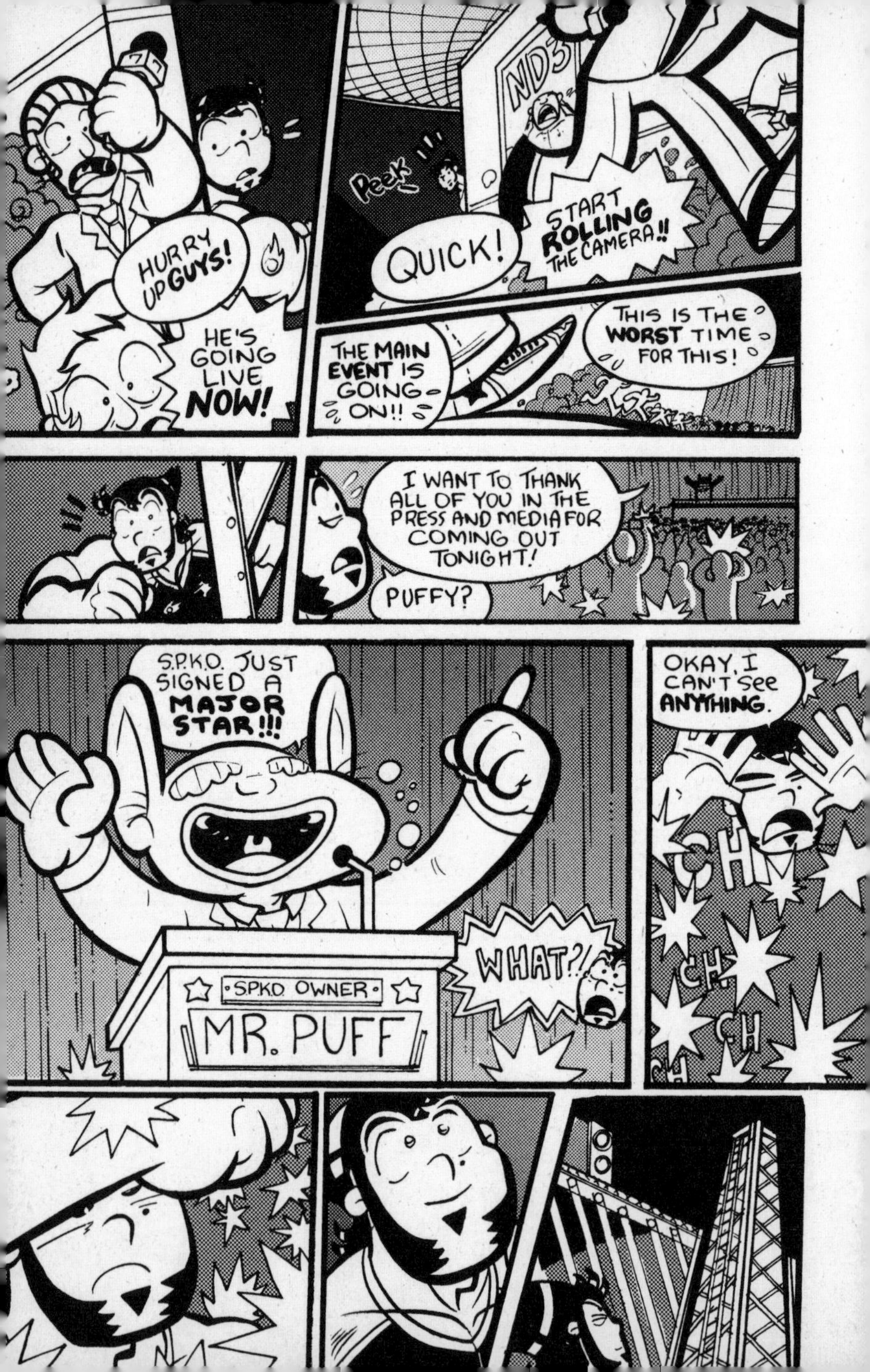

HURRY UP GUYS!
HE'S GOING LIVE NOW!
ND3
Peek
QUICK!
START ROLLING THE CAMERA!!
THE MAIN EVENT IS GOING ON!!
THIS IS THE WORST TIME FOR THIS!
I WANT TO THANK ALL OF YOU IN THE PRESS AND MEDIA FOR COMING OUT TONIGHT!
PUFFY?
S.P.K.O. JUST SIGNED A MAJOR STAR!!!
S.P.K.O. OWNER
MR. PUFF
WHAT?!
OKAY, I CAN'T see ANYTHING.
CH
CH
CH

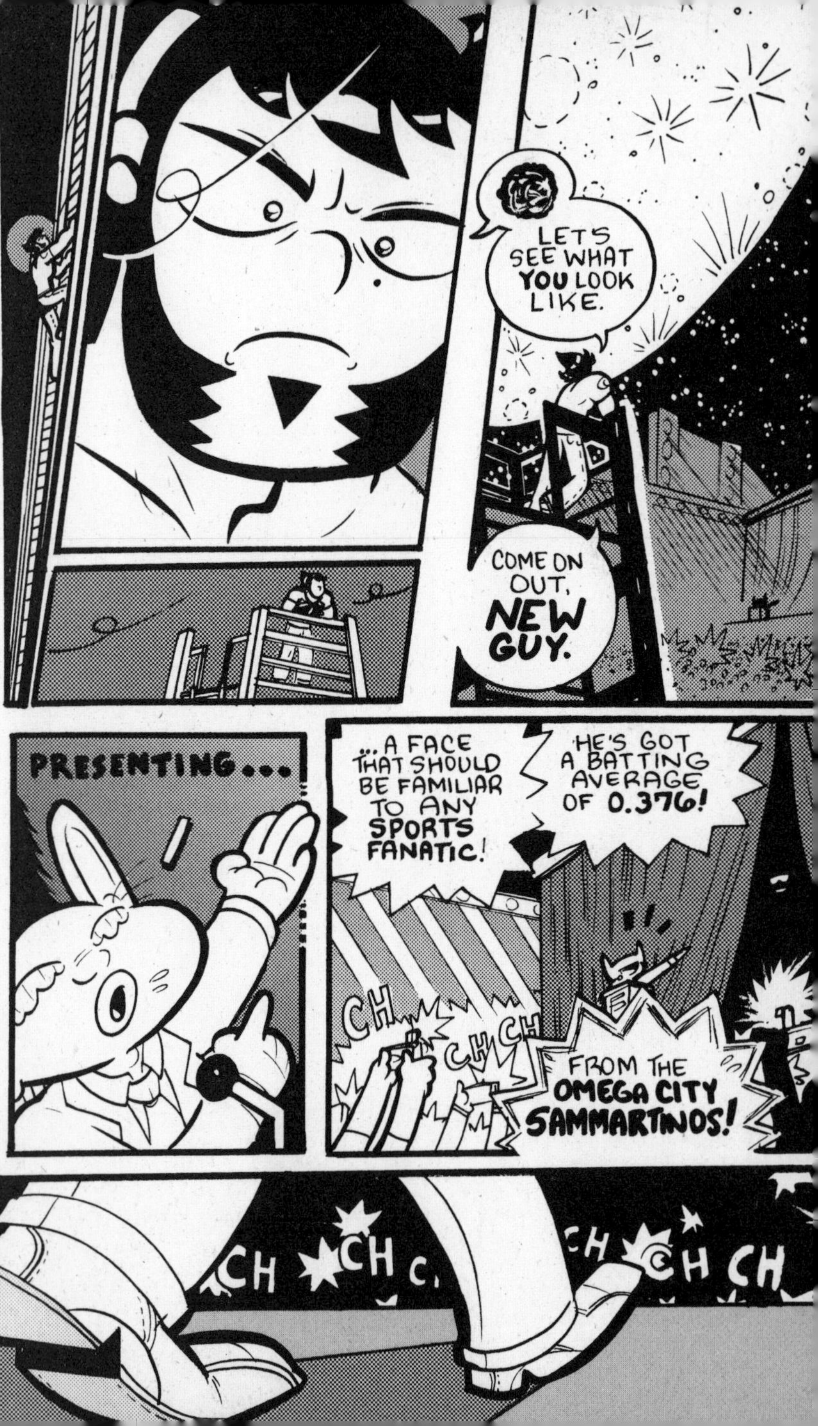
LETS SEE WHAT YOU LOOK LIKE.
COME ON OUT, NEW GUY.
PRESENTING...
...A FACE THAT SHOULD BE FAMILIAR TO ANY SPORTS FANATIC!
HE'S GOT A BATTING AVERAGE OF 0.376!
CH CH CH CH
FROM THE OMEGA CITY SAMMARTINOS!
CH CH CH C CH CH CH CH

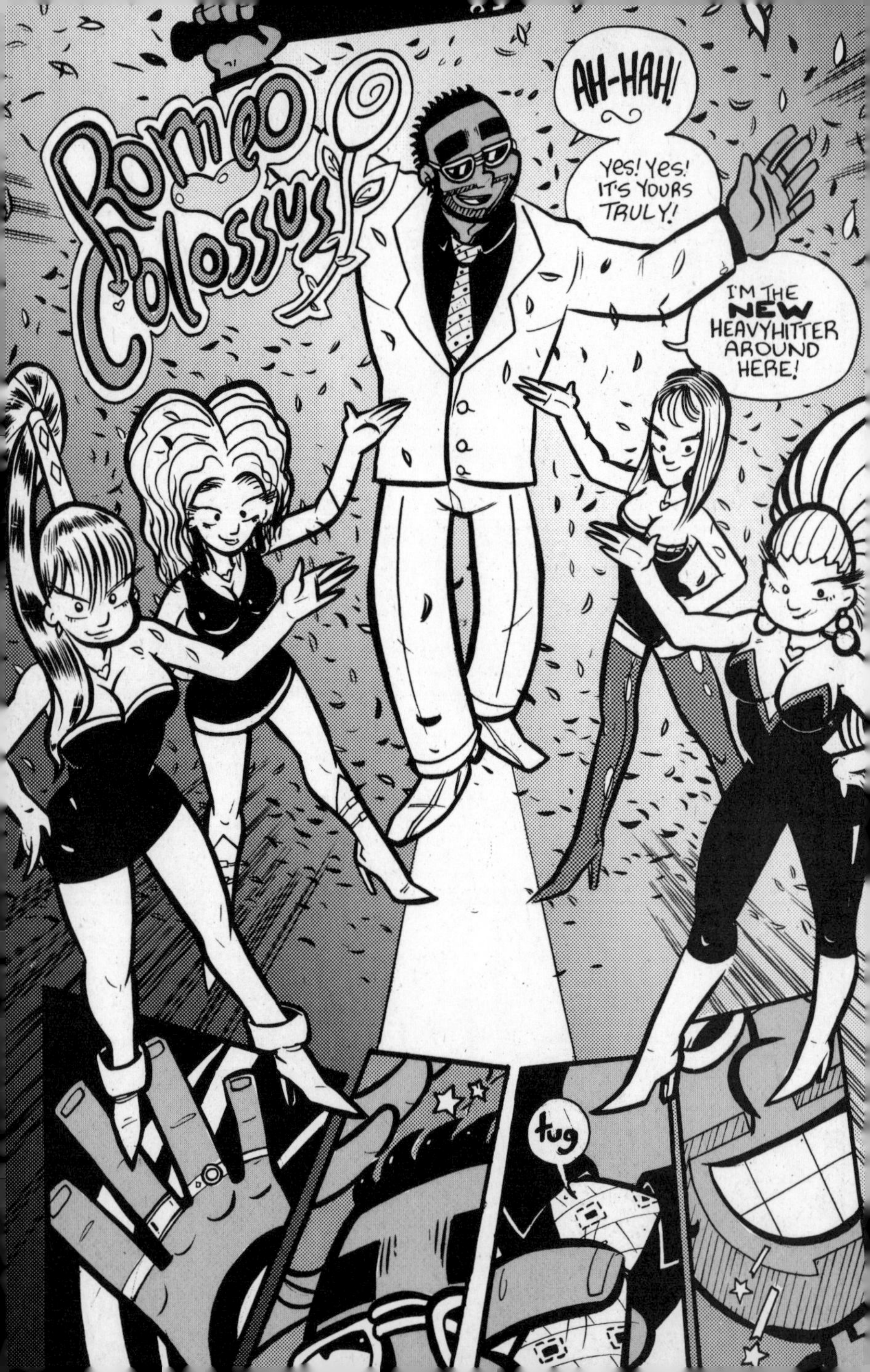
Romeo Colossus
AH-HAH!
YES! YES! IT'S YOURS TRULY!
I'M THE NEW HEAVYHITTER AROUND HERE!
tug

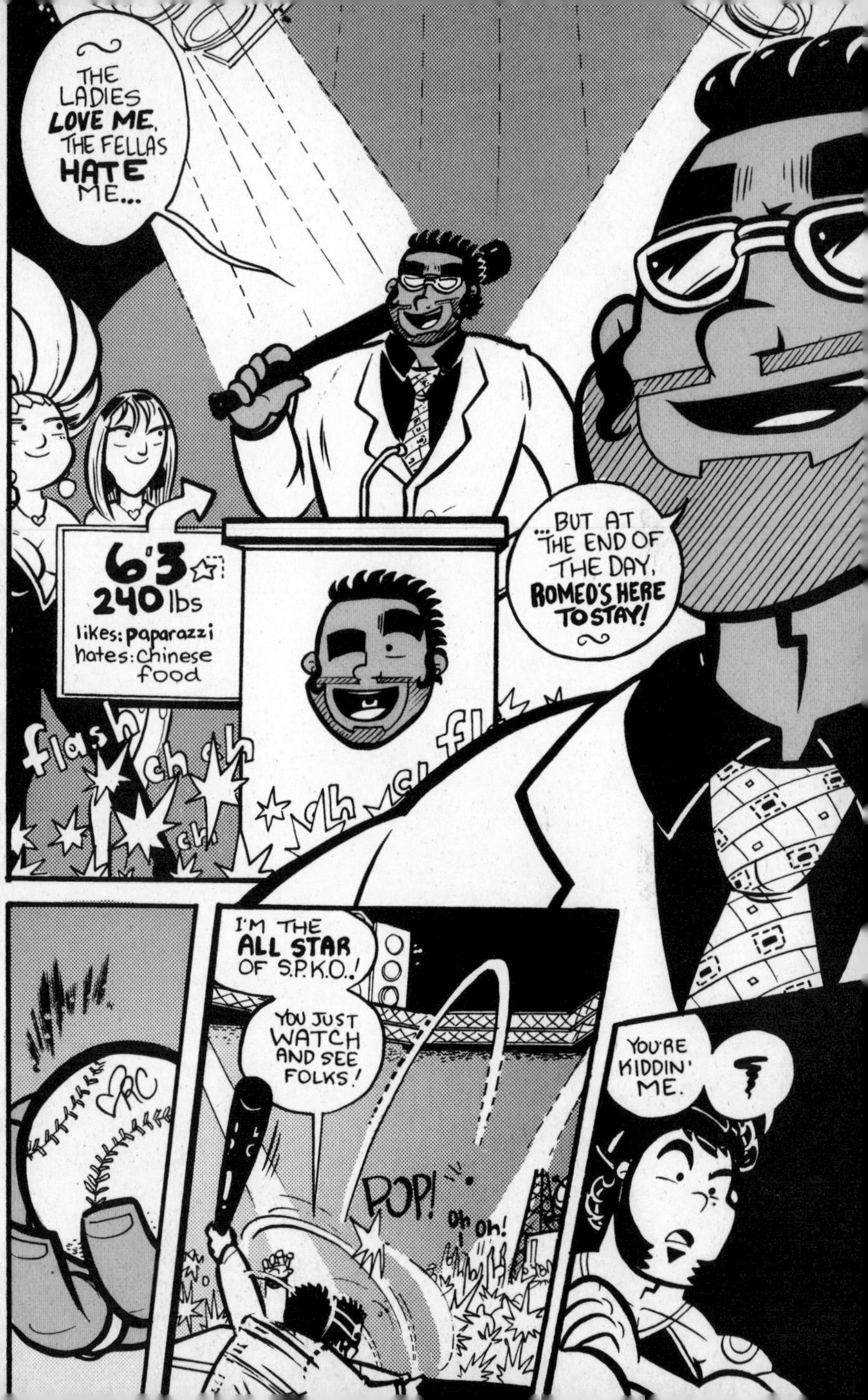
THE LADIES **LOVE ME**, THE FELLAS **HATE** ME...
6'3
240 lbs
likes: paparazzi
hates: chinese food
flash
ch ch
...BUT AT THE END OF THE DAY, **ROMEO'S HERE TO STAY!**
I'M THE **ALL STAR** OF S.P.K.O.!
YOU JUST WATCH AND SEE FOLKS!
POP!
Oh Oh!
YOU'RE KIDDIN' ME.

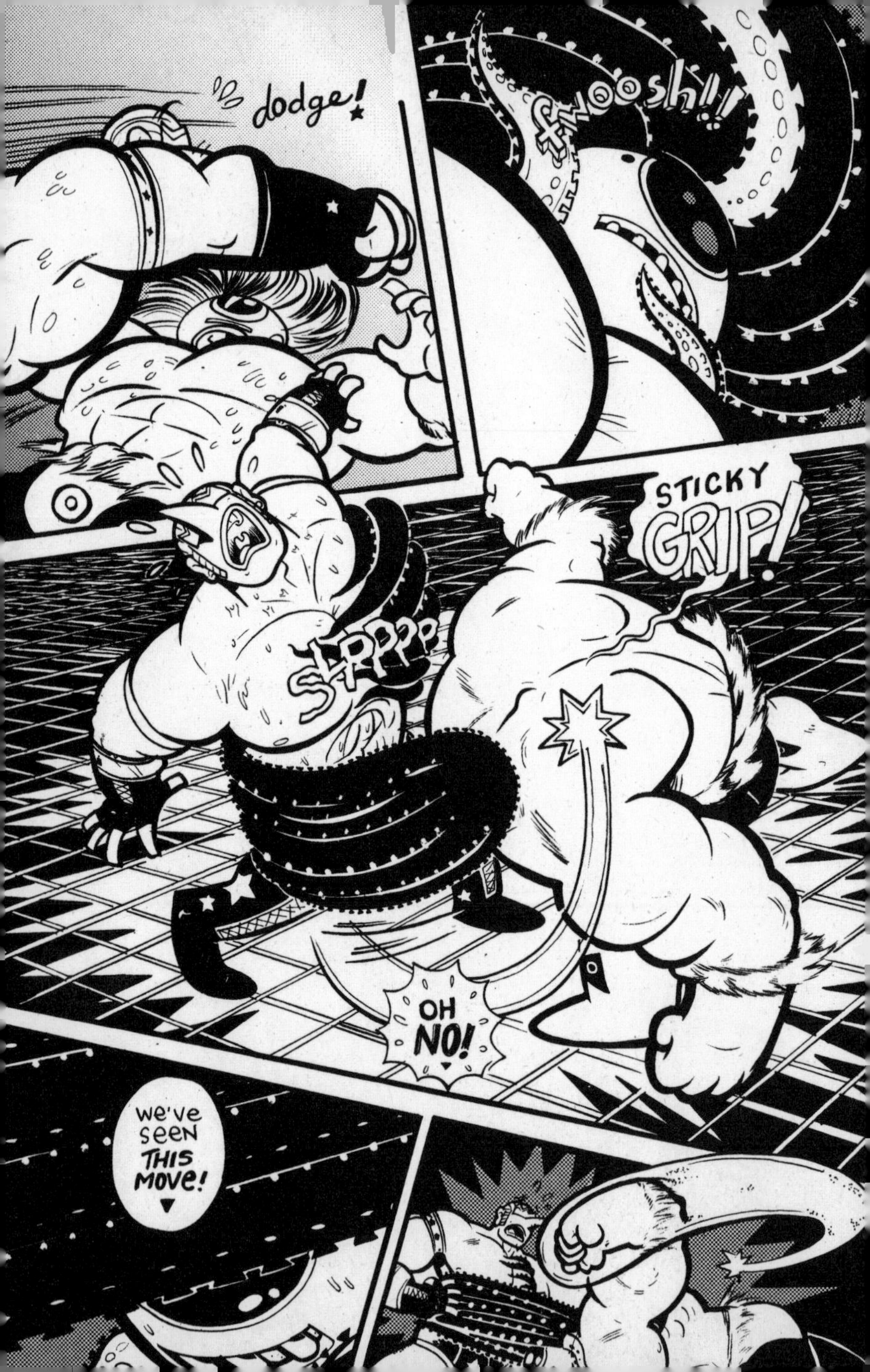
dodge!
fwoosh!!
STICKY GRIP!
SHRPPP
OH NO!
we've seen THIS move!

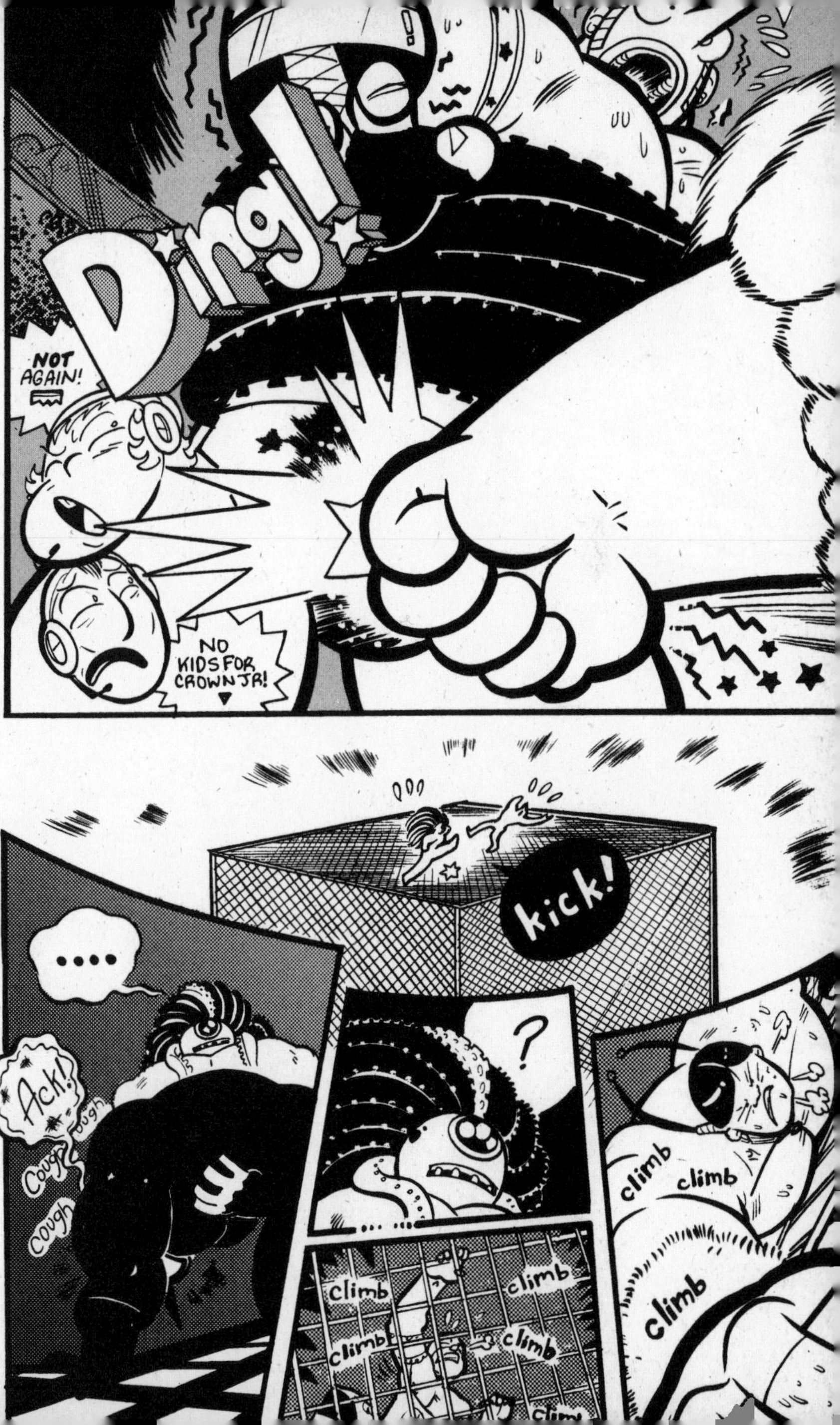
Ding!
NOT AGAIN!
NO KIDS FOR CROWN JR!
kick!
....
Ack!
cough
cough
cough
?
...
climb
climb
climb
climb
climb
climb
climb

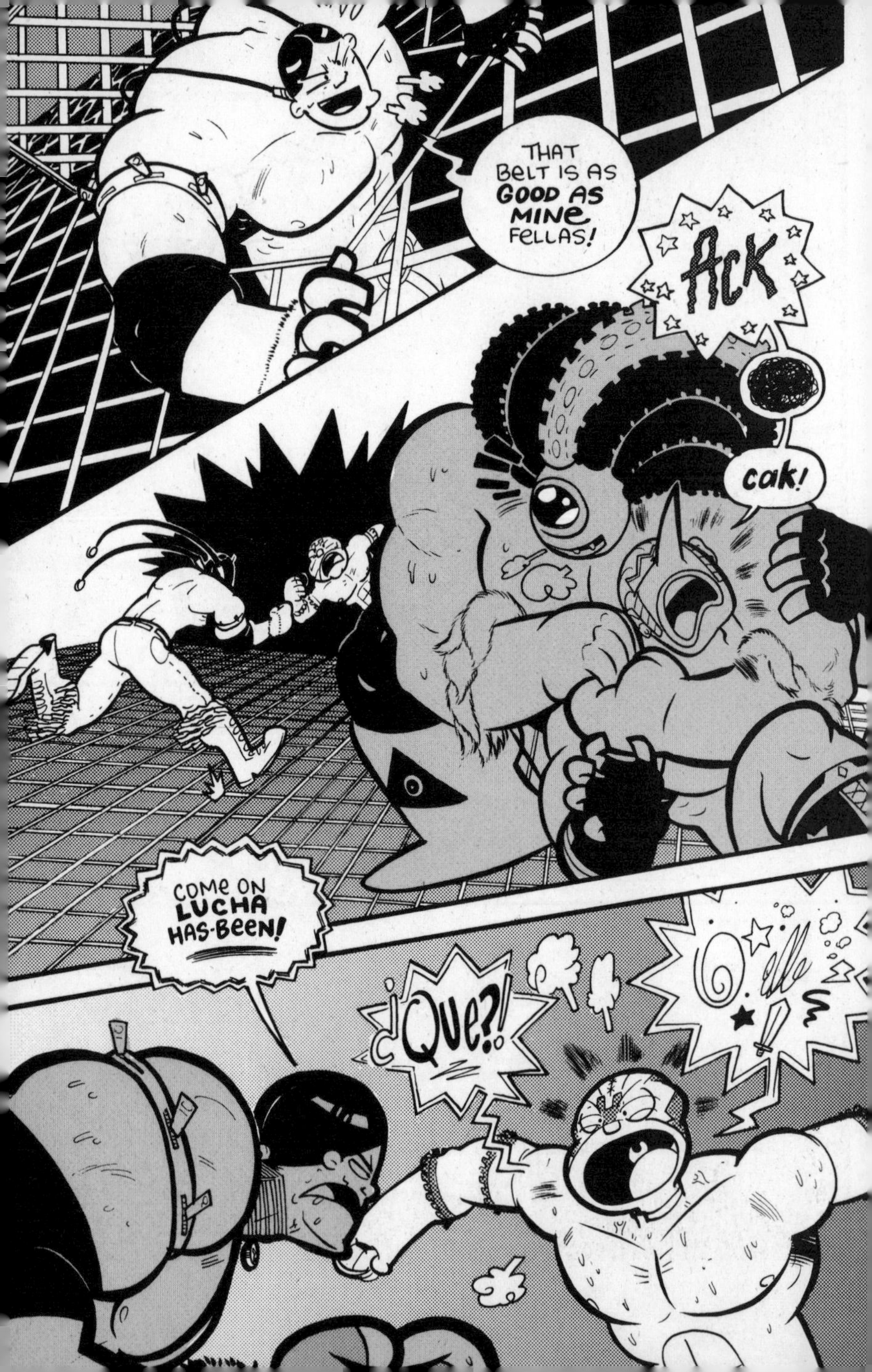
THAT BELT IS AS GOOD AS MINE FELLAS!
ACK
cak!
COME ON LUCHA HAS-BEEN!
¿QUE?!

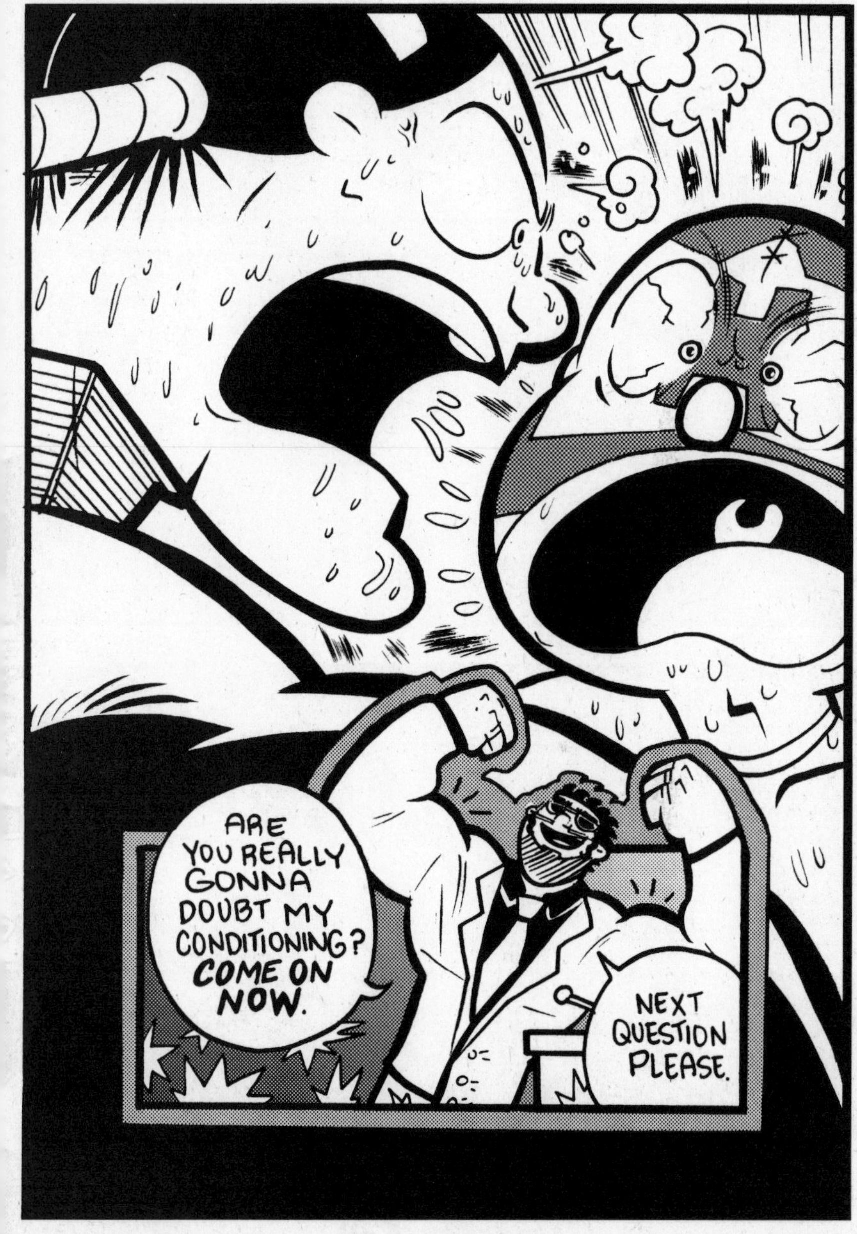
ARE YOU REALLY GONNA DOUBT MY CONDITIONING? COME ON NOW.
NEXT QUESTION PLEASE.

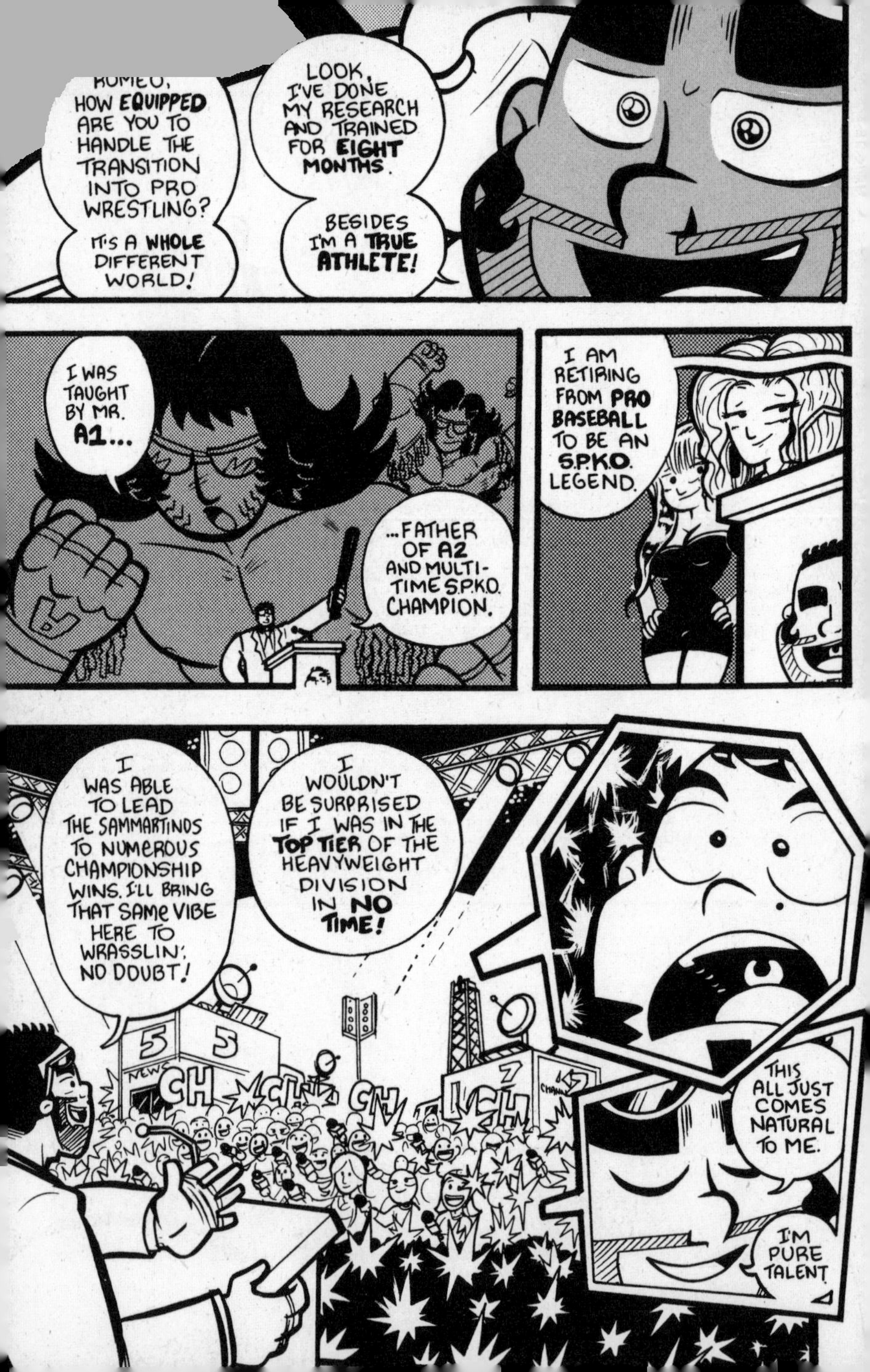
ROMEO, HOW EQUIPPED ARE YOU TO HANDLE THE TRANSITION INTO PRO WRESTLING?
IT'S A WHOLE DIFFERENT WORLD!
LOOK, I'VE DONE MY RESEARCH AND TRAINED FOR EIGHT MONTHS.
BESIDES I'M A TRUE ATHLETE!
I WAS TAUGHT BY MR. A1...
...FATHER OF A2 AND MULTI-TIME S.P.K.O. CHAMPION.
I AM RETIRING FROM PRO BASEBALL TO BE AN S.P.K.O. LEGEND.
I WAS ABLE TO LEAD THE SAMMARTINOS TO NUMEROUS CHAMPIONSHIP WINS. I'LL BRING THAT SAME VIBE HERE TO WRASSLIN', NO DOUBT!
I WOULDN'T BE SURPRISED IF I WAS IN THE TOP TIER OF THE HEAVYWEIGHT DIVISION IN NO TIME!
THIS ALL JUST COMES NATURAL TO ME.
I'M PURE TALENT.

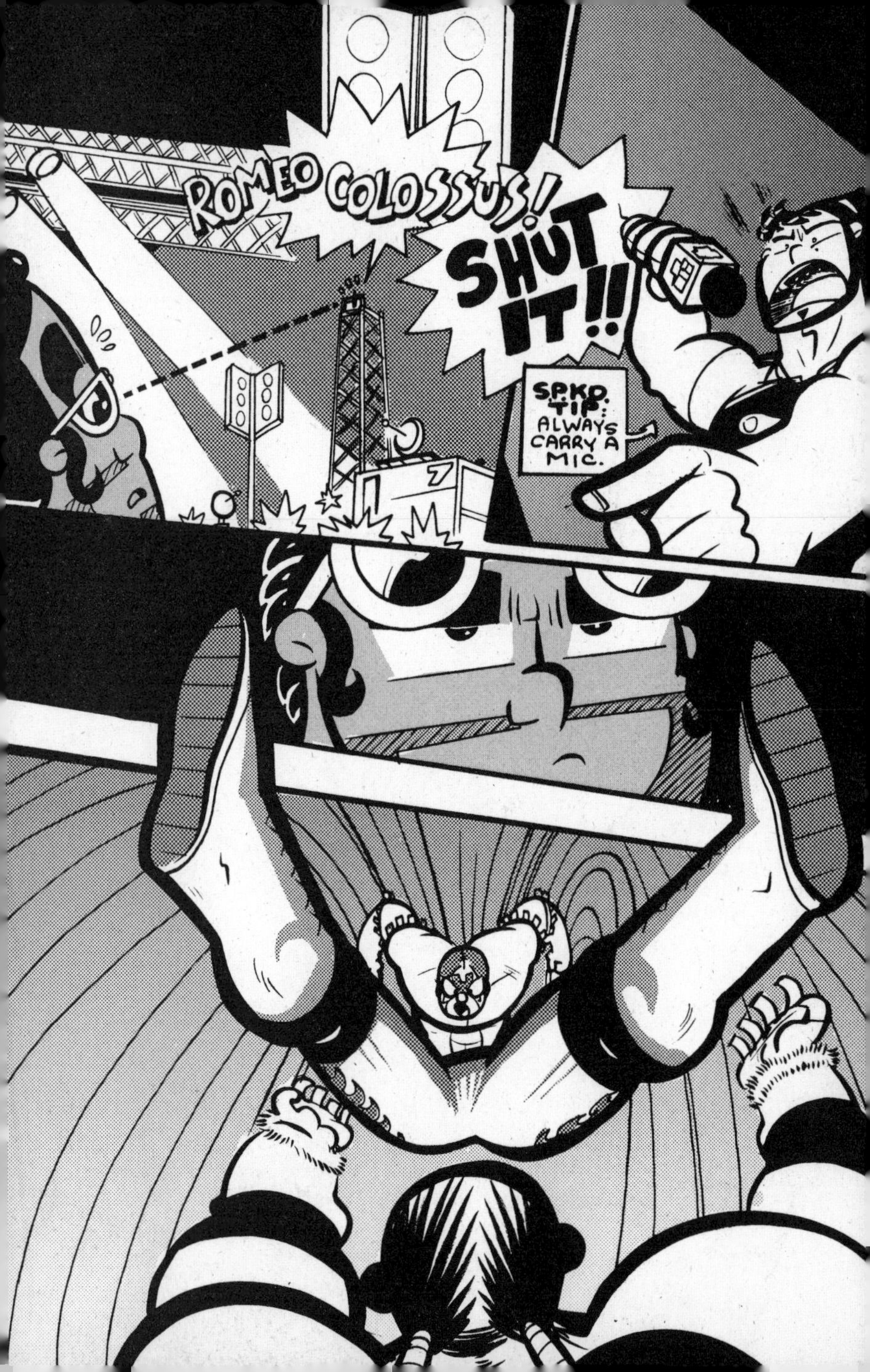
ROMEO COLOSSUS!
SHUT IT!!
SP.KD. TIP: ALWAYS CARRY A MIC.

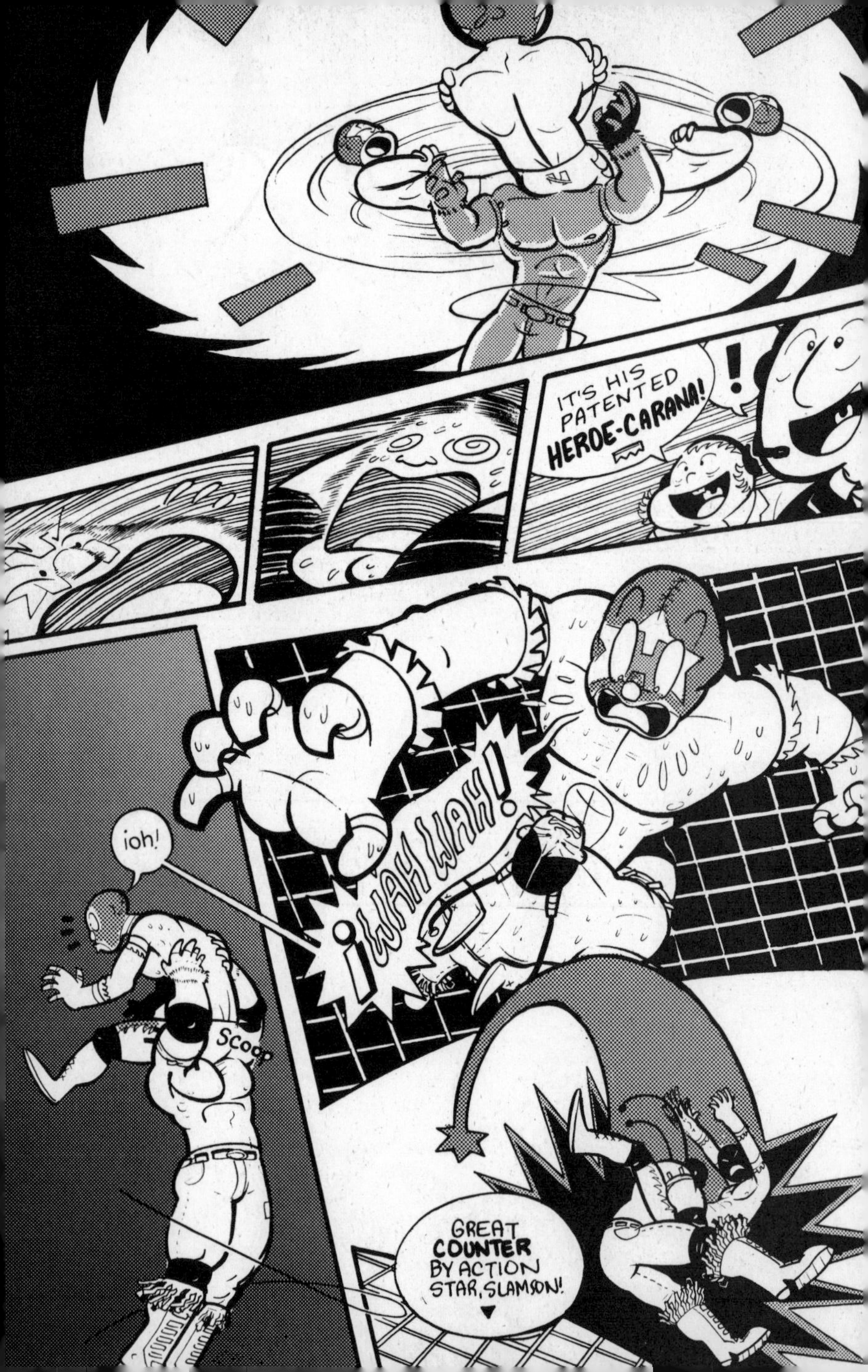

IT'S HIS PATENTED HEROE-CARANA!
!
¡oh!
¡WAH WAH!
Scoop
GREAT COUNTER BY ACTION STAR, SLAMSON!

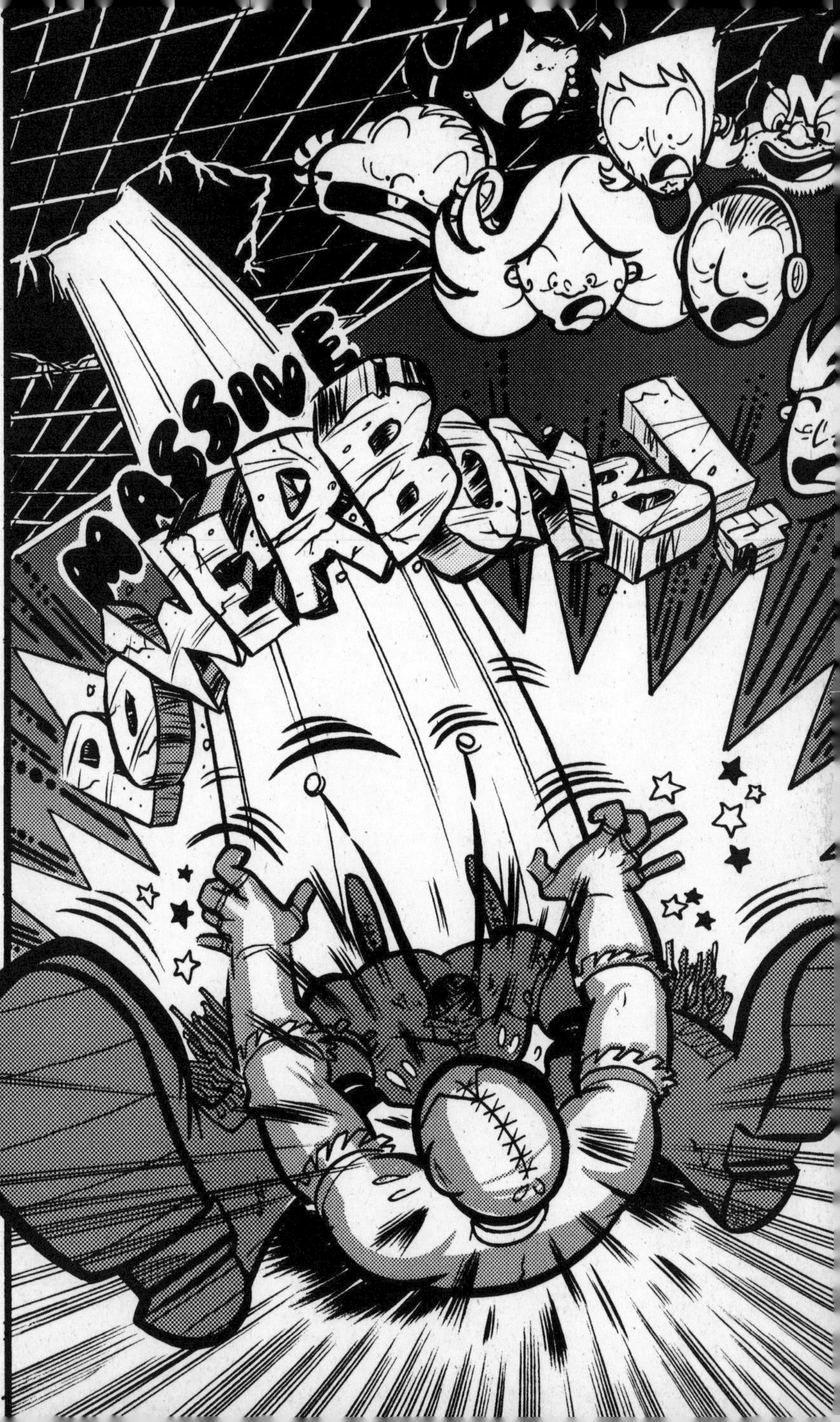
MASSIVE
POWERBOMB!

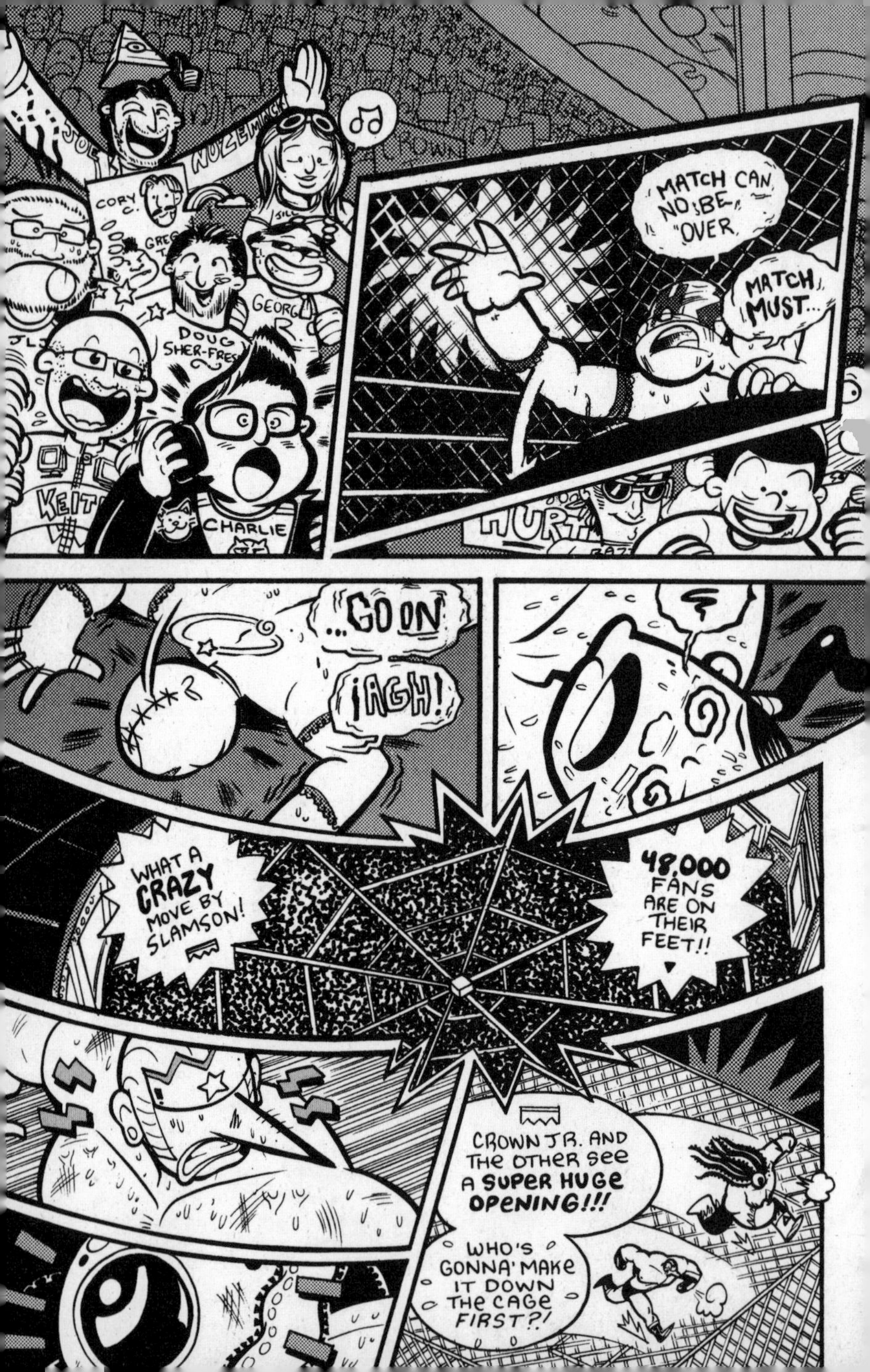
JOE
NOZEMINCH
CORY C.
GREG T.
JILL
GEORGE R.
DOUG SHER-FRESH
KEITH
CHARLIE
CROWN
HURT
MATCH CAN NO BE "OVER
MATCH MUST...
...GO ON
¡AGH!
WHAT A CRAZY MOVE BY SLAMSON!
48,000 FANS ARE ON THEIR FEET!!
CROWN JR. AND THE OTHER SEE A SUPER HUGE OPENING!!!
WHO'S GONNA' MAKE IT DOWN THE CAGE FIRST?!

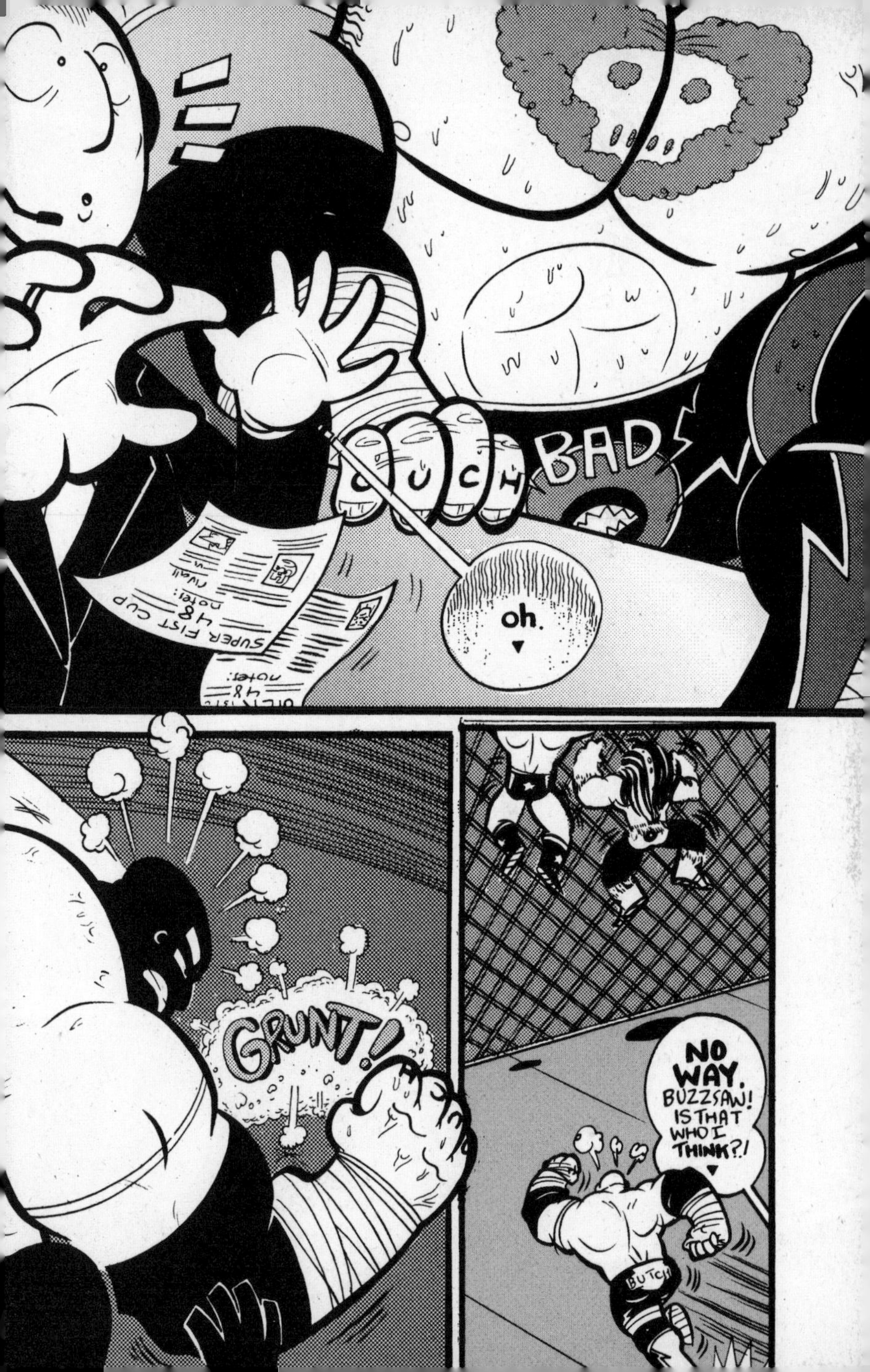
OUCH
BAD
SUPER FIST CUP
48
notes:
oh.
GRUNT!
NO WAY. BUZZSAW! IS THAT WHO I THINK?!
BUTCH

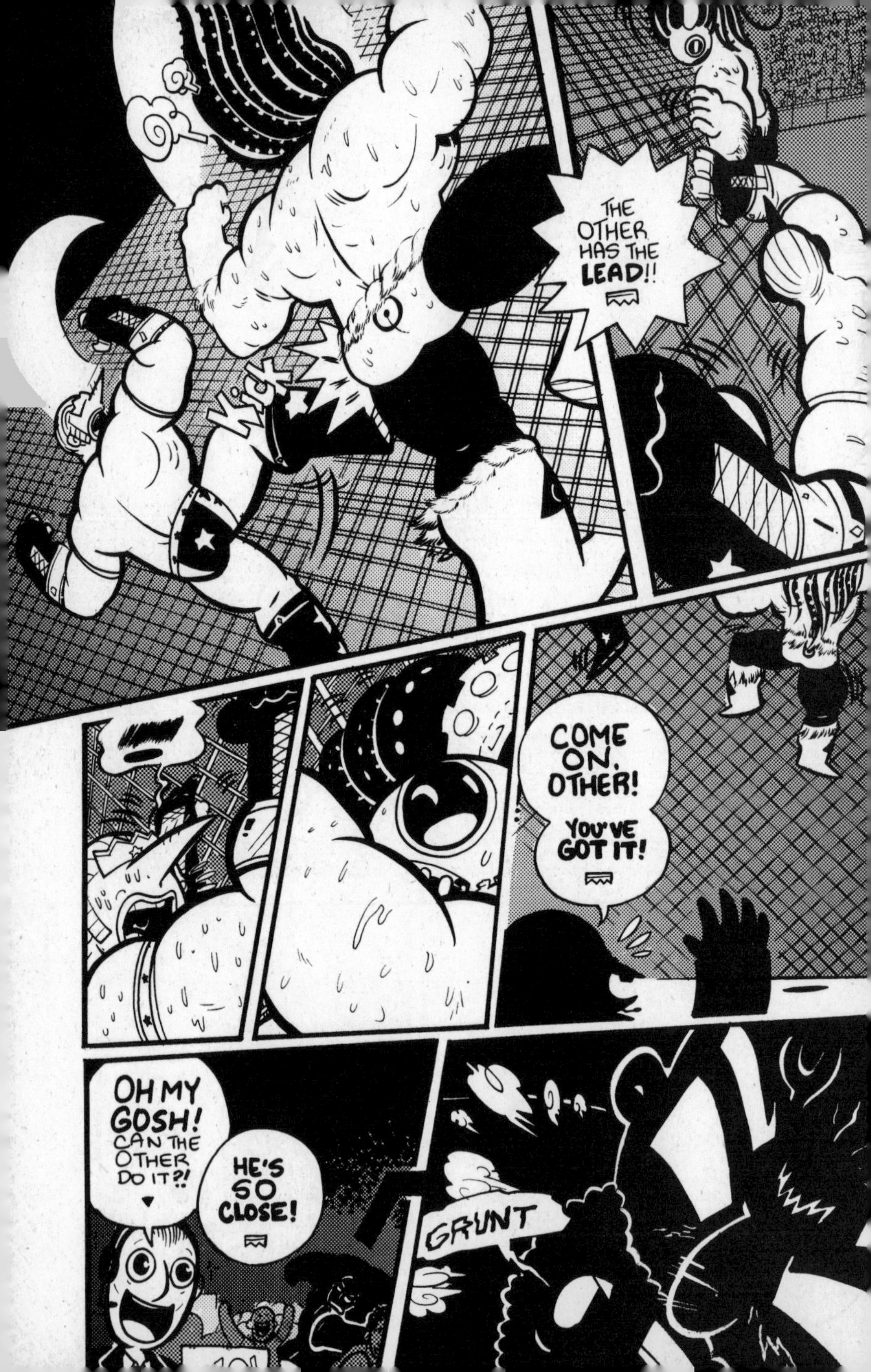
KICK
THE OTHER HAS THE LEAD!!
COME ON, OTHER!
YOU'VE GOT IT!
OH MY GOSH! CAN THE OTHER DO IT?!
HE'S SO CLOSE!
GRUNT

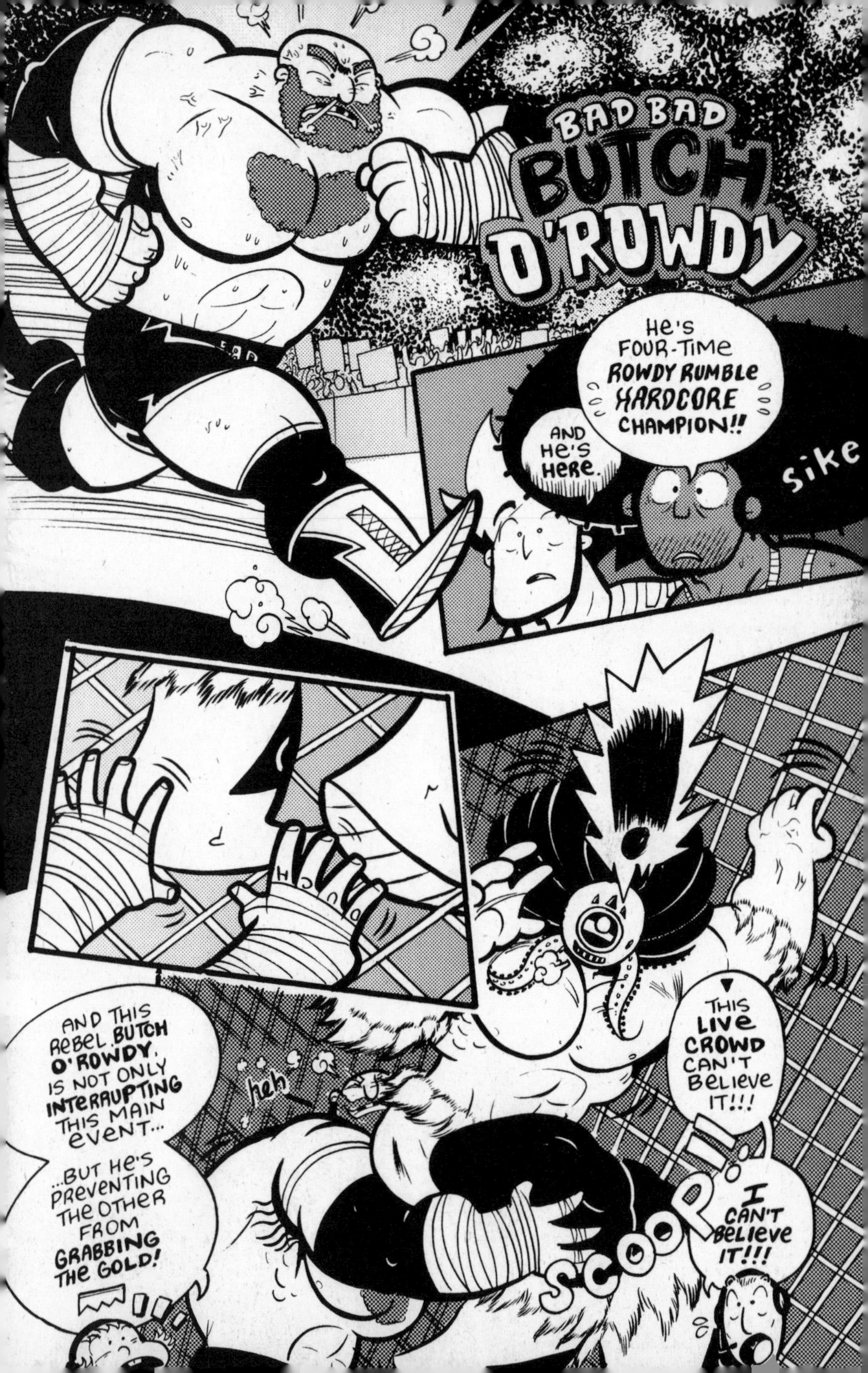

BAD BAD BUTCH O'ROWDY
He's FOUR-TIME ROWDY RUMBLE HARDCORE CHAMPION!!
AND He's HERE.
sike
AND THIS Rebel, BUTCH O'ROWDY, IS NOT ONLY INTERRUPTING THIS MAIN event...
...BUT He's PREVENTING THE OTHER FROM GRABBING THE GOLD!
heh
THIS LIVE CROWD CAN'T Believe IT!!!
SCOOP!!
I CAN'T Believe IT!!!

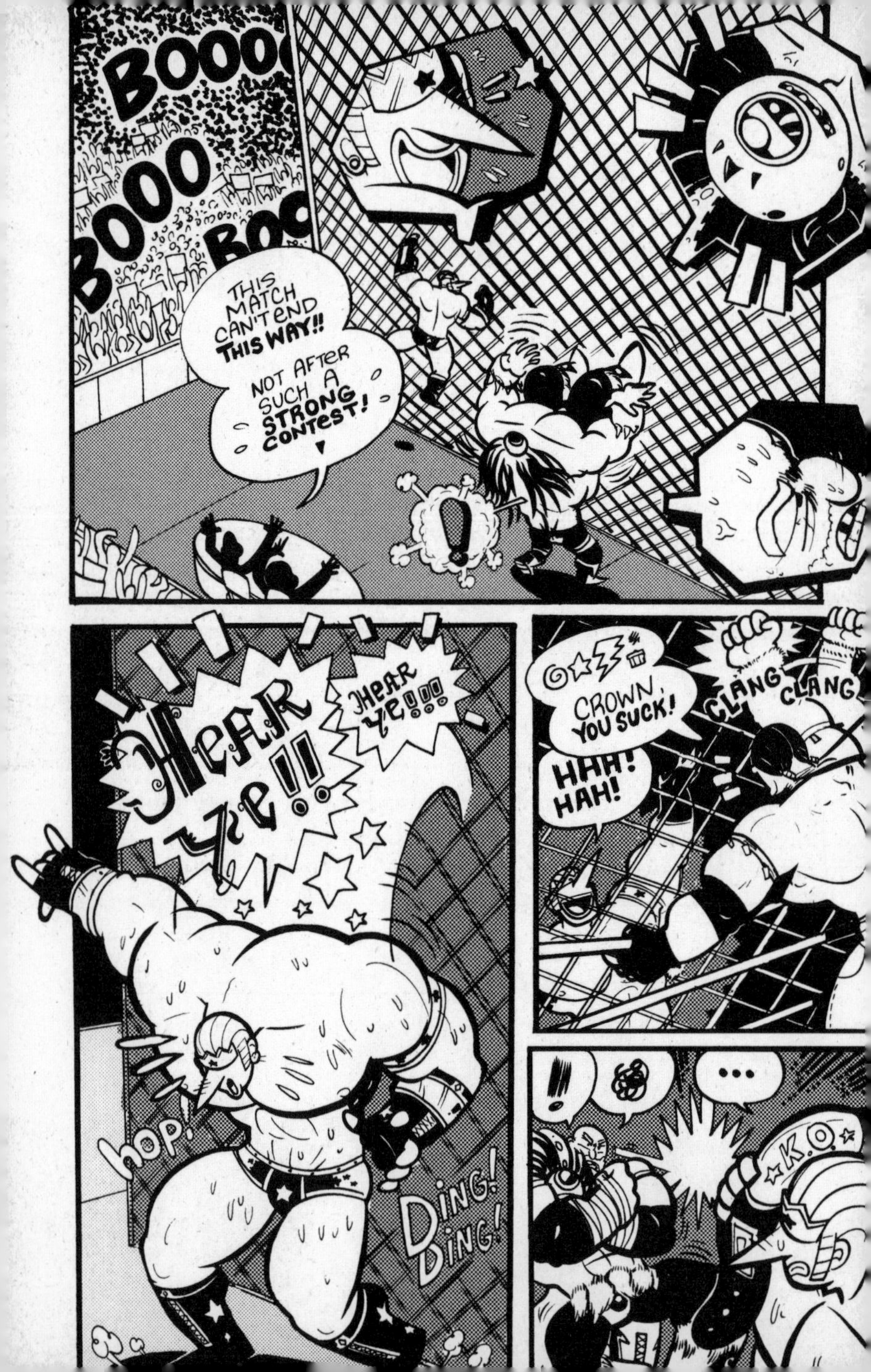
BOOOO
BOOO
BOOO
BOO
THIS MATCH CAN'T END THIS WAY!!
NOT AFTER SUCH A STRONG CONTEST!
!
HEAR YE!!
HEAR YE!!!
hop!
DING! DING!
CROWN, YOU SUCK!
HAH! HAH!
CLANG CLANG
!
...
K.O.

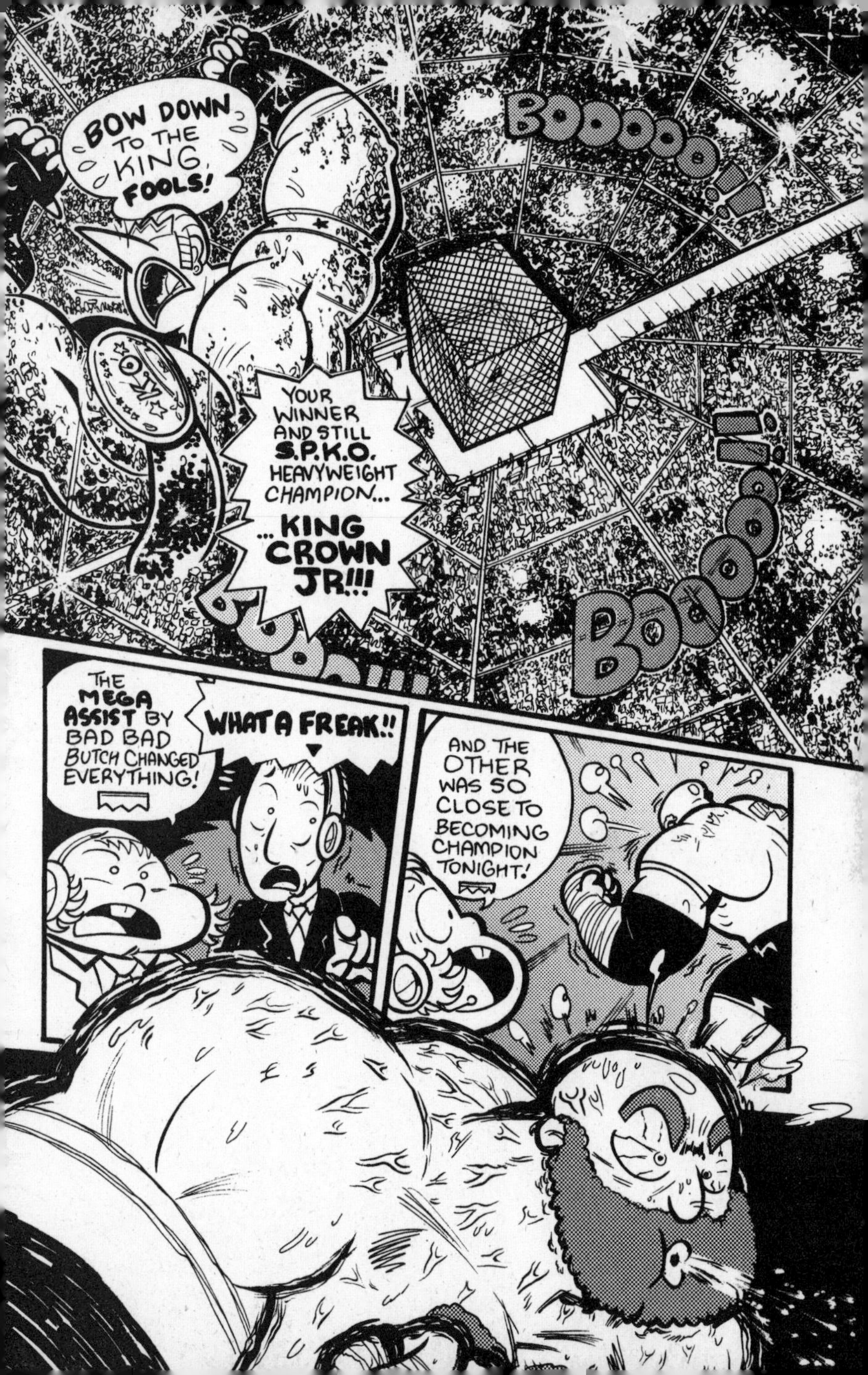
BOW DOWN TO THE KING, FOOLS!
BOOOOO!!
YOUR WINNER AND STILL S.P.K.O. HEAVYWEIGHT CHAMPION...
...KING CROWN JR!!!
BOOOOOO!!
THE MEGA ASSIST BY BAD BAD BUTCH CHANGED EVERYTHING!
WHAT A FREAK!!
AND THE OTHER WAS SO CLOSE TO BECOMING CHAMPION TONIGHT!

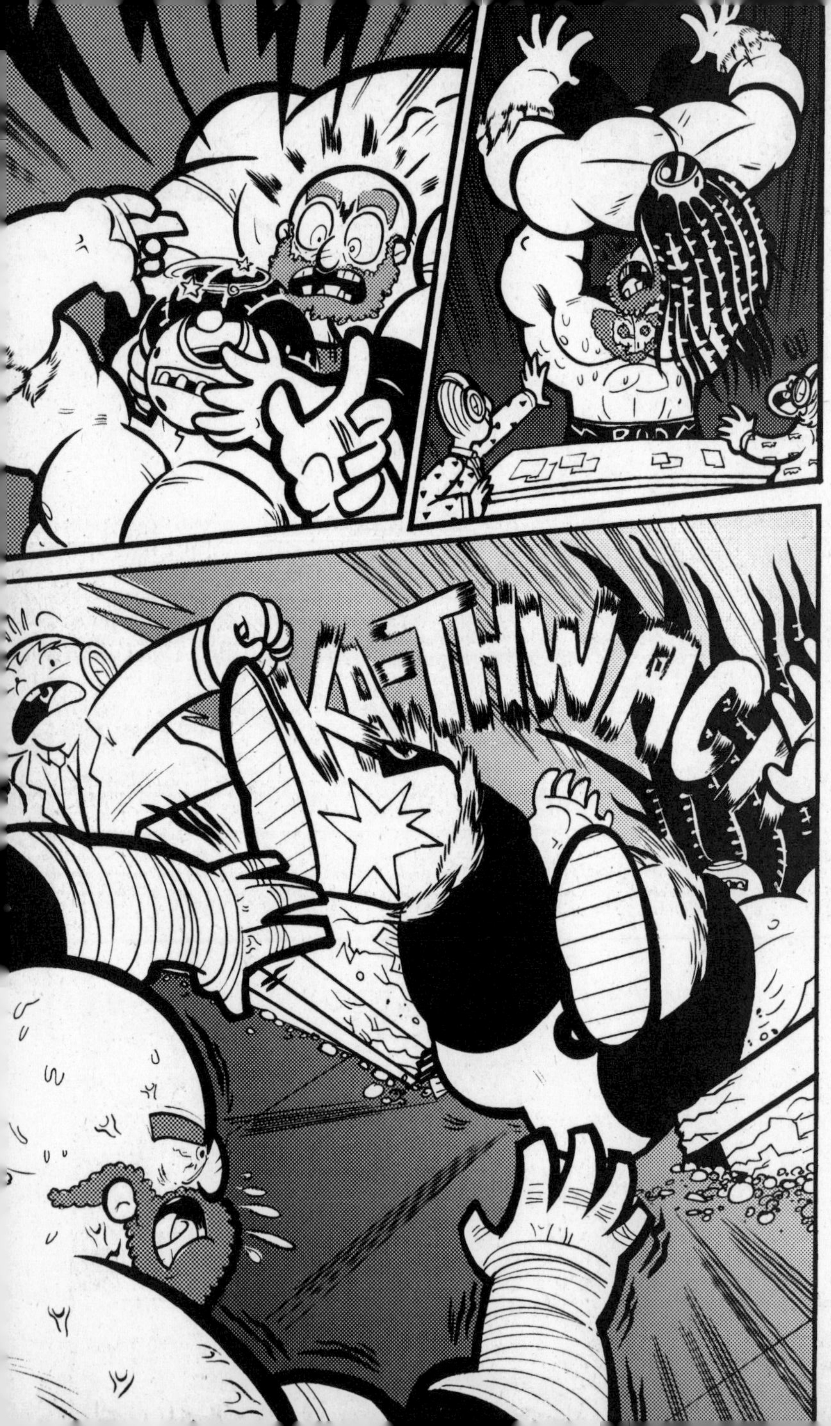
KA-THWACK

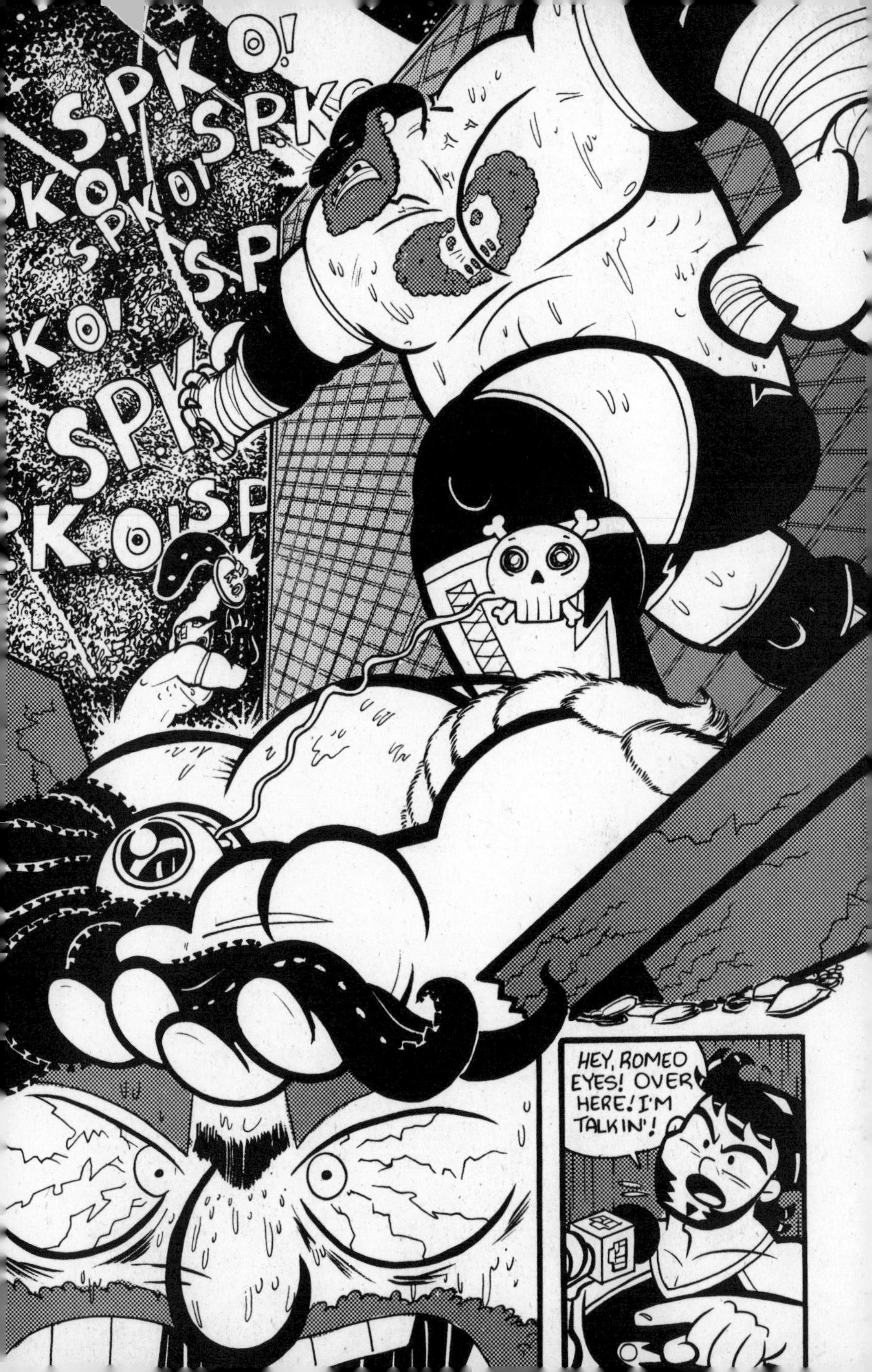
SPKO! SPKO! SPKO!
HEY, ROMEO EYES! OVER HERE! I'M TALKIN'!

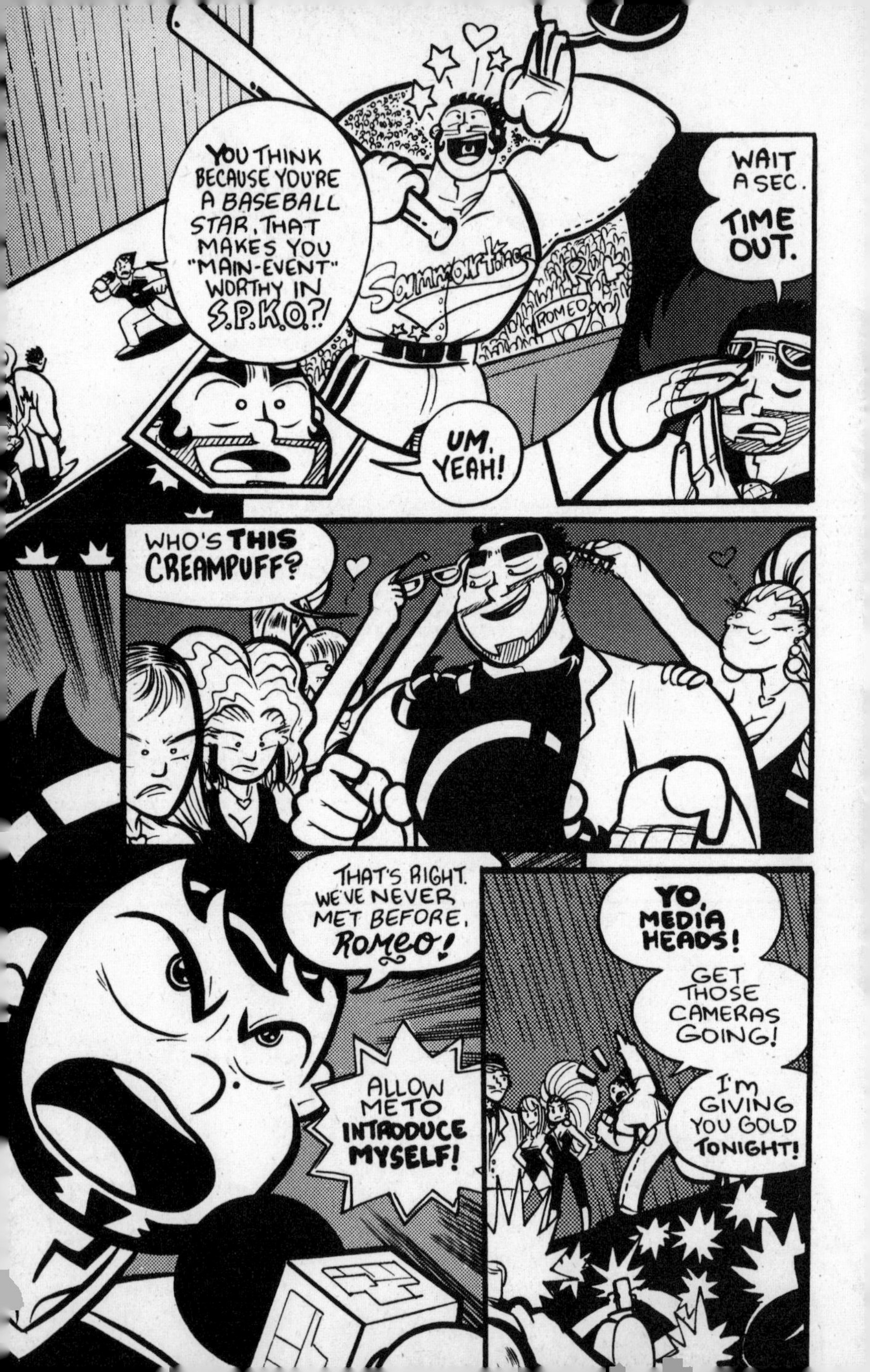
YOU THINK BECAUSE YOU'RE A BASEBALL STAR, THAT MAKES YOU "MAIN-EVENT" WORTHY IN S.P.K.O.?!
UM, YEAH!
WAIT A SEC.
TIME OUT.
ROMEO
WHO'S THIS CREAMPUFF?
THAT'S RIGHT. WE'VE NEVER MET BEFORE, ROMEO!
ALLOW ME TO INTRODUCE MYSELF!
YO, MEDIA HEADS!
GET THOSE CAMERAS GOING!
I'M GIVING YOU GOLD TONIGHT!

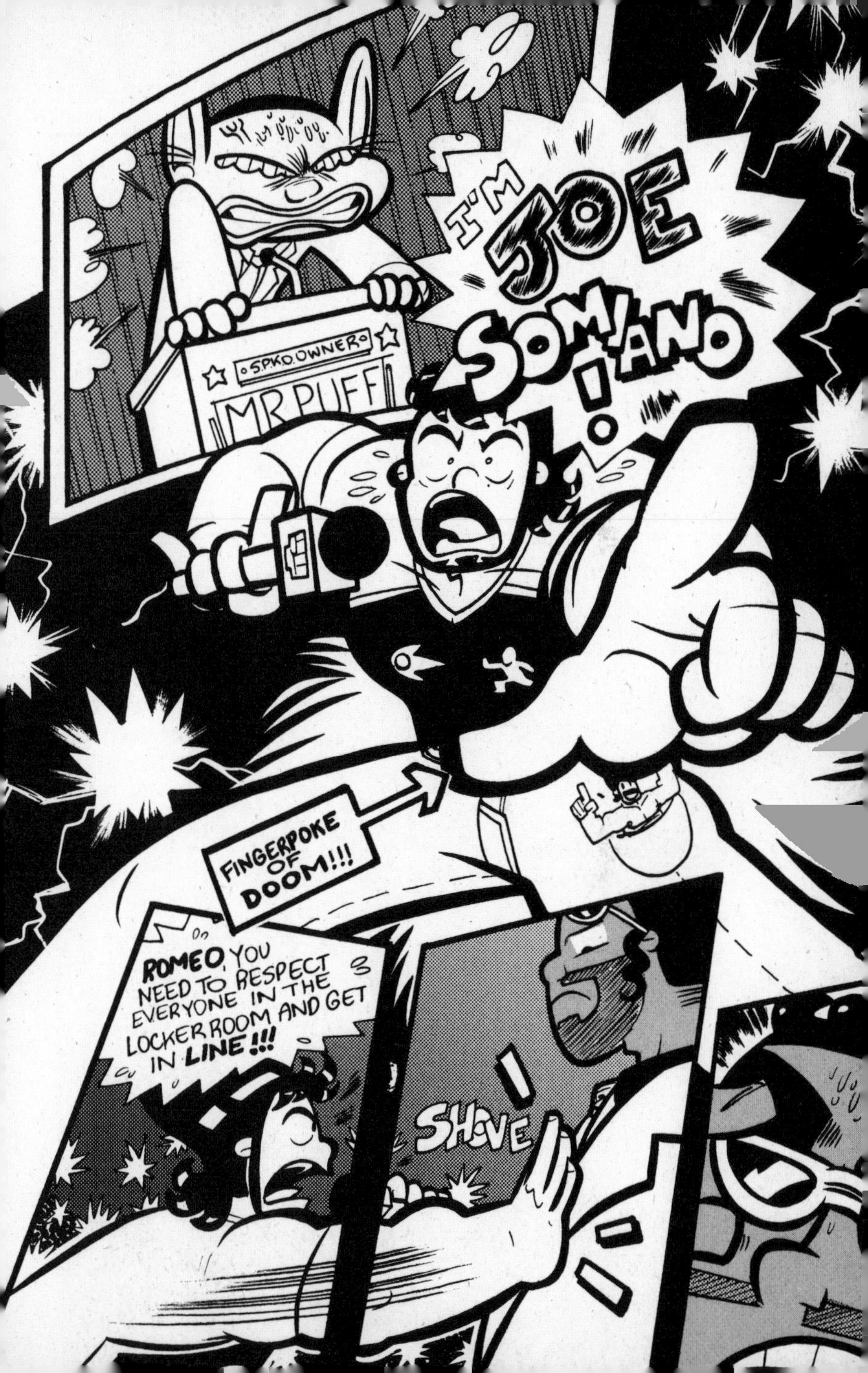

S.P.K.O. OWNER
MR PUFF
I'M JOE SOMIANO!
FINGERPOKE OF DOOM!!!
ROMEO, YOU NEED TO RESPECT EVERYONE IN THE LOCKER ROOM AND GET IN LINE!!!
SHOVE

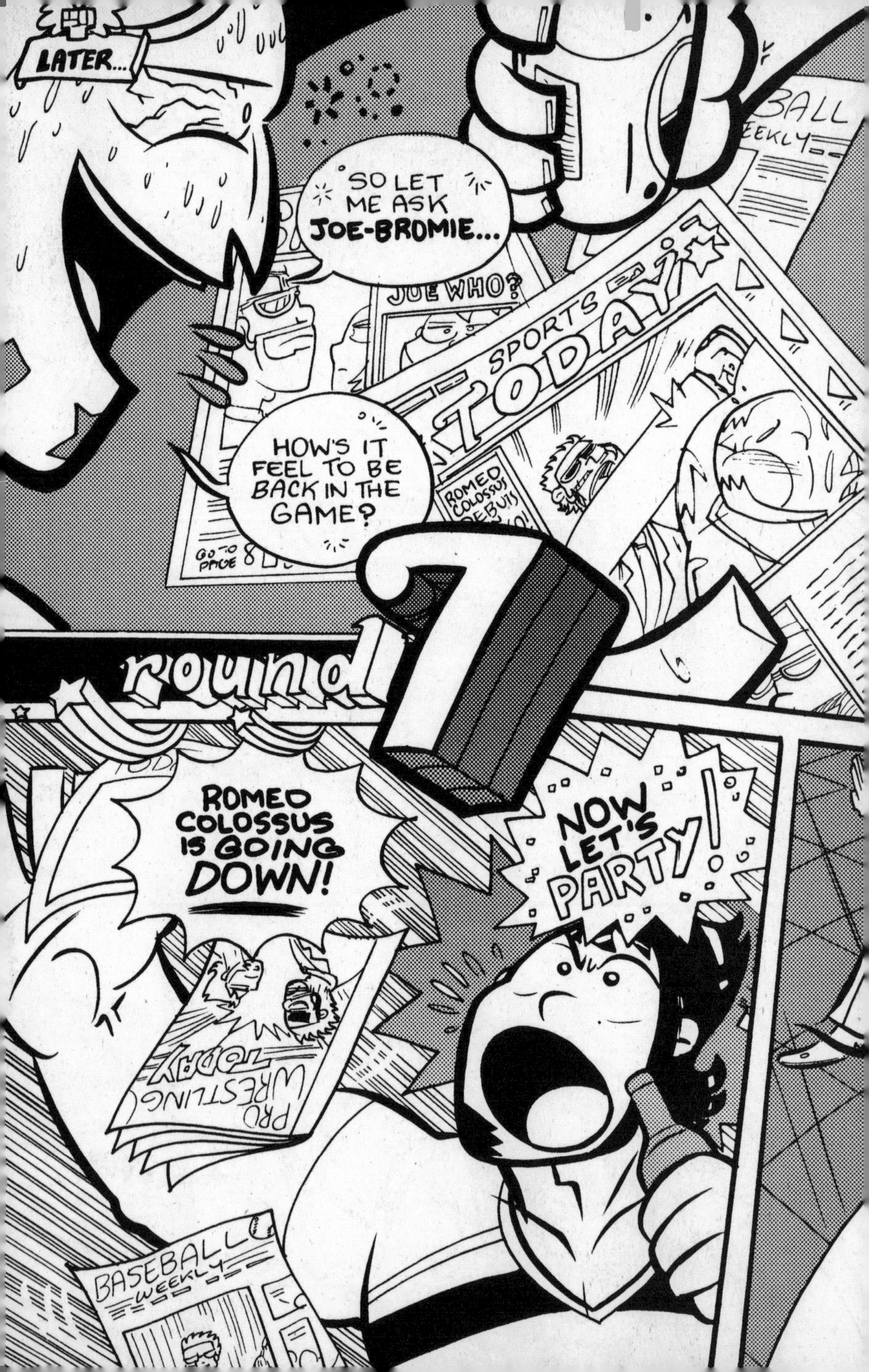
LATER...
SO LET ME ASK JOE-BROMIE...
HOW'S IT FEEL TO BE BACK IN THE GAME?
JOE WHO?
SPORTS TODAY
ROMEO COLOSSUS
GO TO PAGE 8
BALL WEEKLY
round 7
ROMEO COLOSSUS IS GOING DOWN!
NOW LET'S PARTY!
PRO WRESTLING TODAY
BASEBALL WEEKLY

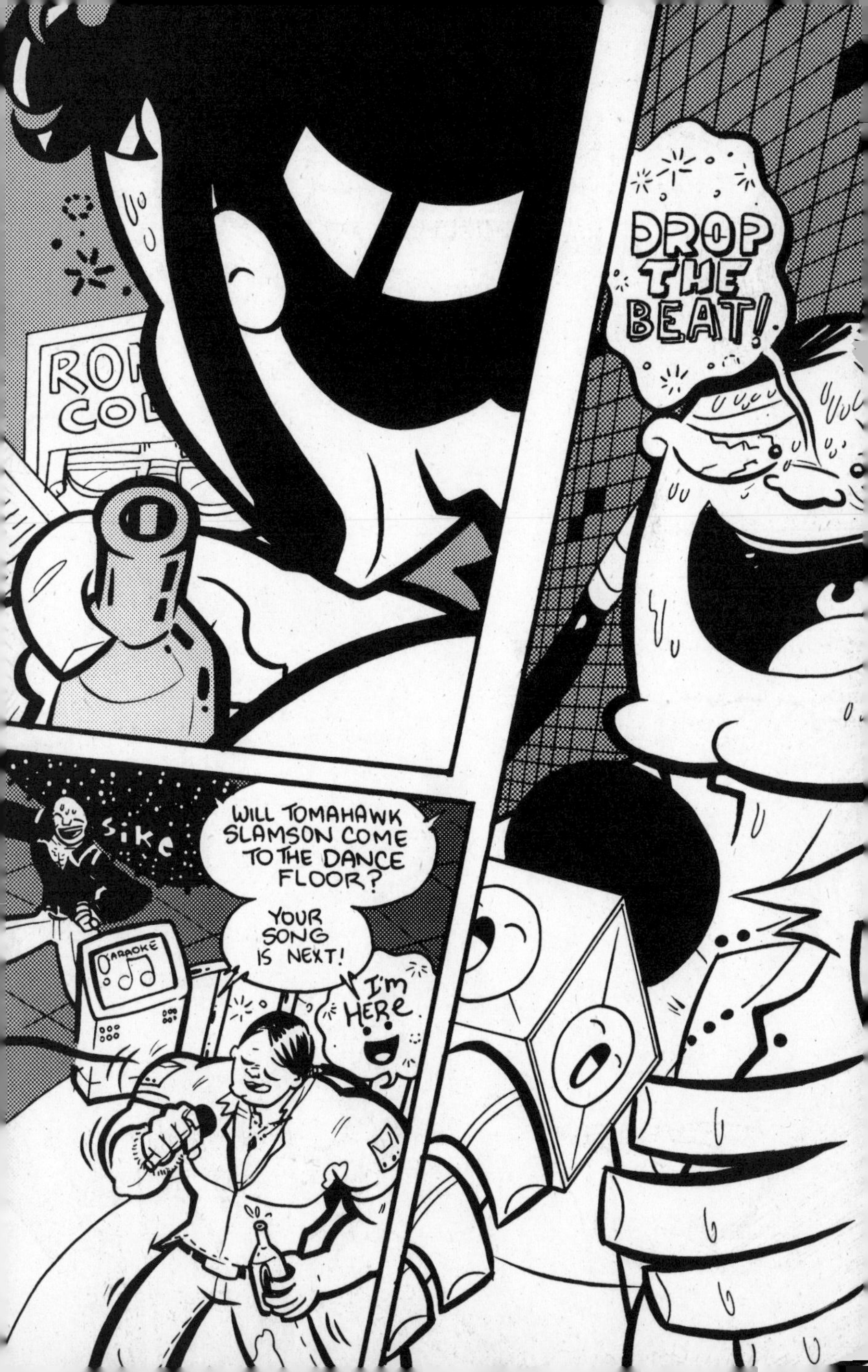
DROP THE BEAT!
WILL TOMAHAWK SLAMSON COME TO THE DANCE FLOOR?
YOUR SONG IS NEXT!
I'm HERE
SIKE
KARAOKE

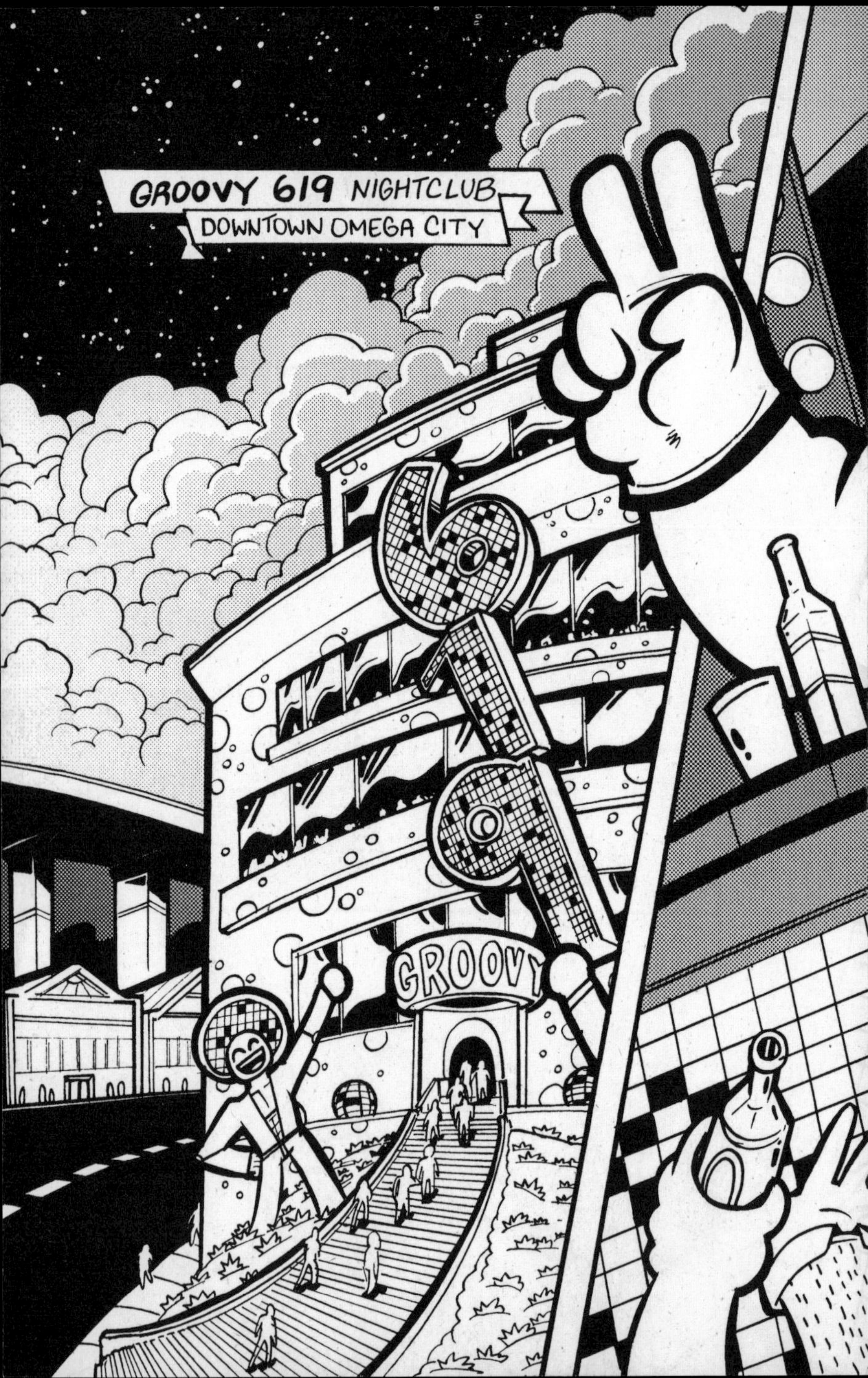

GROOVY 619 NIGHTCLUB
DOWNTOWN OMEGA CITY
GROOVY

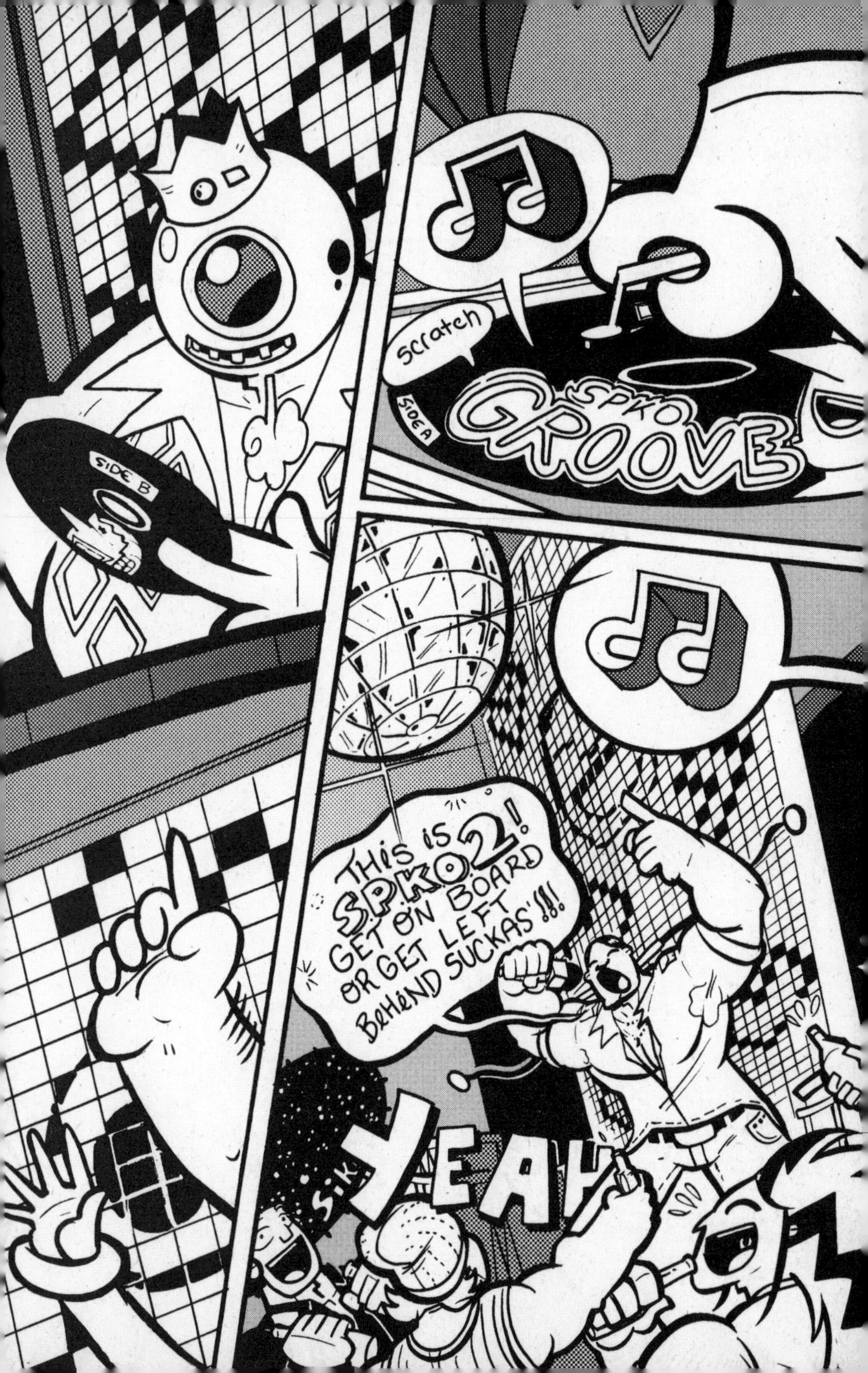
SIDE B
Scratch
SIDE A
SPKO GROOVE
THIS IS SPKO 2! GET ON BOARD OR GET LEFT BEHIND SUCKAS'!!!
YEAH

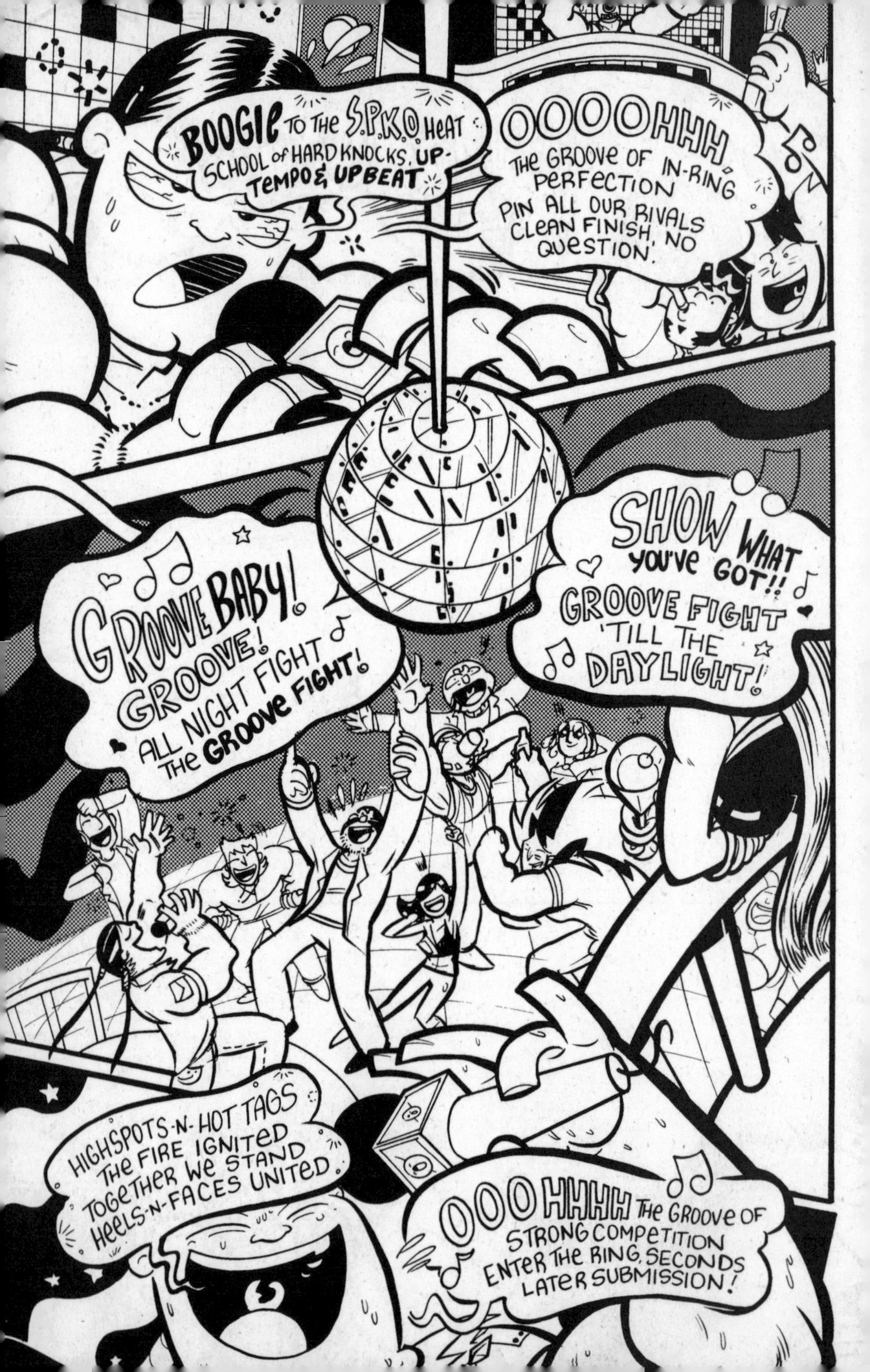

BOOGIE TO THE S.P.K.O. HEAT SCHOOL OF HARD KNOCKS, UP-TEMPO & UPBEAT
OOOOHHH THE GROOVE OF IN-RING PERFECTION PIN ALL OUR RIVALS CLEAN FINISH, NO QUESTION.
GROOVE BABY! GROOVE! ALL NIGHT FIGHT THE GROOVE FIGHT!
SHOW WHAT YOU'VE GOT!! GROOVE FIGHT 'TILL THE DAYLIGHT!
HIGHSPOTS-N-HOT TAGS THE FIRE IGNITED TOGETHER WE STAND HEELS-N-FACES UNITED
OOOHHHH THE GROOVE OF STRONG COMPETITION ENTER THE RING, SECONDS LATER SUBMISSION!

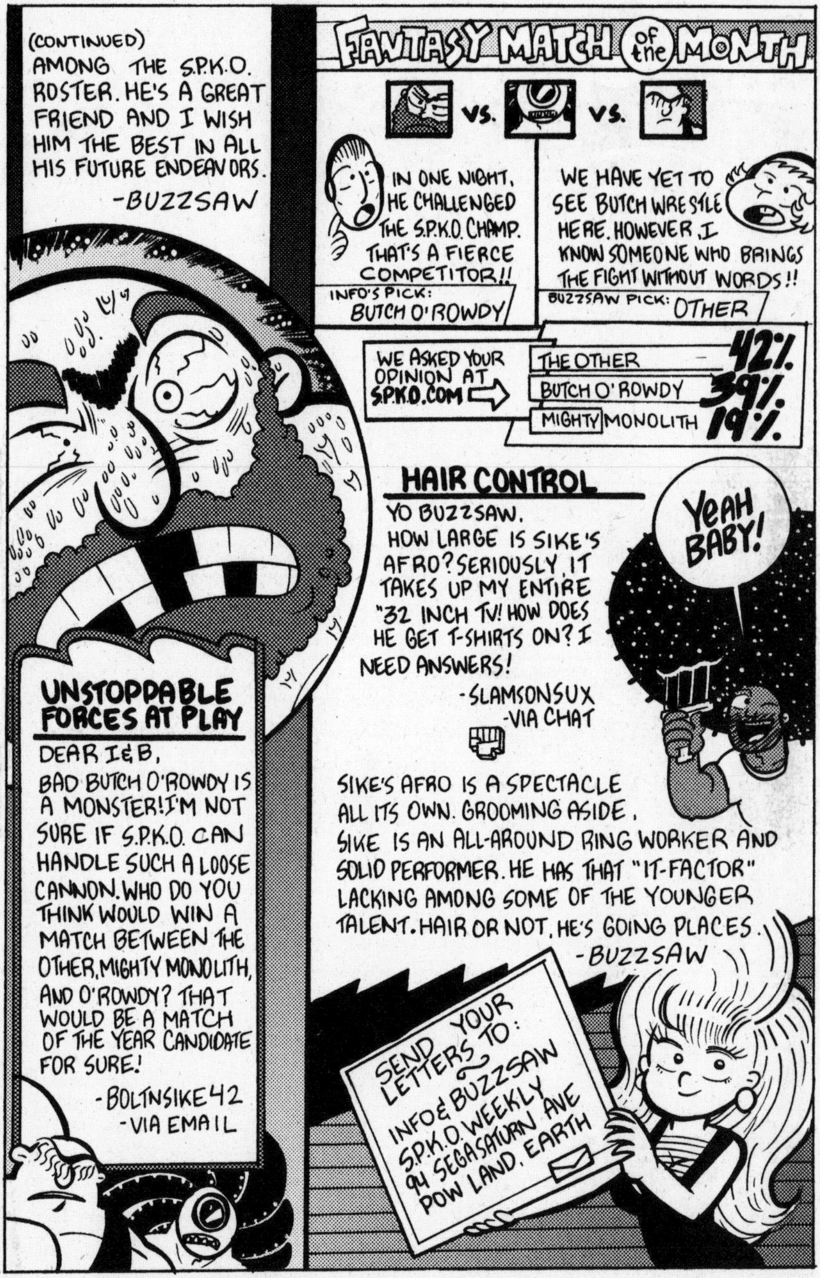
(CONTINUED)
AMONG THE S.P.K.O. ROSTER. HE'S A GREAT FRIEND AND I WISH HIM THE BEST IN ALL HIS FUTURE ENDEAVORS.
-BUZZSAW
FANTASY MATCH of the MONTH
VS.
VS.
IN ONE NIGHT, HE CHALLENGED THE S.P.K.O. CHAMP. THAT'S A FIERCE COMPETITOR!!
INFO'S PICK: BUTCH O'ROWDY
WE HAVE YET TO SEE BUTCH WRESTLE HERE. HOWEVER, I KNOW SOMEONE WHO BRINGS THE FIGHT WITHOUT WORDS!!
BUZZSAW PICK: OTHER
WE ASKED YOUR OPINION AT S.P.K.O.COM
THE OTHER 42%.
BUTCH O'ROWDY 39%.
MIGHTY MONOLITH 19%.
HAIR CONTROL
YO BUZZSAW.
HOW LARGE IS SIKE'S AFRO? SERIOUSLY, IT TAKES UP MY ENTIRE "32 INCH TV! HOW DOES HE GET T-SHIRTS ON? I NEED ANSWERS!
-SLAMSONSUX
-VIA CHAT
YEAH BABY!
SIKE'S AFRO IS A SPECTACLE ALL ITS OWN. GROOMING ASIDE, SIKE IS AN ALL-AROUND RING WORKER AND SOLID PERFORMER. HE HAS THAT "IT-FACTOR" LACKING AMONG SOME OF THE YOUNGER TALENT. HAIR OR NOT, HE'S GOING PLACES.
-BUZZSAW
UNSTOPPABLE FORCES AT PLAY
DEAR I&B,
BAD BUTCH O'ROWDY IS A MONSTER! I'M NOT SURE IF S.P.K.O. CAN HANDLE SUCH A LOOSE CANNON. WHO DO YOU THINK WOULD WIN A MATCH BETWEEN THE OTHER, MIGHTY MONOLITH, AND O'ROWDY? THAT WOULD BE A MATCH OF THE YEAR CANDIDATE FOR SURE!
-BOLTNSIKE42
-VIA EMAIL
SEND YOUR LETTERS TO:
INFO & BUZZSAW
S.P.K.O. WEEKLY
94 SEGASATURN AVE
POW LAND, EARTH

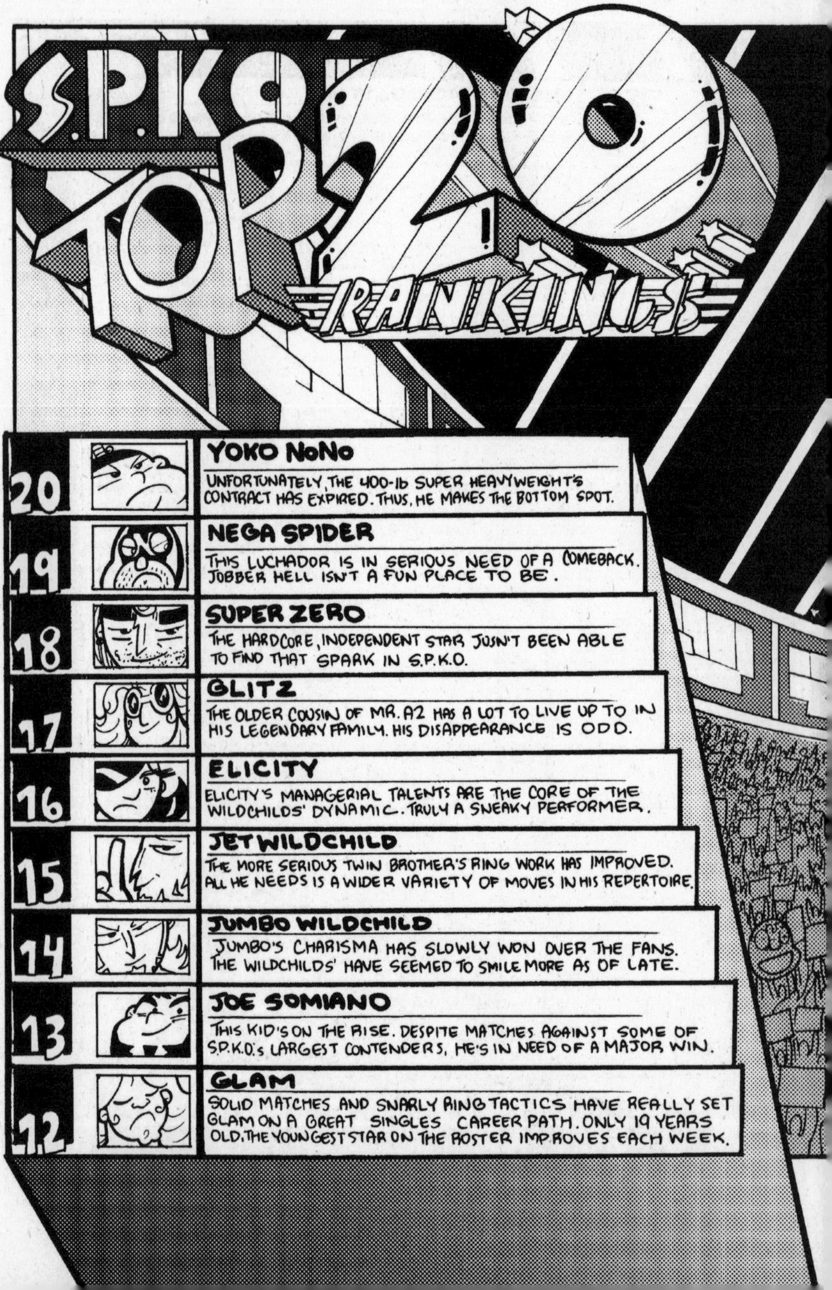
S.P.K.O.
TOP 20
RANKINGS
20
YOKO NoNo
UNFORTUNATELY, THE 400-lb SUPER HEAVYWEIGHT'S CONTRACT HAS EXPIRED. THUS, HE MAKES THE BOTTOM SPOT.
19
NEGA SPIDER
THIS LUCHADOR IS IN SERIOUS NEED OF A COMEBACK. JOBBER HELL ISN'T A FUN PLACE TO BE.
18
SUPER ZERO
THE HARDCORE, INDEPENDENT STAR JUSN'T BEEN ABLE TO FIND THAT SPARK IN S.P.K.O.
17
GLITZ
THE OLDER COUSIN OF MR. A2 HAS A LOT TO LIVE UP TO IN HIS LEGENDARY FAMILY. HIS DISAPPEARANCE IS ODD.
16
ELICITY
ELICITY'S MANAGERIAL TALENTS ARE THE CORE OF THE WILDCHILDS' DYNAMIC. TRULY A SNEAKY PERFORMER.
15
JET WILDCHILD
THE MORE SERIOUS TWIN BROTHER'S RING WORK HAS IMPROVED. ALL HE NEEDS IS A WIDER VARIETY OF MOVES IN HIS REPERTOIRE.
14
JUMBO WILDCHILD
JUMBO'S CHARISMA HAS SLOWLY WON OVER THE FANS. THE WILDCHILDS' HAVE SEEMED TO SMILE MORE AS OF LATE.
13
JOE SOMIANO
THIS KID'S ON THE RISE. DESPITE MATCHES AGAINST SOME OF S.P.K.O.'s LARGEST CONTENDERS, HE'S IN NEED OF A MAJOR WIN.
12
GLAM
SOLID MATCHES AND SNARLY RING TACTICS HAVE REALLY SET GLAM ON A GREAT SINGLES CAREER PATH. ONLY 19 YEARS OLD, THE YOUNGEST STAR ON THE ROSTER IMPROVES EACH WEEK.

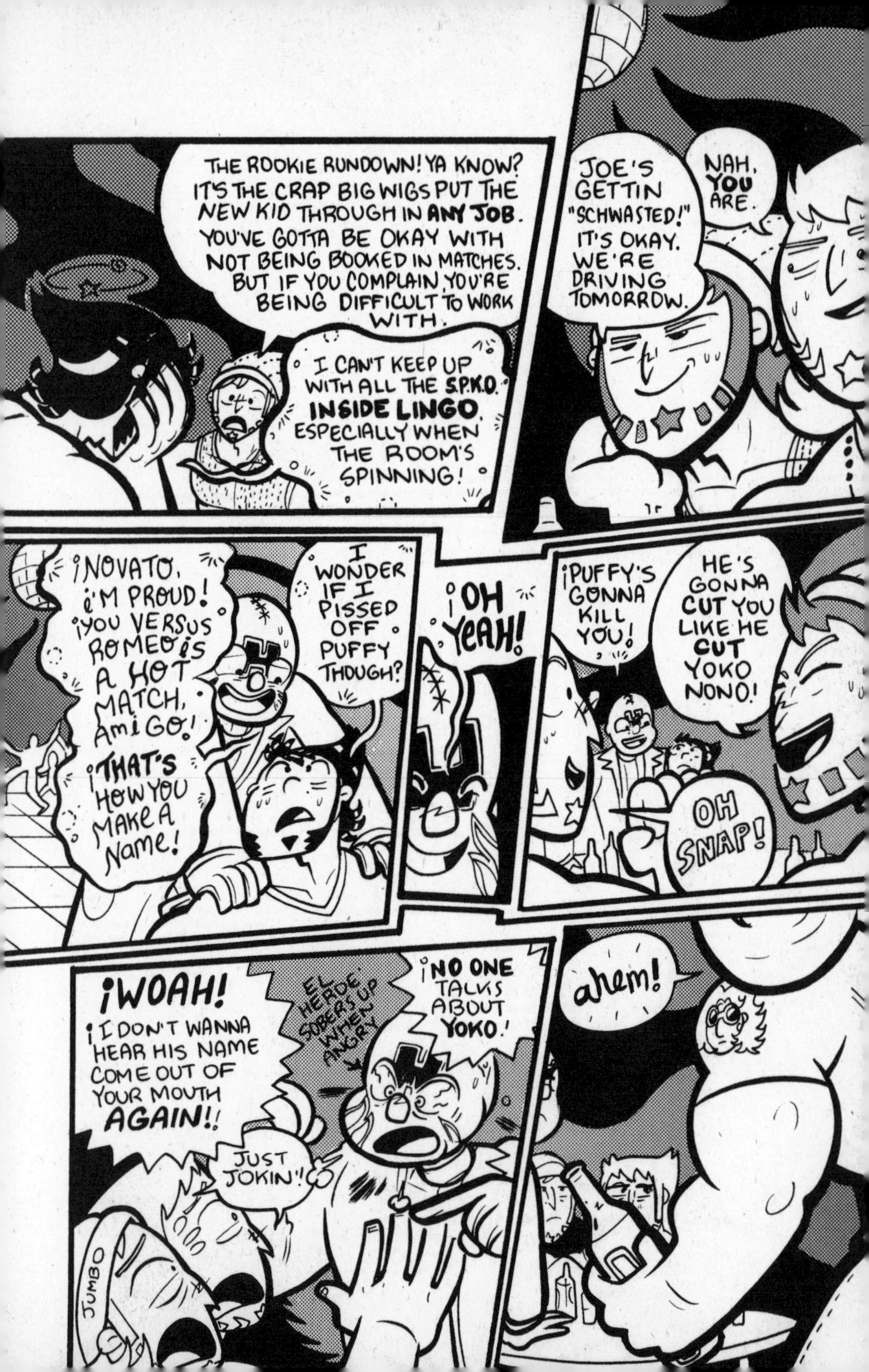
THE ROOKIE RUNDOWN! YA KNOW? IT'S THE CRAP BIG WIGS PUT THE NEW KID THROUGH IN ANY JOB. YOU'VE GOTTA BE OKAY WITH NOT BEING BOOKED IN MATCHES. BUT IF YOU COMPLAIN, YOU'RE BEING DIFFICULT TO WORK WITH.
I CAN'T KEEP UP WITH ALL THE S.P.K.O. INSIDE LINGO, ESPECIALLY WHEN THE ROOM'S SPINNING!
JOE'S GETTIN "SCHWASTED!" IT'S OKAY. WE'RE DRIVING TOMORROW.
NAH, YOU ARE.
¡NOVATO, ¿'M PROUD! ¡YOU VERSUS ROMEO IS A HOT MATCH, AMIGO! ¡THAT'S HOW YOU MAKE A NAME!
I WONDER IF I PISSED OFF PUFFY THOUGH?
¡OH YEAH!
¡PUFFY'S GONNA KILL YOU!
HE'S GONNA CUT YOU LIKE HE CUT YOKO NONO!
OH SNAP!
¡WOAH! ¡I DON'T WANNA HEAR HIS NAME COME OUT OF YOUR MOUTH AGAIN!!
EL HEROE SOBERS UP WHEN ANGRY
¡NO ONE TALKS ABOUT YOKO!
JUST JOKIN'!
ahem!
JUMBO

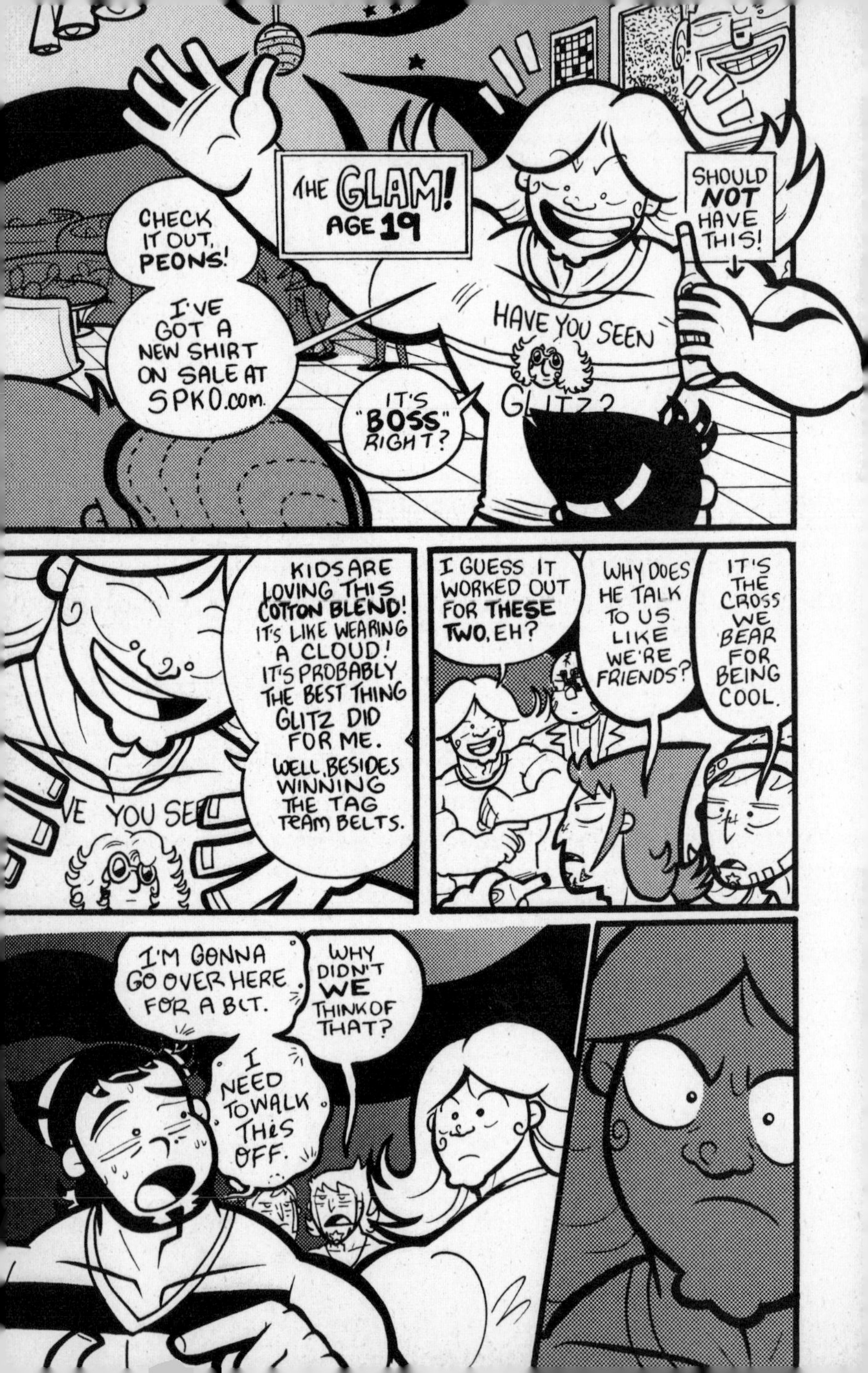
THE GLAM! AGE 19
SHOULD NOT HAVE THIS!
CHECK IT OUT, PEONS!
I'VE GOT A NEW SHIRT ON SALE AT SPKO.com.
HAVE YOU SEEN GLITZ?
IT'S "BOSS" RIGHT?
KIDS ARE LOVING THIS COTTON BLEND! IT'S LIKE WEARING A CLOUD! IT'S PROBABLY THE BEST THING GLITZ DID FOR ME.
WELL, BESIDES WINNING THE TAG TEAM BELTS.
I GUESS IT WORKED OUT FOR THESE TWO, EH?
WHY DOES HE TALK TO US LIKE WE'RE FRIENDS?
IT'S THE CROSS WE BEAR FOR BEING COOL.
I'M GONNA GO OVER HERE FOR A BLT.
I NEED TO WALK THIS OFF.
WHY DIDN'T WE THINK OF THAT?

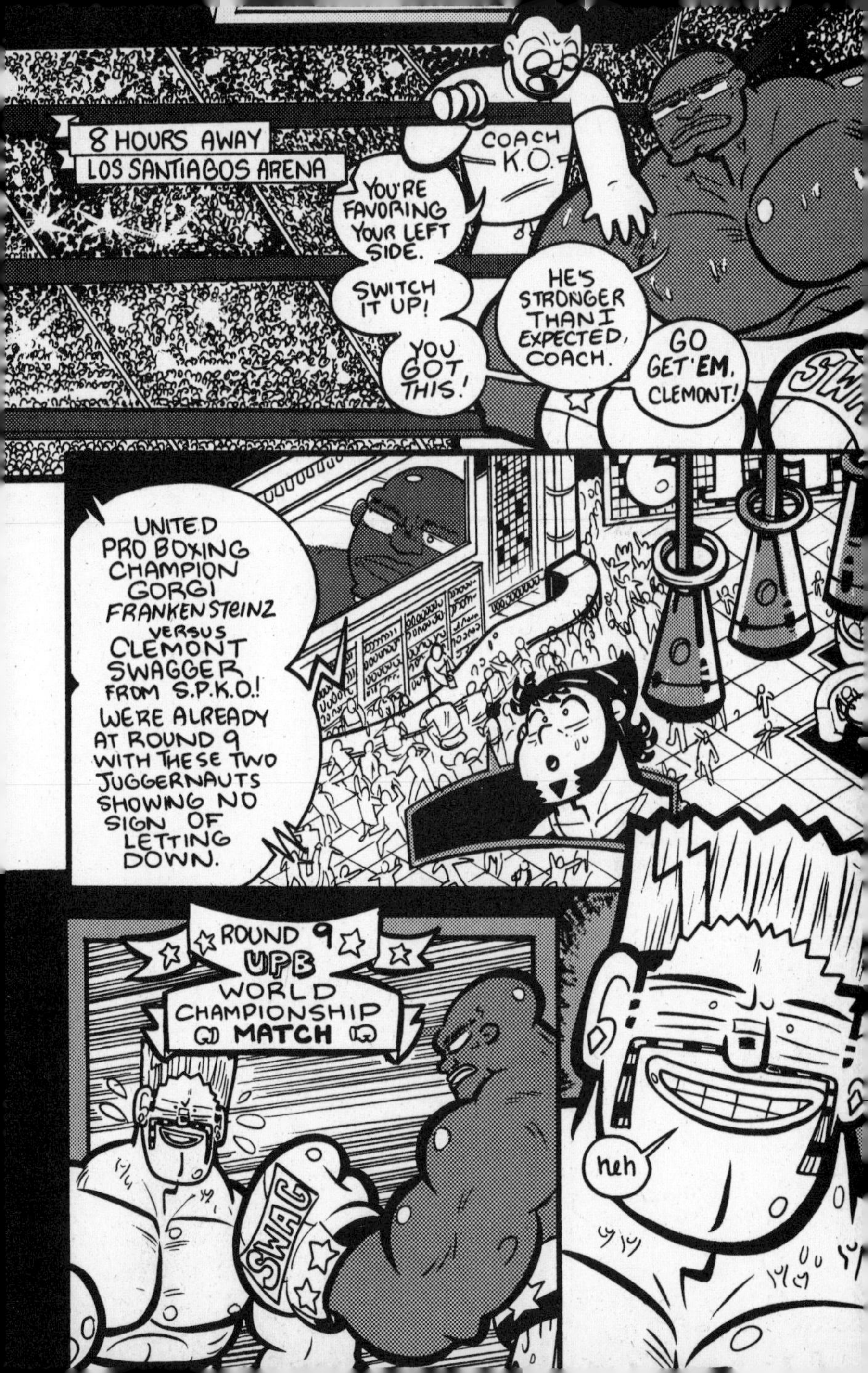
8 HOURS AWAY
LOS SANTIAGOS ARENA
COACH K.O.
YOU'RE FAVORING YOUR LEFT SIDE.
SWITCH IT UP!
YOU GOT THIS!
HE'S STRONGER THAN I EXPECTED, COACH.
GO GET 'EM, CLEMONT!
UNITED PRO BOXING CHAMPION GORGI FRANKENSTEINZ VERSUS CLEMONT SWAGGER FROM S.P.K.O.! WERE ALREADY AT ROUND 9 WITH THESE TWO JUGGERNAUTS SHOWING NO SIGN OF LETTING DOWN.
ROUND 9 UPB WORLD CHAMPIONSHIP MATCH
SWAG
neh

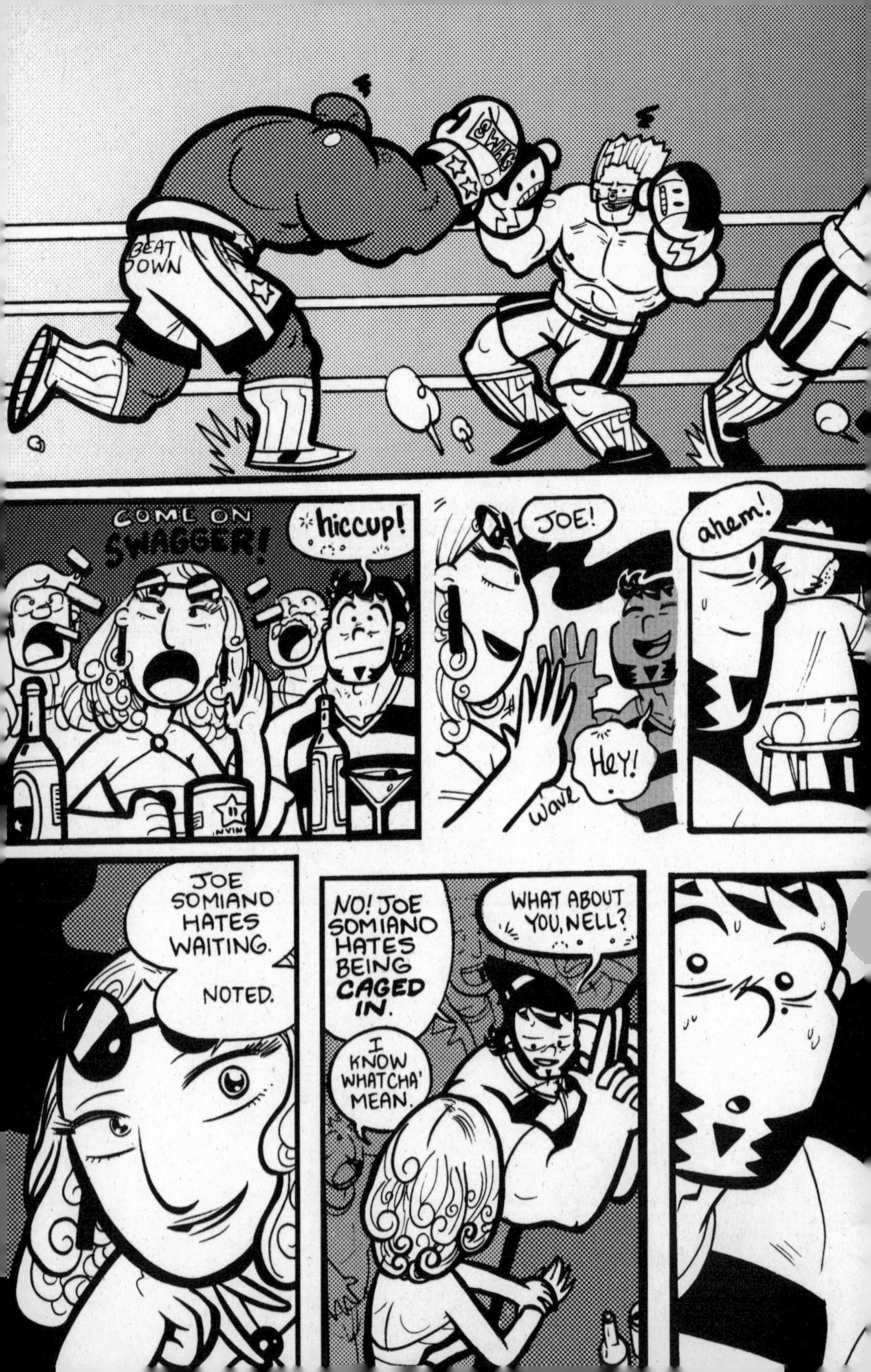

SWAG
BEAT DOWN
COME ON SWAGGER!
hiccup!
JOE!
HEY!
wave
ahem!
JOE SOMIANO HATES WAITING.
NOTED.
NO! JOE SOMIANO HATES BEING CAGED IN.
WHAT ABOUT YOU, NELL?
I KNOW WHATCHA' MEAN.

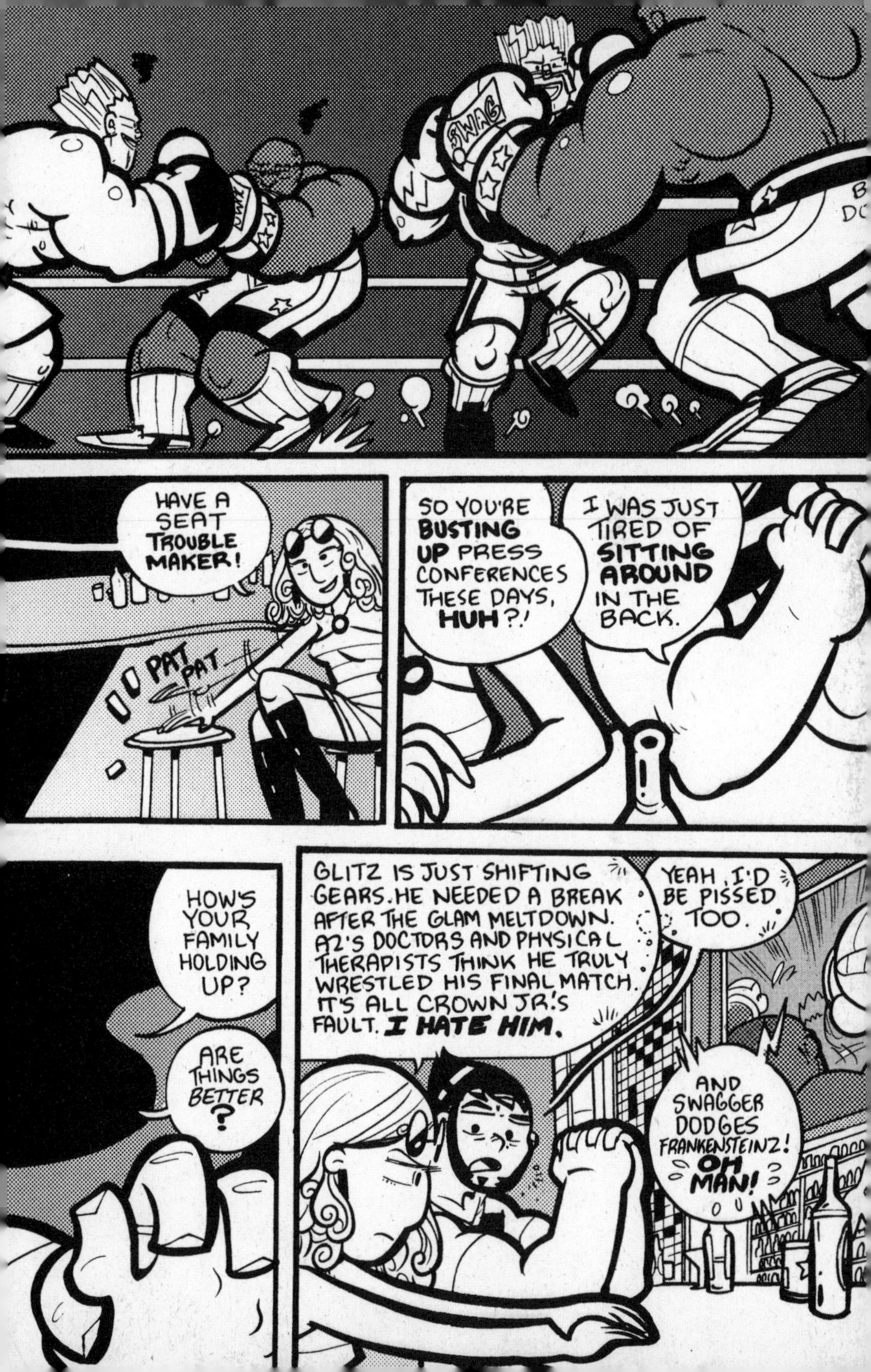
HAVE A SEAT TROUBLE MAKER!
PAT PAT
SO YOU'RE BUSTING UP PRESS CONFERENCES THESE DAYS, HUH?!
I WAS JUST TIRED OF SITTING AROUND IN THE BACK.
HOW'S YOUR FAMILY HOLDING UP?
ARE THINGS BETTER?
GLITZ IS JUST SHIFTING GEARS. HE NEEDED A BREAK AFTER THE GLAM MELTDOWN. AZ'S DOCTORS AND PHYSICAL THERAPISTS THINK HE TRULY WRESTLED HIS FINAL MATCH. IT'S ALL CROWN JR.'S FAULT. I HATE HIM.
YEAH, I'D BE PISSED TOO.
AND SWAGGER DODGES FRANKENSTEINZ! OH MAN!

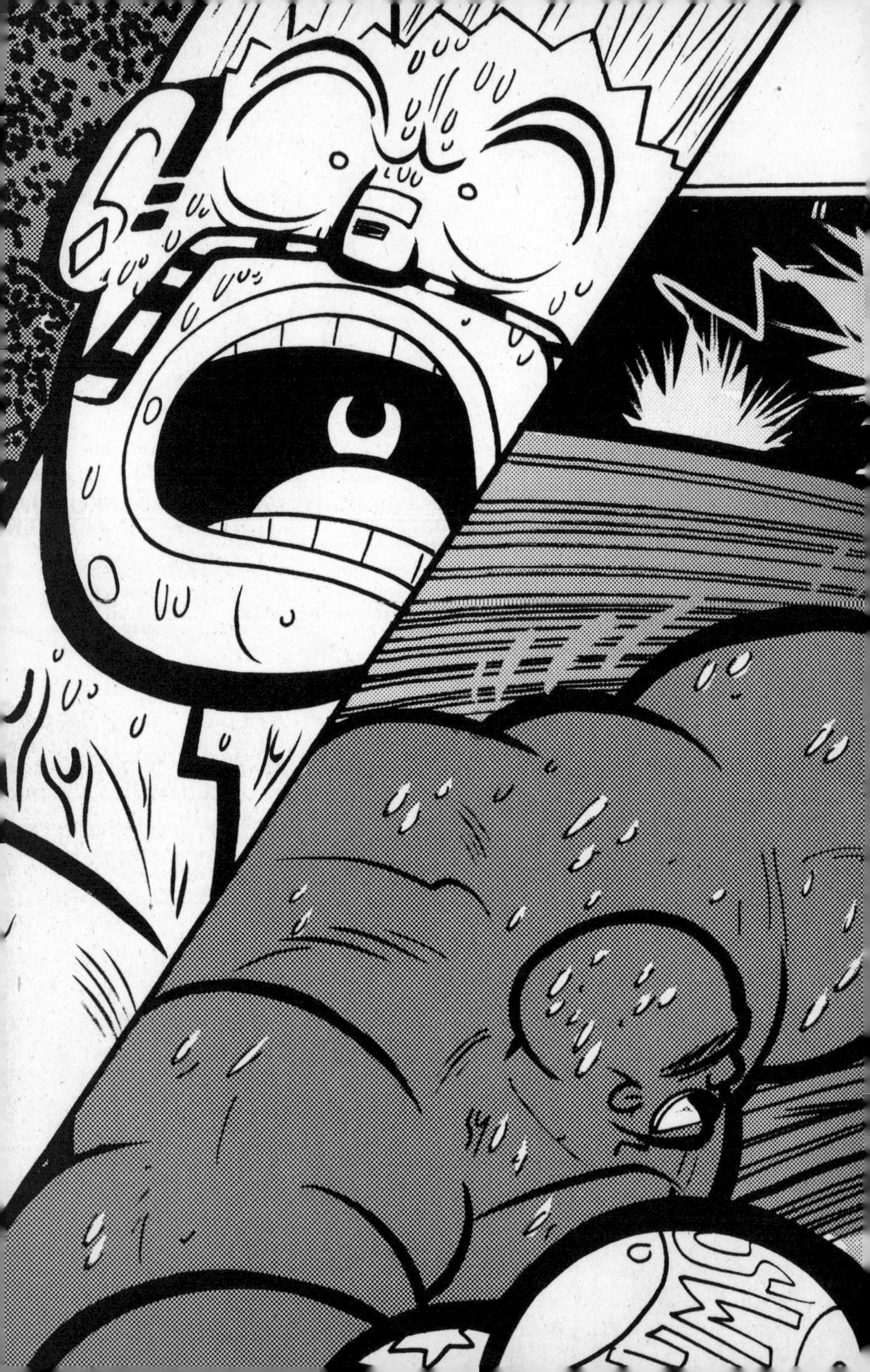

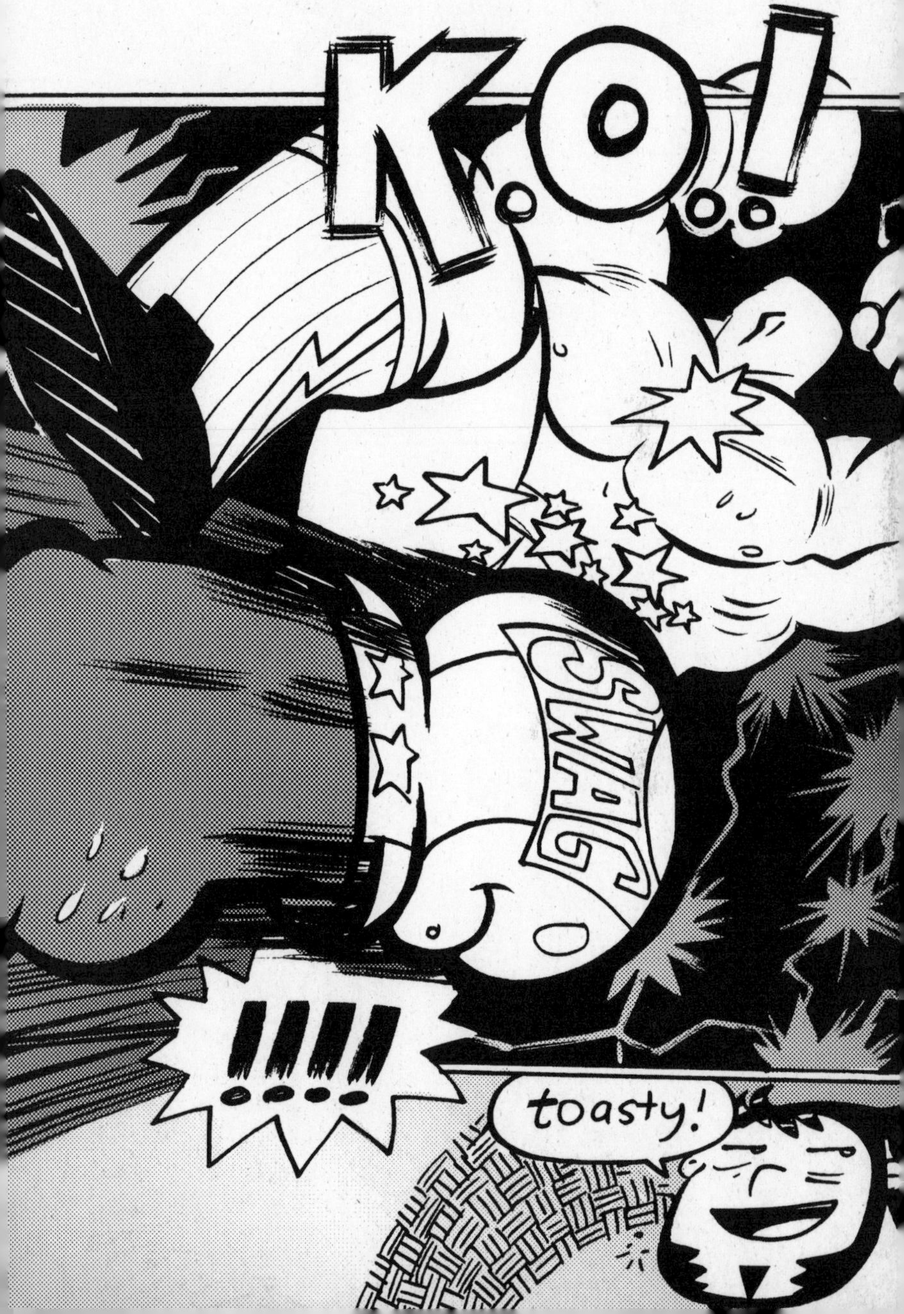
K.O.!
SWAG
!!!!!
toasty!

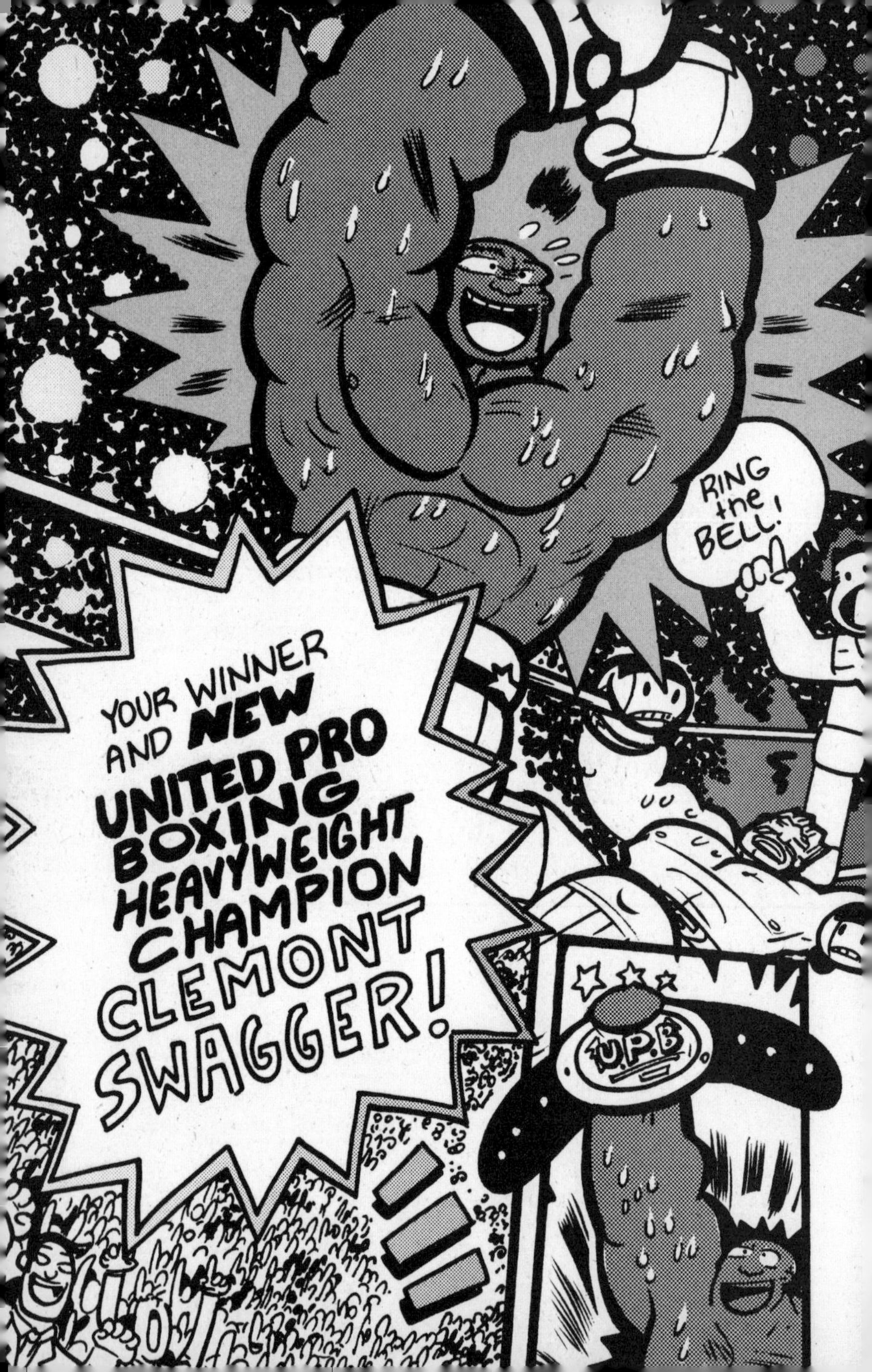
YOUR WINNER AND NEW UNITED PRO BOXING HEAVYWEIGHT CHAMPION CLEMONT SWAGGER!
RING the BELL!
U.P.B

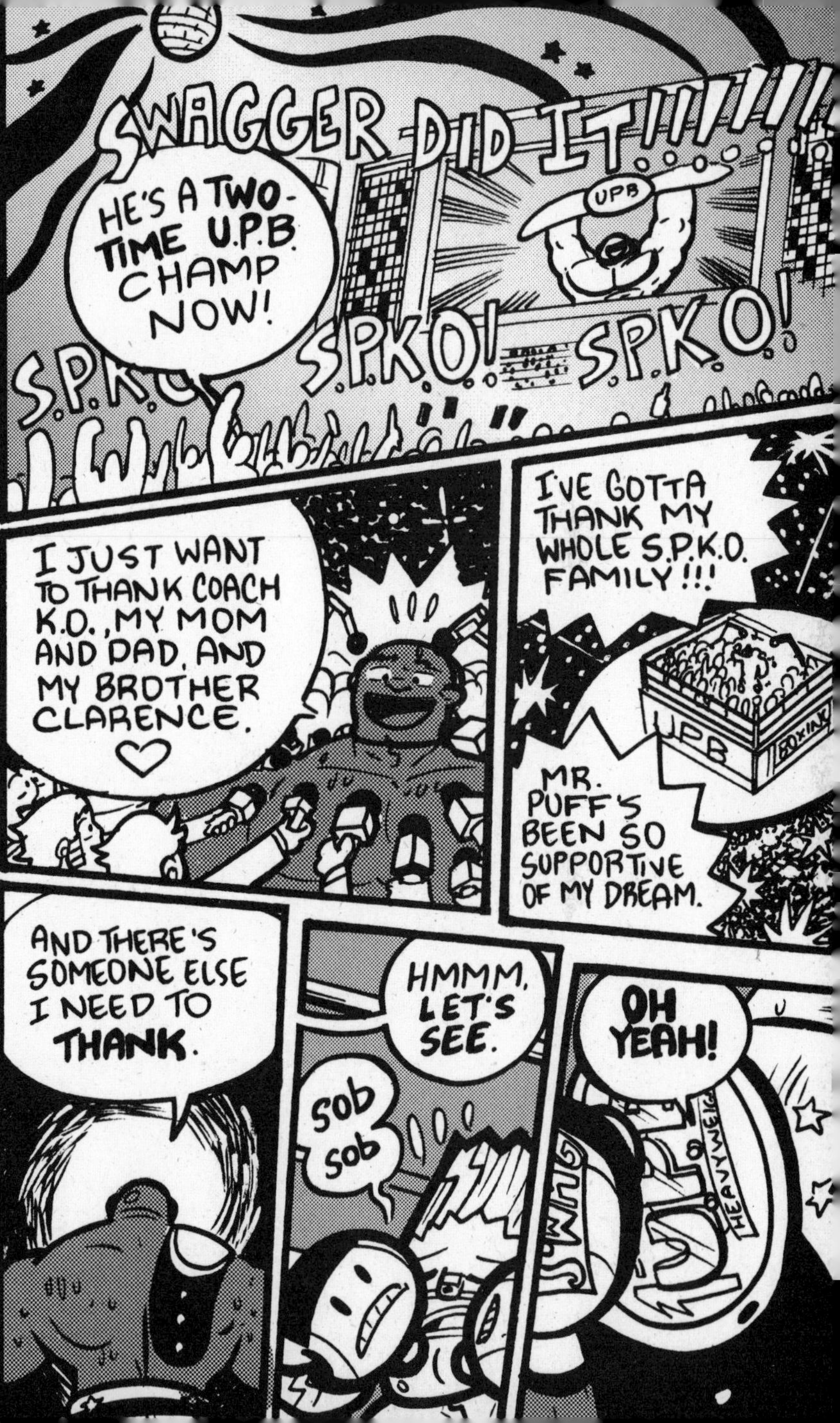
SWAGGER DID IT!!!!!!!
HE'S A TWO-TIME U.P.B. CHAMP NOW!
UPB
S.P.K.O! S.P.K.O! S.P.K.O!
I JUST WANT TO THANK COACH K.O., MY MOM AND DAD, AND MY BROTHER CLARENCE.
I'VE GOTTA THANK MY WHOLE S.P.K.O. FAMILY!!!
UPB
BOXING
MR. PUFF'S BEEN SO SUPPORTIVE OF MY DREAM.
AND THERE'S SOMEONE ELSE I NEED TO THANK.
HMMM, LET'S SEE.
sob sob
OH YEAH!
HEAVYWEIGHT

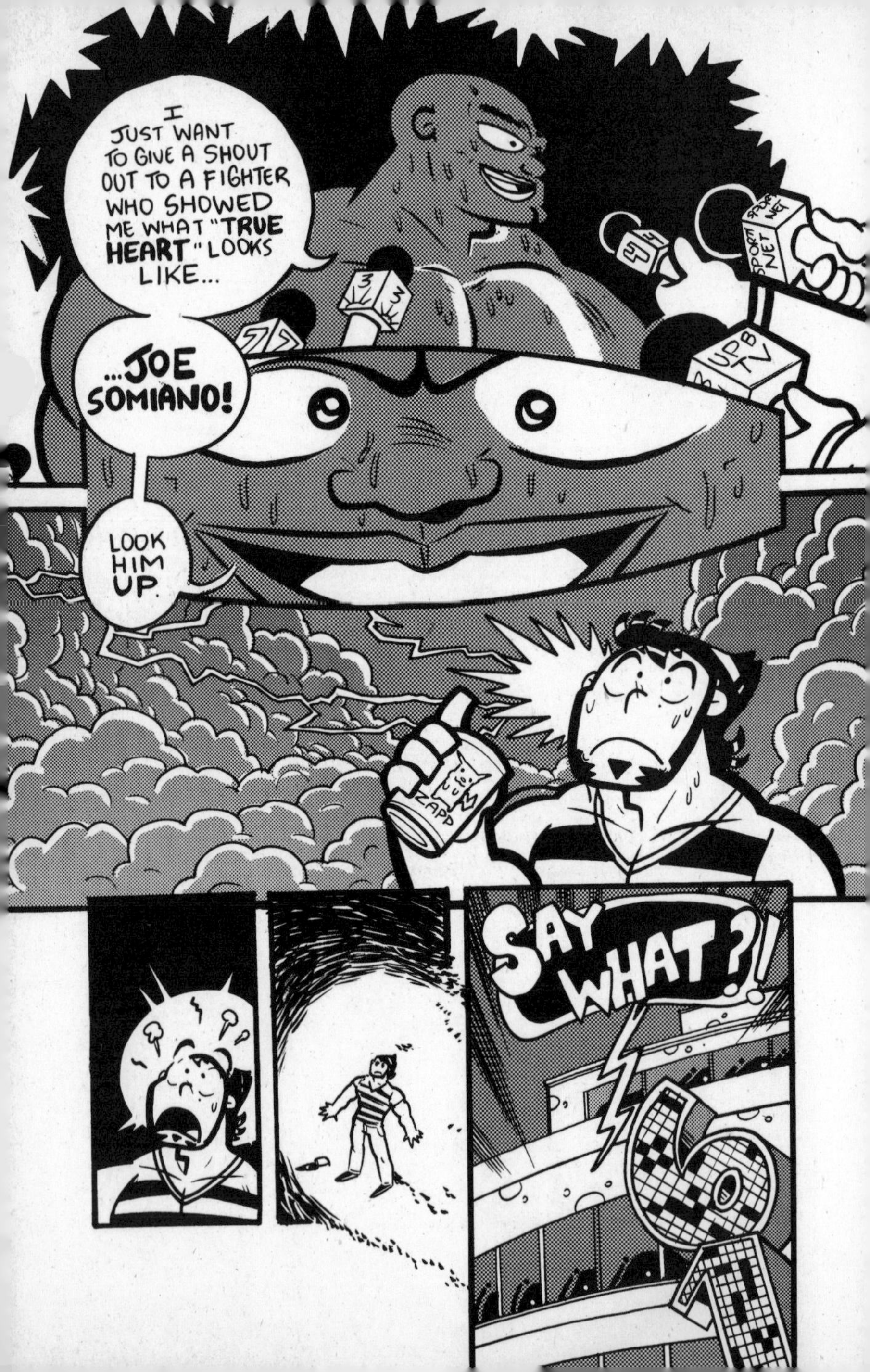
I JUST WANT TO GIVE A SHOUT OUT TO A FIGHTER WHO SHOWED ME WHAT "TRUE HEART" LOOKS LIKE...
...JOE SOMIANO!
LOOK HIM UP.
ZAPP
SAY WHAT?!

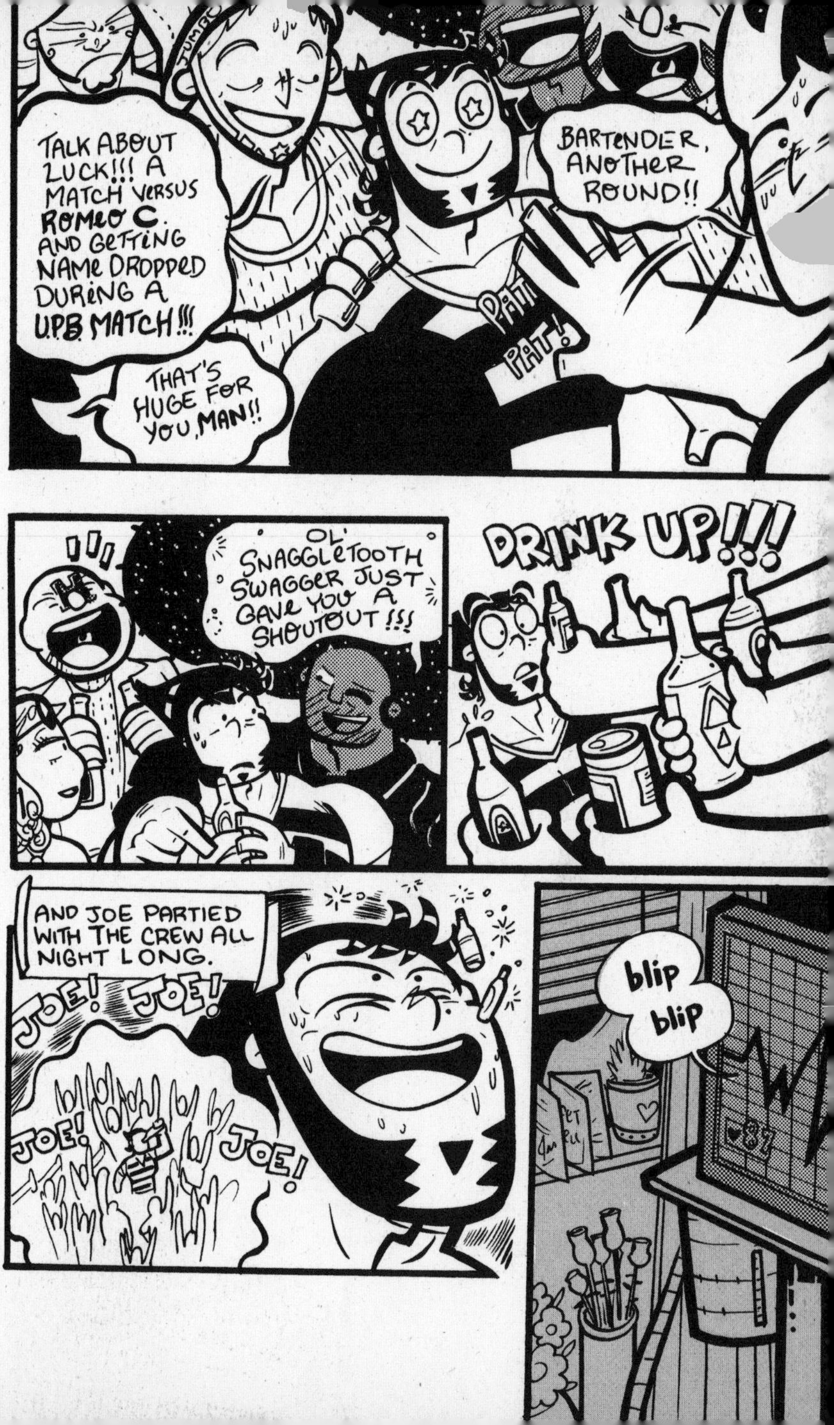
TALK ABOUT LUCK!!! A MATCH VERSUS ROMEO C. AND GETTING NAME DROPPED DURING A U.P.B. MATCH!!!
THAT'S HUGE FOR YOU, MAN!!
BARTENDER, ANOTHER ROUND!!
PAT!
PAT!
OL' SNAGGLETOOTH SWAGGER JUST GAVE YOU A SHOUTOUT!!!
DRINK UP!!!
AND JOE PARTIED WITH THE CREW ALL NIGHT LONG.
JOE! JOE!
JOE! JOE!
blip blip

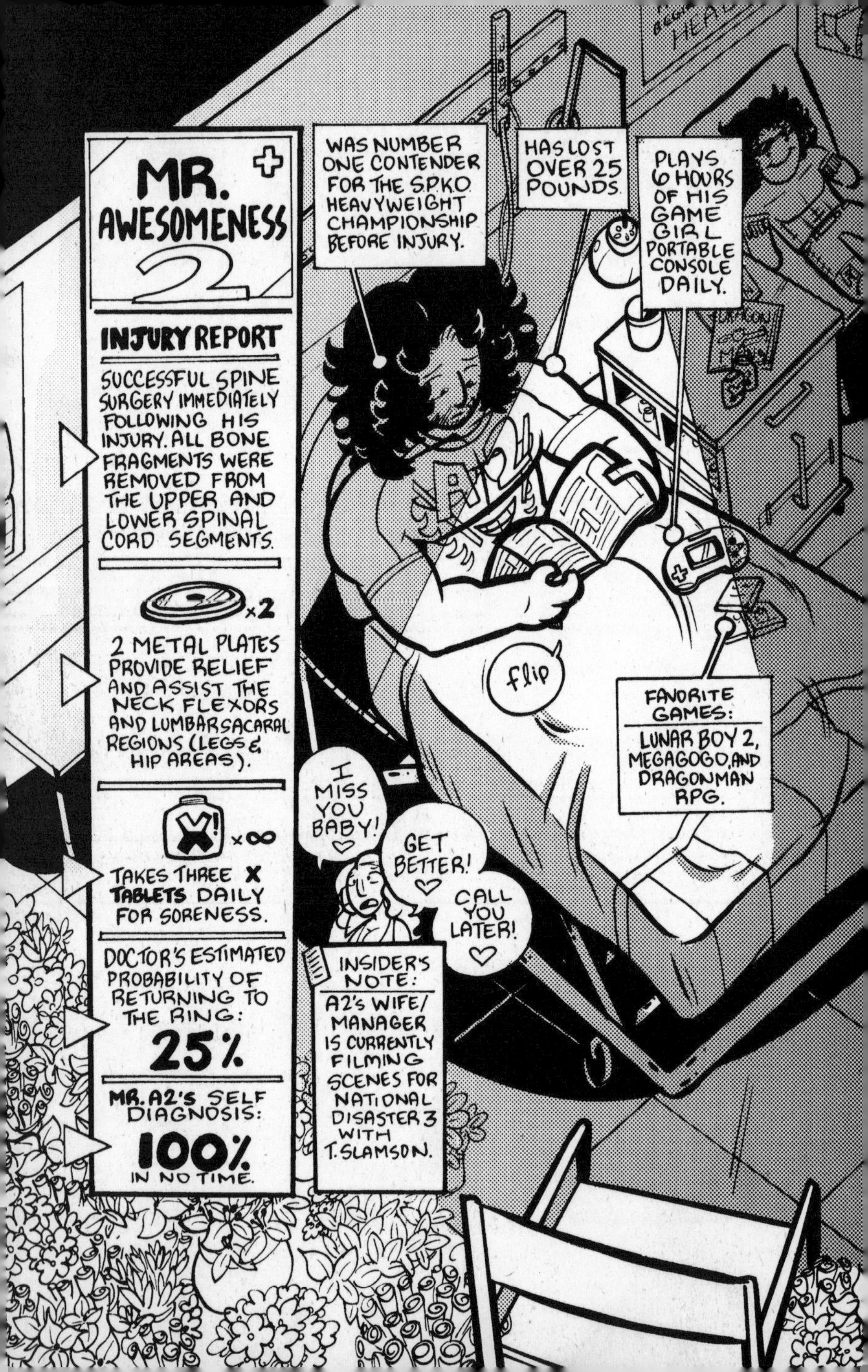

MR. AWESOMENESS 2
INJURY REPORT
SUCCESSFUL SPINE SURGERY IMMEDIATELY FOLLOWING HIS INJURY. ALL BONE FRAGMENTS WERE REMOVED FROM THE UPPER AND LOWER SPINAL CORD SEGMENTS.
×2
2 METAL PLATES PROVIDE RELIEF AND ASSIST THE NECK FLEXORS AND LUMBARSACARAL REGIONS (LEGS & HIP AREAS).
×∞
TAKES THREE X TABLETS DAILY FOR SORENESS.
DOCTOR'S ESTIMATED PROBABILITY OF RETURNING TO THE RING: 25%
MR. A2'S SELF DIAGNOSIS: 100% IN NO TIME.
WAS NUMBER ONE CONTENDER FOR THE S.P.K.O. HEAVYWEIGHT CHAMPIONSHIP BEFORE INJURY.
HAS LOST OVER 25 POUNDS.
PLAYS 6 HOURS OF HIS GAME GIRL PORTABLE CONSOLE DAILY.
flip
FAVORITE GAMES: LUNAR BOY 2, MEGAGOGO, AND DRAGONMAN RPG.
I MISS YOU BABY!
GET BETTER!
CALL YOU LATER!
INSIDER'S NOTE: A2'S WIFE/MANAGER IS CURRENTLY FILMING SCENES FOR NATIONAL DISASTER 3 WITH T. SLAMSON.

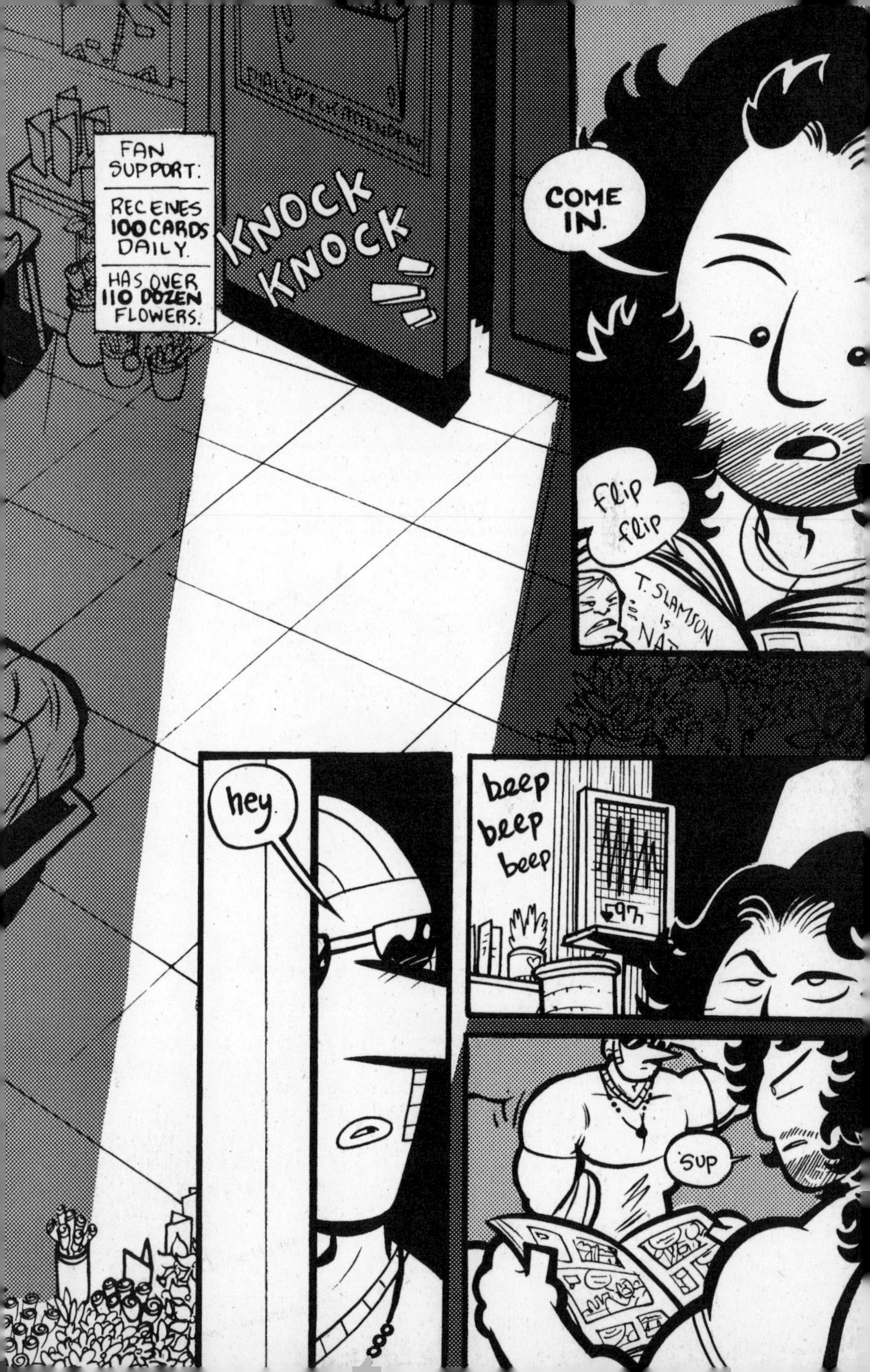
DIALYSIS TECH ATTENDENT
FAN SUPPORT:
RECEIVES 100 CARDS DAILY.
HAS OVER 110 DOZEN FLOWERS.
KNOCK KNOCK
COME IN.
flip flip
T. SLAMSON is NAT
hey.
beep beep beep
97
'SUP

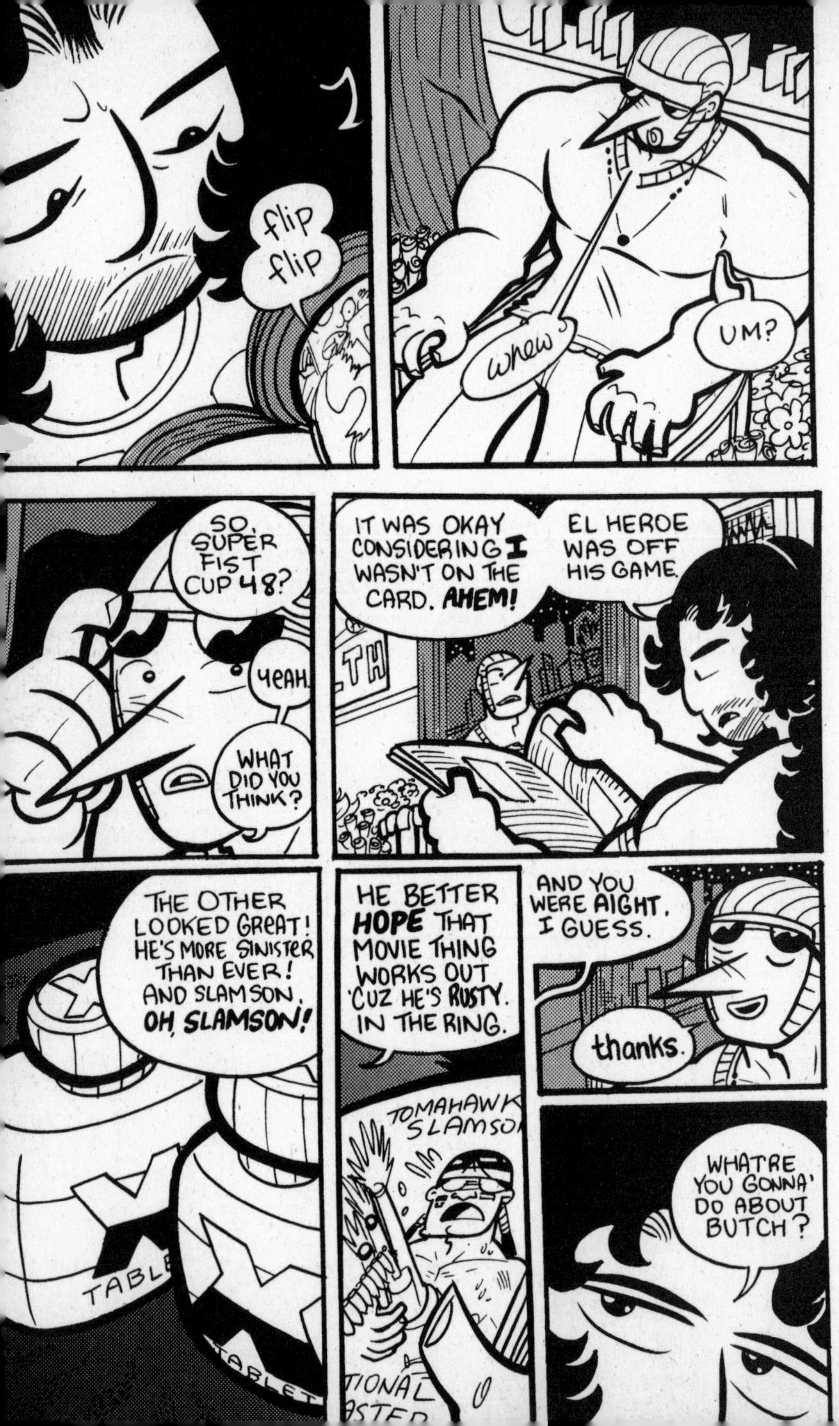

flip flip
whew
UM?
SO, SUPER FIST CUP 48?
yeah.
WHAT DID YOU THINK?
IT WAS OKAY CONSIDERING I WASN'T ON THE CARD. AHEM!
EL HEROE WAS OFF HIS GAME.
LTH
THE OTHER LOOKED GREAT! HE'S MORE SINISTER THAN EVER! AND SLAMSON. OH, SLAMSON!
HE BETTER HOPE THAT MOVIE THING WORKS OUT 'CUZ HE'S RUSTY. IN THE RING.
AND YOU WERE AIGHT, I GUESS.
thanks.
WHATRE YOU GONNA' DO ABOUT BUTCH?
TABLE
TABLET

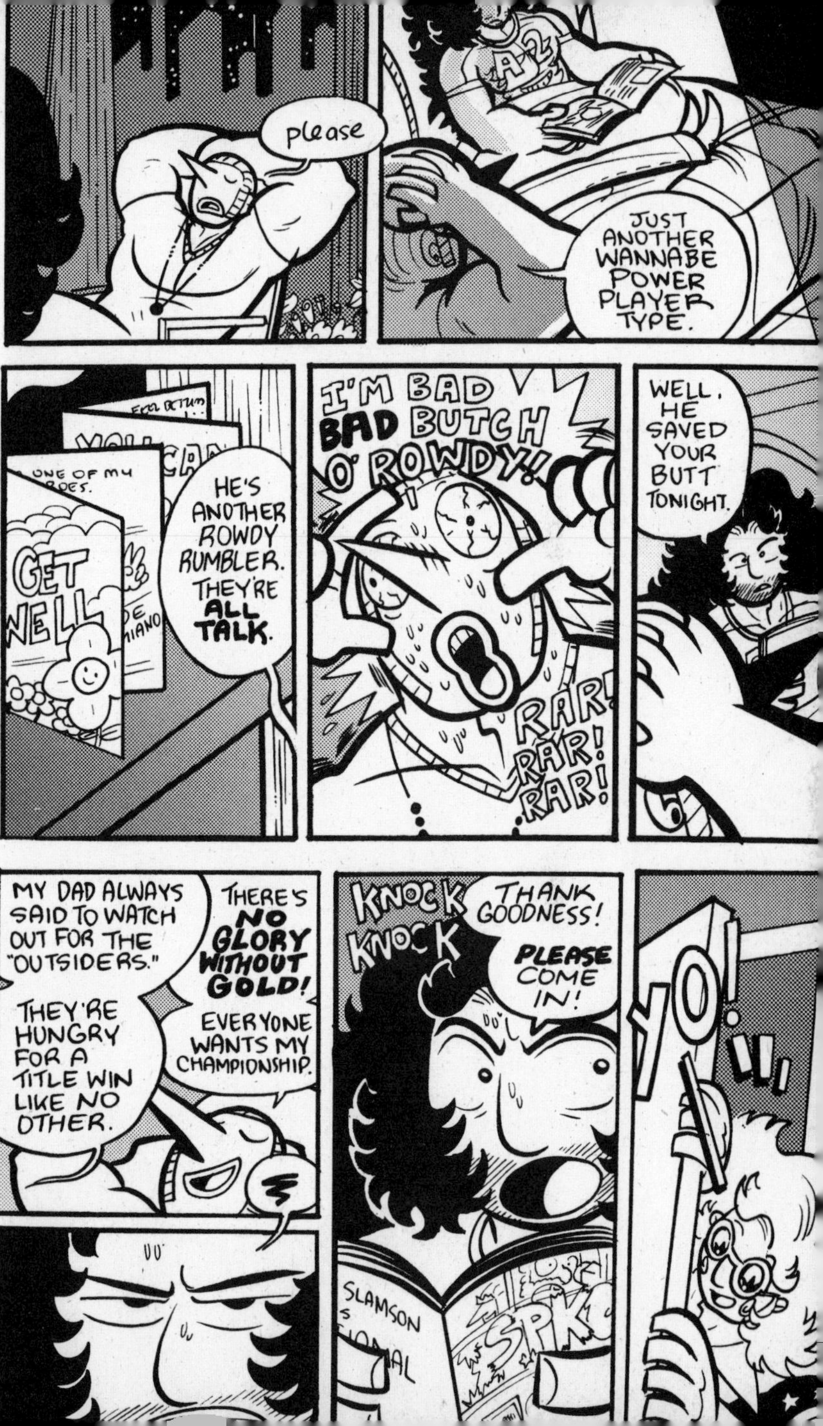
please
JUST ANOTHER WANNABE POWER PLAYER TYPE.
HE'S ANOTHER ROWDY RUMBLER. THEY'RE ALL TALK.
GET WELL
I'M BAD BAD BUTCH O'ROWDY!
RAR! RAR! RAR!
WELL, HE SAVED YOUR BUTT TONIGHT.
MY DAD ALWAYS SAID TO WATCH OUT FOR THE "OUTSIDERS."
THEY'RE HUNGRY FOR A TITLE WIN LIKE NO OTHER.
THERE'S NO GLORY WITHOUT GOLD!
EVERYONE WANTS MY CHAMPIONSHIP.
KNOCK KNOCK
THANK GOODNESS!
PLEASE COME IN!
SLAMSON
YO!

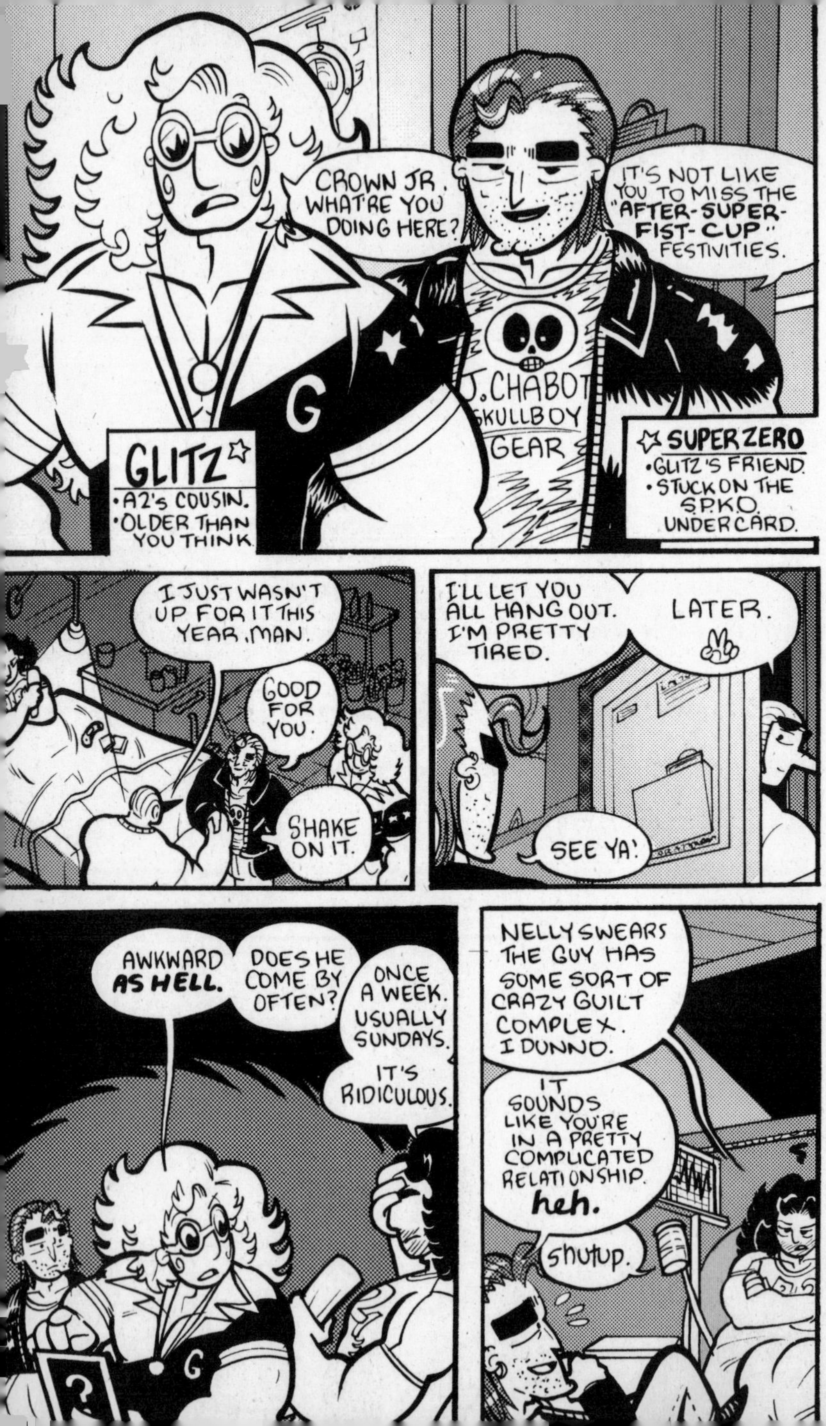
CROWN JR. WHAT'RE YOU DOING HERE?
IT'S NOT LIKE YOU TO MISS THE "AFTER-SUPER-FIST-CUP" FESTIVITIES.
J. CHABOT SKULLBOY GEAR
GLITZ
•A2's COUSIN.
•OLDER THAN YOU THINK.
SUPER ZERO
•GLITZ'S FRIEND.
•STUCK ON THE S.P.K.O. UNDERCARD.
I JUST WASN'T UP FOR IT THIS YEAR, MAN.
GOOD FOR YOU.
SHAKE ON IT.
I'LL LET YOU ALL HANG OUT. I'M PRETTY TIRED.
LATER.
SEE YA'.
AWKWARD AS HELL.
DOES HE COME BY OFTEN?
ONCE A WEEK. USUALLY SUNDAYS.
IT'S RIDICULOUS.
NELLY SWEARS THE GUY HAS SOME SORT OF CRAZY GUILT COMPLEX. I DUNNO.
IT SOUNDS LIKE YOU'RE IN A PRETTY COMPLICATED RELATIONSHIP. heh.
shutup.

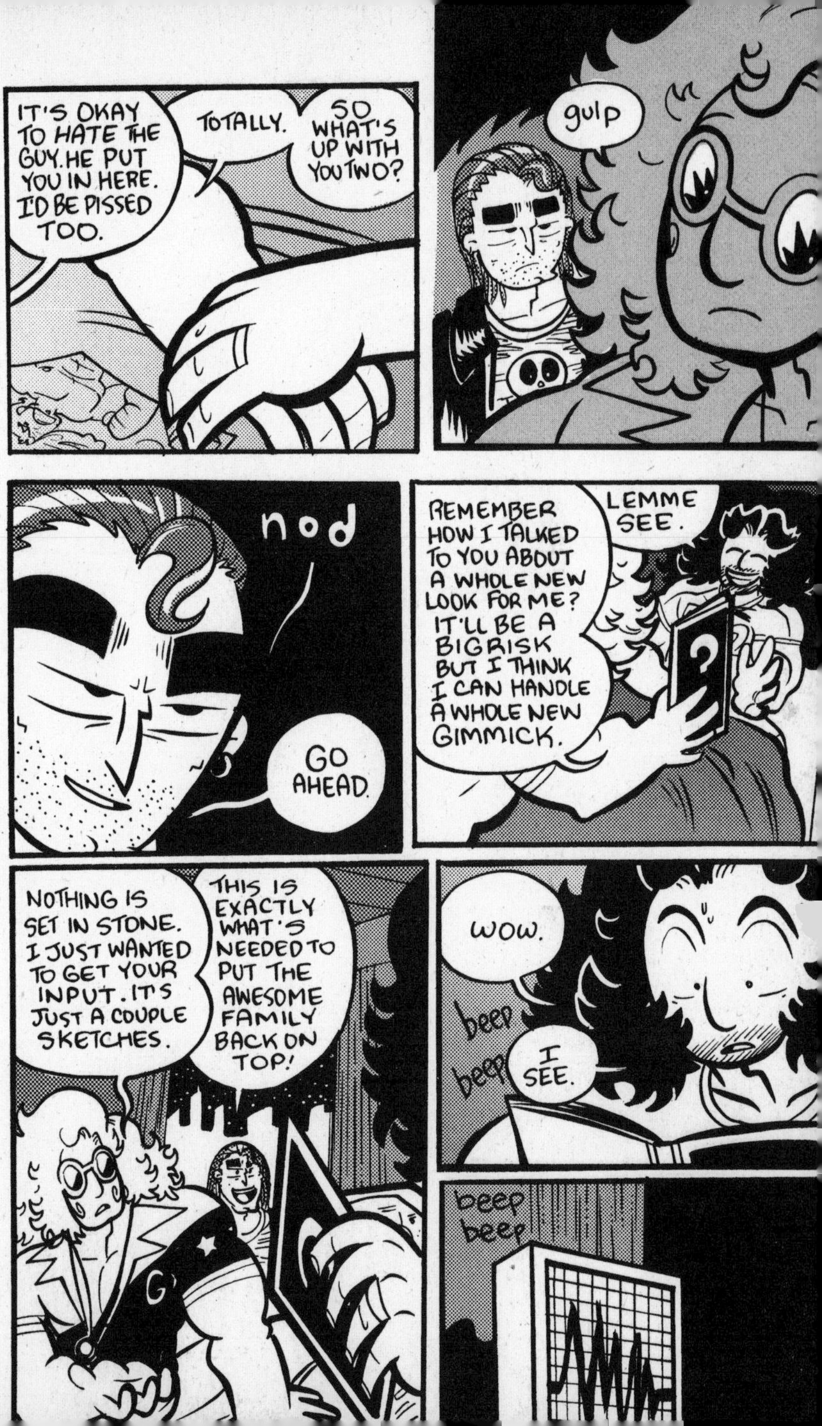
IT'S OKAY TO HATE THE GUY. HE PUT YOU IN HERE. I'D BE PISSED TOO.
TOTALLY.
SO WHAT'S UP WITH YOU TWO?
gulp
nod
GO AHEAD.
REMEMBER HOW I TALKED TO YOU ABOUT A WHOLE NEW LOOK FOR ME? IT'LL BE A BIG RISK BUT I THINK I CAN HANDLE A WHOLE NEW GIMMICK.
LEMME SEE.
NOTHING IS SET IN STONE. I JUST WANTED TO GET YOUR INPUT. IT'S JUST A COUPLE SKETCHES.
THIS IS EXACTLY WHAT'S NEEDED TO PUT THE AWESOME FAMILY BACK ON TOP!
WOW.
beep
beep
I SEE.
beep
beep

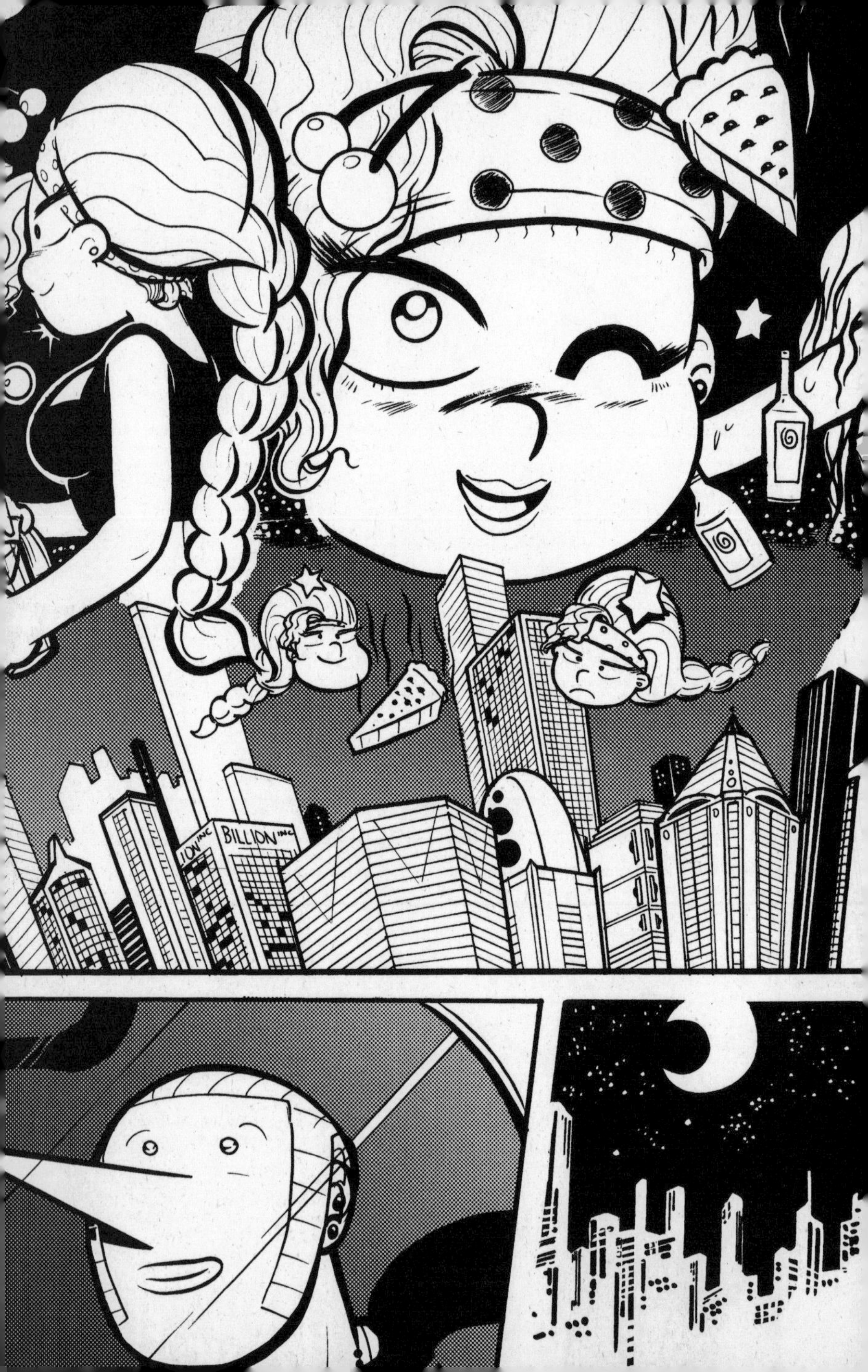
BILLION INC

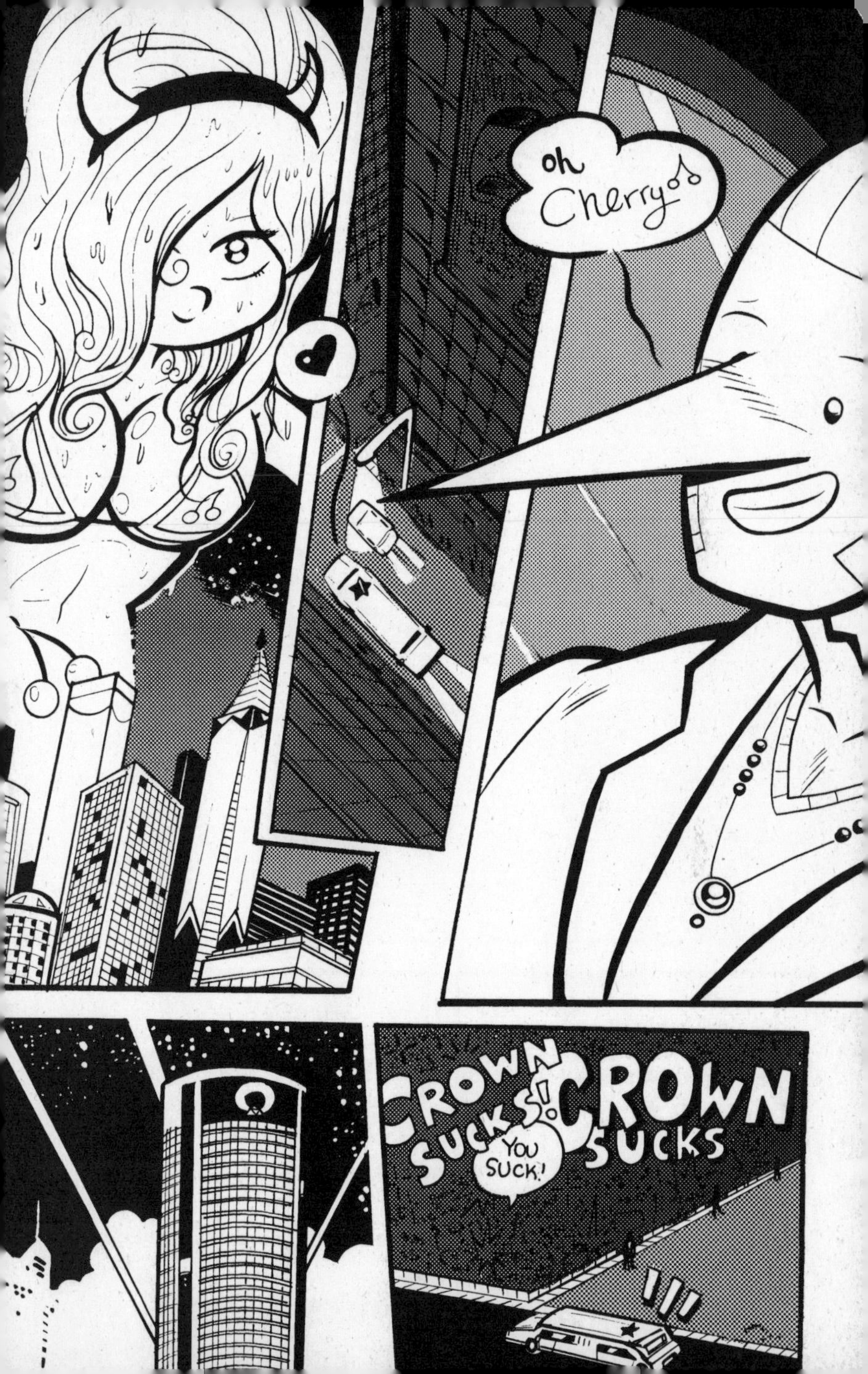

oh Cherry♫
CROWN SUCKS!
YOU SUCK!
CROWN SUCKS

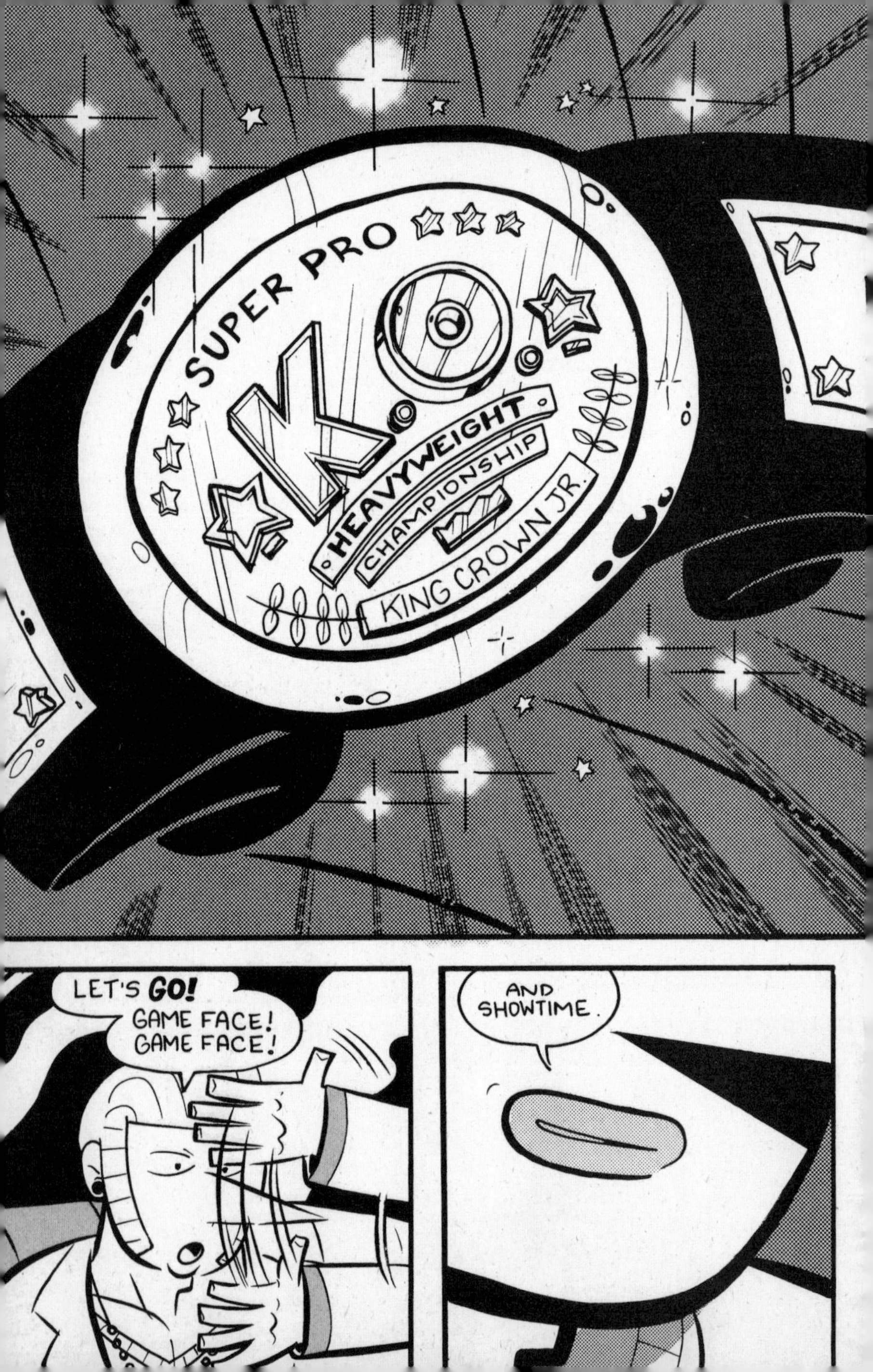
SUPER PRO
K.O.
HEAVYWEIGHT
CHAMPIONSHIP
KING CROWN JR.
LET'S GO!
GAME FACE!
GAME FACE!
AND
SHOWTIME.

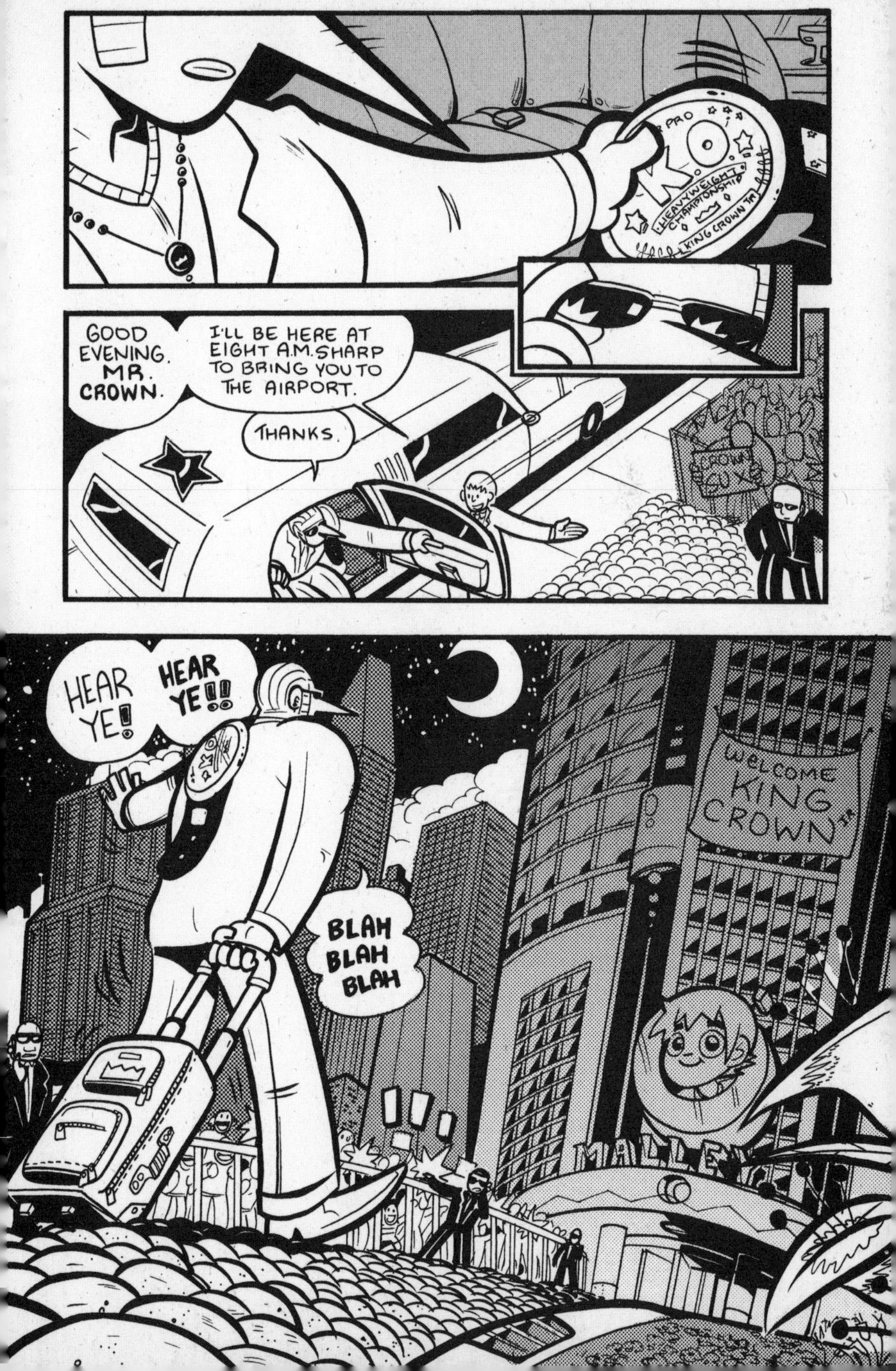
PRO K.O.
HEAVYWEIGHT CHAMPIONSHIP
KING CROWN TM
GOOD EVENING. MR. CROWN.
I'LL BE HERE AT EIGHT A.M. SHARP TO BRING YOU TO THE AIRPORT.
THANKS.
HEAR YE!
HEAR YE!!
BLAH BLAH BLAH
WELCOME KING CROWN TM

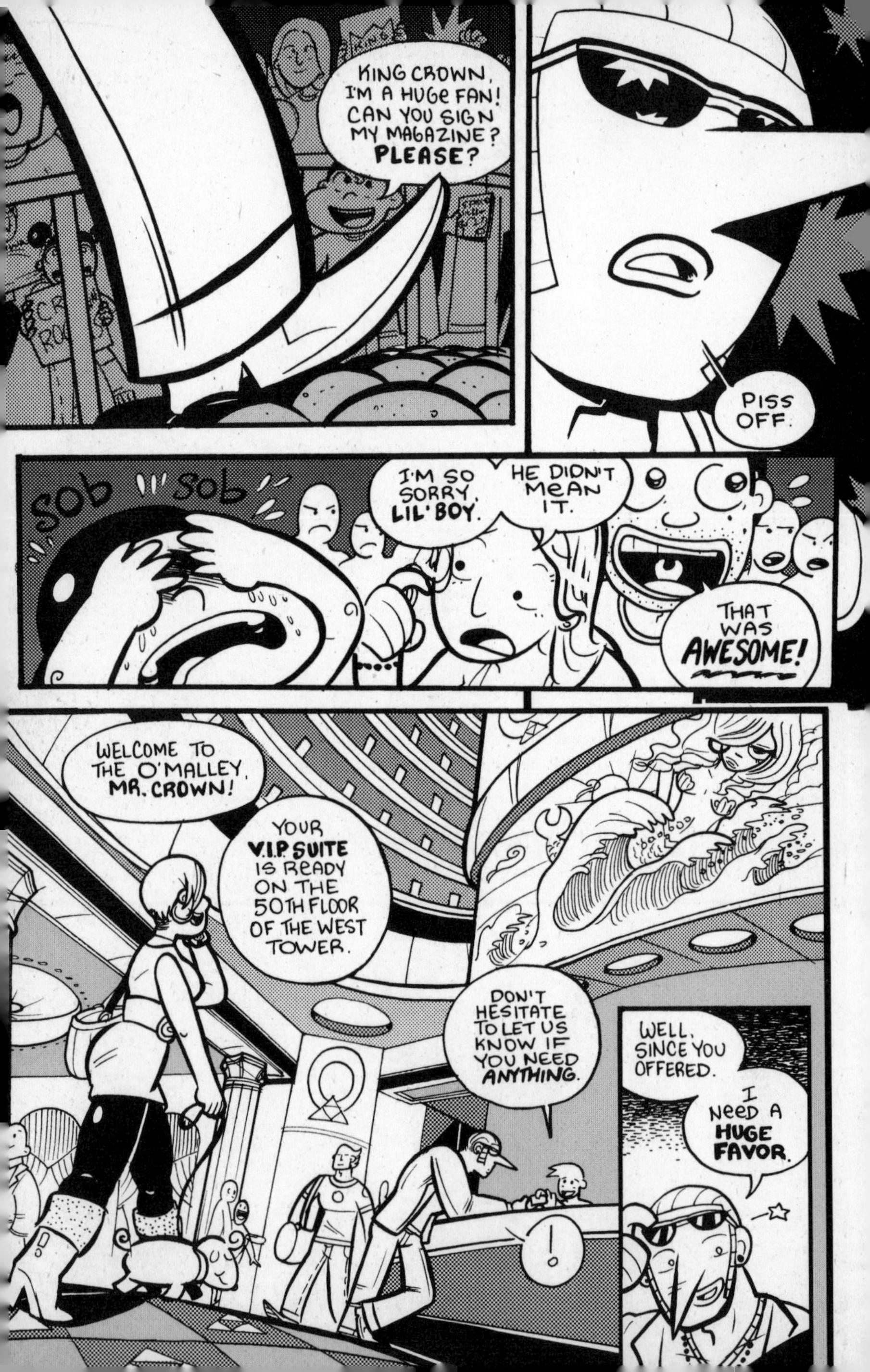
KING CROWN, I'M A HUGE FAN! CAN YOU SIGN MY MAGAZINE? PLEASE?
PISS OFF.
SOB SOB
I'M SO SORRY, LIL' BOY.
HE DIDN'T MEAN IT.
THAT WAS AWESOME!
WELCOME TO THE O'MALLEY, MR. CROWN!
YOUR V.I.P. SUITE IS READY ON THE 50TH FLOOR OF THE WEST TOWER.
DON'T HESITATE TO LET US KNOW IF YOU NEED ANYTHING.
!
WELL, SINCE YOU OFFERED.
I NEED A HUGE FAVOR.

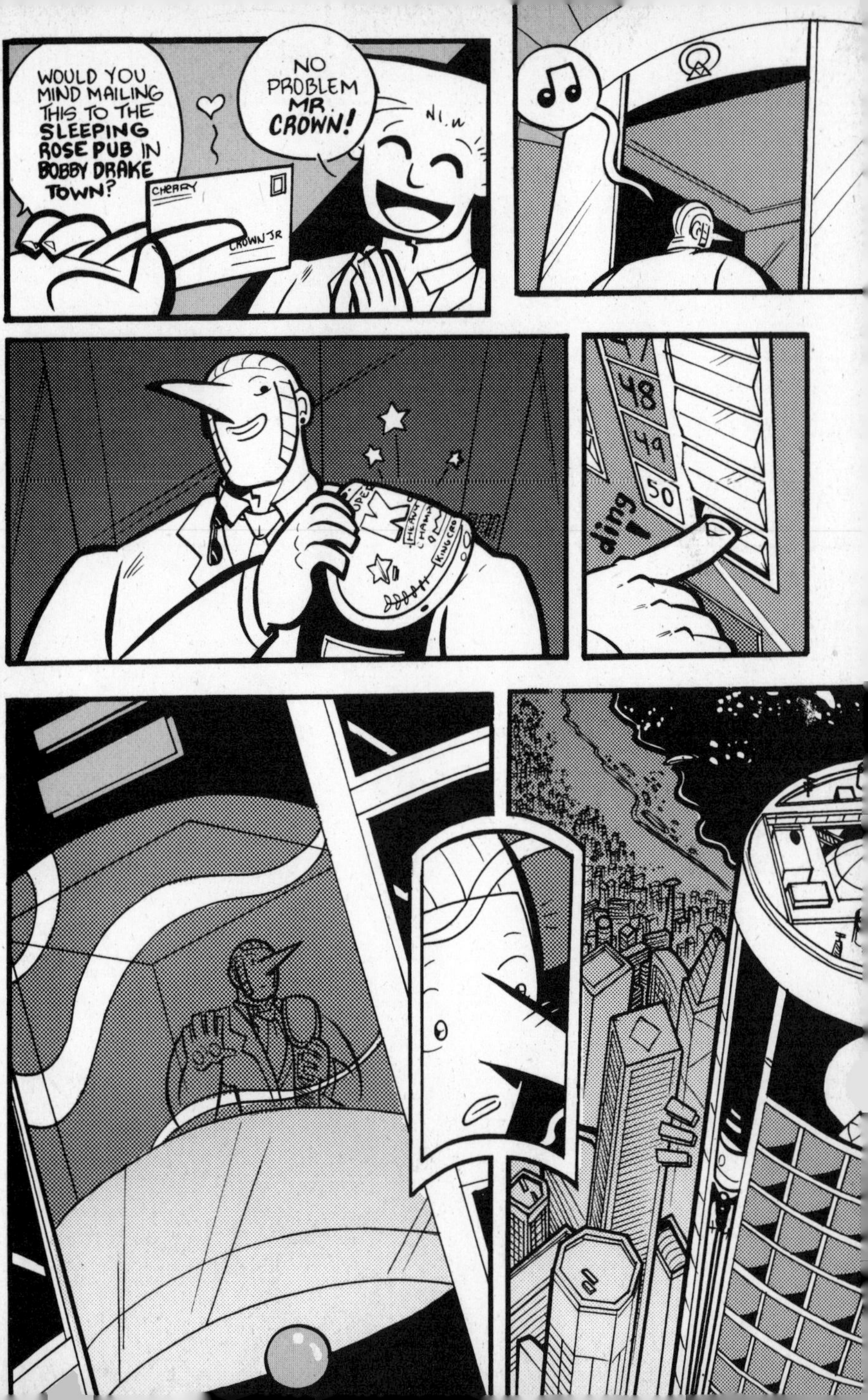

WOULD YOU MIND MAILING THIS TO THE SLEEPING ROSE PUB IN BOBBY DRAKE TOWN?
NO PROBLEM MR. CROWN!
CHERRY
CROWN JR
48
49
50
ding

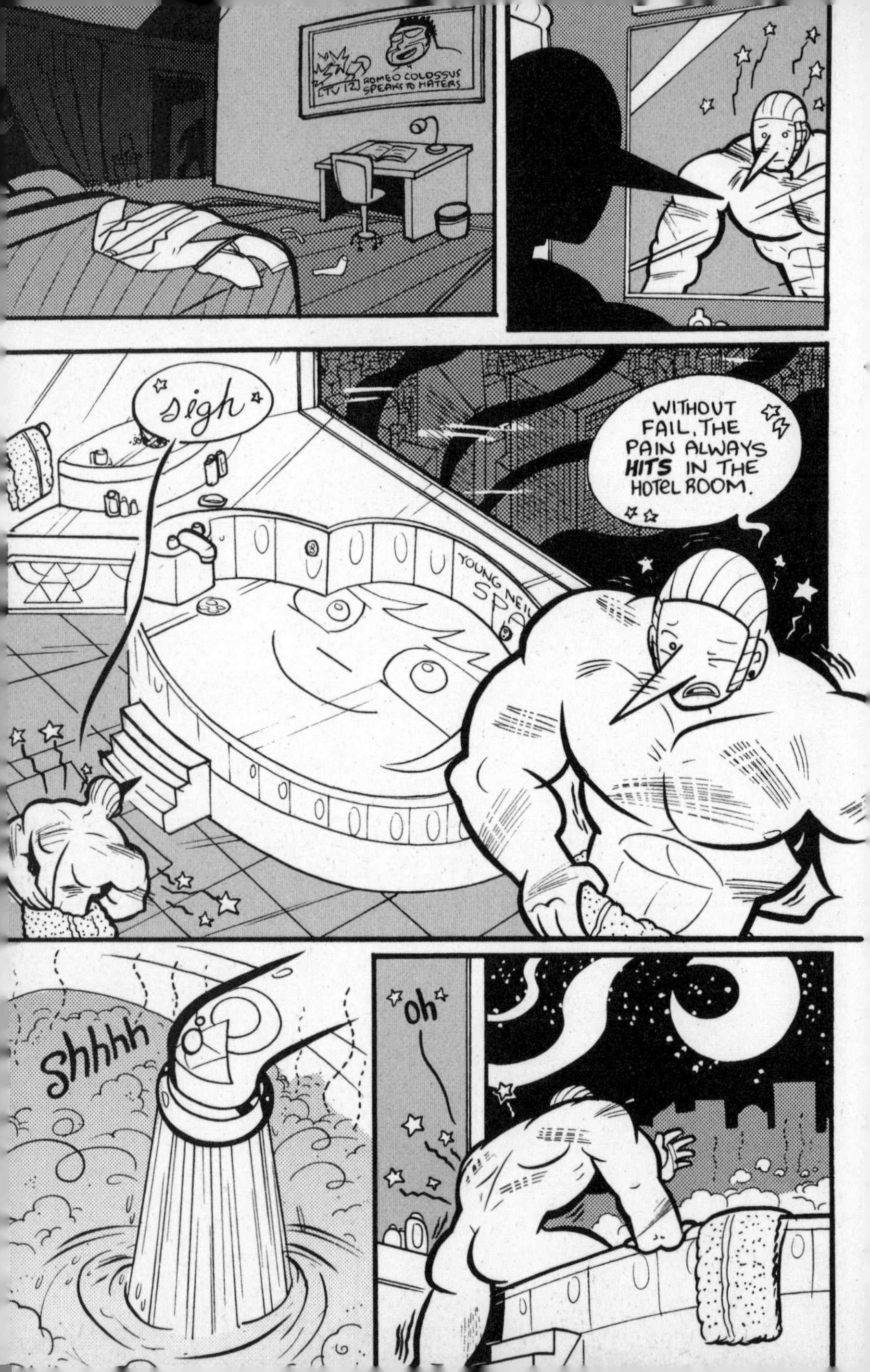
[TV 12] ROMEO COLOSSUS SPEAKS TO MATERS
sigh
WITHOUT FAIL, THE PAIN ALWAYS **HITS** IN THE HOTEL ROOM.
YOUNG NEIL SPA
Shhhh
oh

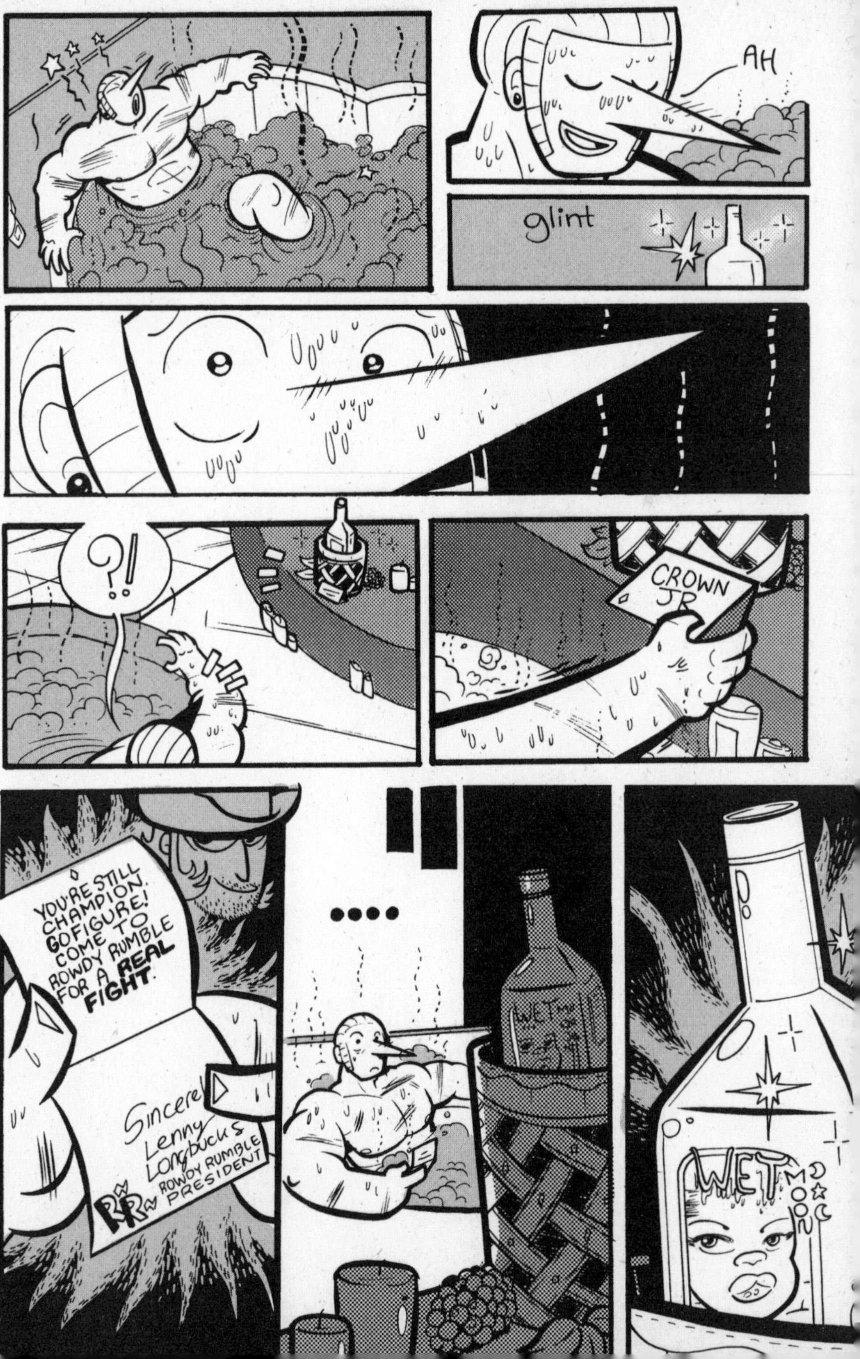
AH
glint
?!
CROWN JR
YOU'RE STILL CHAMPION. GO FIGURE! COME TO ROWDY RUMBLE FOR A REAL FIGHT.
Sincerel
Lenny Longbucks
ROWDY RUMBLE PRESIDENT
RR
....
WET MOON

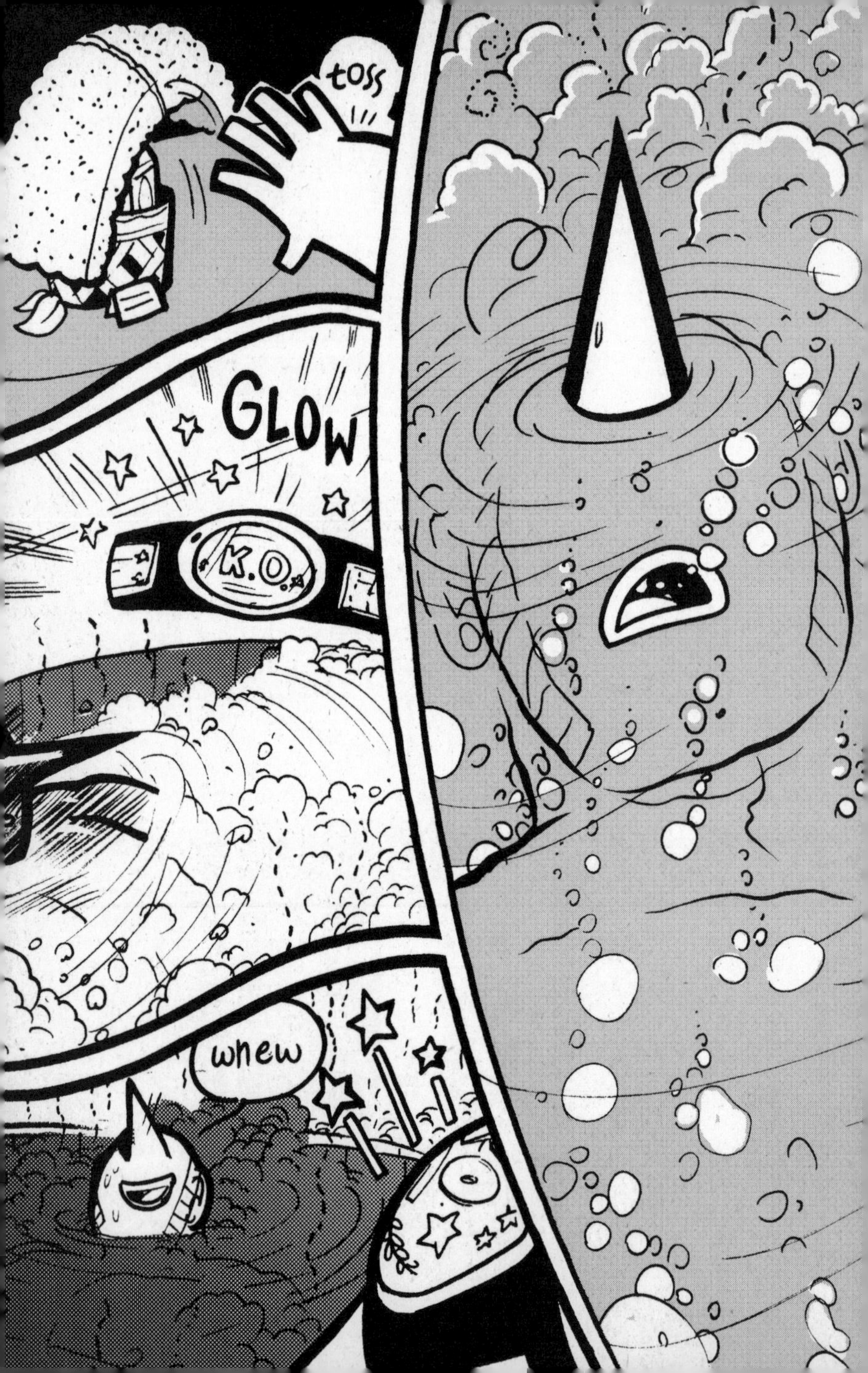
toss
GLOW
K.O.
whew

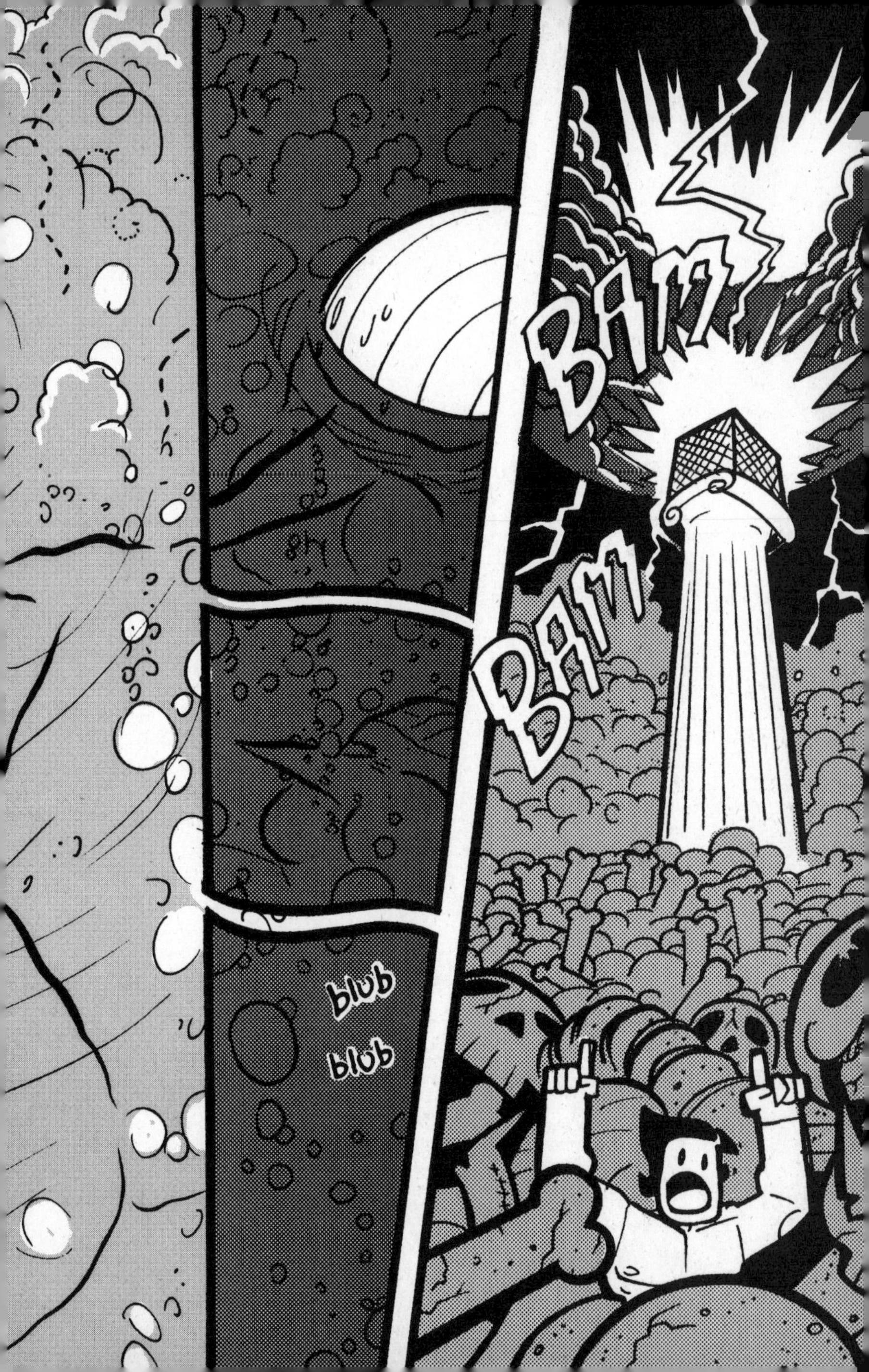
blub
blub
BAM
BAM

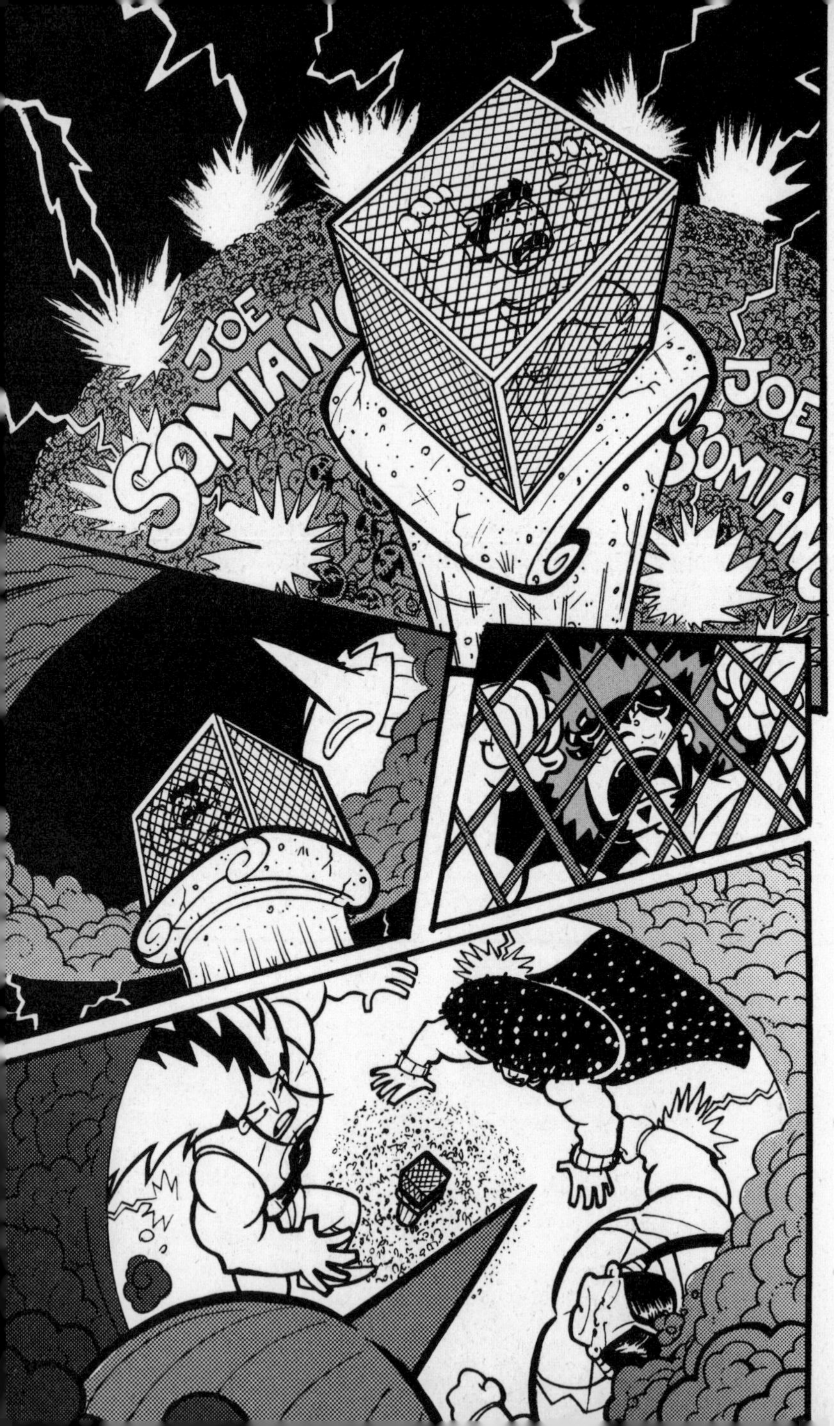
JOE SOMIANO
JOE SOMIANO

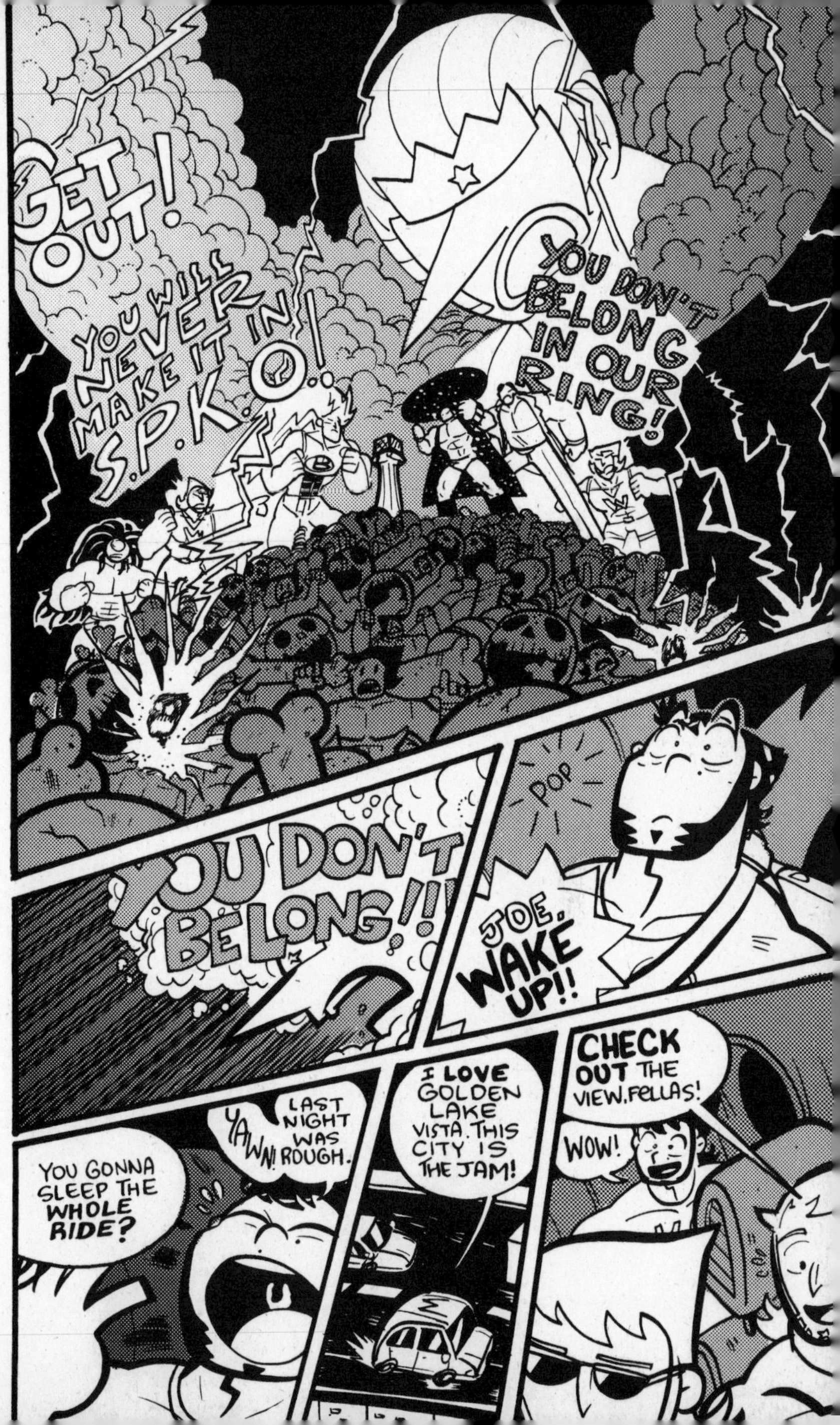
GET OUT!
YOU WILL NEVER MAKE IT IN S.P.K.O.!
YOU DON'T BELONG IN OUR RING!
YOU DON'T BELONG!!!
POP
JOE. WAKE UP!!
YOU GONNA SLEEP THE WHOLE RIDE?
YAWN!
LAST NIGHT WAS ROUGH.
I LOVE GOLDEN LAKE VISTA. THIS CITY IS THE JAM!
CHECK OUT THE VIEW, FELLAS!
WOW!

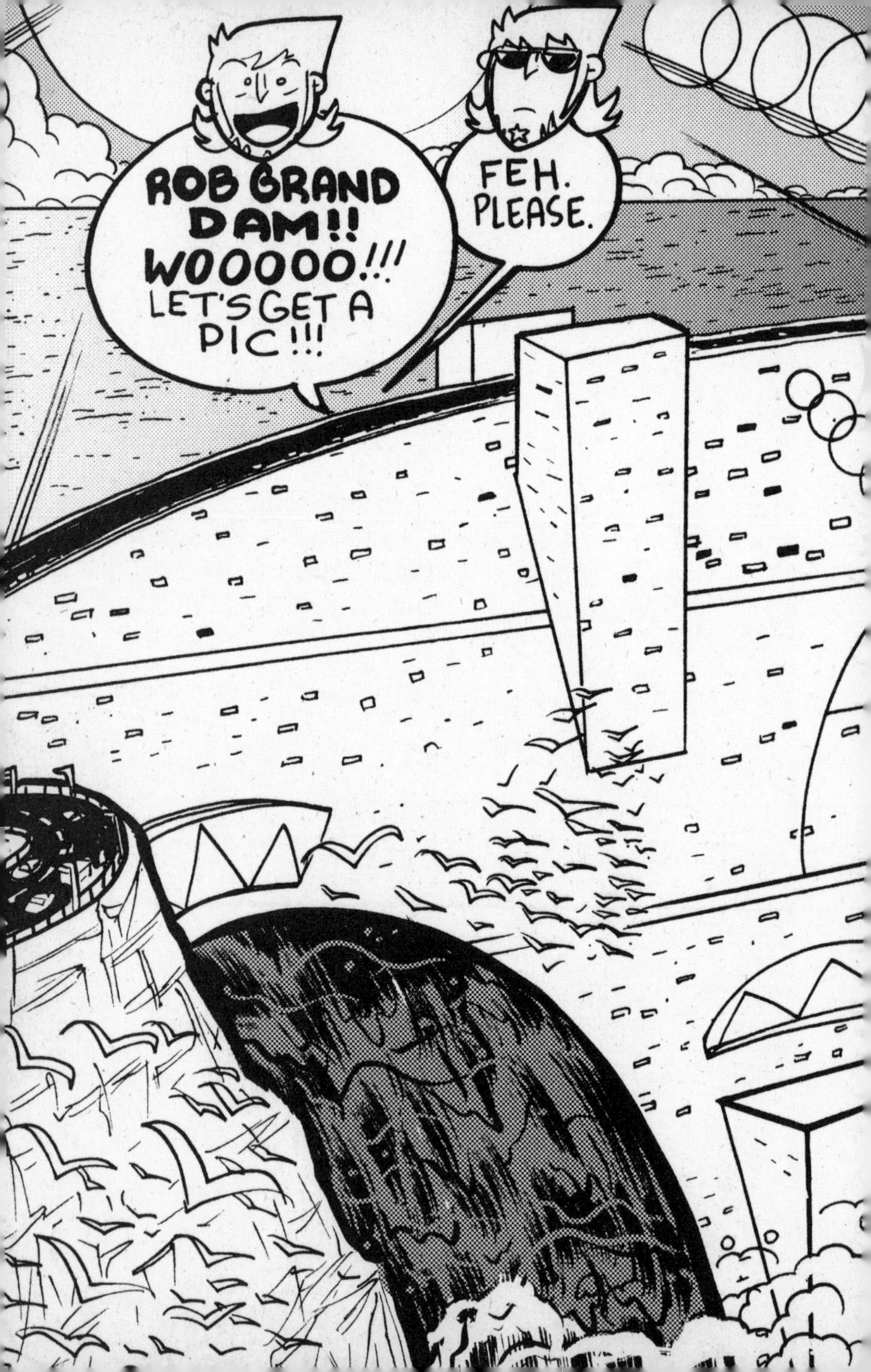
ROB GRAND DAM!! WOOOOO!!! LET'S GET A PIC!!!
FEH. PLEASE.

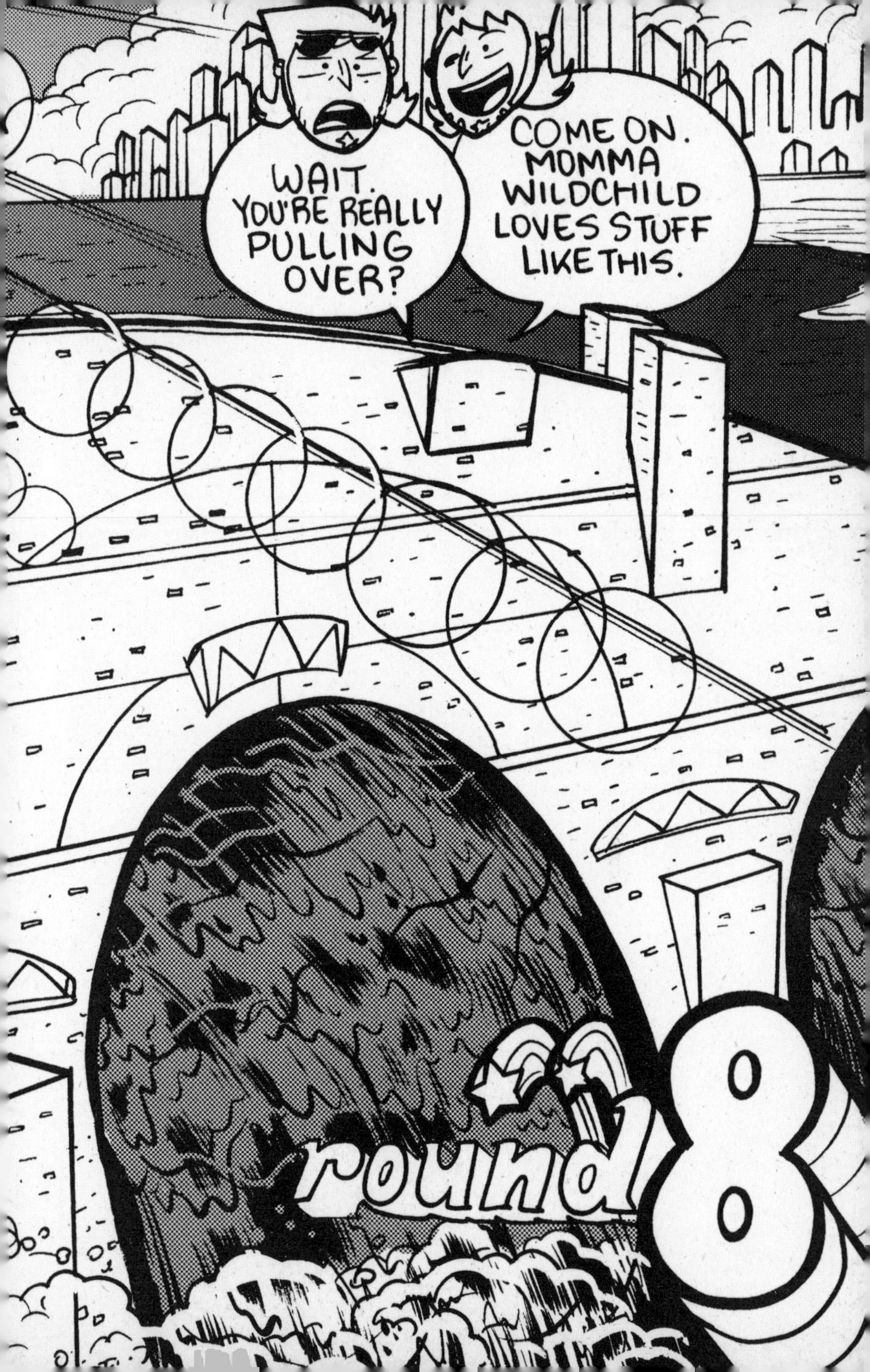
WAIT. YOU'RE REALLY PULLING OVER?
COME ON. MOMMA WILDCHILD LOVES STUFF LIKE THIS.
round 8

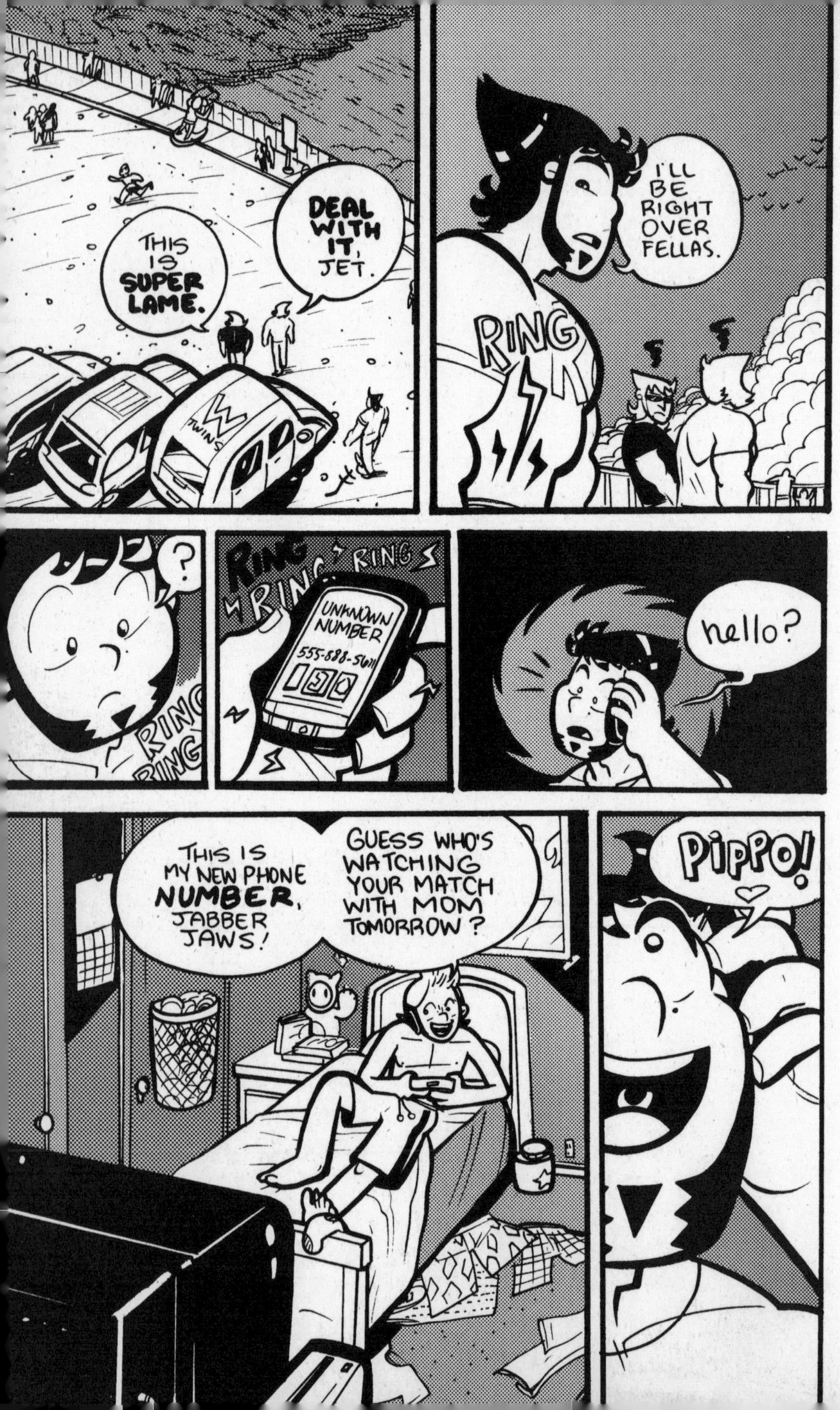
THIS IS SUPER LAME.
DEAL WITH IT, JET.
TWINS
I'LL BE RIGHT OVER FELLAS.
RING
?
RING RING
RING RING RING
UNKNOWN NUMBER
555-888-5611
hello?
THIS IS MY NEW PHONE NUMBER, JABBER JAWS!
GUESS WHO'S WATCHING YOUR MATCH WITH MOM TOMORROW?
PIPPO!

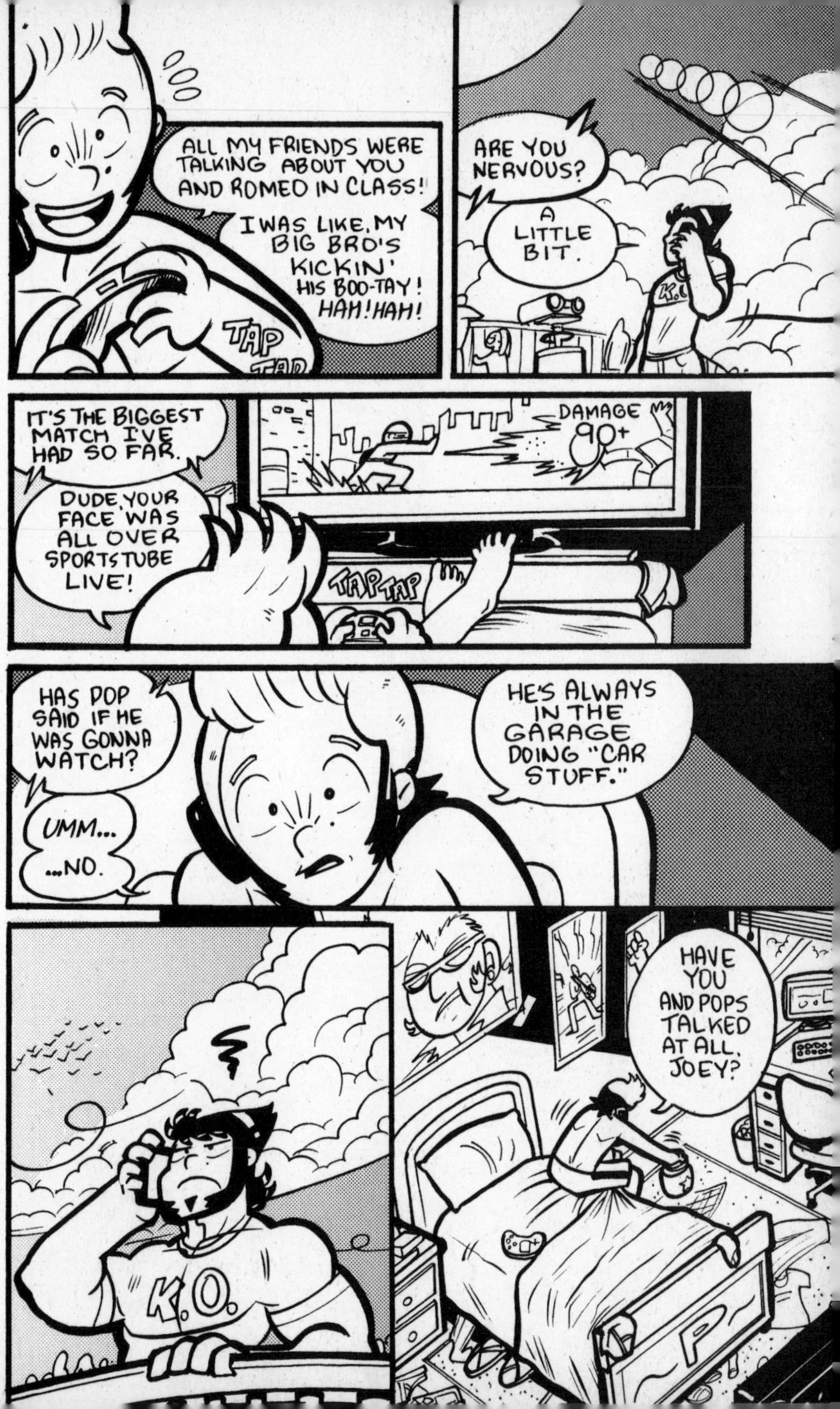
ALL MY FRIENDS WERE TALKING ABOUT YOU AND ROMEO IN CLASS!
I WAS LIKE, MY BIG BRO'S KICKIN' HIS BOO-TAY! HAH! HAH!
TAP TAP
ARE YOU NERVOUS?
A LITTLE BIT.
K.O.
IT'S THE BIGGEST MATCH I'VE HAD SO FAR.
DAMAGE 90+
DUDE, YOUR FACE WAS ALL OVER SPORTSTUBE LIVE!
TAP TAP
HAS POP SAID IF HE WAS GONNA WATCH?
UMM...
...NO.
HE'S ALWAYS IN THE GARAGE DOING "CAR STUFF."
HAVE YOU AND POPS TALKED AT ALL, JOEY?
K.O.

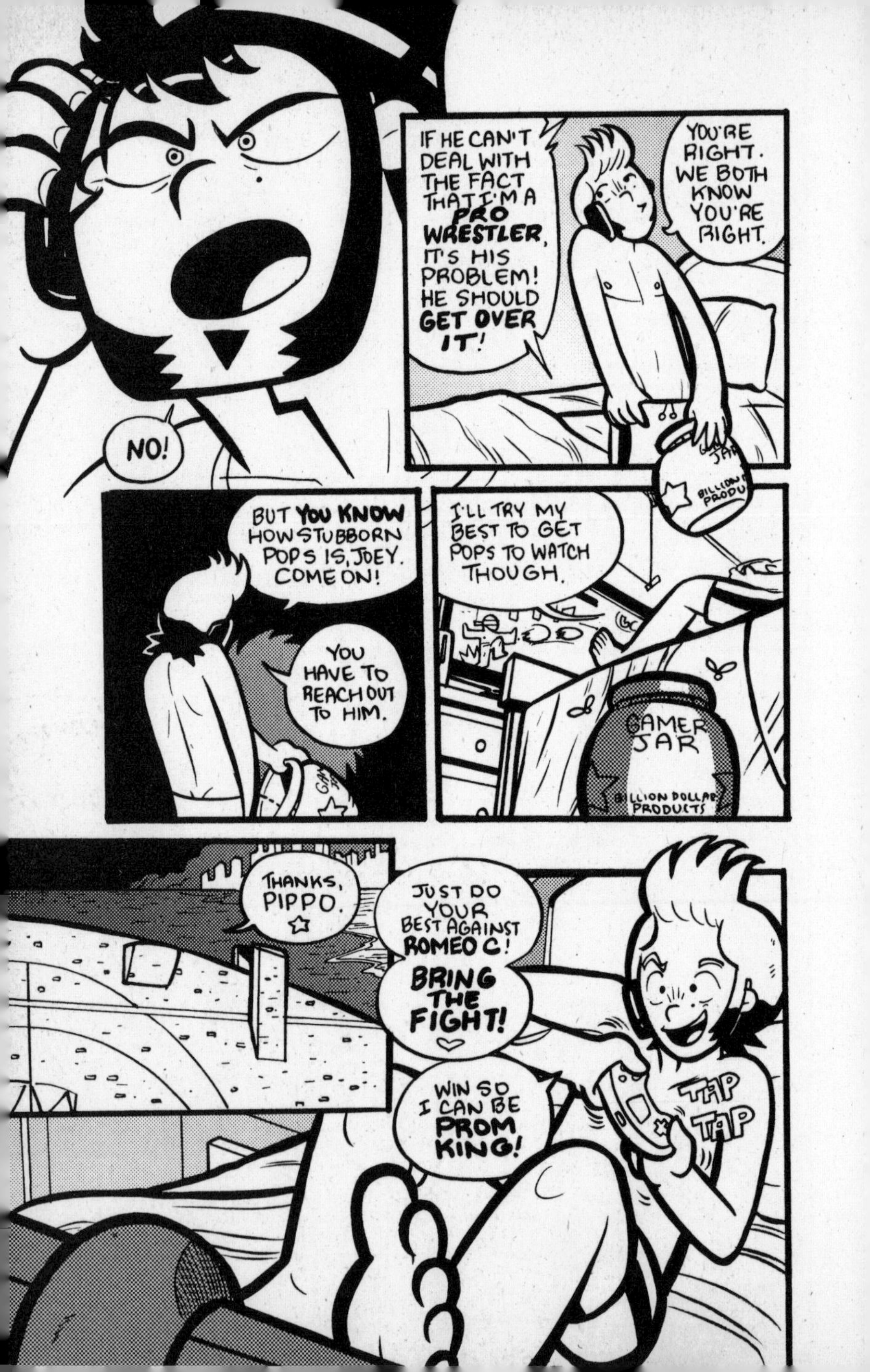
NO!
IF HE CAN'T DEAL WITH THE FACT THAT I'M A PRO WRESTLER, IT'S HIS PROBLEM! HE SHOULD GET OVER IT!
YOU'RE RIGHT. WE BOTH KNOW YOU'RE RIGHT.
BUT YOU KNOW HOW STUBBORN POPS IS, JOEY. COME ON!
YOU HAVE TO REACH OUT TO HIM.
I'LL TRY MY BEST TO GET POPS TO WATCH THOUGH.
GAMER JAR
BILLION DOLLAR PRODUCTS
THANKS, PIPPO.
JUST DO YOUR BEST AGAINST ROMEO C!
BRING THE FIGHT!
I WIN SO I CAN BE PROM KING!
TAP TAP

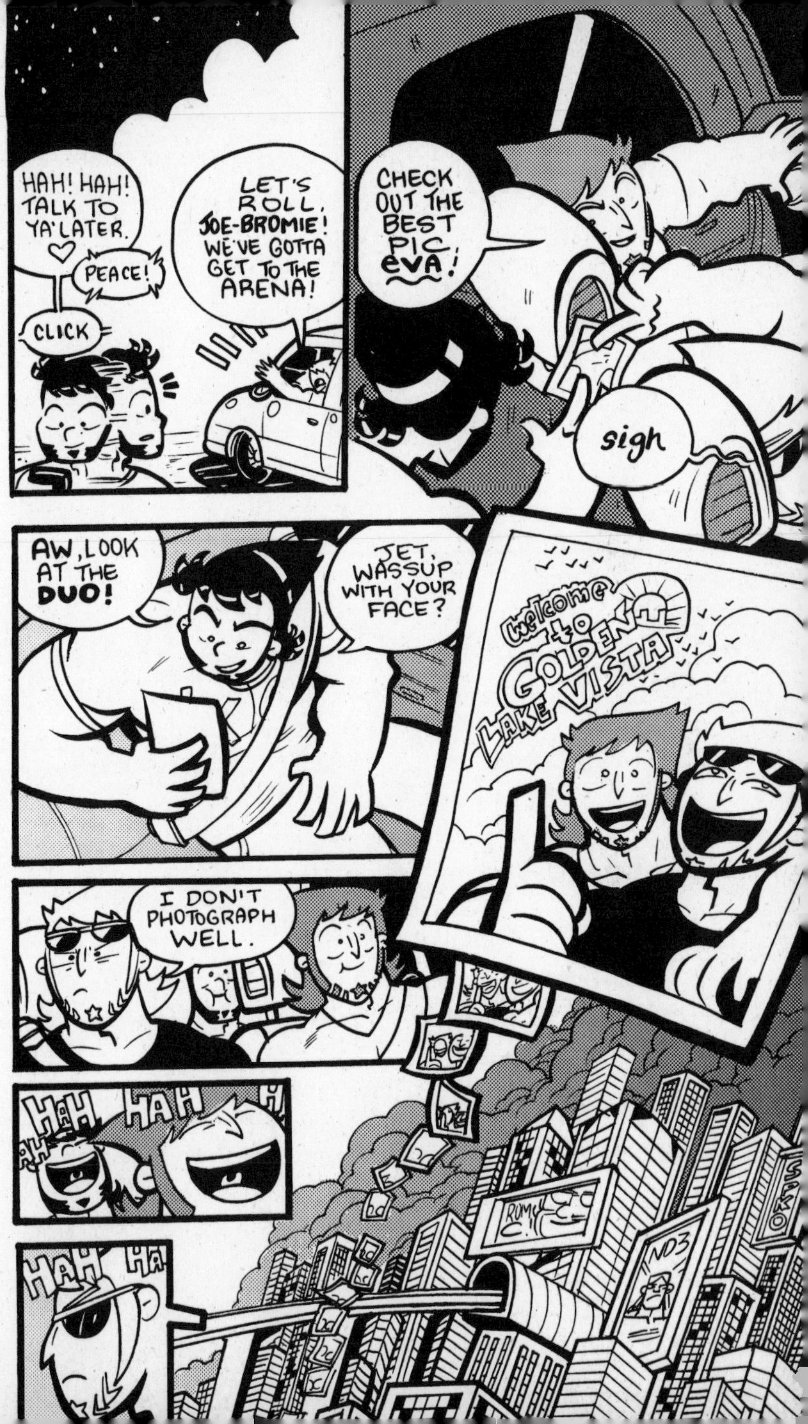

HAH! HAH! TALK TO YA' LATER. ♡
PEACE!
CLICK
LET'S ROLL, JOE-BROMIE! WE'VE GOTTA GET TO THE ARENA!
CHECK OUT THE BEST PIC EVA!
sigh
AW, LOOK AT THE DUO!
JET, WASSUP WITH YOUR FACE?
WELCOME TO GOLDEN LAKE VISTA
I DON'T PHOTOGRAPH WELL.
HAH HAH HAH H
HAH HA

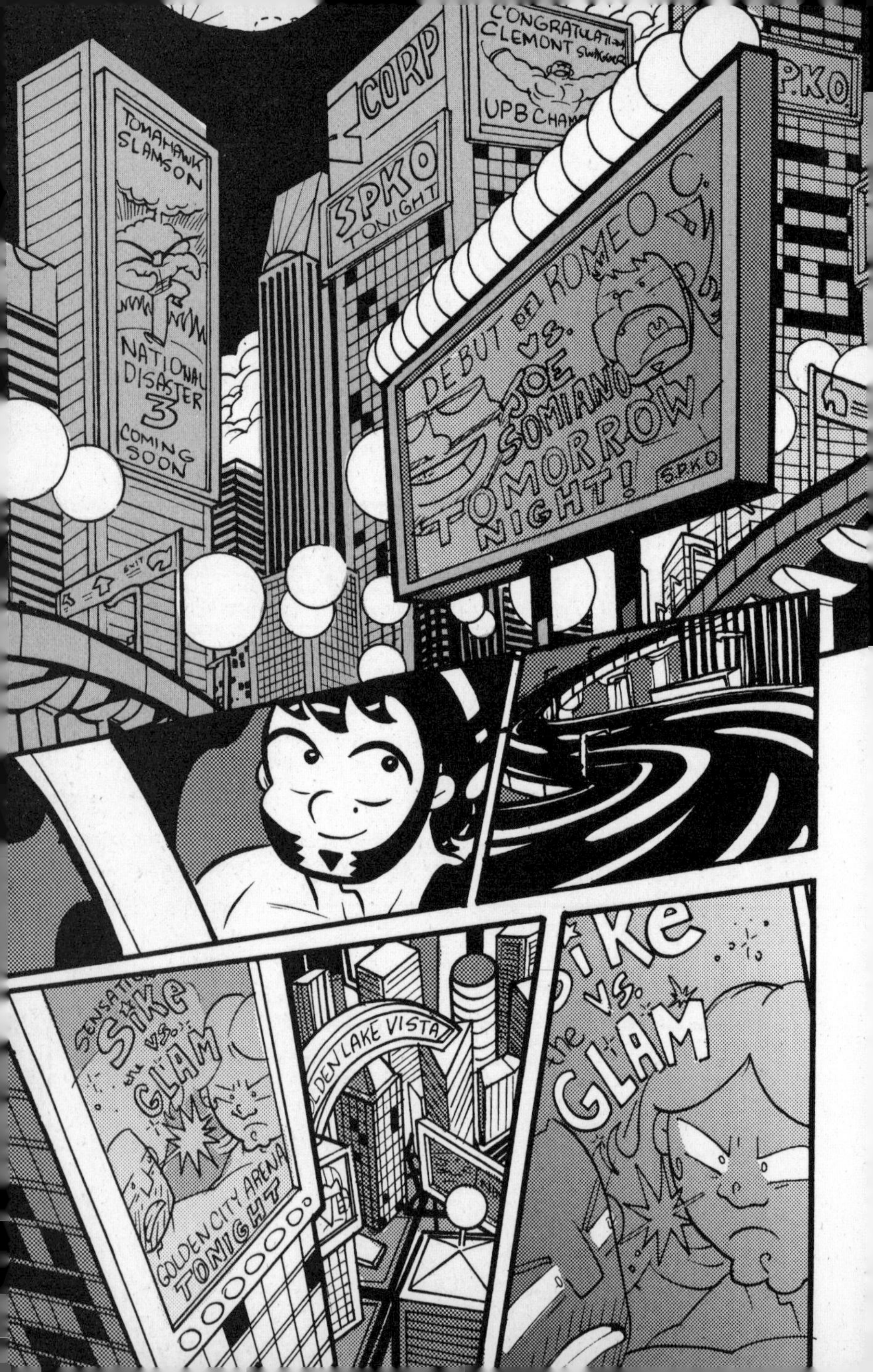

TOMAHAWK SLAMSON
NATIONAL DISASTER 3 COMING SOON
CORP
CONGRATULATIONS CLEMONT
SPKO TONIGHT
P.K.O
DEBUT OF ROMEO C. VS. JOE SOMIANO TOMORROW NIGHT!
SPKO
EXIT
Sike vs. GLAM
GOLDEN CITY ARENA TONIGHT
OLDEN LAKE VISTA
vs.
GLAM

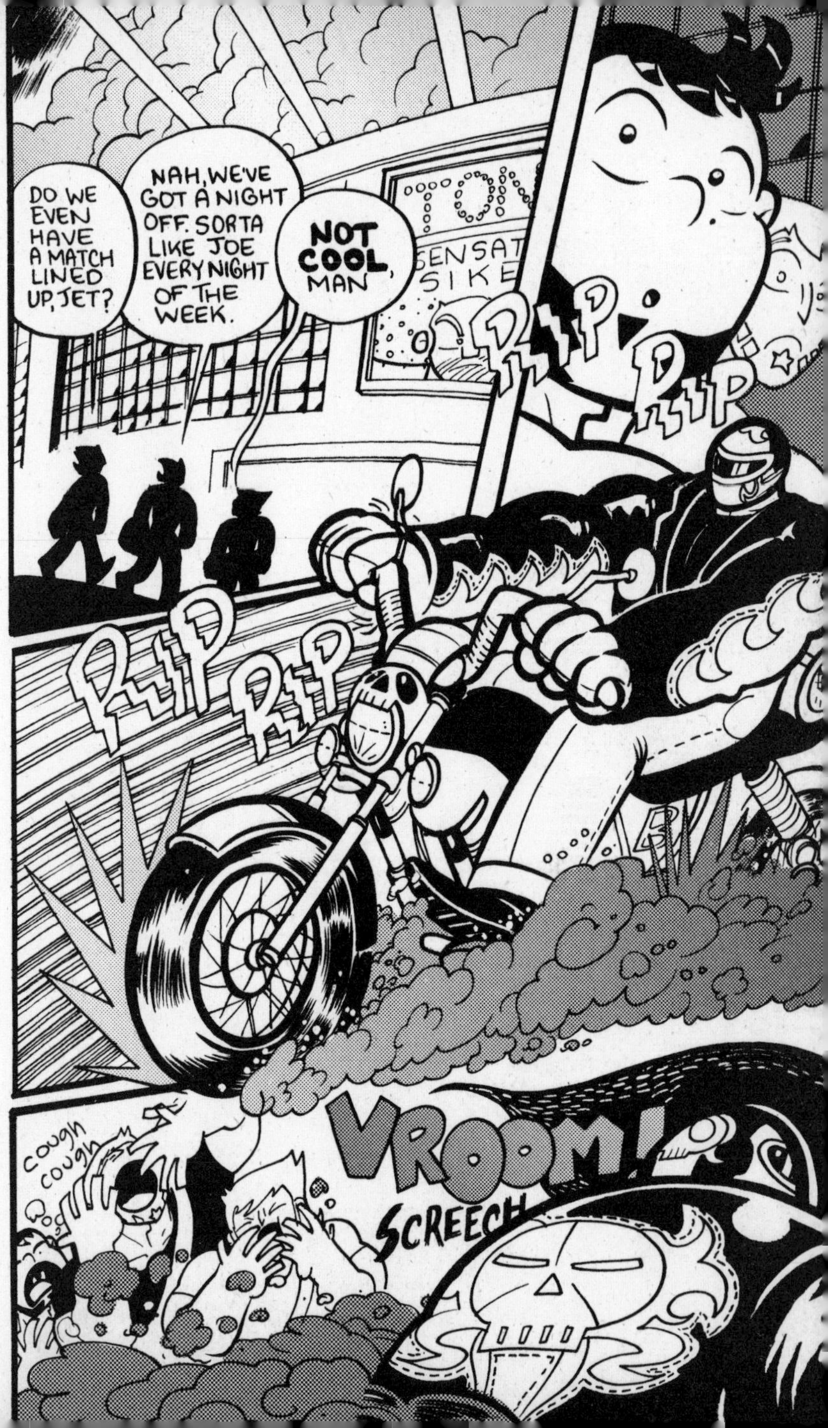
DO WE EVEN HAVE A MATCH LINED UP, JET?
NAH, WE'VE GOT A NIGHT OFF. SORTA LIKE JOE EVERY NIGHT OF THE WEEK.
NOT COOL, MAN
RIP RIP
RIP RIP
VROOM!
SCREECH
cough cough

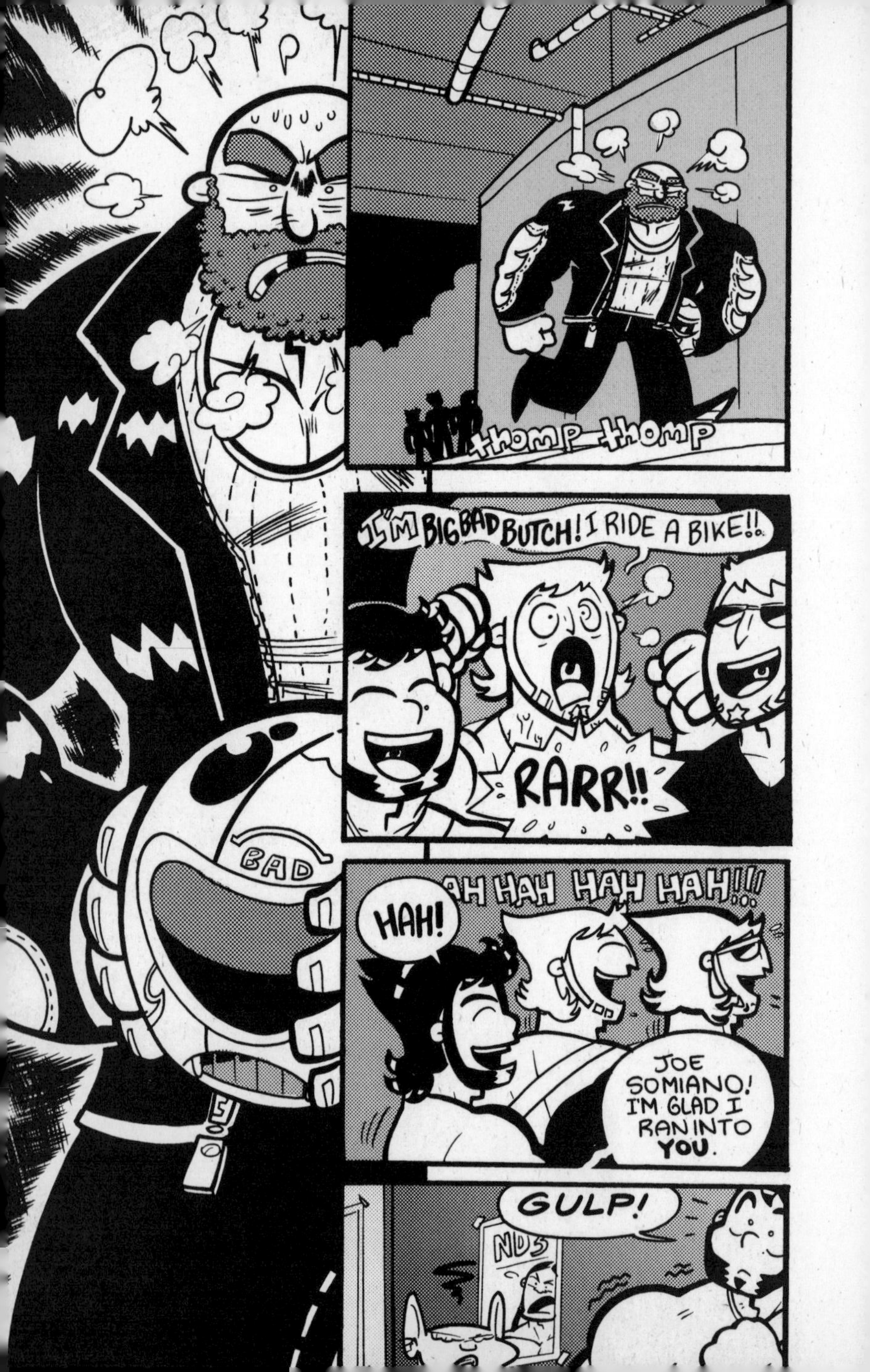
thomp thomp
I'M BIG BAD BUTCH! I RIDE A BIKE!!
RARR!!
BAD
HAH!
AH HAH HAH HAH!!!
JOE SOMIANO! I'M GLAD I RAN INTO **YOU**.
GULP!
NDS

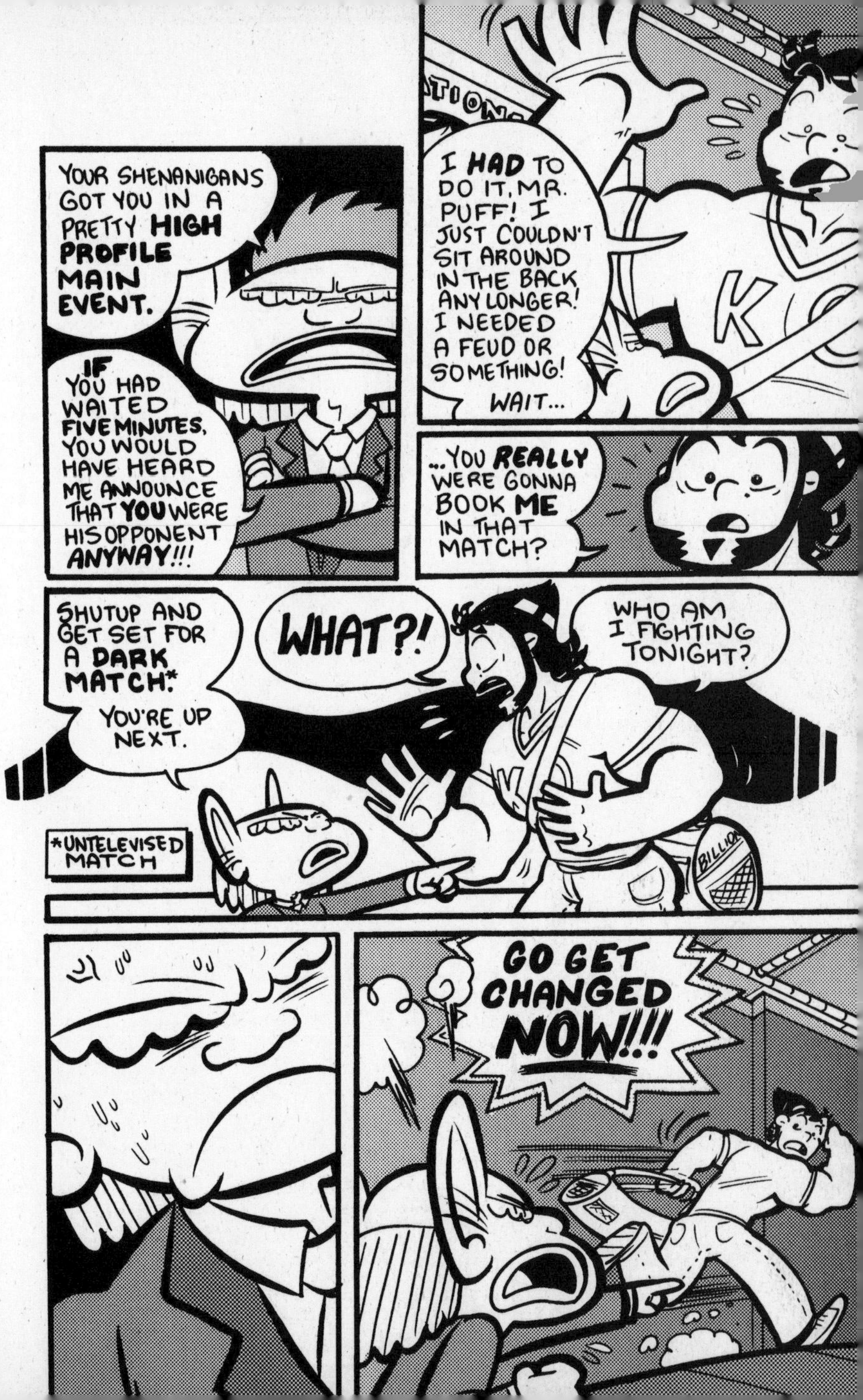
YOUR SHENANIGANS GOT YOU IN A PRETTY HIGH PROFILE MAIN EVENT.
IF YOU HAD WAITED FIVE MINUTES, YOU WOULD HAVE HEARD ME ANNOUNCE THAT YOU WERE HIS OPPONENT ANYWAY!!!
I HAD TO DO IT, MR. PUFF! I JUST COULDN'T SIT AROUND IN THE BACK ANY LONGER! I NEEDED A FEUD OR SOMETHING!
WAIT...
...YOU REALLY WERE GONNA BOOK ME IN THAT MATCH?
SHUTUP AND GET SET FOR A DARK MATCH.*
YOU'RE UP NEXT.
WHAT?!
WHO AM I FIGHTING TONIGHT?
*UNTELEVISED MATCH
GO GET CHANGED NOW!!!

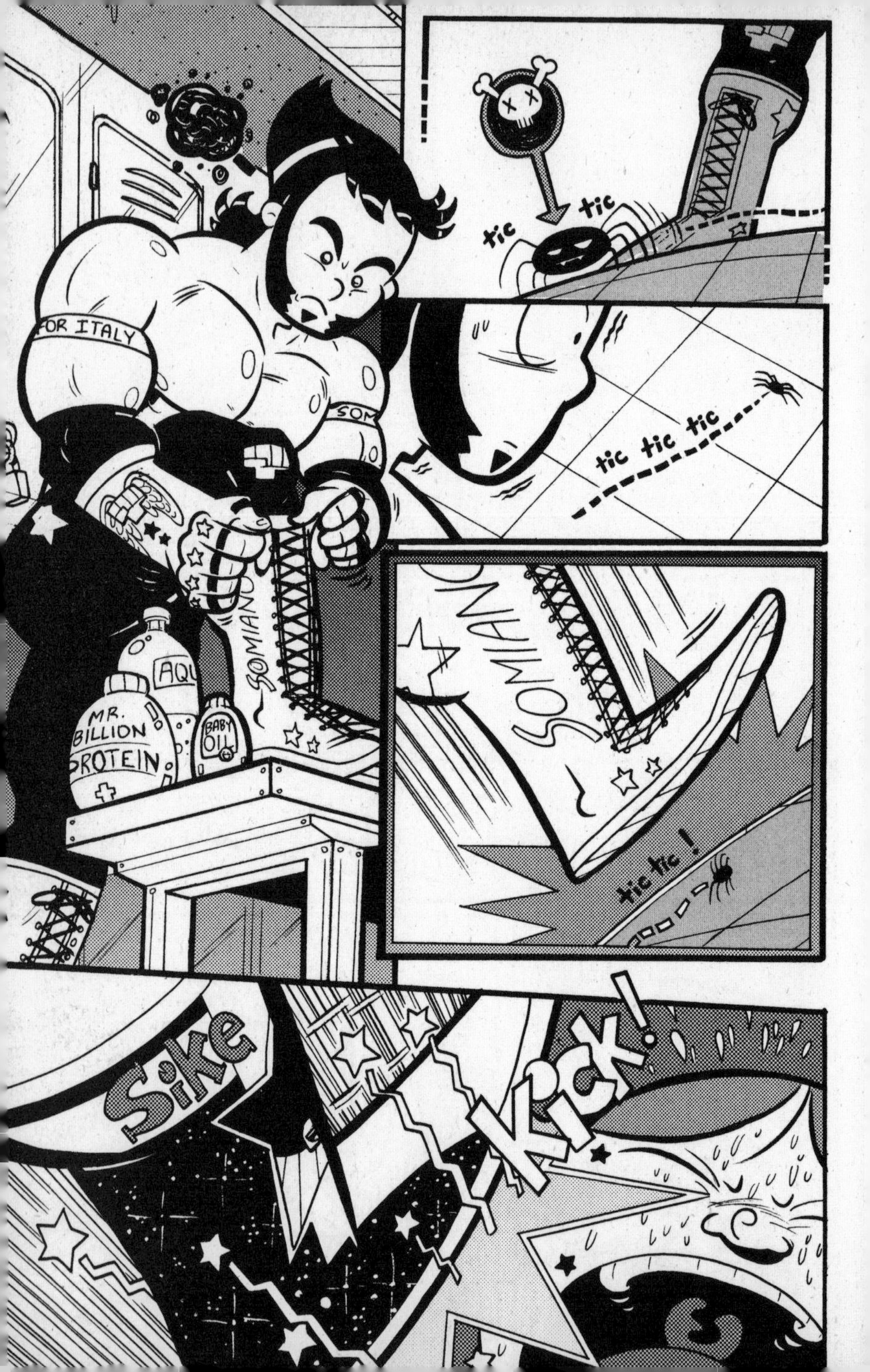

FOR ITALY
SOMIANO
MR. BILLION PROTEIN
AQU
BABY OIL
tic tic
tic tic tic
SOMIANO
tic tic !
Sike
KICK!

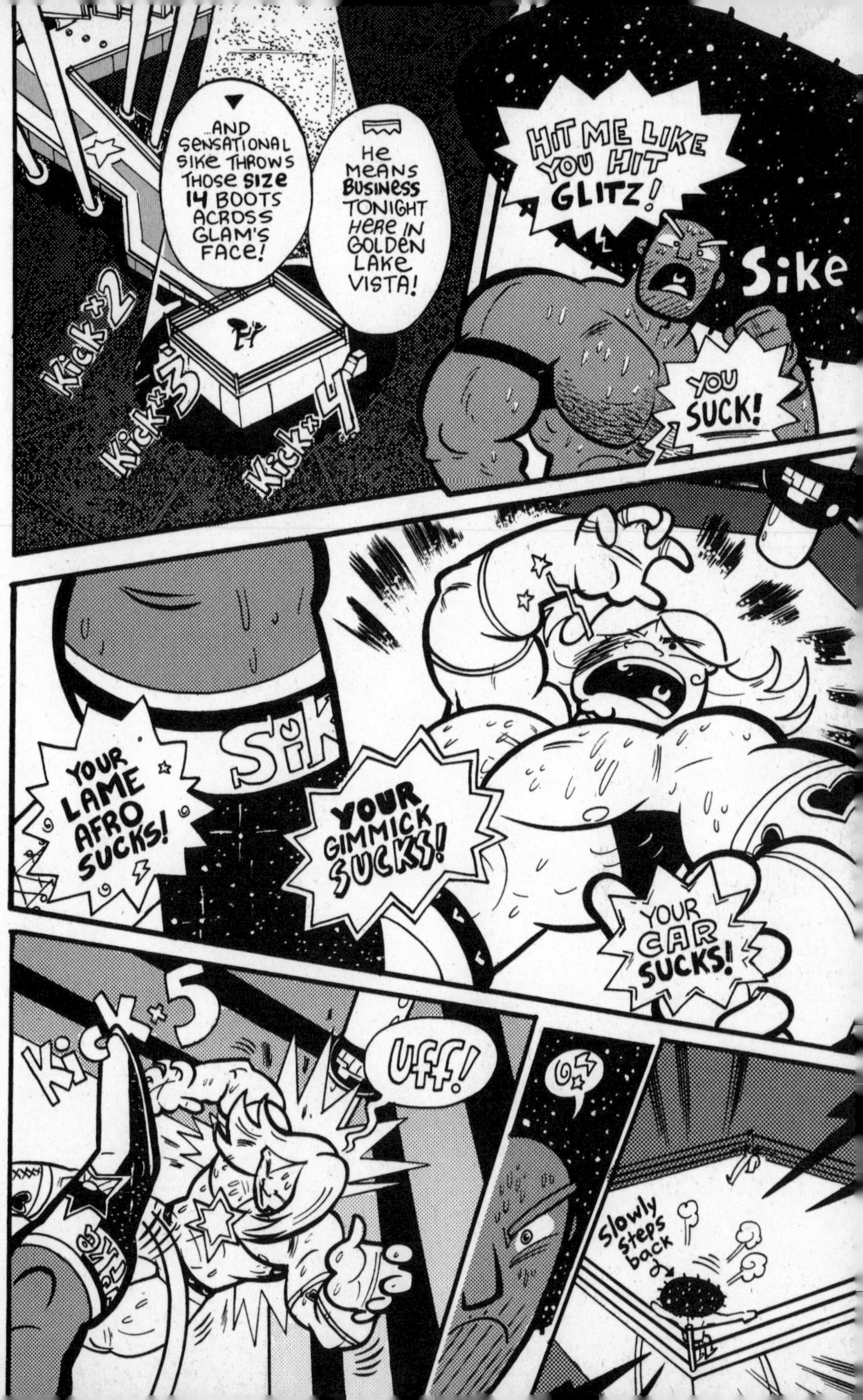...AND SENSATIONAL SIKE THROWS THOSE SIZE 14 BOOTS ACROSS GLAM'S FACE!
HE MEANS BUSINESS TONIGHT HERE IN GOLDEN LAKE VISTA!
HIT ME LIKE YOU HIT GLITZ!
Sike
KICK x 2
KICK x 3
KICK x 4
YOU SUCK!
YOUR LAME AFRO SUCKS!
YOUR GIMMICK SUCKS!
YOUR CAR SUCKS!
KICK x 5
UFF!
Slowly steps back

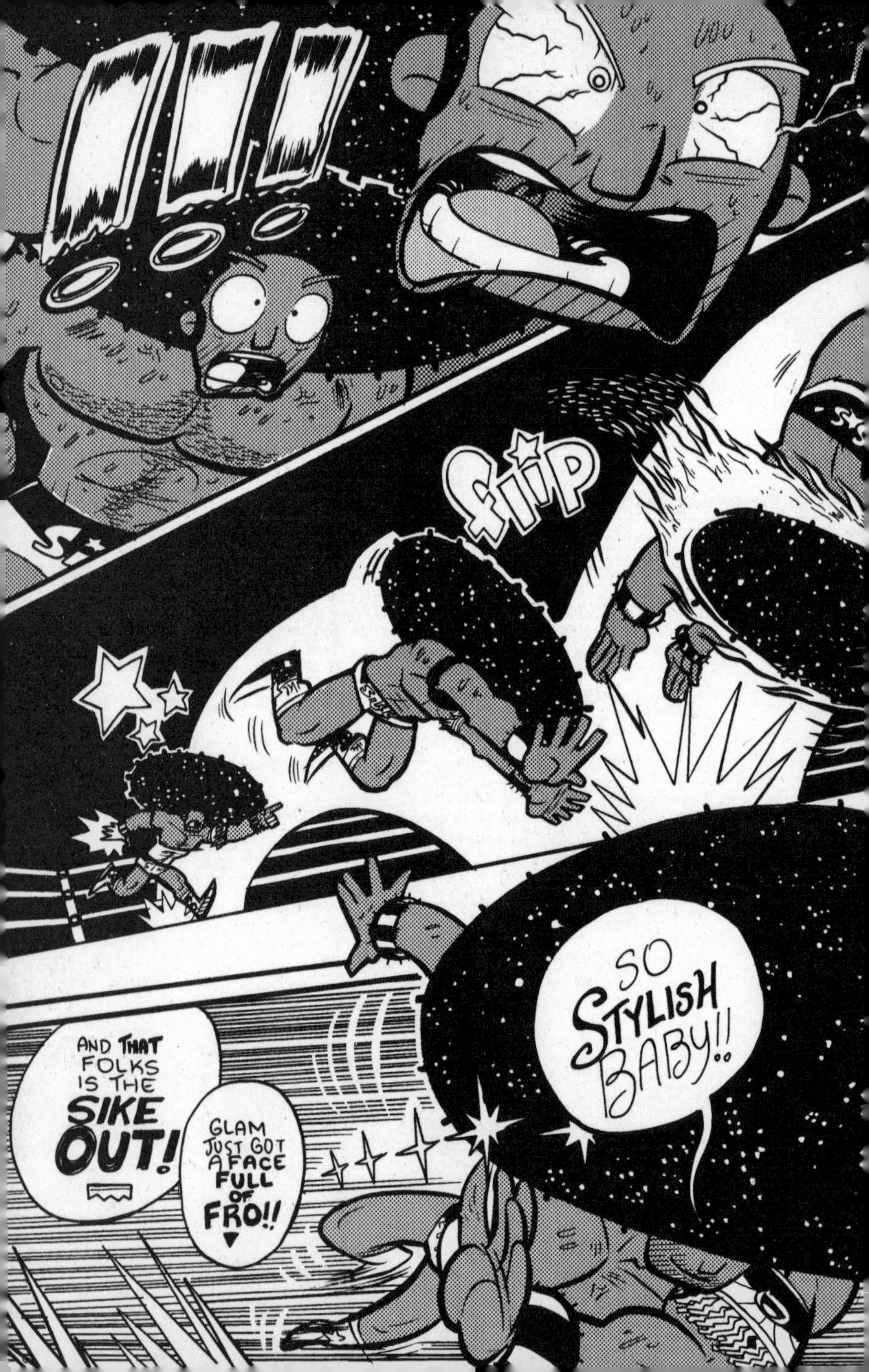
flip
AND THAT FOLKS IS THE SIKE OUT!
GLAM JUST GOT A FACE FULL OF FRO!!
SO STYLISH BABY!!

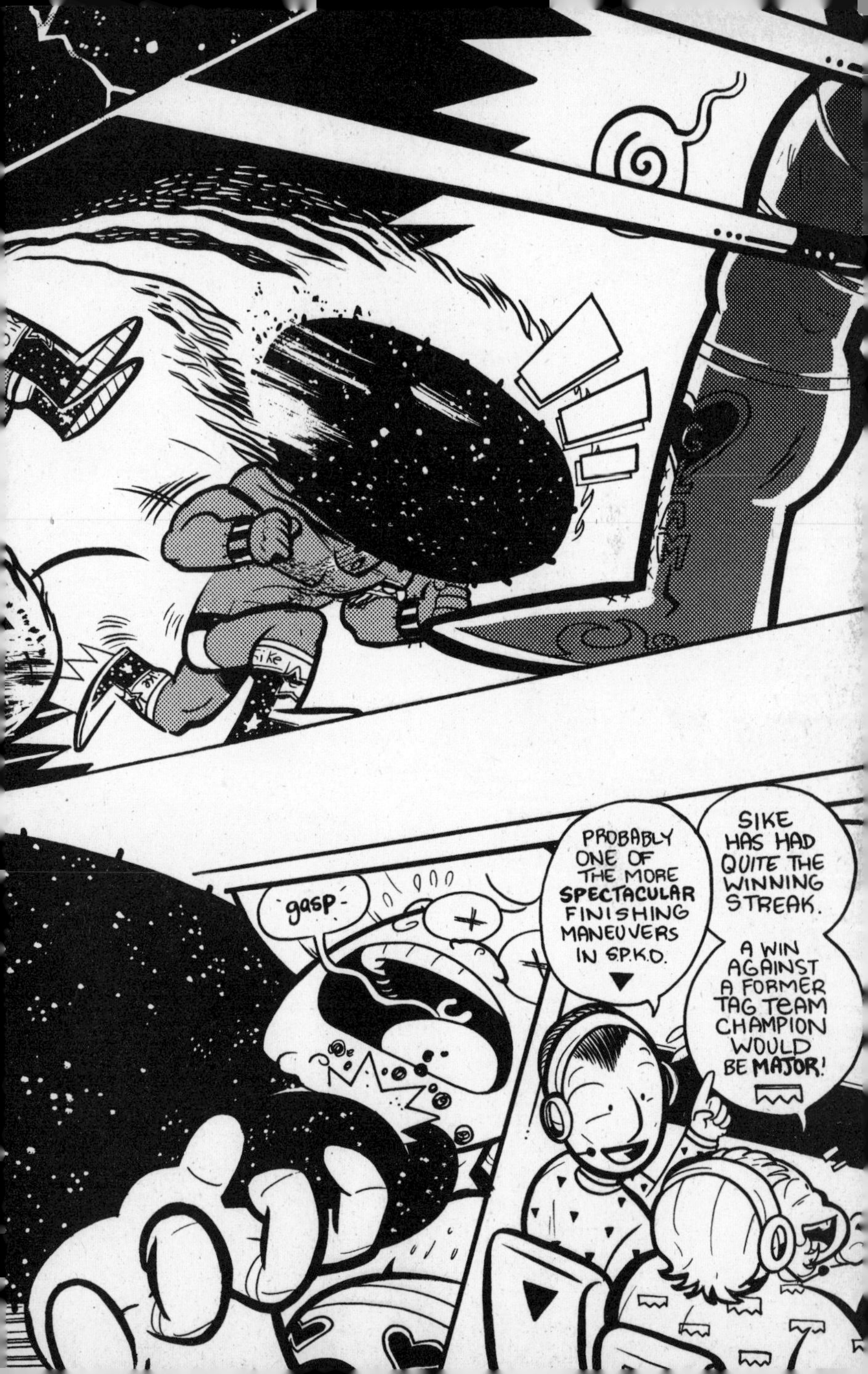

gasp
PROBABLY ONE OF THE MORE SPECTACULAR FINISHING MANEUVERS IN S.P.K.O.
SIKE HAS HAD QUITE THE WINNING STREAK.
A WIN AGAINST A FORMER TAG TEAM CHAMPION WOULD BE MAJOR!

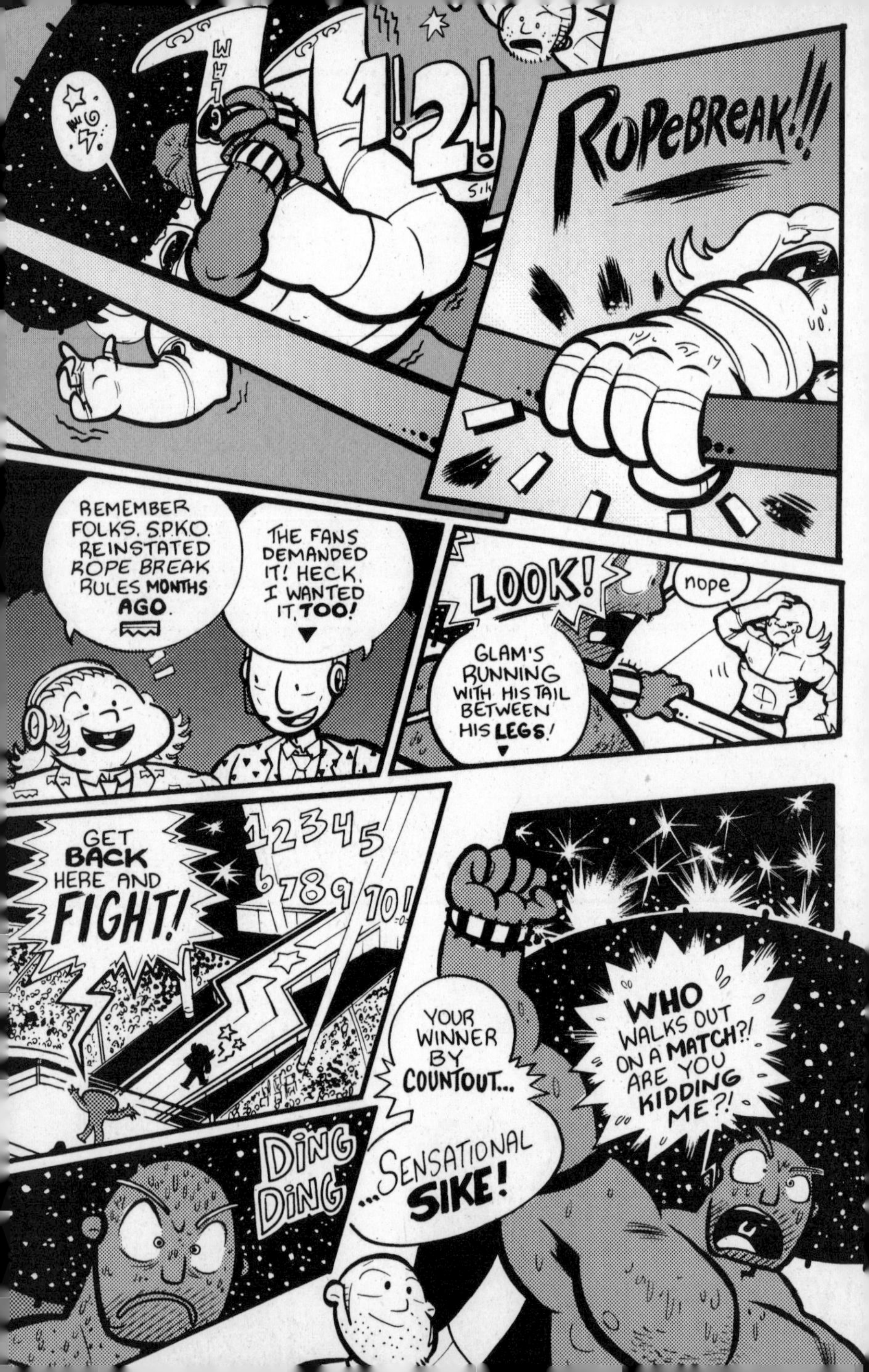

WHU
1! 2!
SIK
ROPEBREAK!!!
REMEMBER FOLKS, S.P.K.O. REINSTATED ROPE BREAK RULES MONTHS AGO.
THE FANS DEMANDED IT! HECK, I WANTED IT, TOO!
LOOK!
nope
GLAM'S RUNNING WITH HIS TAIL BETWEEN HIS LEGS!
GET BACK HERE AND FIGHT!
1 2 3 4 5 6 7 8 9 10!
YOUR WINNER BY COUNTOUT...
WHO WALKS OUT ON A MATCH?! ARE YOU KIDDING ME?!
DING DING
...SENSATIONAL SIKE!

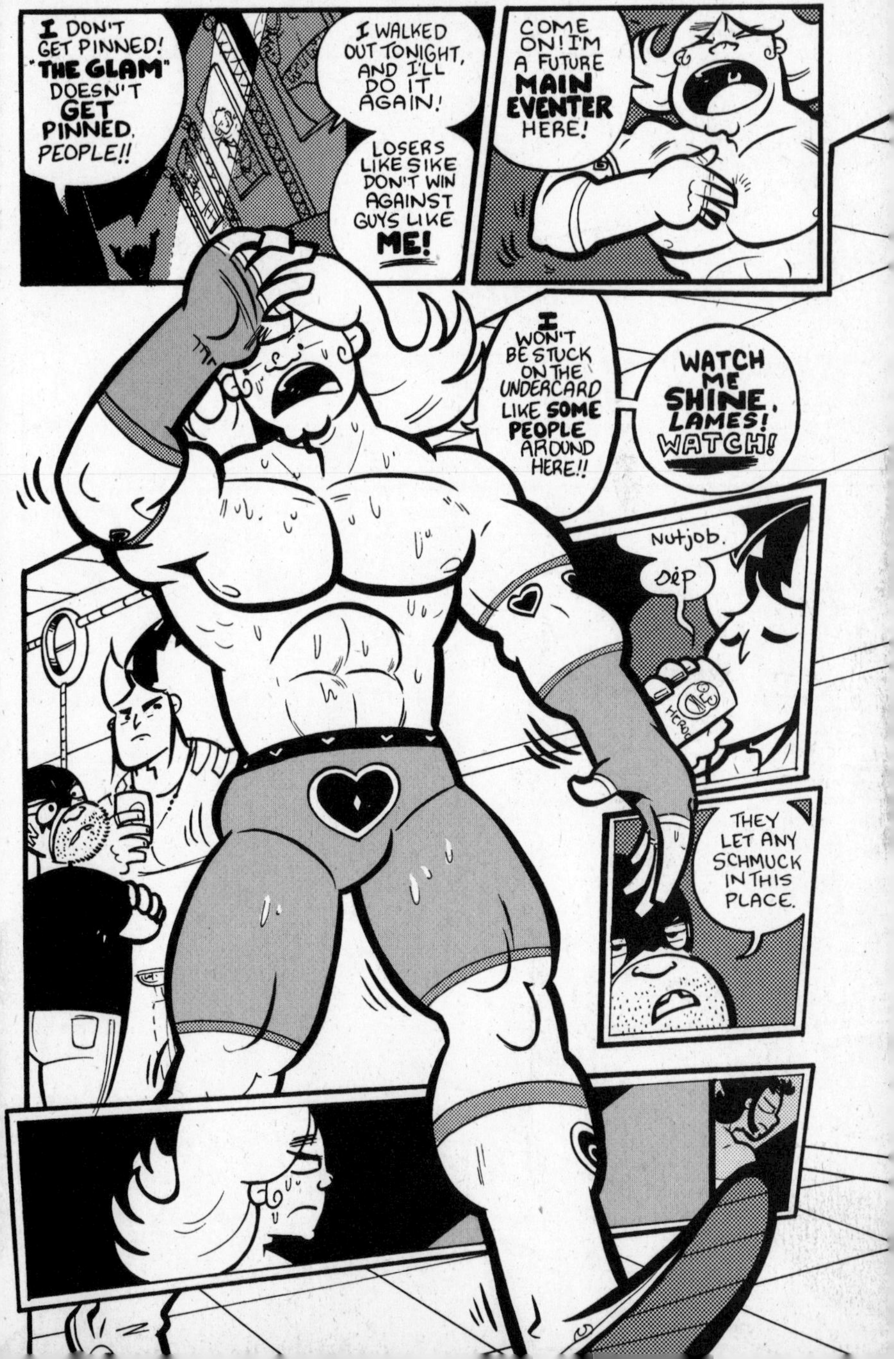
I DON'T GET PINNED! "THE GLAM" DOESN'T GET PINNED, PEOPLE!!
I WALKED OUT TONIGHT, AND I'LL DO IT AGAIN!
LOSERS LIKE SIKE DON'T WIN AGAINST GUYS LIKE ME!
COME ON! I'M A FUTURE MAIN EVENTER HERE!
I WON'T BE STUCK ON THE UNDERCARD LIKE SOME PEOPLE AROUND HERE!!
WATCH ME SHINE, LAMES! WATCH!
Nutjob.
sip
THEY LET ANY SCHMUCK IN THIS PLACE.

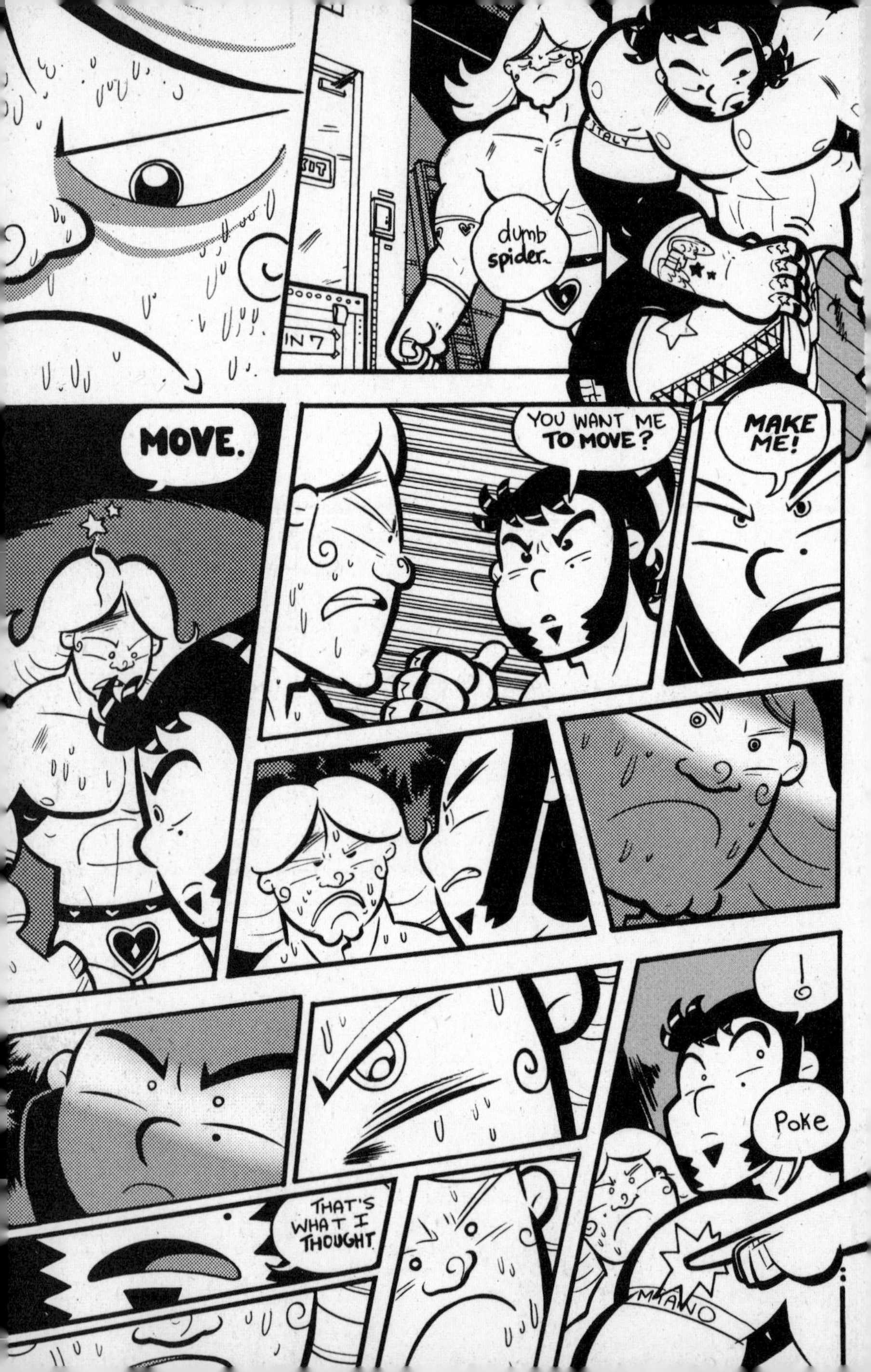

dumb spider.
MOVE.
YOU WANT ME TO MOVE?
MAKE ME!
!
Poke
THAT'S WHAT I THOUGHT.

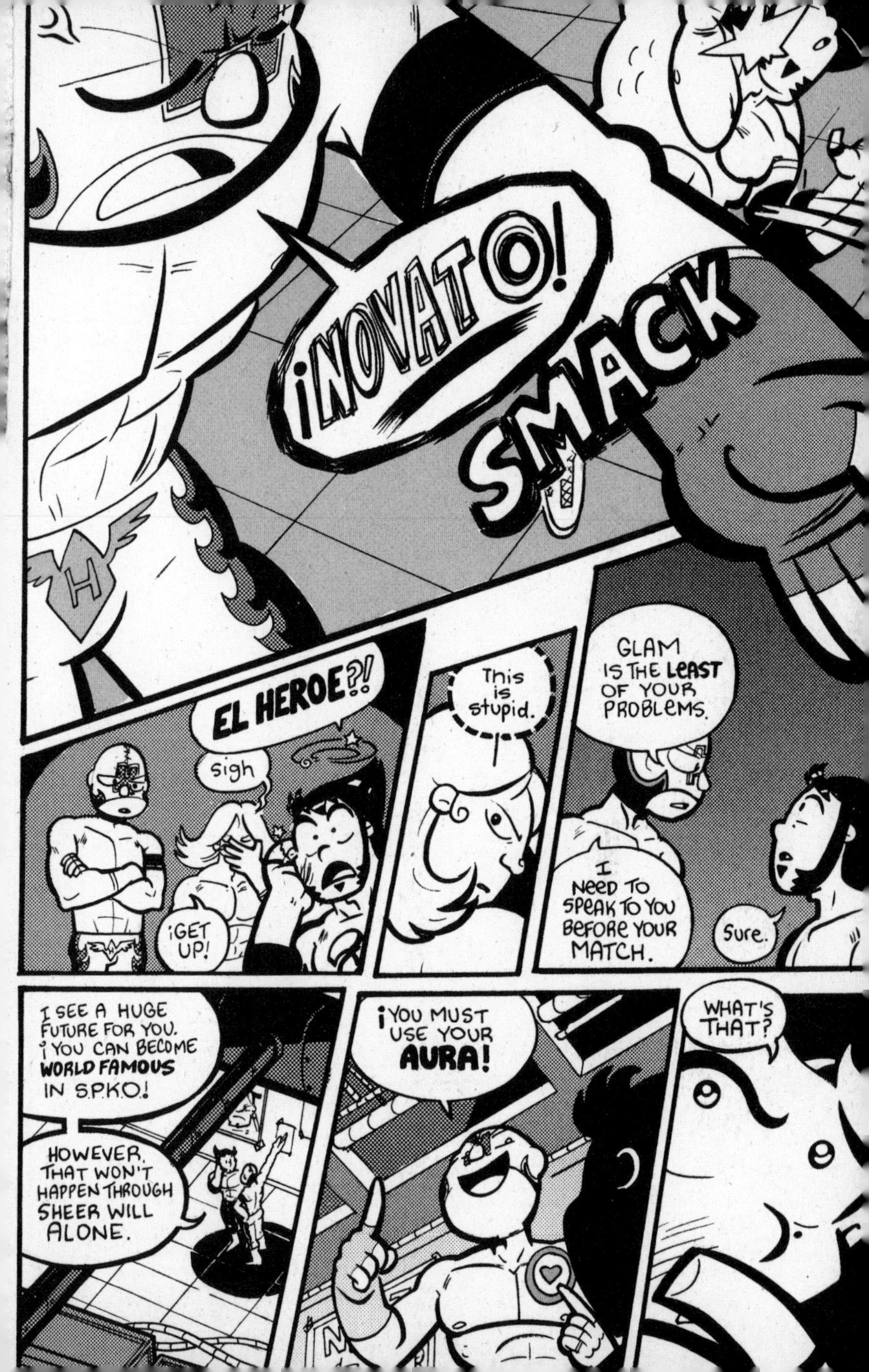

¡NOVATO!
SMACK
EL HEROE?!
sigh
¡GET UP!
This is stupid.
GLAM IS THE LEAST OF YOUR PROBLEMS.
I NEED TO SPEAK TO YOU BEFORE YOUR MATCH.
Sure.
I SEE A HUGE FUTURE FOR YOU. ¡YOU CAN BECOME WORLD FAMOUS IN S.P.K.O.!
HOWEVER, THAT WON'T HAPPEN THROUGH SHEER WILL ALONE.
¡YOU MUST USE YOUR AURA!
WHAT'S THAT?

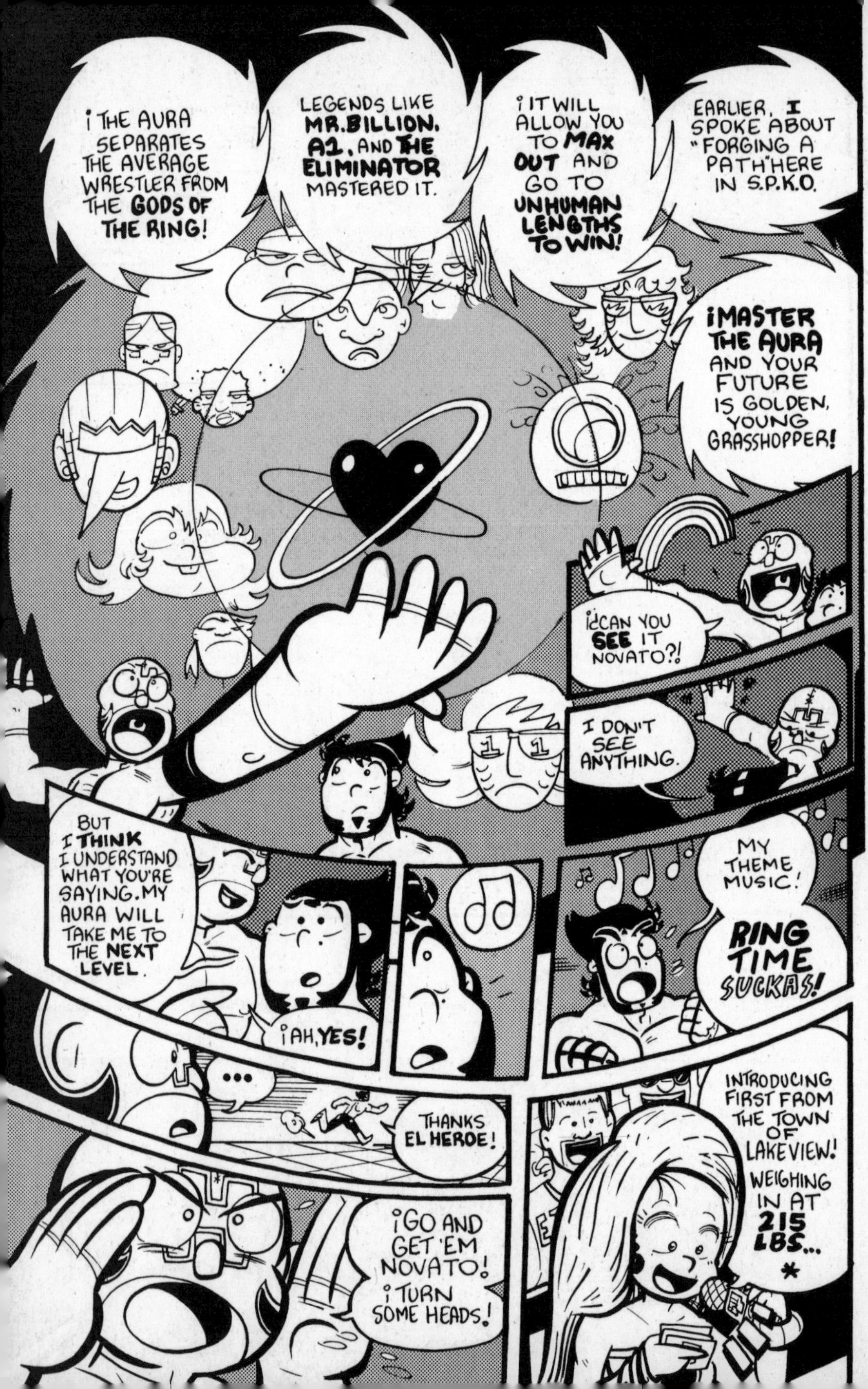

¡THE AURA SEPARATES THE AVERAGE WRESTLER FROM THE GODS OF THE RING!
LEGENDS LIKE MR.BILLION, A1, AND THE ELIMINATOR MASTERED IT.
¡IT WILL ALLOW YOU TO MAX OUT AND GO TO UNHUMAN LENGTHS TO WIN!
EARLIER, I SPOKE ABOUT "FORGING A PATH" HERE IN S.P.K.O.
¡MASTER THE AURA AND YOUR FUTURE IS GOLDEN, YOUNG GRASSHOPPER!
¡¿CAN YOU SEE IT NOVATO?!
I DON'T SEE ANYTHING.
BUT I THINK I UNDERSTAND WHAT YOU'RE SAYING. MY AURA WILL TAKE ME TO THE NEXT LEVEL.
¡AH, YES!
MY THEME MUSIC!
RING TIME SUCKAS!
...
THANKS EL HEROE!
INTRODUCING FIRST FROM THE TOWN OF LAKEVIEW! WEIGHING IN AT 215 LBS...
*
¡GO AND GET 'EM NOVATO! ¡TURN SOME HEADS!

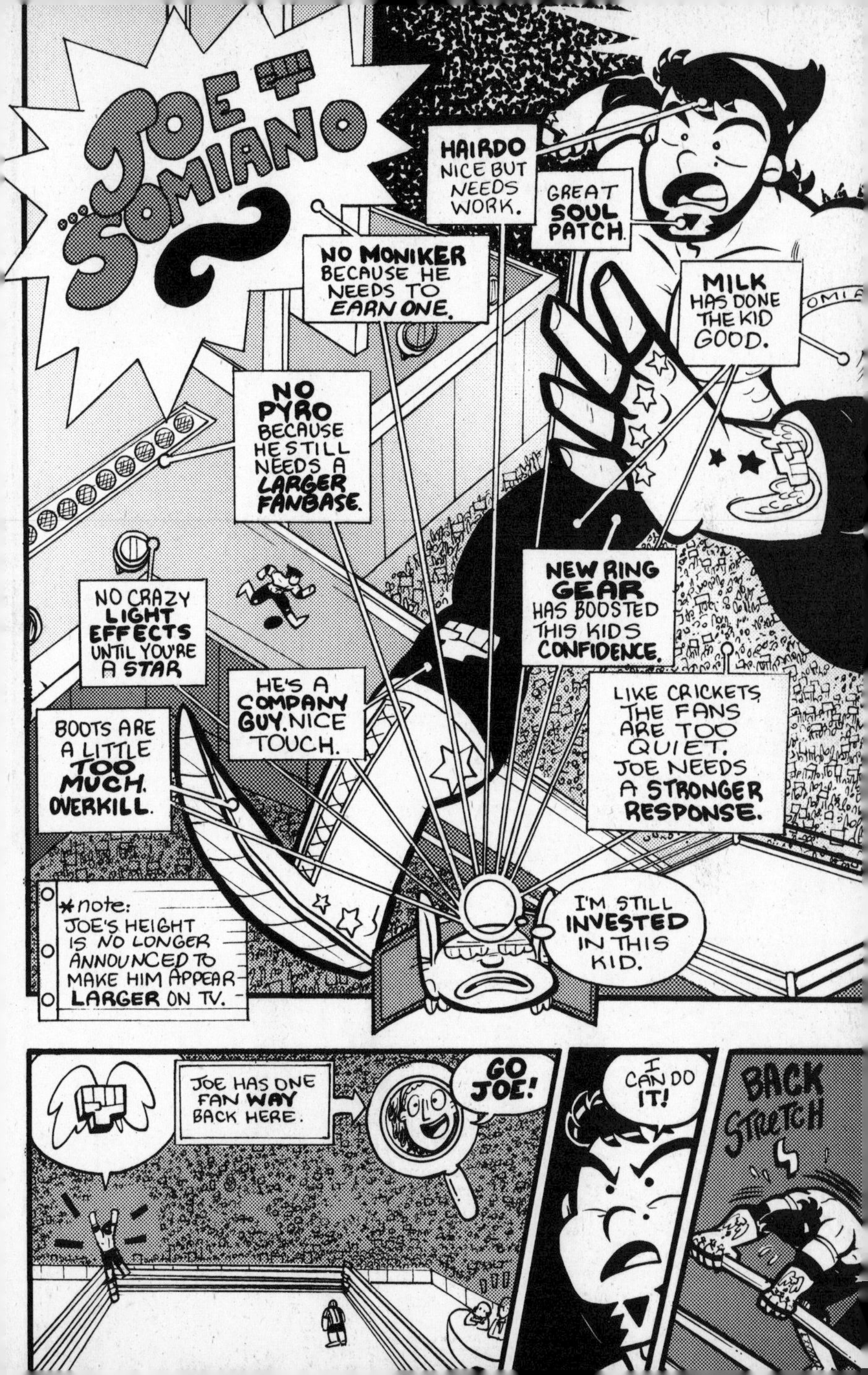
...JOE SOMIANO?
HAIRDO NICE BUT NEEDS WORK.
GREAT SOUL PATCH.
NO MONIKER BECAUSE HE NEEDS TO EARN ONE.
MILK HAS DONE THE KID GOOD.
NO PYRO BECAUSE HE STILL NEEDS A LARGER FANBASE.
NO CRAZY LIGHT EFFECTS UNTIL YOU'RE A STAR
NEW RING GEAR HAS BOOSTED THIS KIDS CONFIDENCE.
HE'S A COMPANY GUY. NICE TOUCH.
LIKE CRICKETS, THE FANS ARE TOO QUIET. JOE NEEDS A STRONGER RESPONSE.
BOOTS ARE A LITTLE TOO MUCH. OVERKILL.
*note: JOE'S HEIGHT IS NO LONGER ANNOUNCED TO MAKE HIM APPEAR LARGER ON TV.
I'M STILL INVESTED IN THIS KID.
JOE HAS ONE FAN WAY BACK HERE.
GO JOE!
I CAN DO IT!
BACK STRETCH

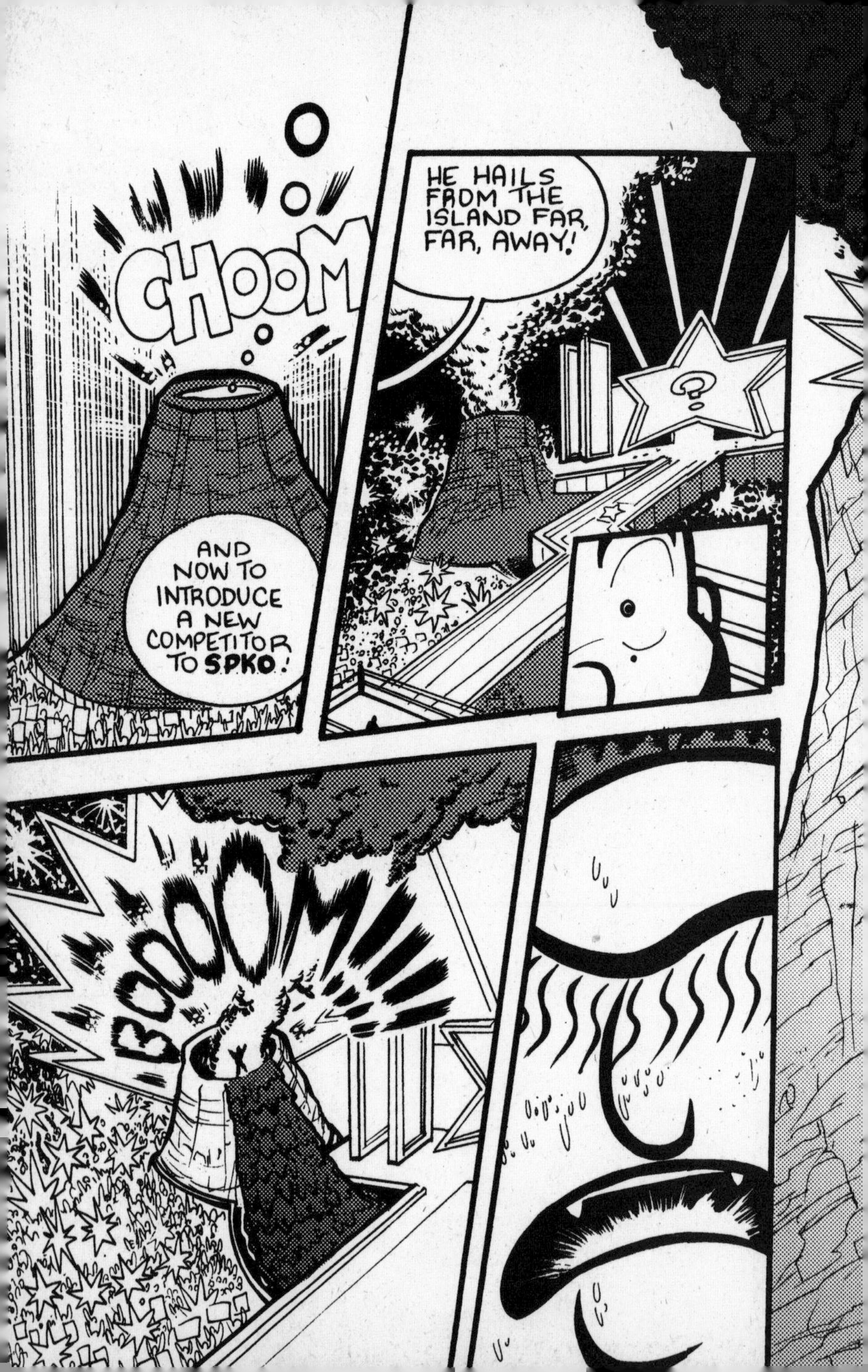
CHOOM
AND NOW TO INTRODUCE A NEW COMPETITOR TO S.P.K.O.!
HE HAILS FROM THE ISLAND FAR, FAR, AWAY!
BOOOOM

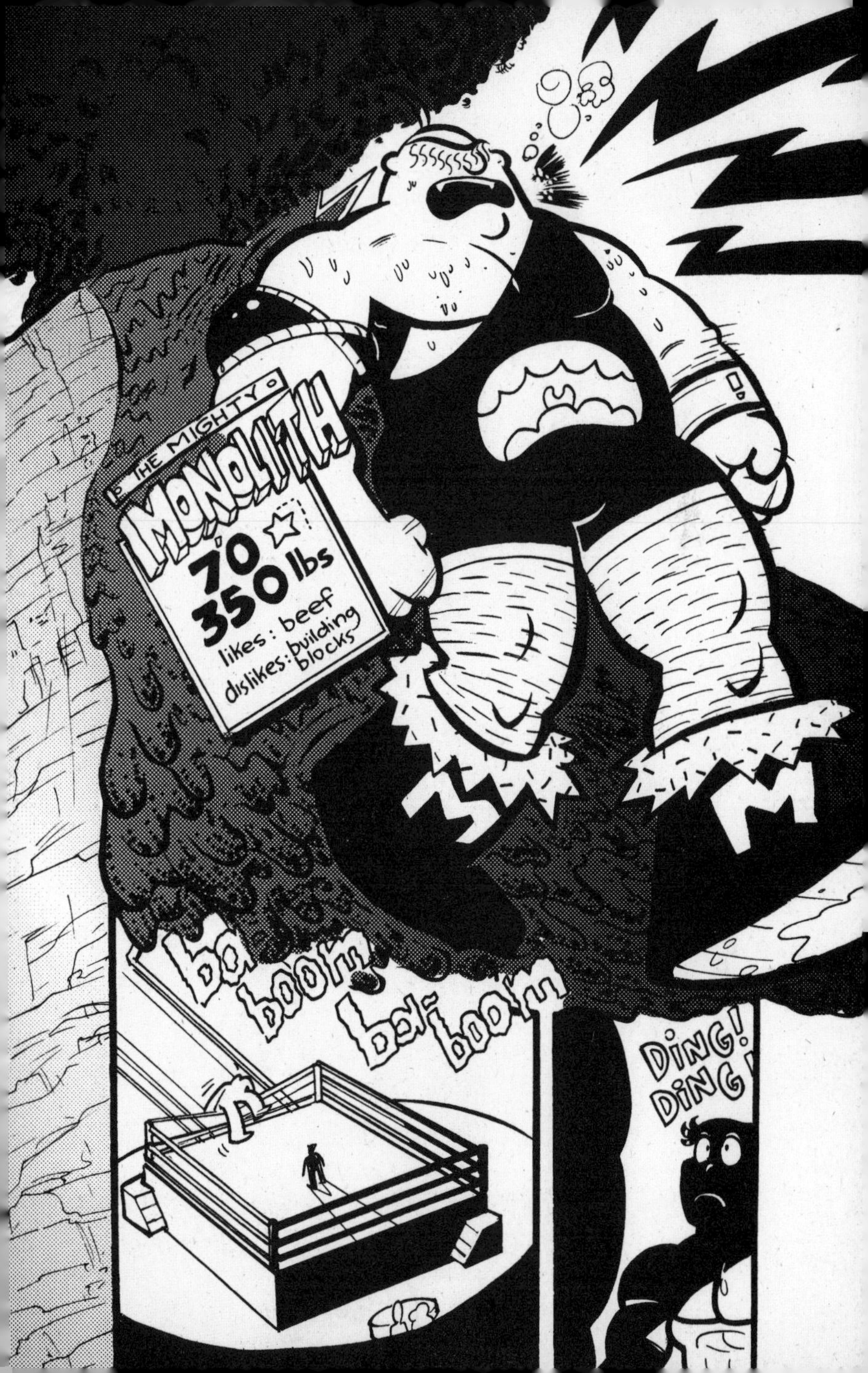

THE MIGHTY
MONOLITH
7'0
350 lbs
likes: beef
dislikes: building blocks
ba boom ba boom
DING! DING!

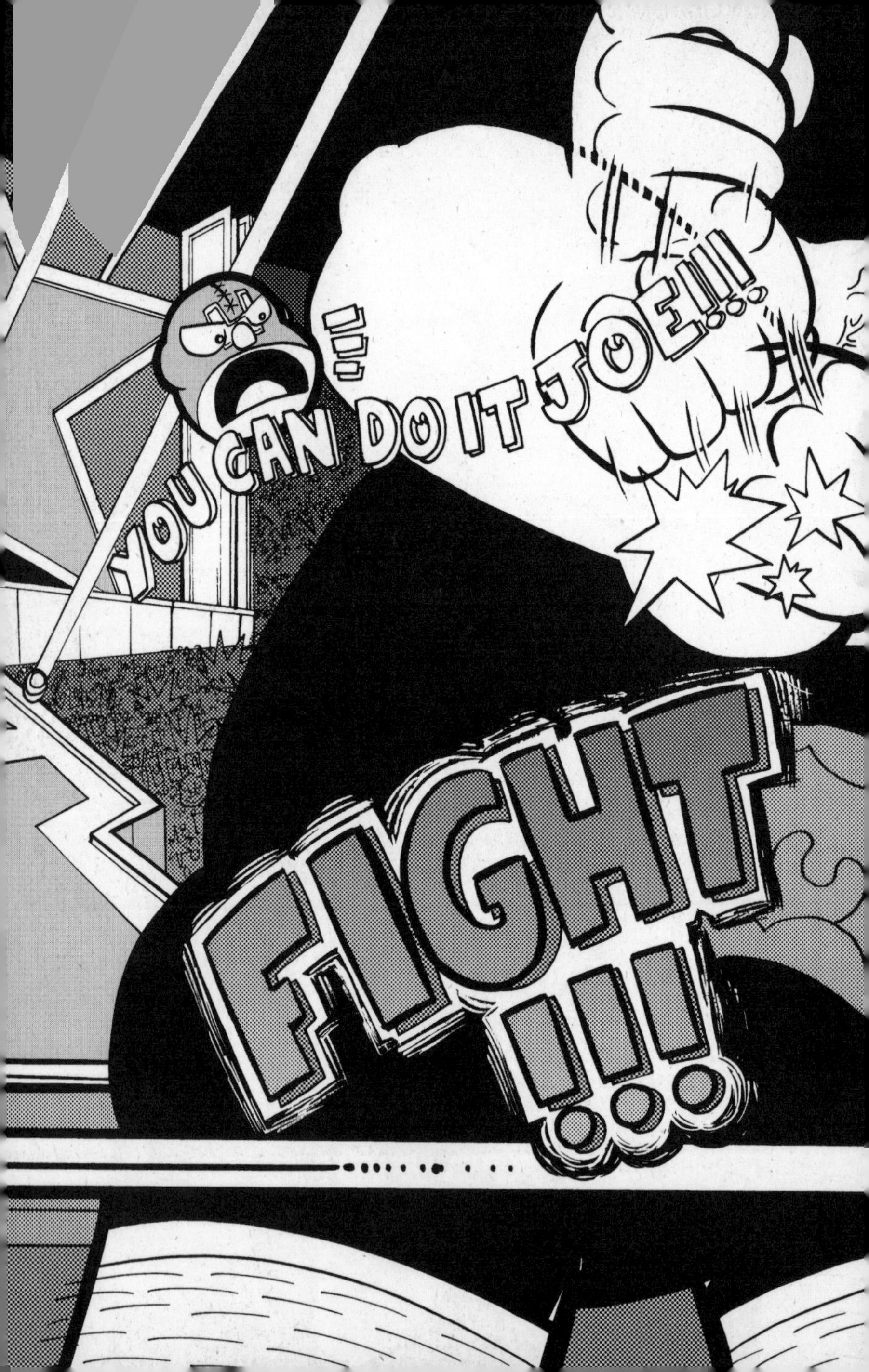
YOU CAN DO IT JOE!!!...
FIGHT!!!...

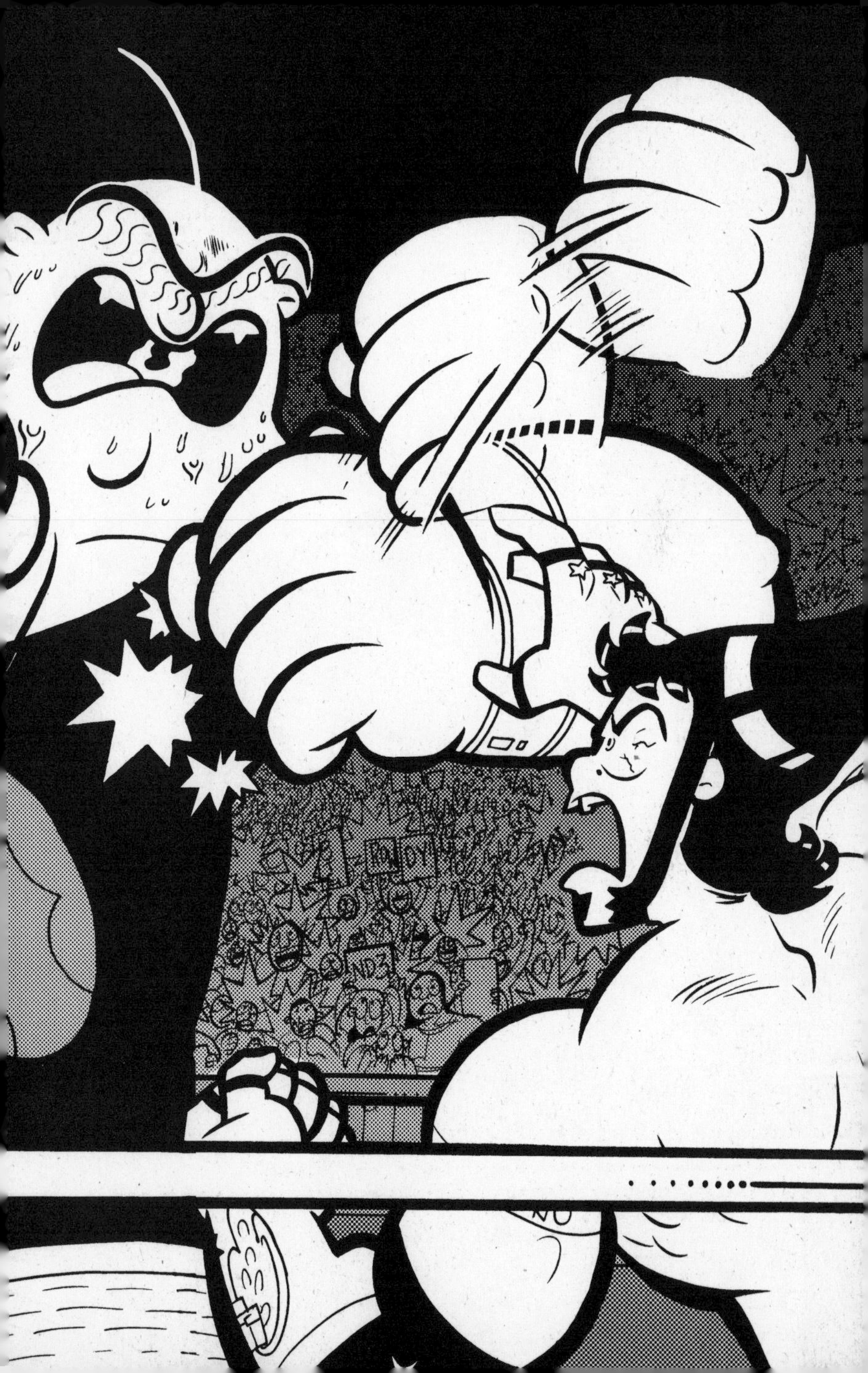

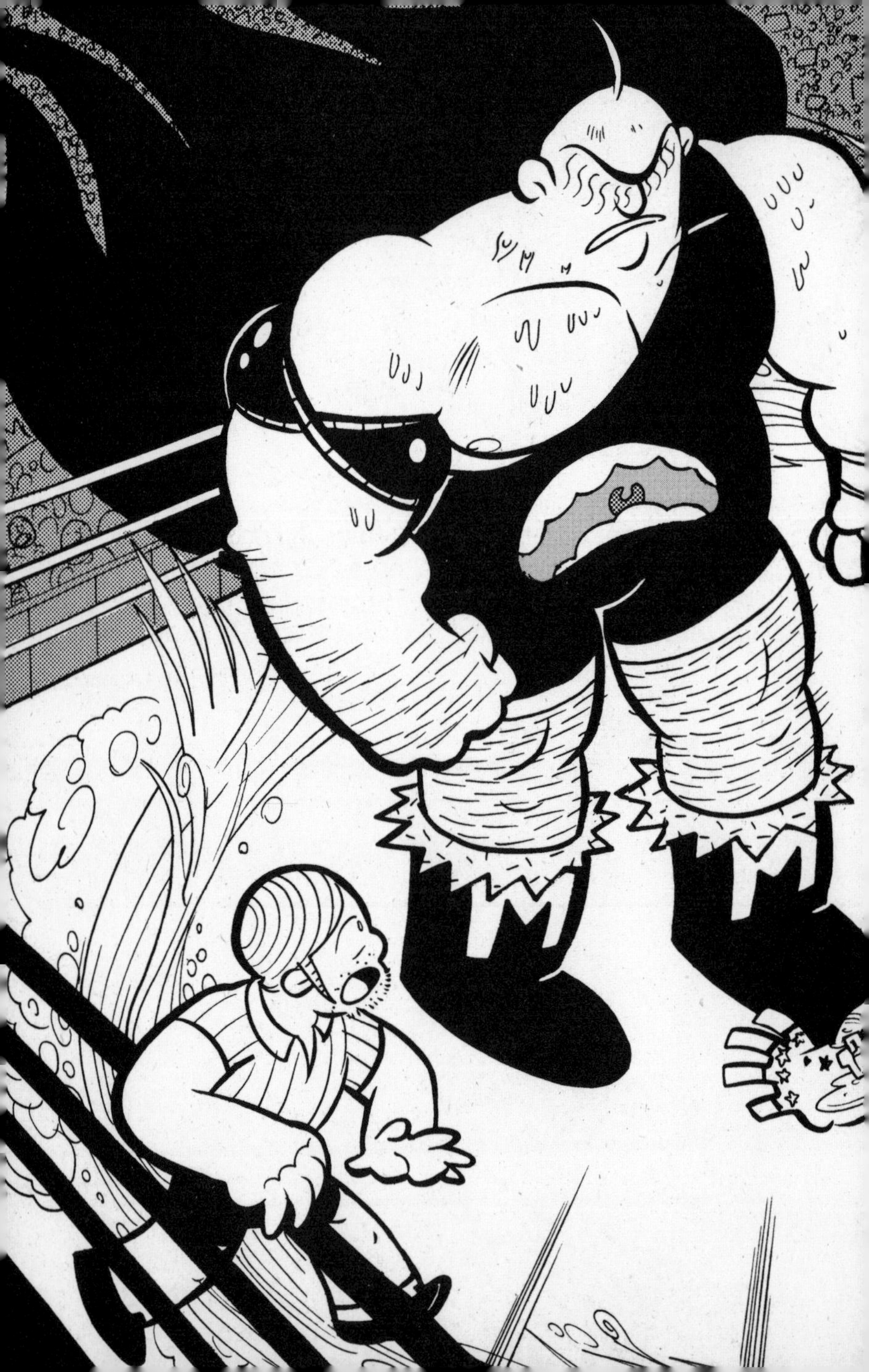

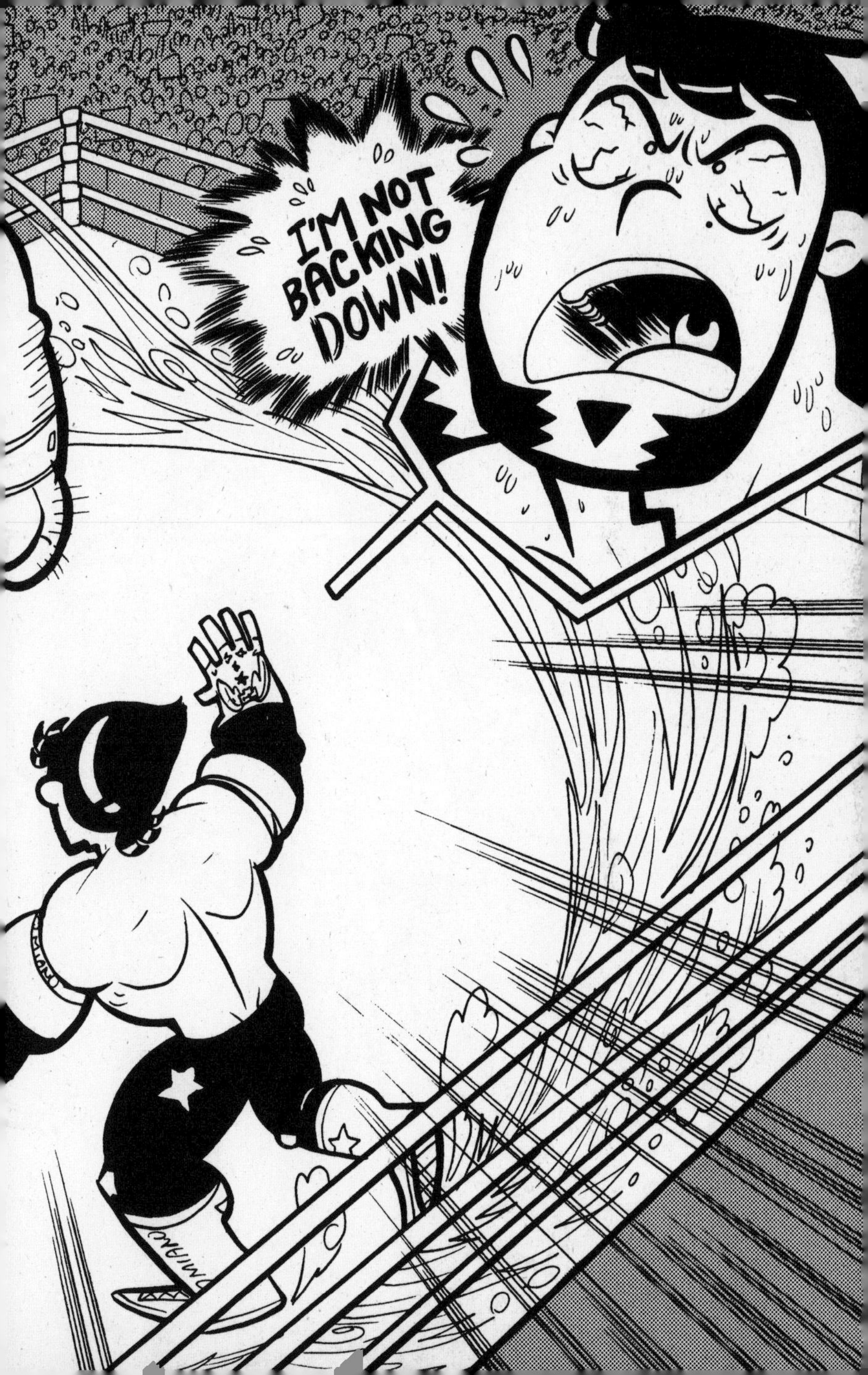
I'M NOT BACKING DOWN!

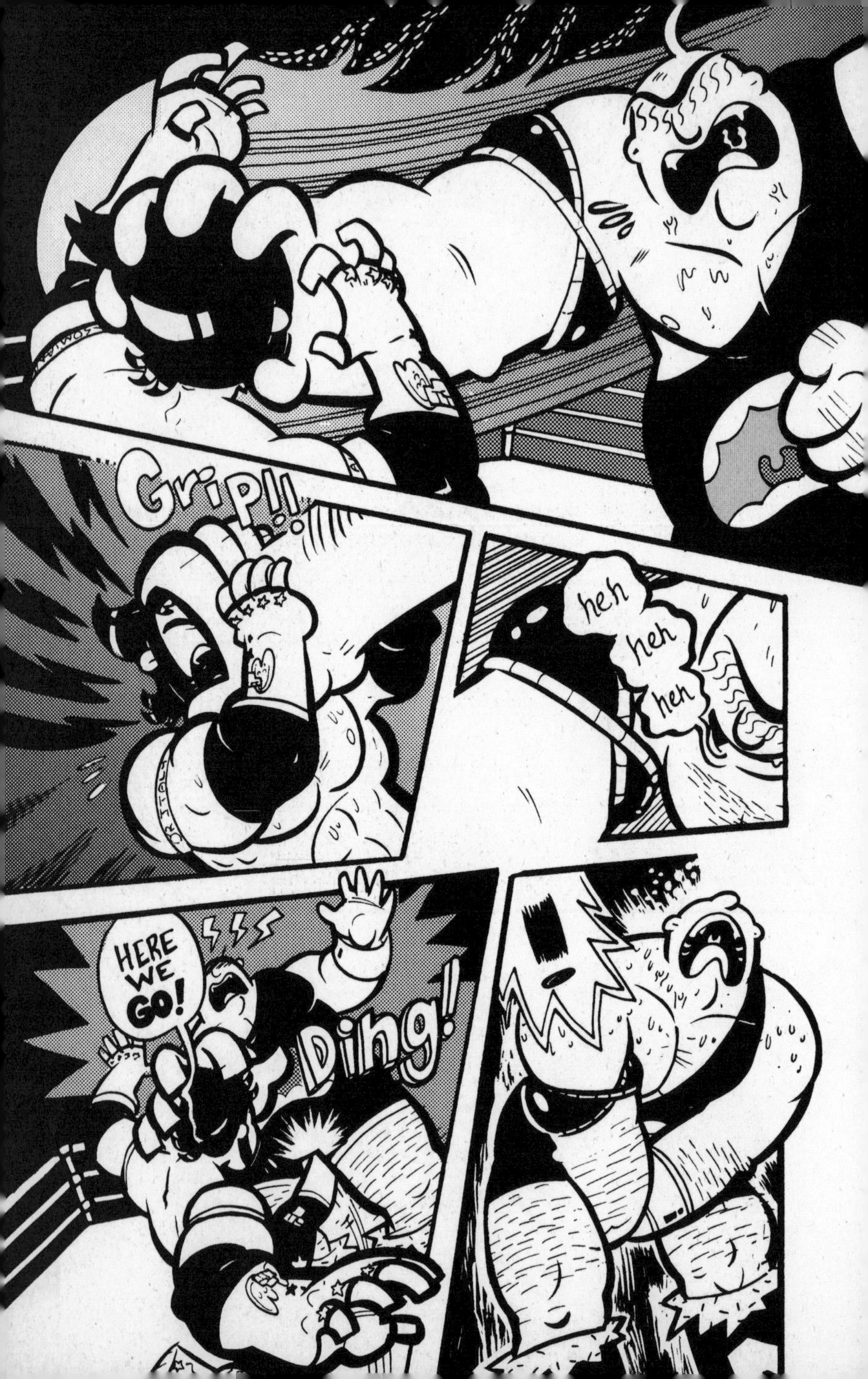
Grip!!
heh
heh
heh
HERE WE GO!
Ding!

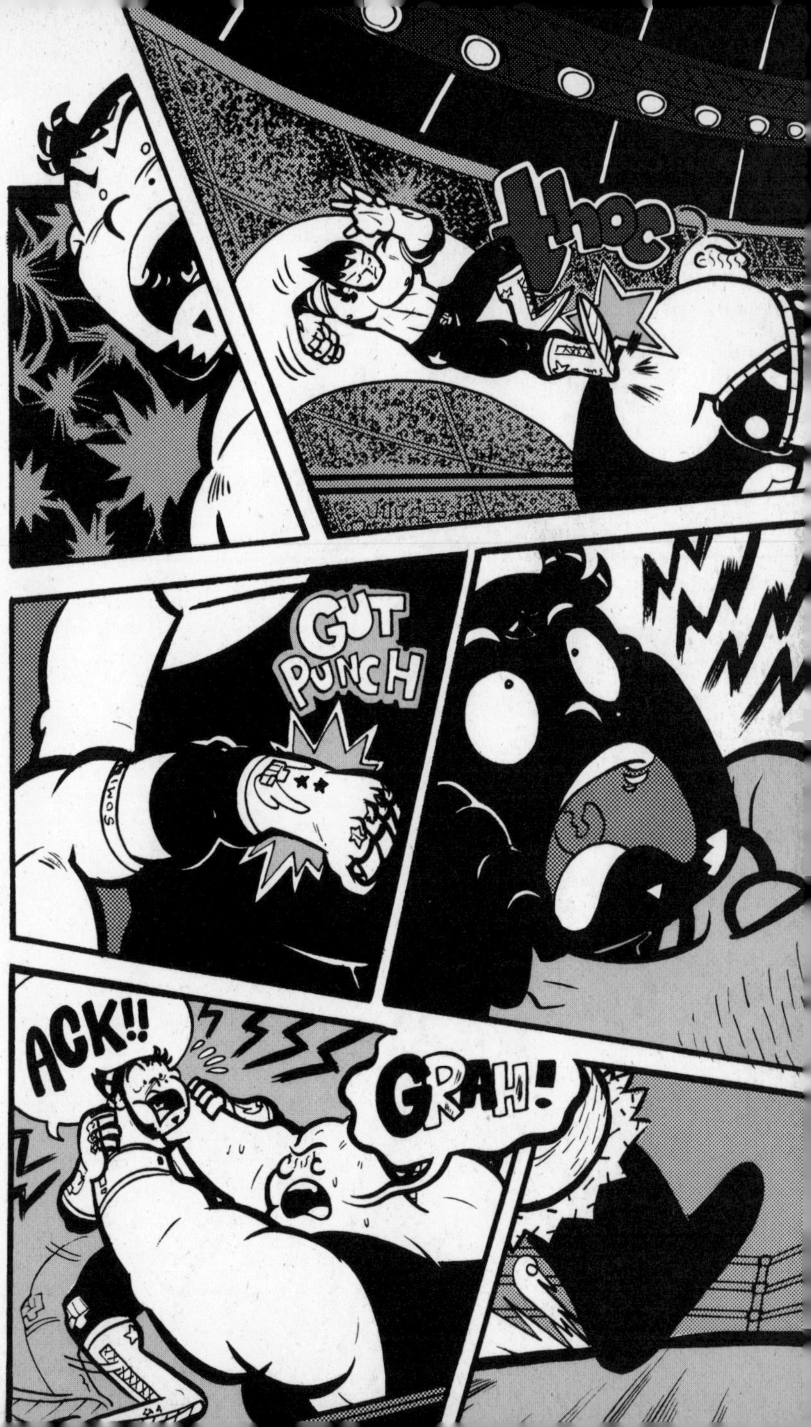

THOC
GUT PUNCH
ACK!!
GRAH!

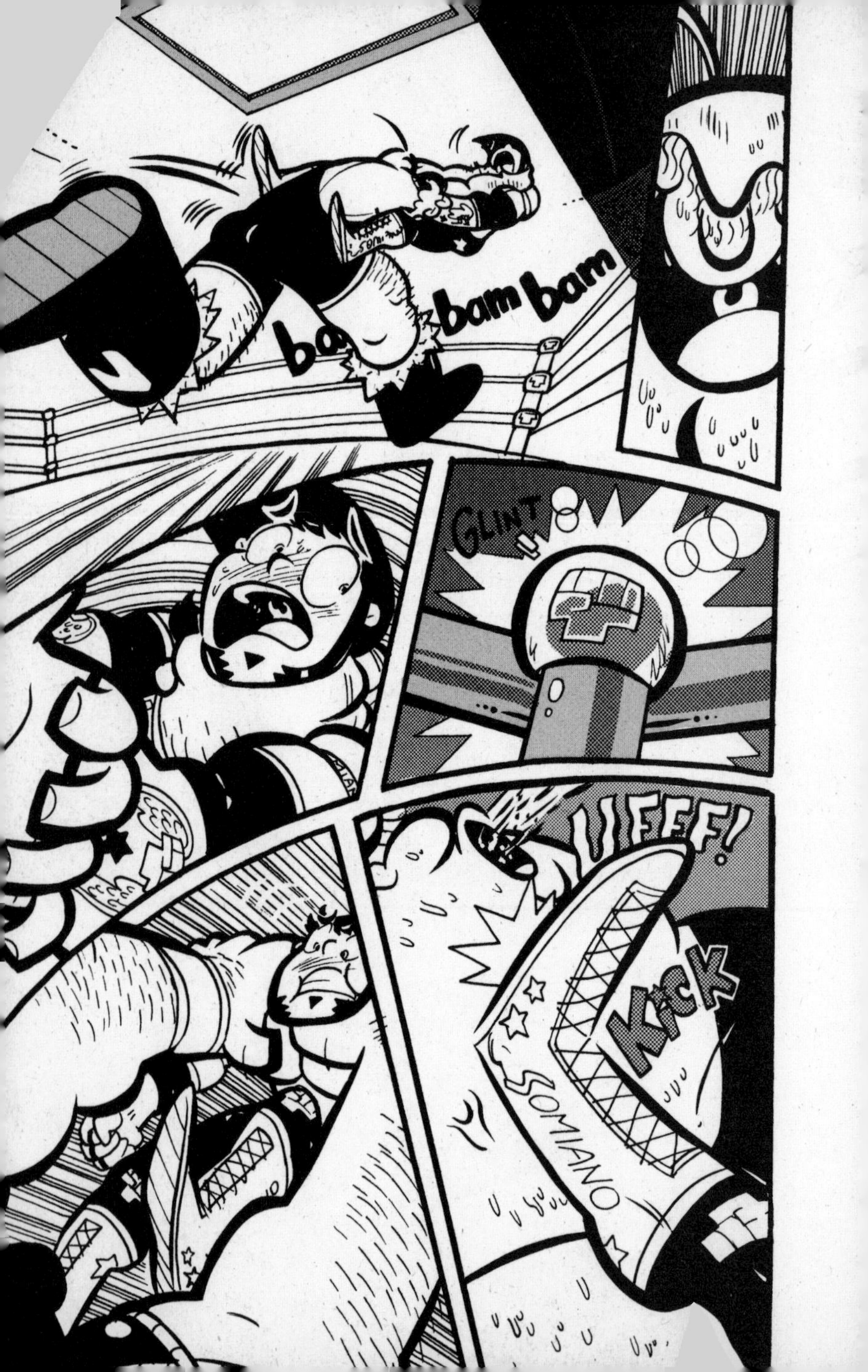
ba
bam bam
GLINT
UFFF!
KICK
SOMIANO

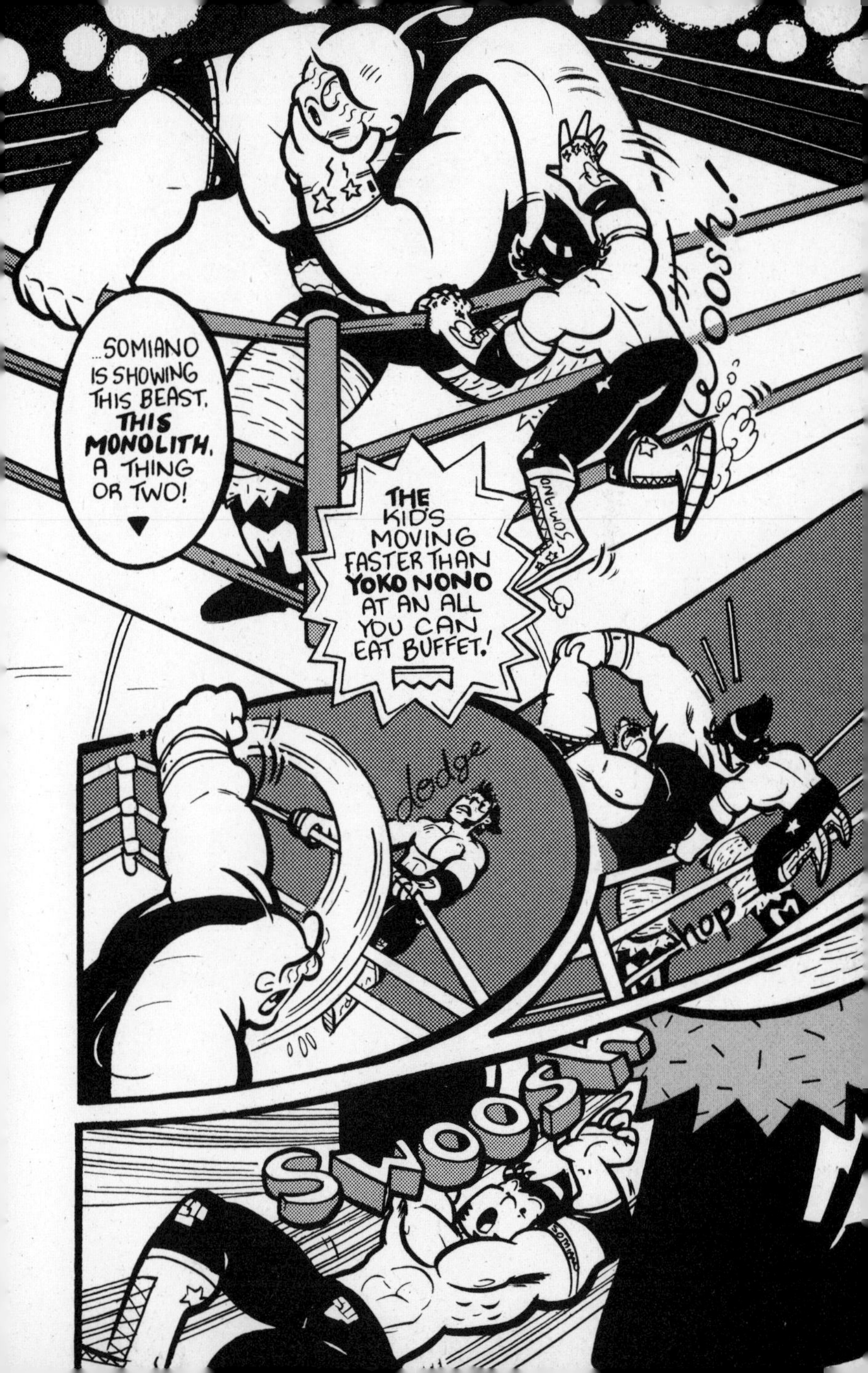
...SOMIANO IS SHOWING THIS BEAST, **THIS MONOLITH**, A THING OR TWO!
THE KID'S MOVING FASTER THAN **YOKO NONO** AT AN ALL YOU CAN EAT BUFFET!
oosh!
dodge
hop
SWOOSH

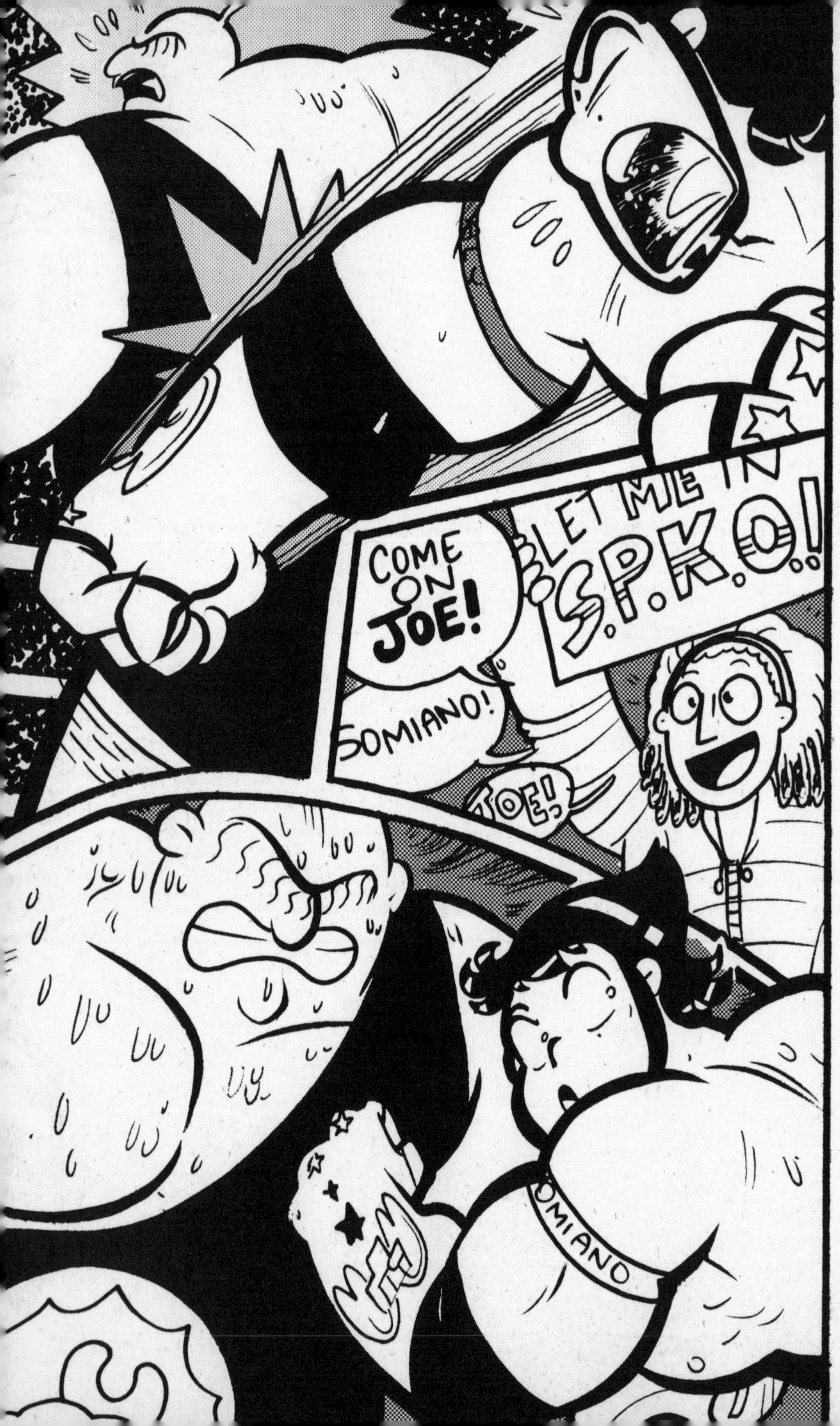
LET ME IN S.P.K.O.!
COME ON JOE!
SOMIANO!
JOE!
OMIANO

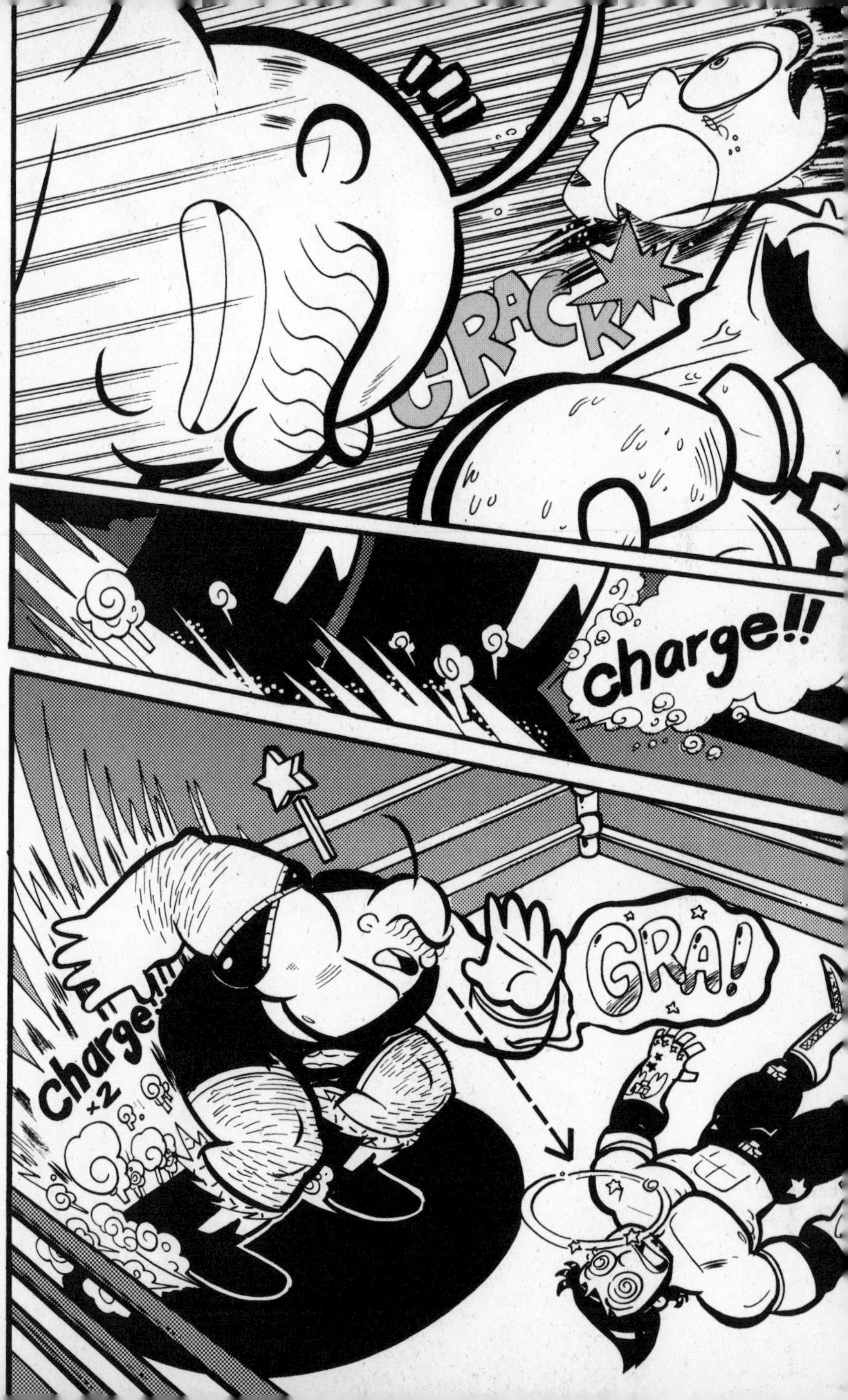
CRACK
charge!!
charge!!
×2
GRA!

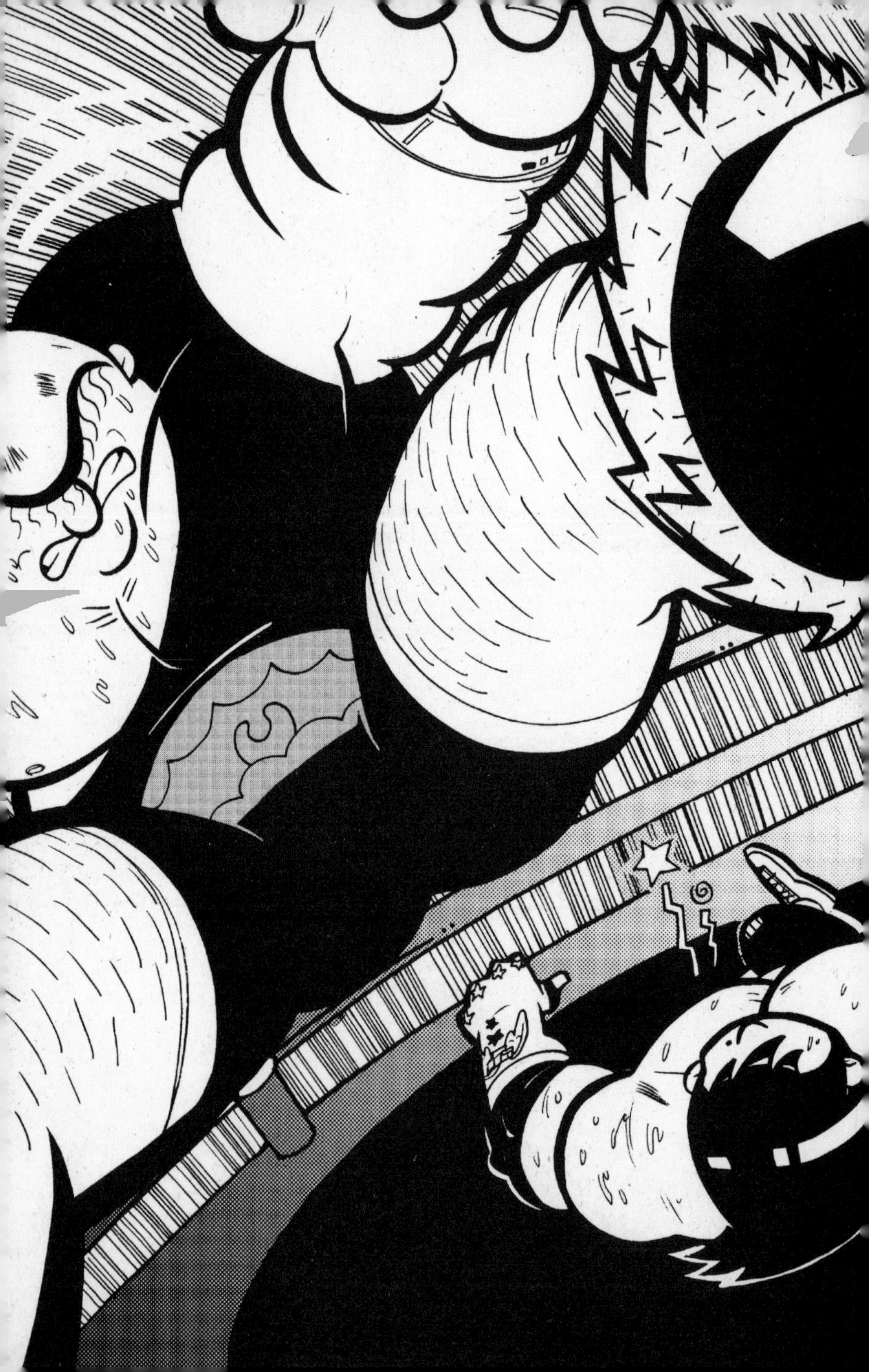

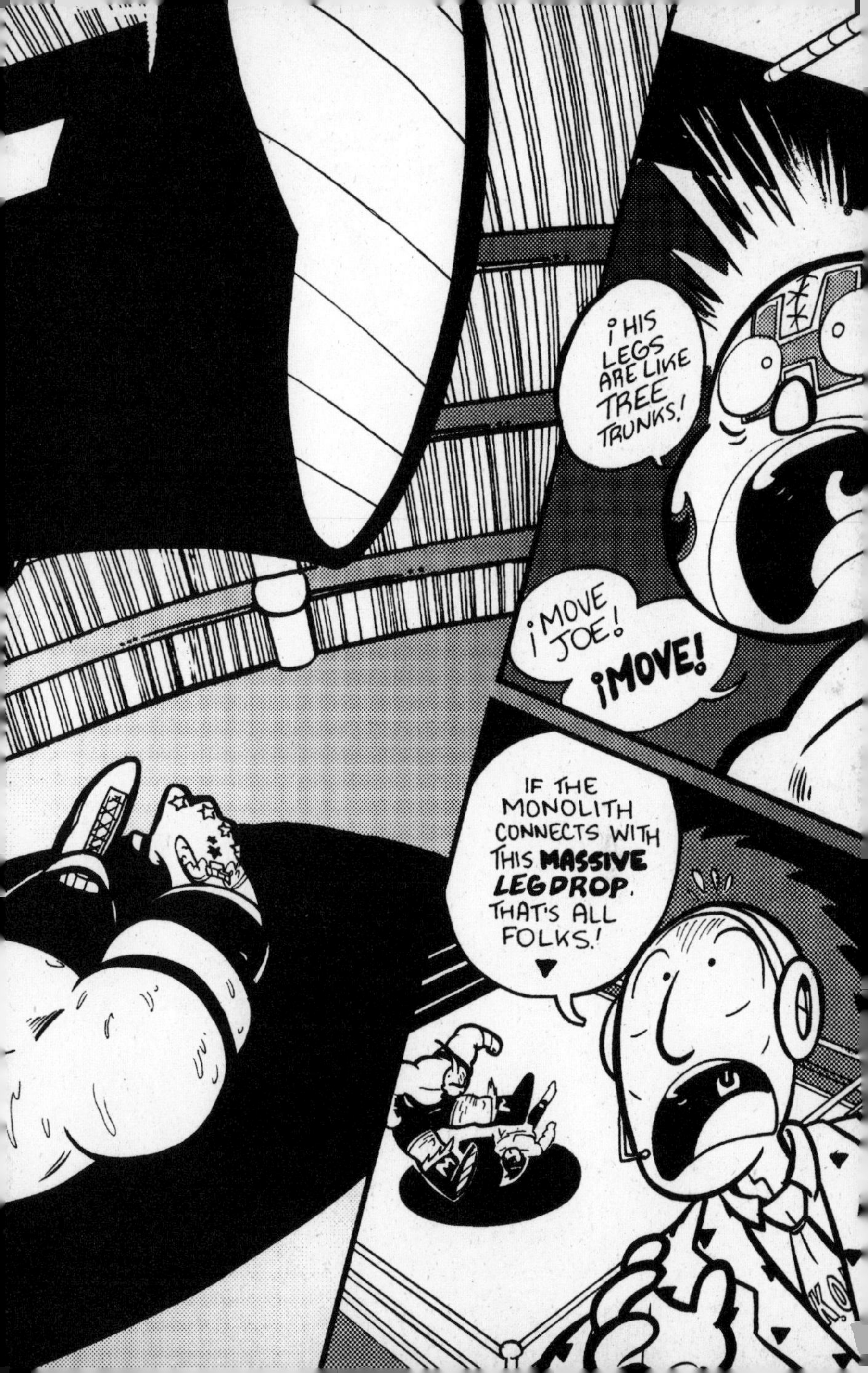
¡HIS LEGS ARE LIKE TREE TRUNKS!
¡MOVE JOE! ¡MOVE!
IF THE MONOLITH CONNECTS WITH THIS **MASSIVE LEGDROP**, THAT'S ALL FOLKS!

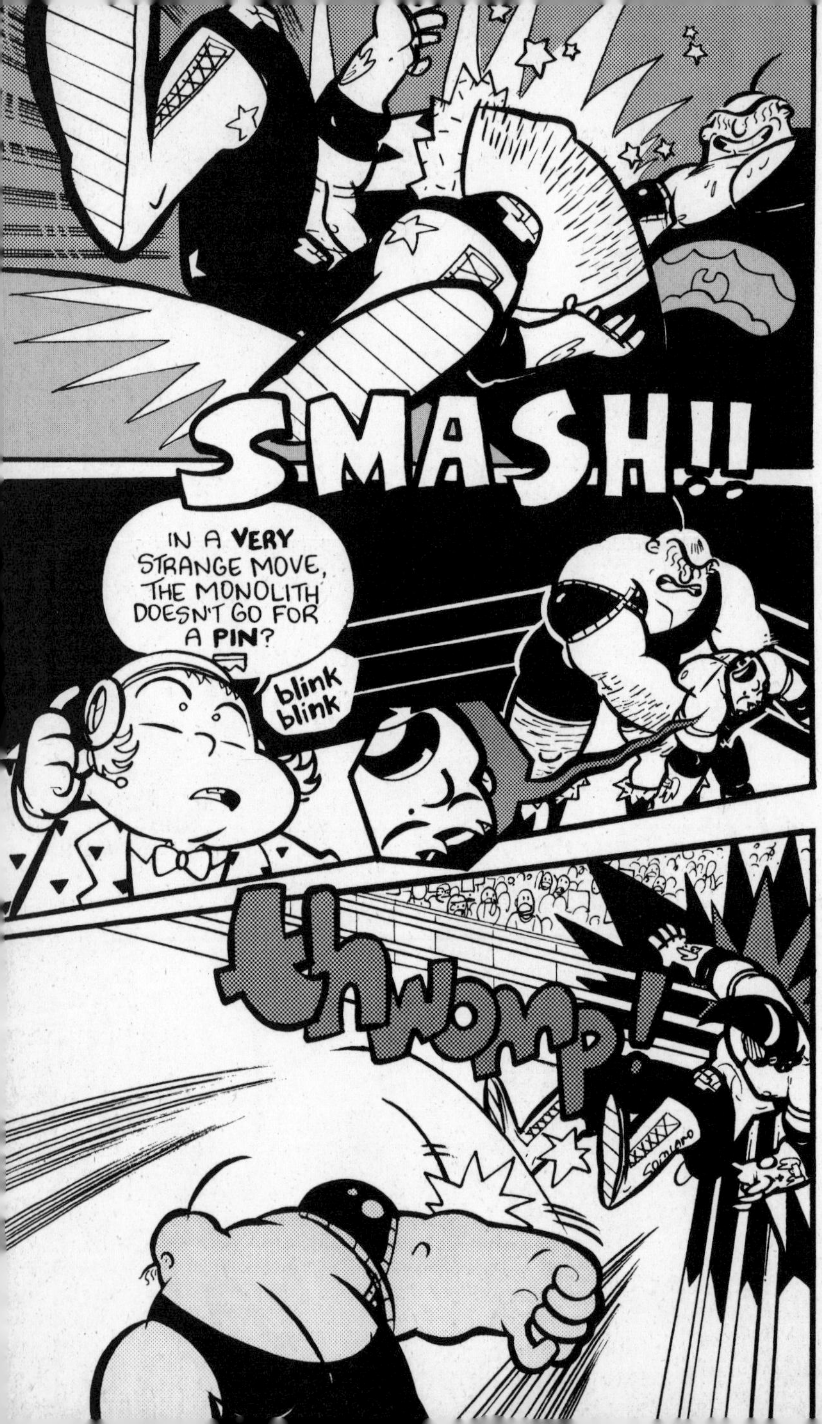
SMASH!!
IN A VERY STRANGE MOVE, THE MONOLITH DOESN'T GO FOR A PIN?
blink blink
thwomp!

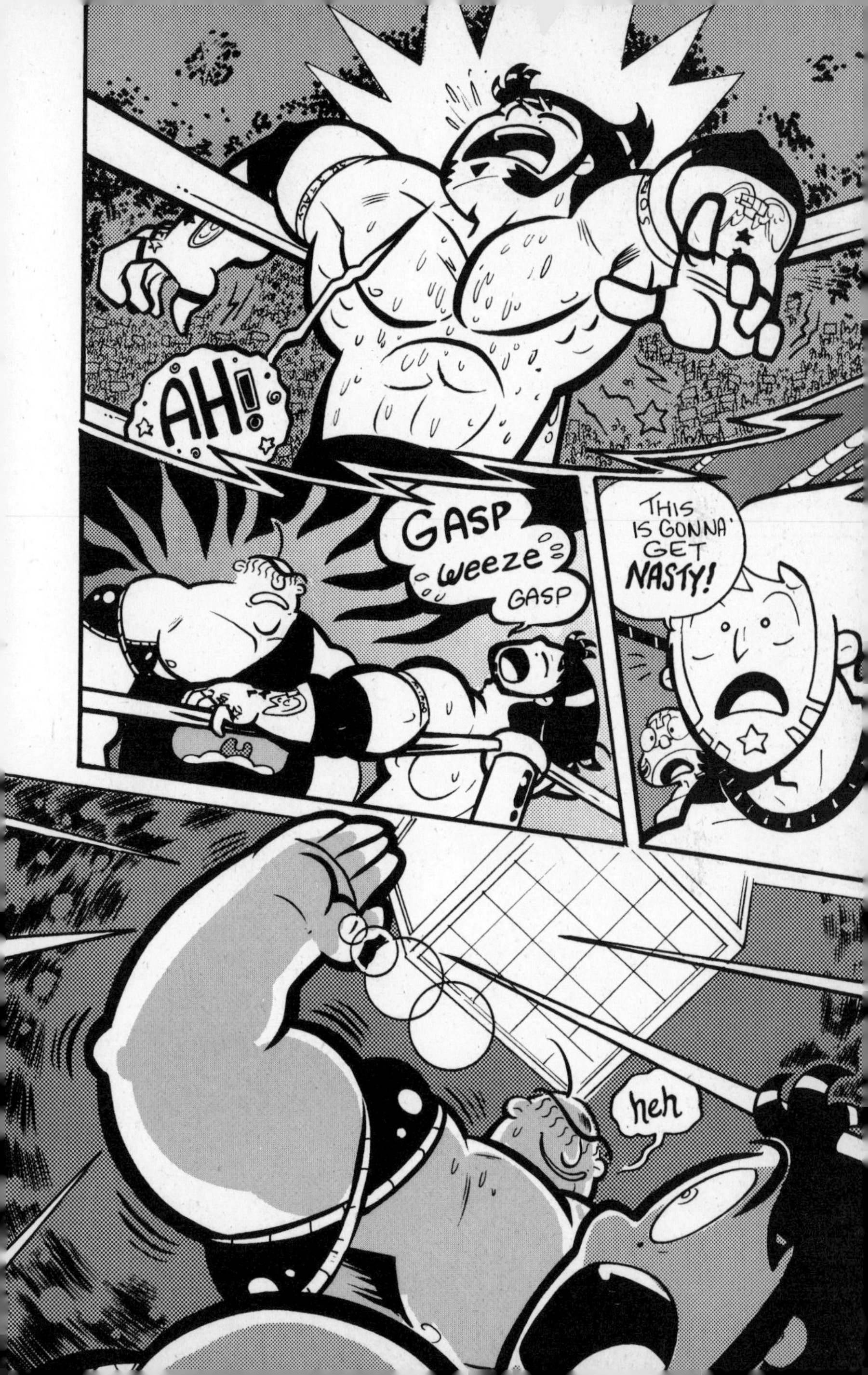
AH!
GASP
weeze
GASP
THIS IS GONNA' GET NASTY!
heh

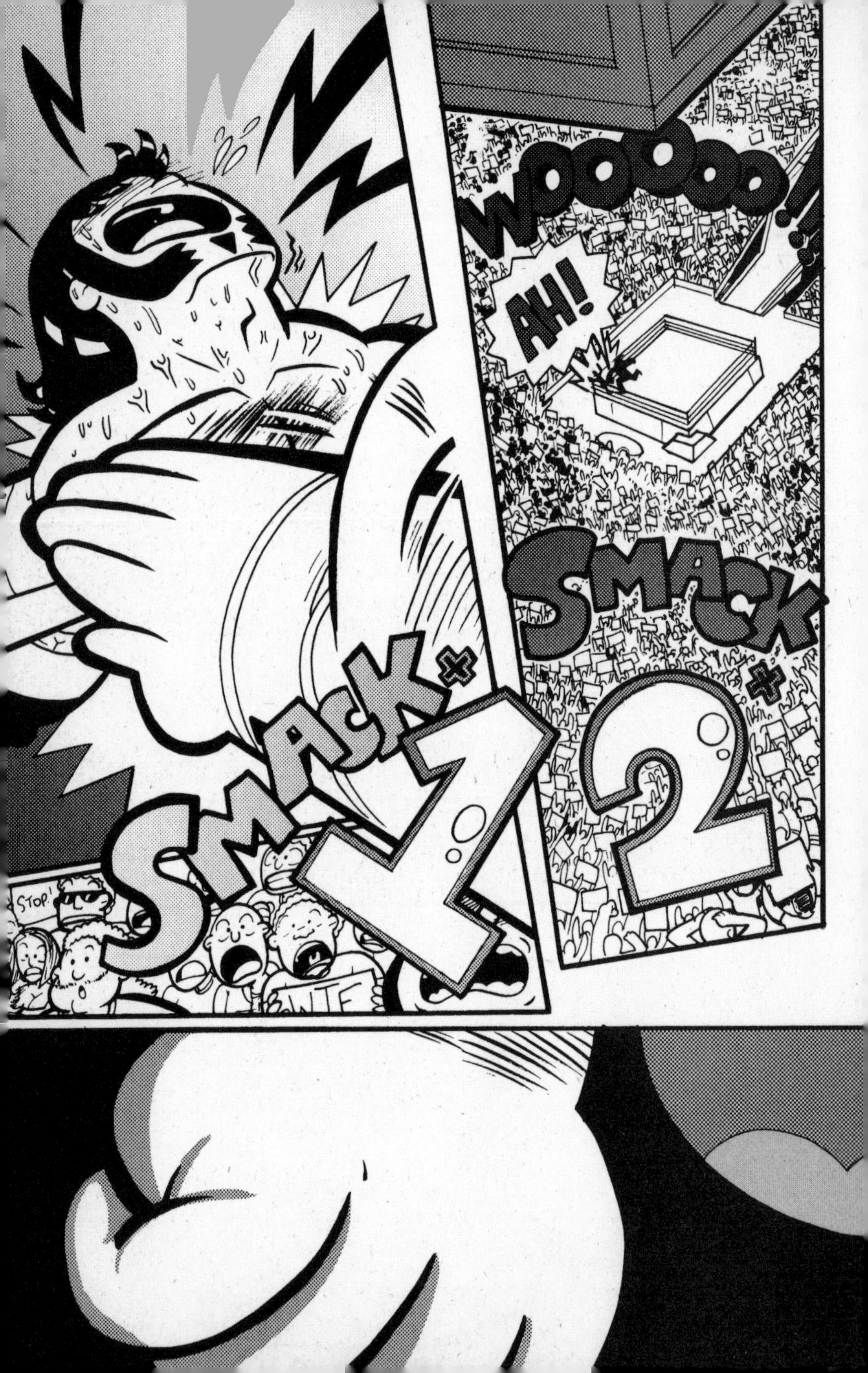
WOOOOOO!!
AH!
SMACK
1
SMACK
2
STOP!

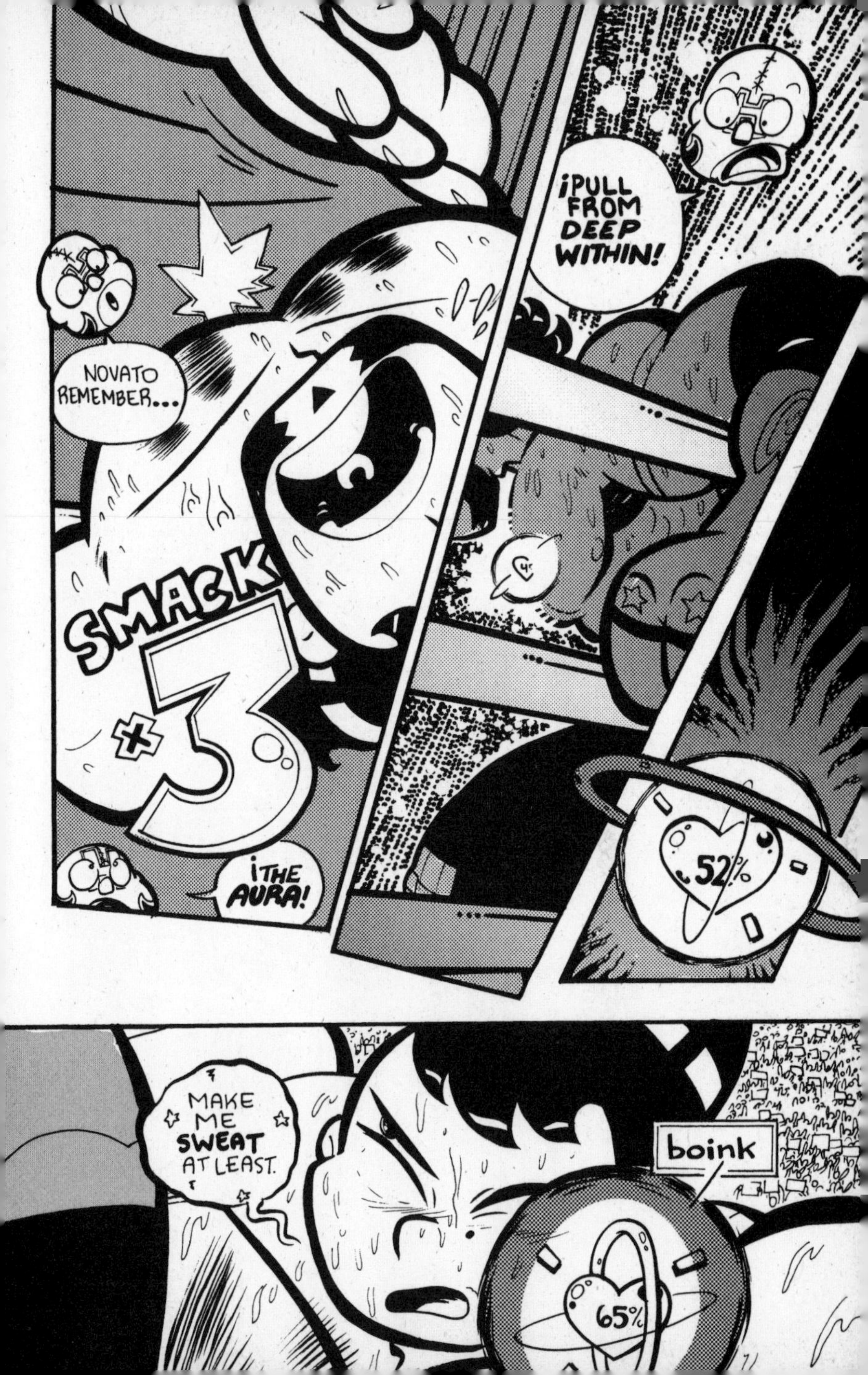
NOVATO REMEMBER...
¡PULL FROM DEEP WITHIN!
SMACK
x3
¡THE AURA!
52%
MAKE ME SWEAT AT LEAST.
boink
65%

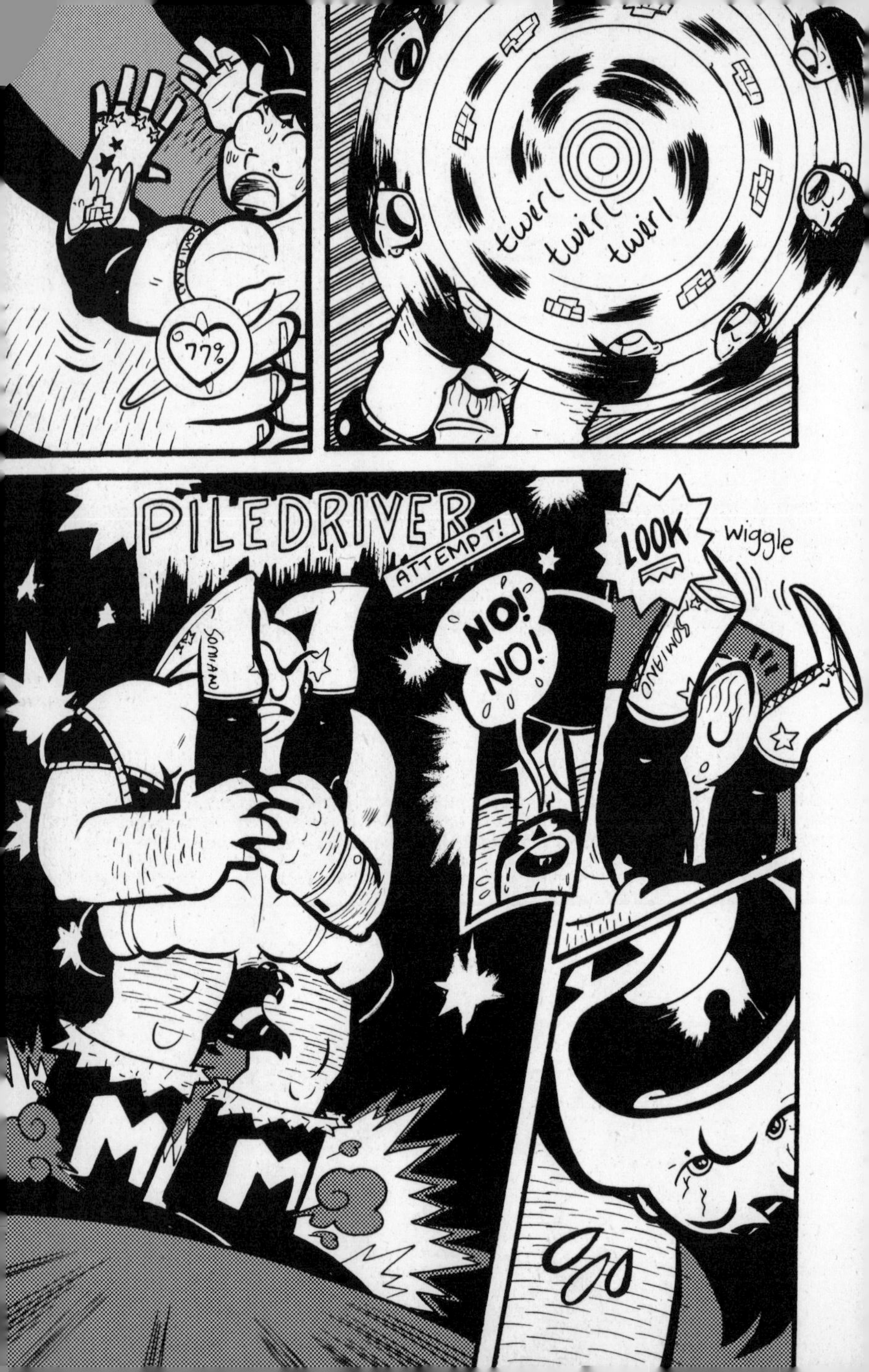

77%
twirl
twirl
twirl
SOMIANO
PILEDRIVER
ATTEMPT!
NO!
NO!
LOOK
wiggle

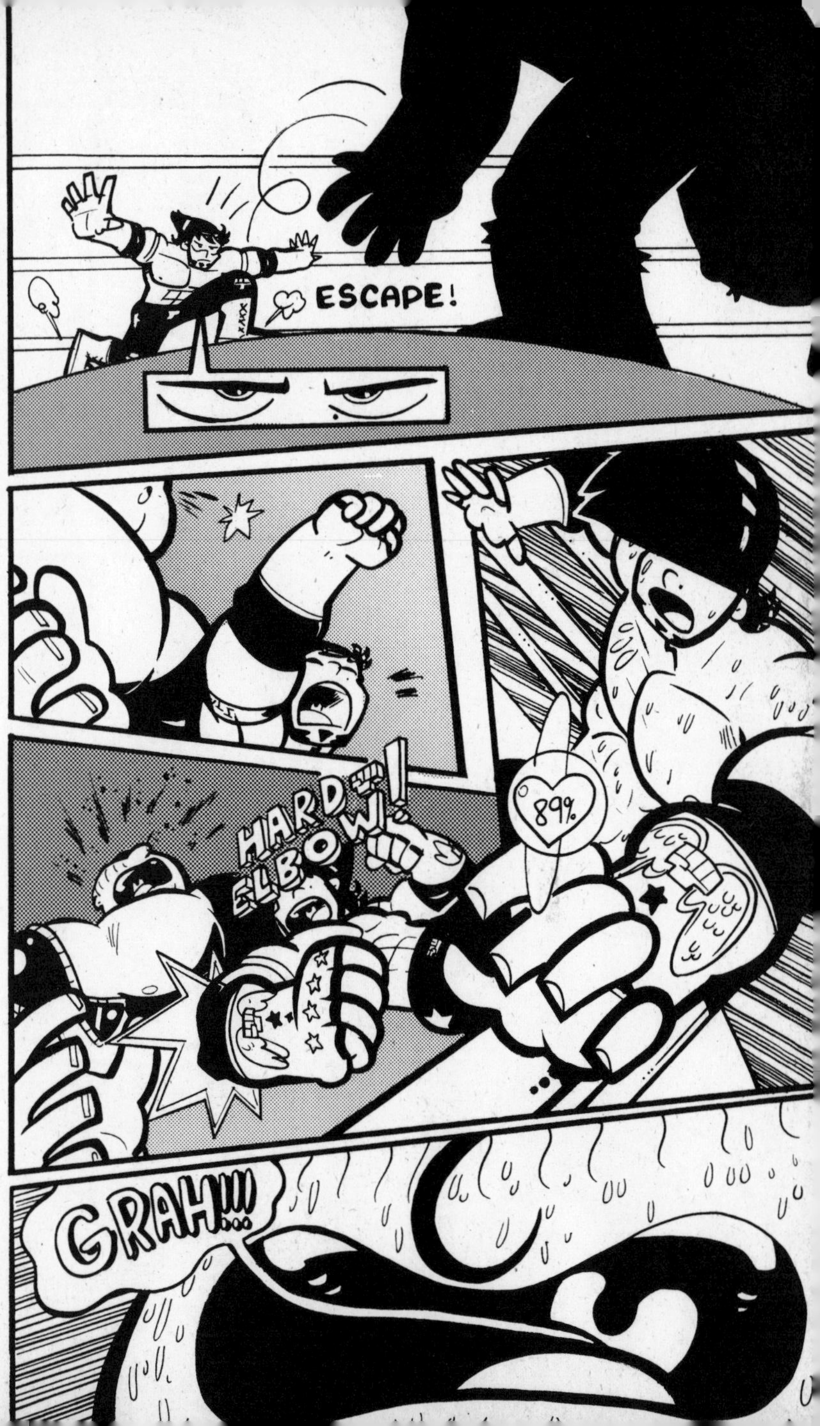

ESCAPE!
HARD ELBOW!
89%
GRAH!!!

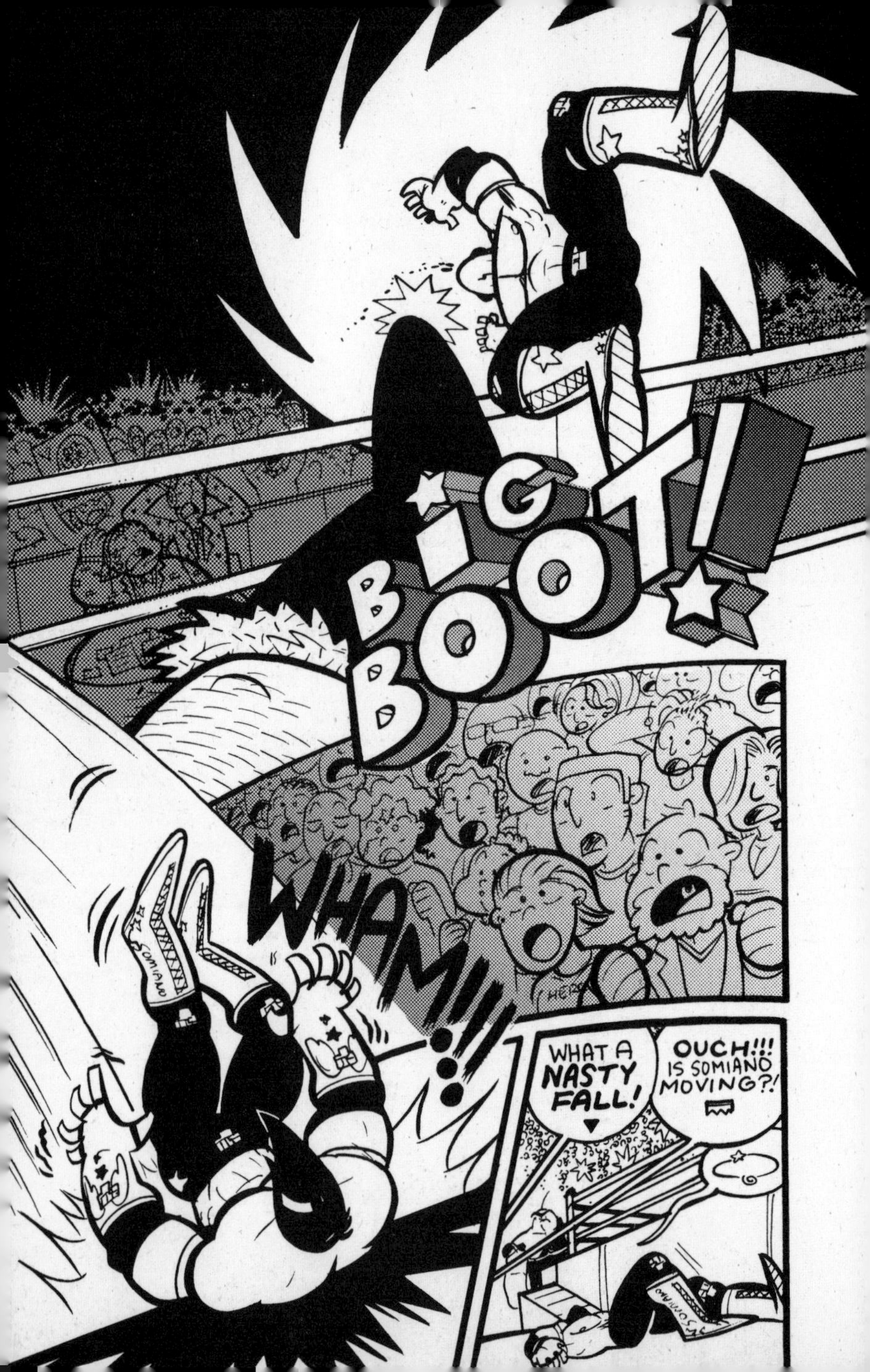

BIG BOOT!
WHAM!!!!
WHAT A NASTY FALL!
OUCH!!! IS SOMIANO MOVING?!

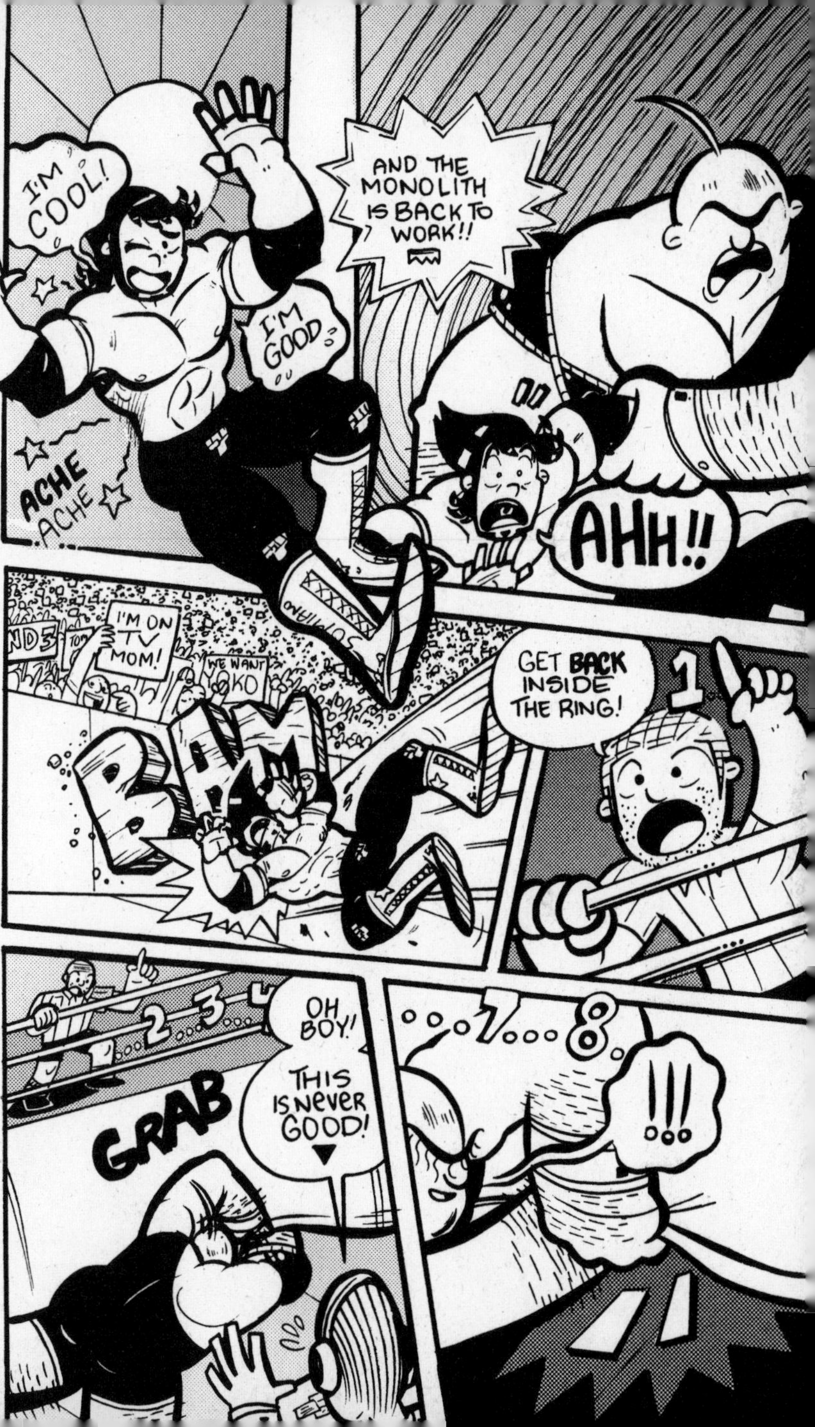

I'M COOL!
I'M GOOD
ACHE ACHE
AND THE MONOLITH IS BACK TO WORK!!
AHH!!
I'M ON TV MOM!
WE WANT YOKO
BAM
GET BACK INSIDE THE RING!
1
2...3...4
OH BOY!
THIS IS NEVER GOOD!
GRAB
...7...8...
!!!...

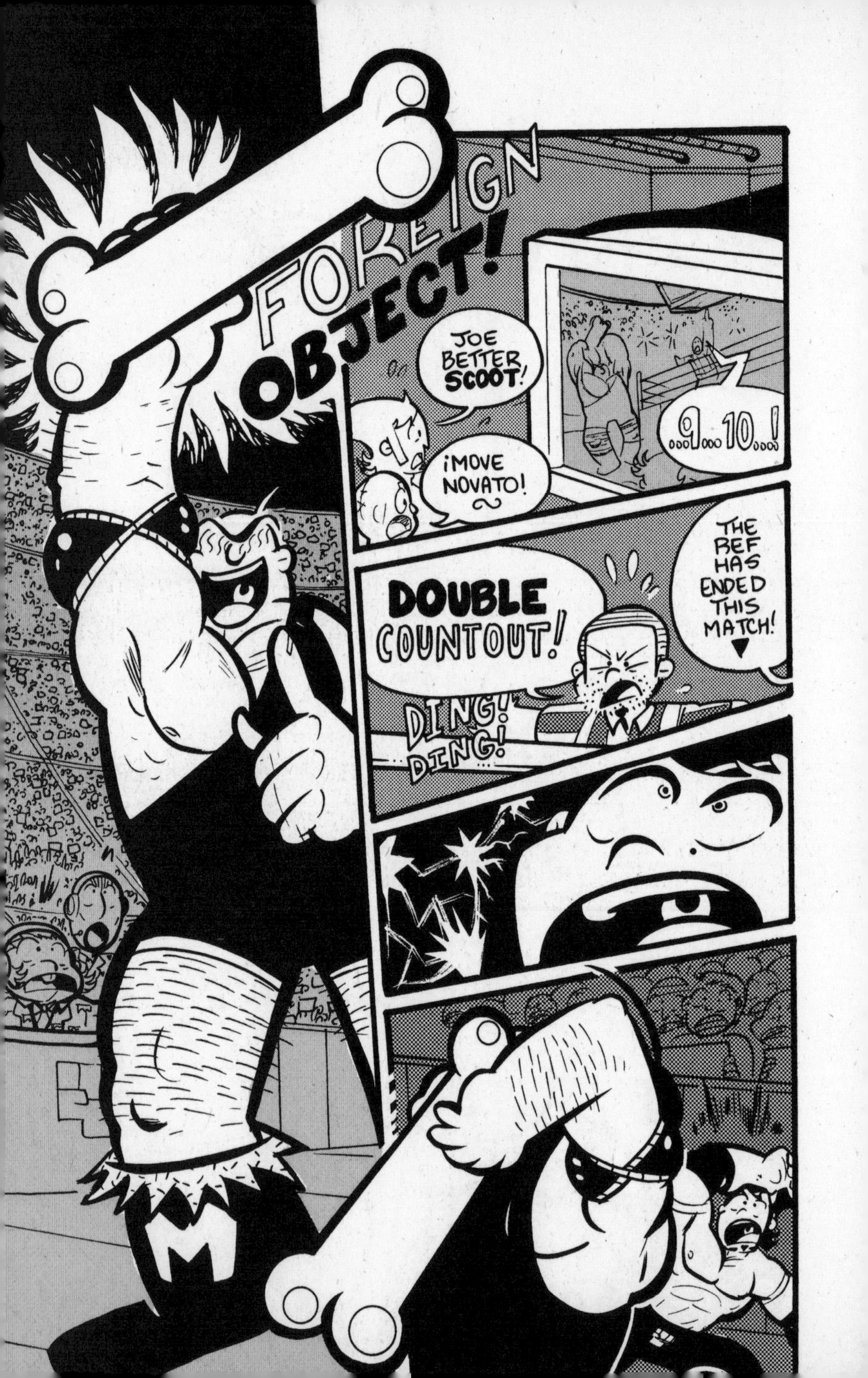
FOREIGN OBJECT!
JOE BETTER SCOOT!
¡MOVE NOVATO!
...9...10...!
DOUBLE COUNTOUT!
THE REF HAS ENDED THIS MATCH!
DING! DING!

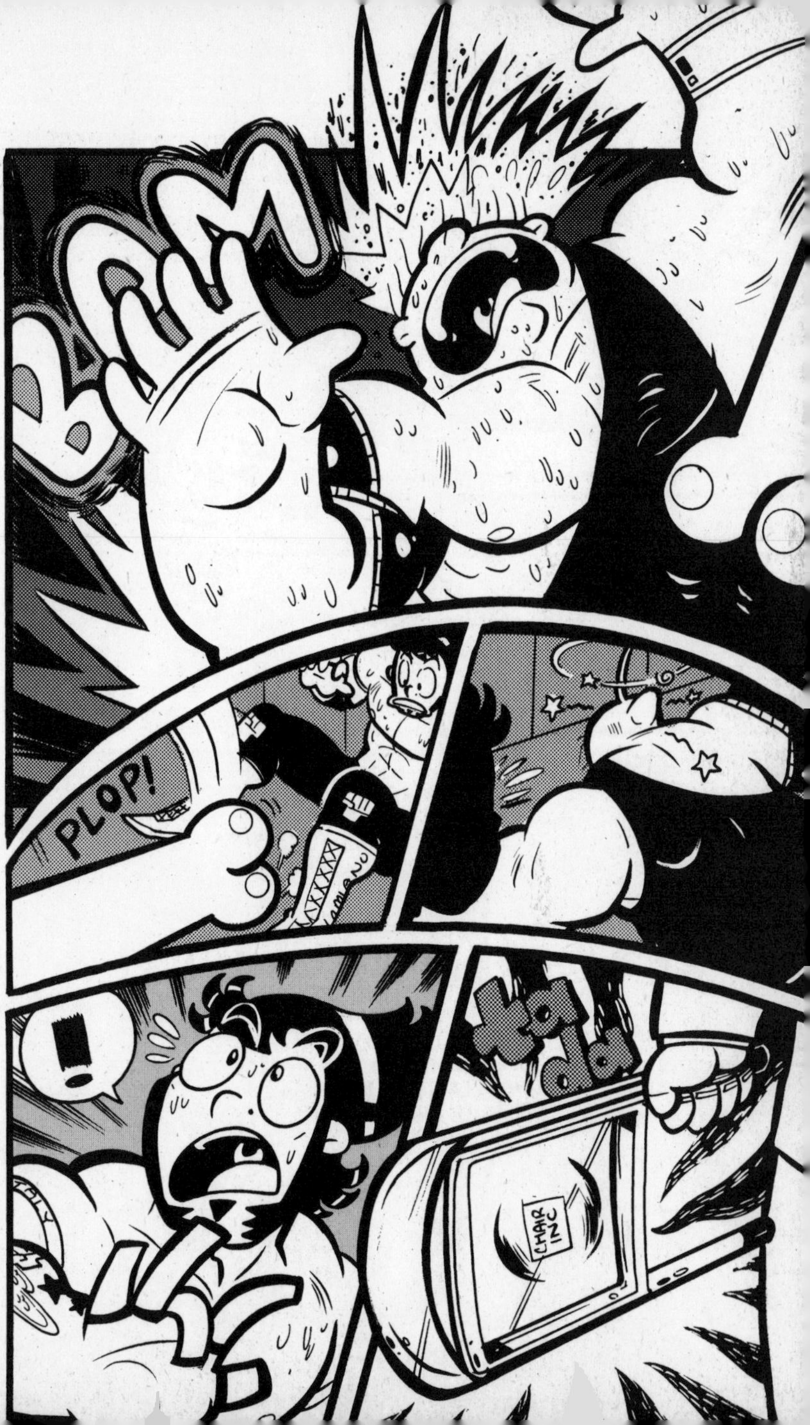
PLOP!
!
CHAIR INC

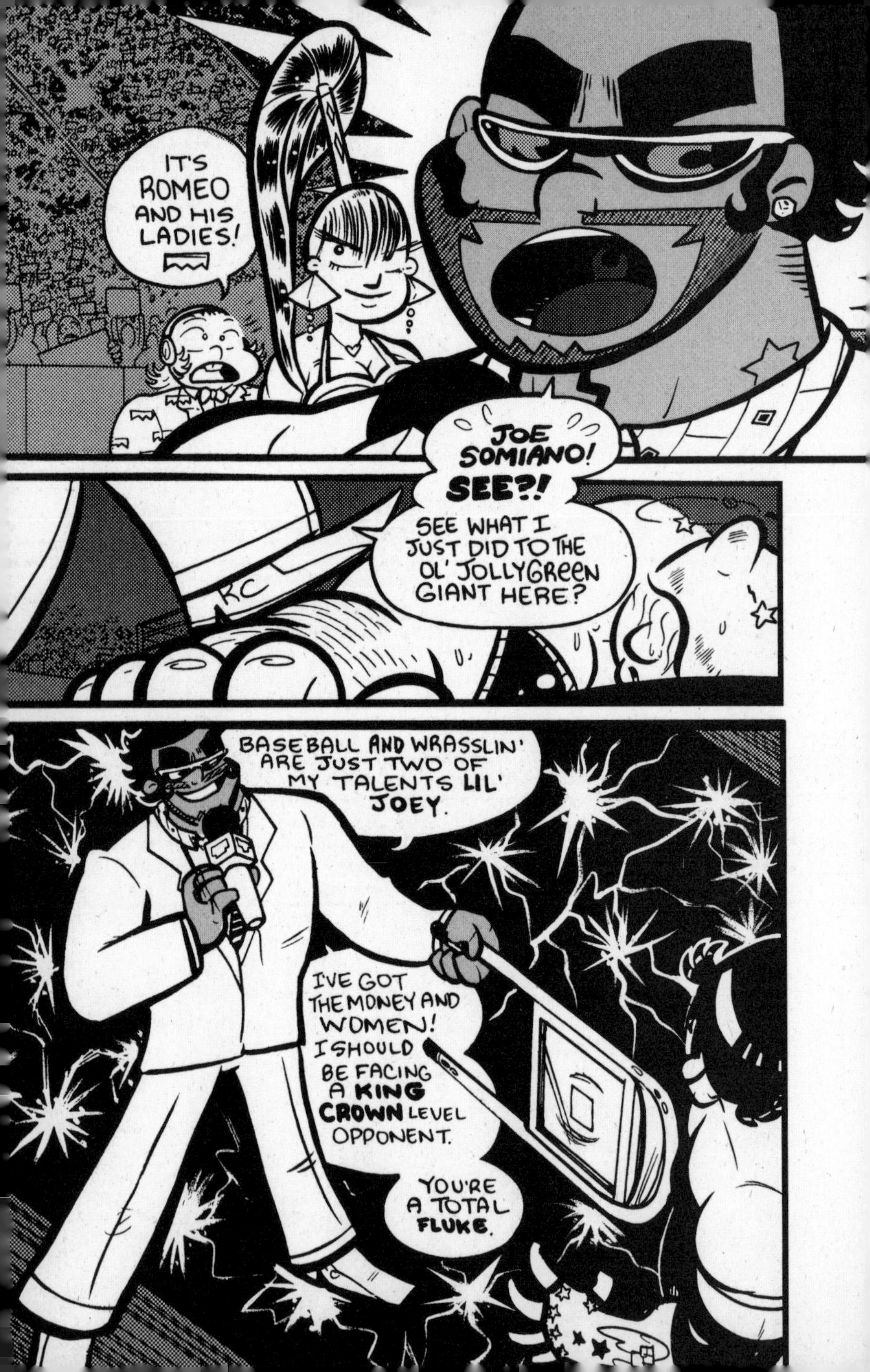
IT'S ROMEO AND HIS LADIES!
JOE SOMIANO! SEE?!
SEE WHAT I JUST DID TO THE OL' JOLLY GREEN GIANT HERE?
BASEBALL AND WRASSLIN' ARE JUST TWO OF MY TALENTS LIL' JOEY.
I'VE GOT THE MONEY AND WOMEN! I SHOULD BE FACING A KING CROWN LEVEL OPPONENT.
YOU'RE A TOTAL FLUKE.

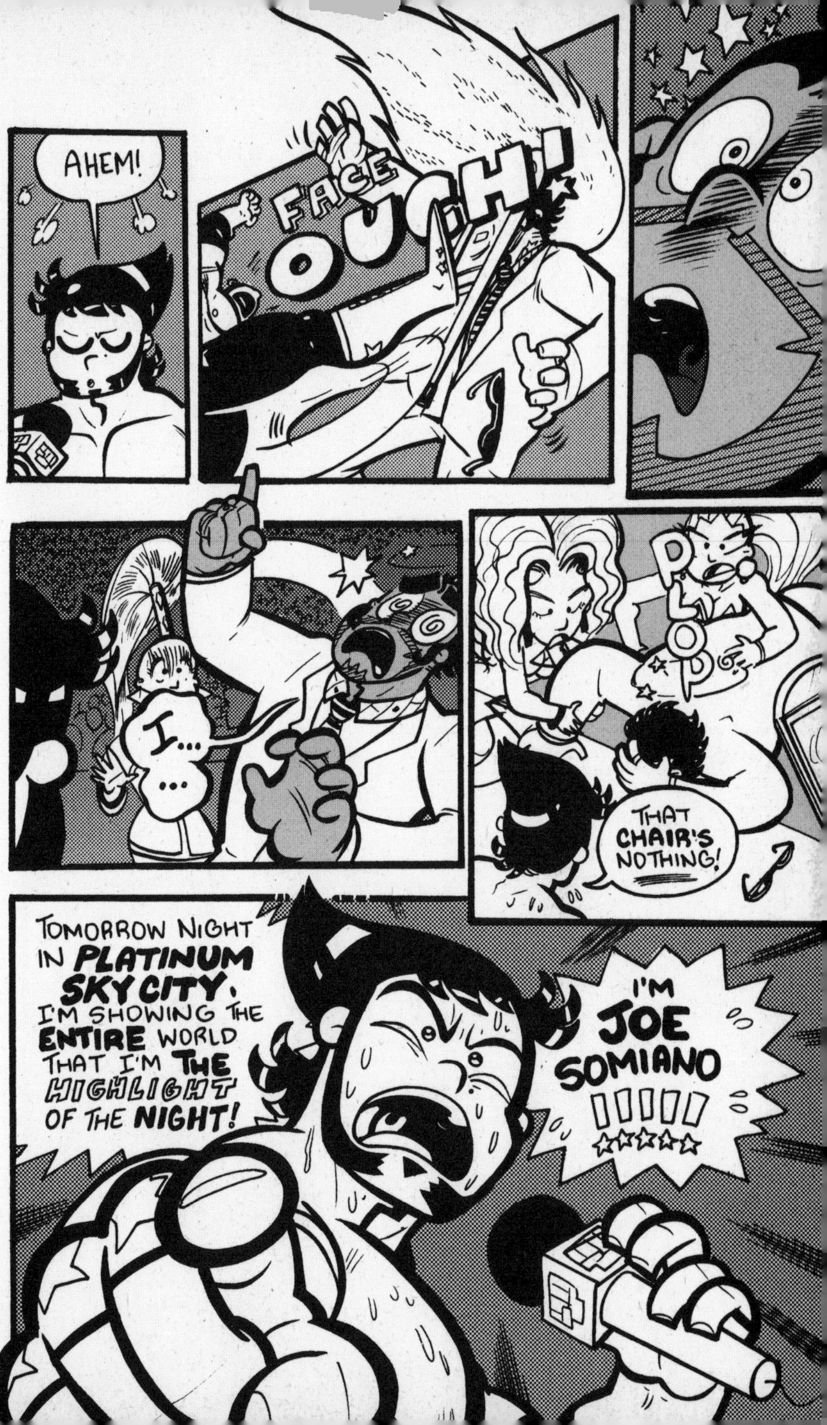
AHEM!
FACE
OUCH!
I... ...
PLOP
THAT CHAIR'S NOTHING!
TOMORROW NIGHT IN PLATINUM SKY CITY, I'M SHOWING THE ENTIRE WORLD THAT I'M THE HIGHLIGHT OF THE NIGHT!
I'M JOE SOMIANO !!!!!

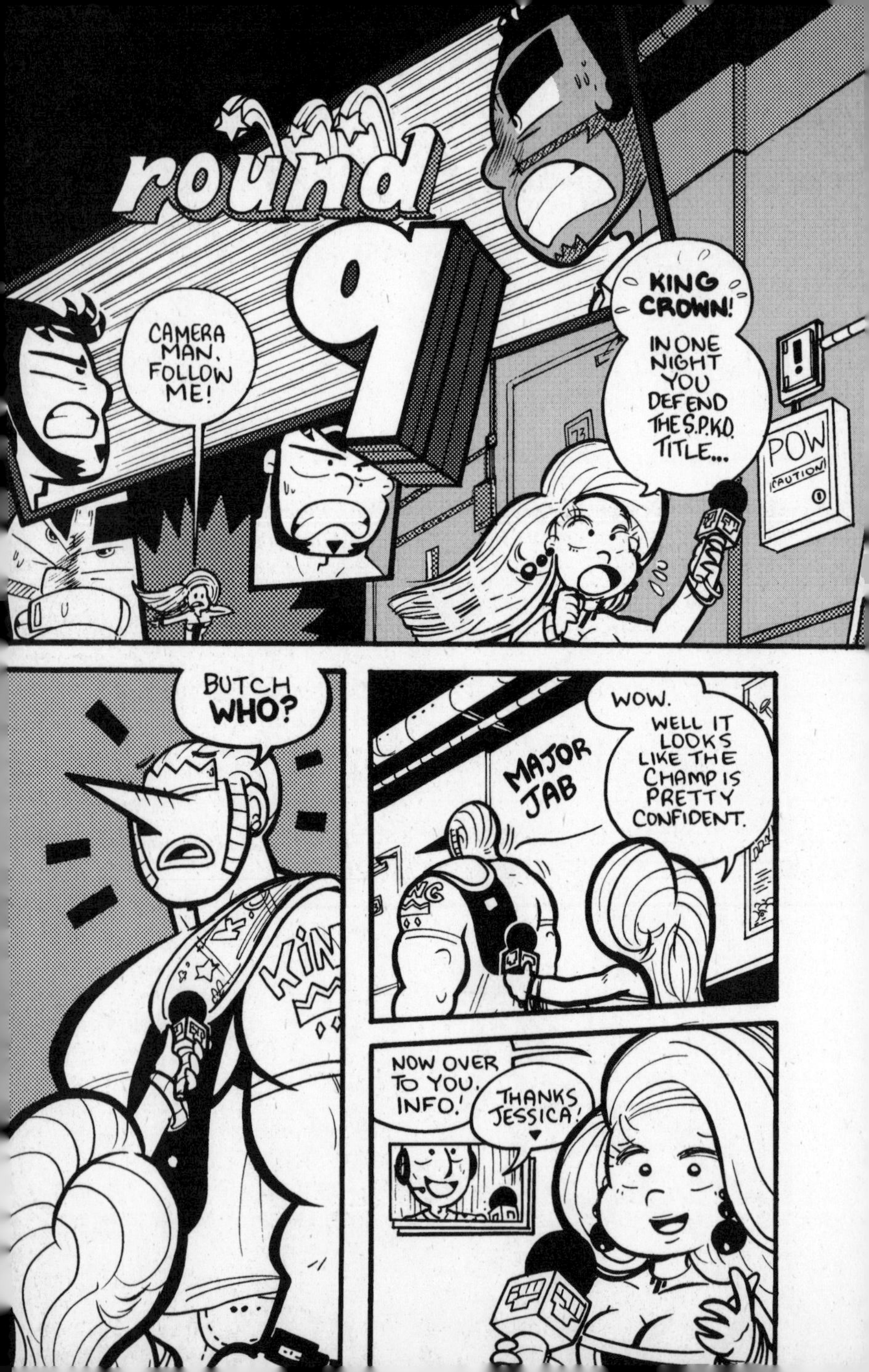

round 9
CAMERA MAN. FOLLOW ME!
KING CROWN!
IN ONE NIGHT YOU DEFEND THE S.P.K.O. TITLE...
POW
CAUTION
BUTCH WHO?
MAJOR JAB
WOW.
WELL IT LOOKS LIKE THE CHAMP IS PRETTY CONFIDENT.
NOW OVER TO YOU, INFO!
THANKS JESSICA!

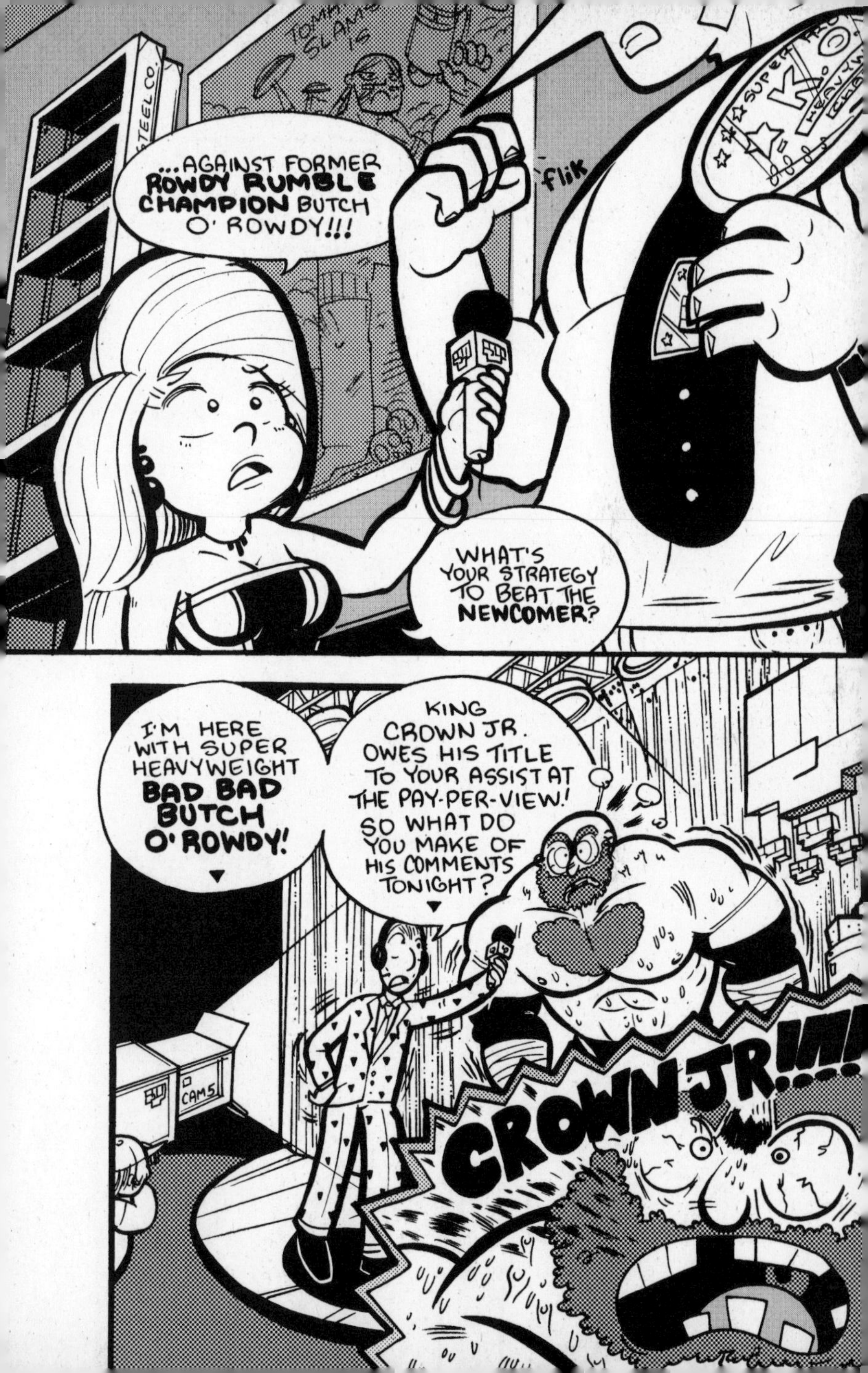

TOMMY SLAMS IS
STEEL CO.
...AGAINST FORMER **ROWDY RUMBLE CHAMPION** BUTCH O' ROWDY!!!
flik
WHAT'S YOUR STRATEGY TO BEAT THE **NEWCOMER**?
I'M HERE WITH SUPER HEAVYWEIGHT **BAD BAD BUTCH O' ROWDY!**
KING CROWN JR. OWES HIS TITLE TO YOUR ASSIST AT THE PAY-PER-VIEW! SO WHAT DO YOU MAKE OF HIS COMMENTS TONIGHT?
CAM 5
CROWN JR.!!!...

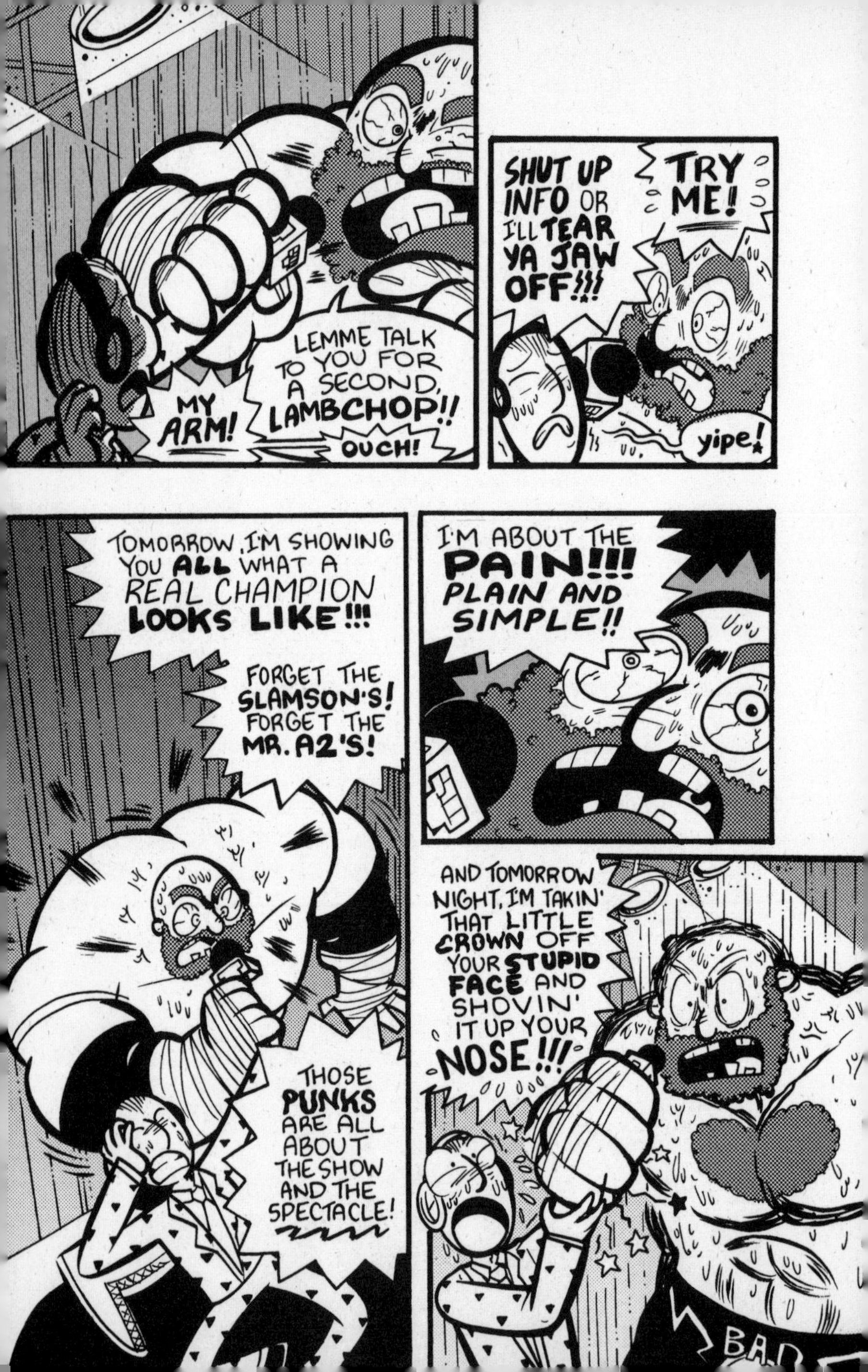

LEMME TALK TO YOU FOR A SECOND, LAMBCHOP!!
MY ARM!
OUCH!
SHUT UP INFO OR I'LL TEAR YA JAW OFF!!!
TRY ME!
yipe!
TOMORROW, I'M SHOWING YOU ALL WHAT A REAL CHAMPION LOOKS LIKE!!!
FORGET THE SLAMSON'S! FORGET THE MR. A2'S!
THOSE PUNKS ARE ALL ABOUT THE SHOW AND THE SPECTACLE!
I'M ABOUT THE PAIN!!! PLAIN AND SIMPLE!!
AND TOMORROW NIGHT, I'M TAKIN' THAT LITTLE CROWN OFF YOUR STUPID FACE AND SHOVIN' IT UP YOUR NOSE!!!
BAD

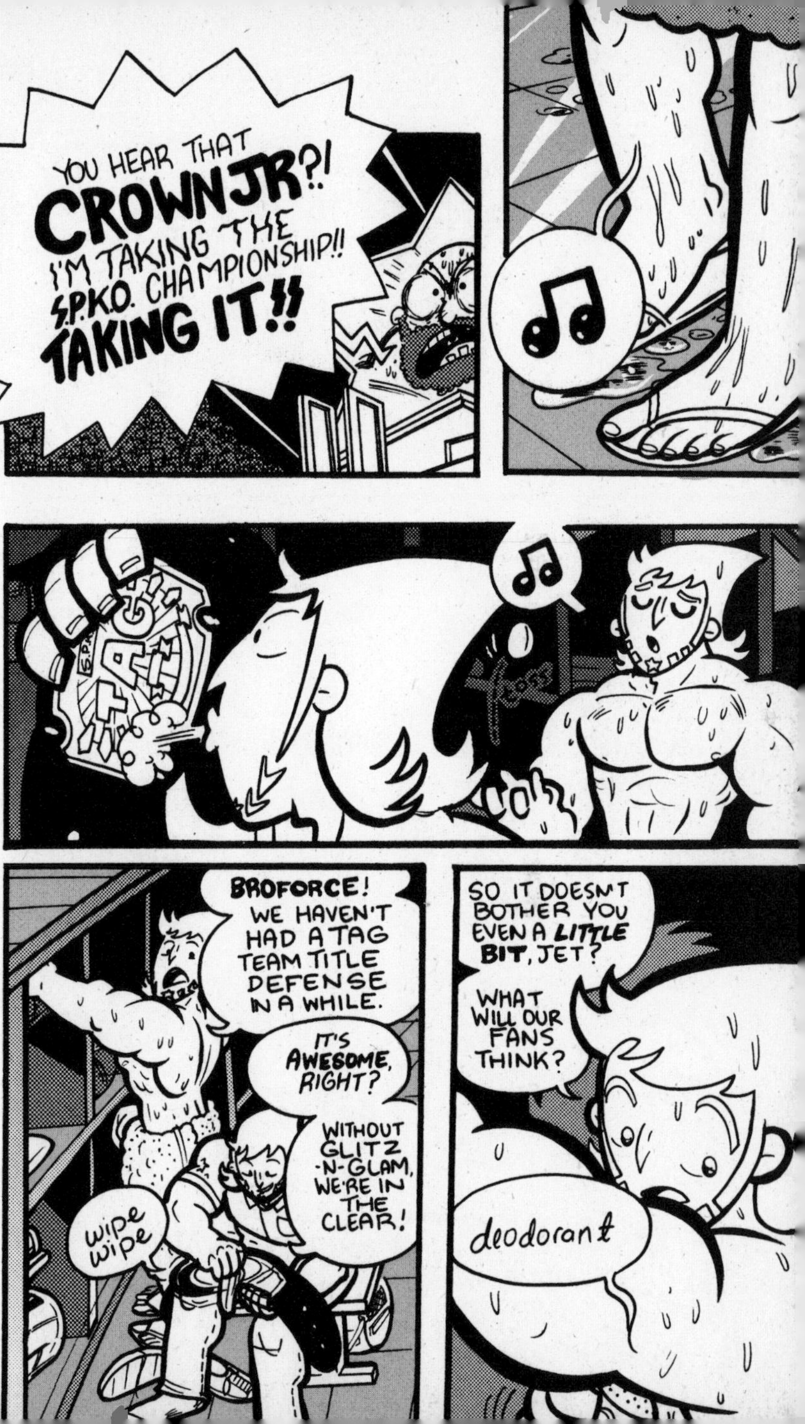

YOU HEAR THAT CROWNJR?! I'M TAKING THE S.P.K.O. CHAMPIONSHIP!! TAKING IT!!
BROFORCE! WE HAVEN'T HAD A TAG TEAM TITLE DEFENSE IN A WHILE.
IT'S AWESOME, RIGHT?
WITHOUT GLITZ-N-GLAM, WE'RE IN THE CLEAR!
wipe wipe
SO IT DOESN'T BOTHER YOU EVEN A LITTLE BIT, JET?
WHAT WILL OUR FANS THINK?
deodorant

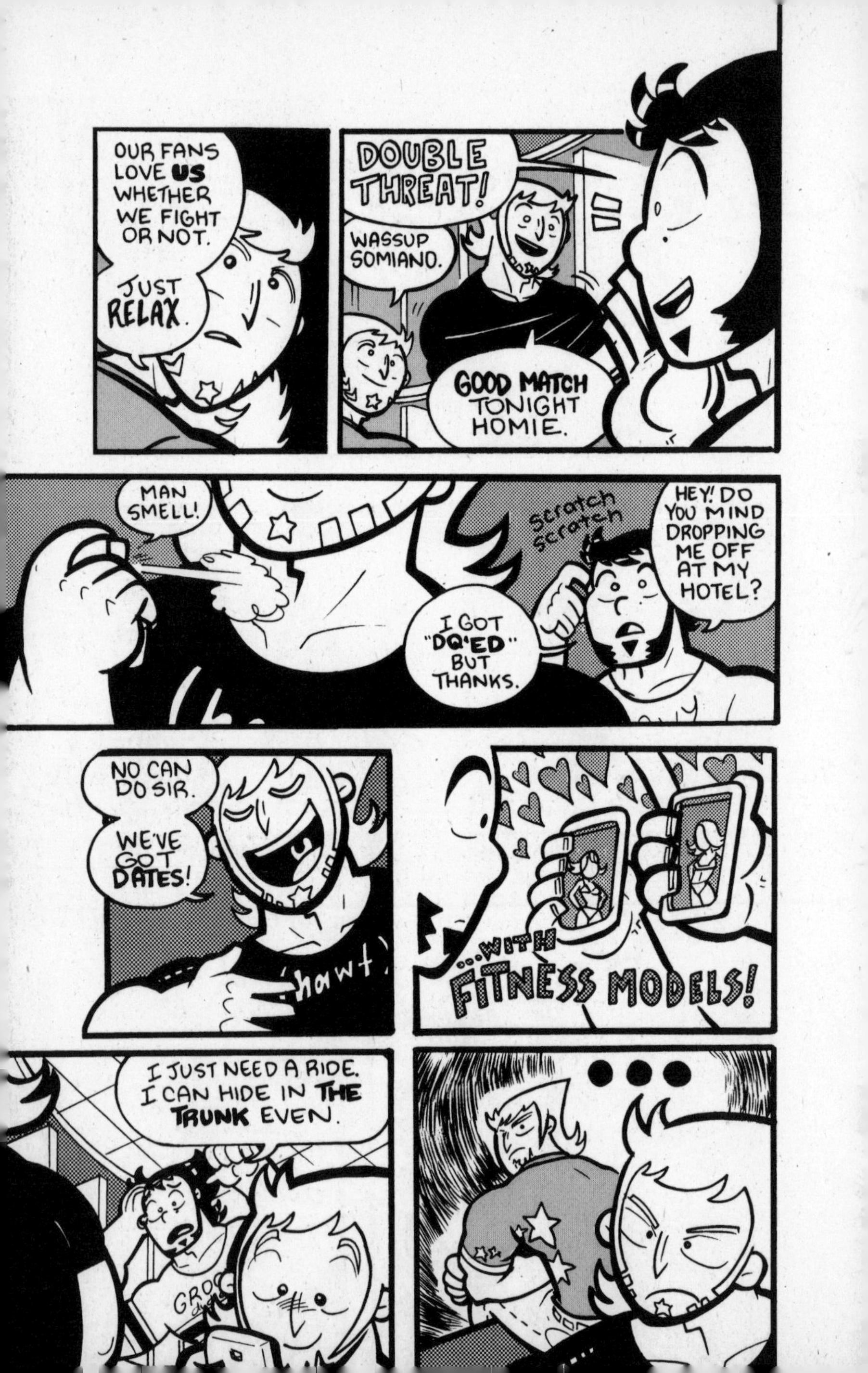
OUR FANS LOVE US WHETHER WE FIGHT OR NOT.
JUST RELAX.
DOUBLE THREAT!
WASSUP SOMIANO.
GOOD MATCH TONIGHT HOMIE.
MAN SMELL!
SCRATCH SCRATCH
HEY! DO YOU MIND DROPPING ME OFF AT MY HOTEL?
I GOT "DQ'ED" BUT THANKS.
NO CAN DO SIR.
WE'VE GOT DATES!
...WITH FITNESS MODELS!
I JUST NEED A RIDE. I CAN HIDE IN THE TRUNK EVEN.
• • •

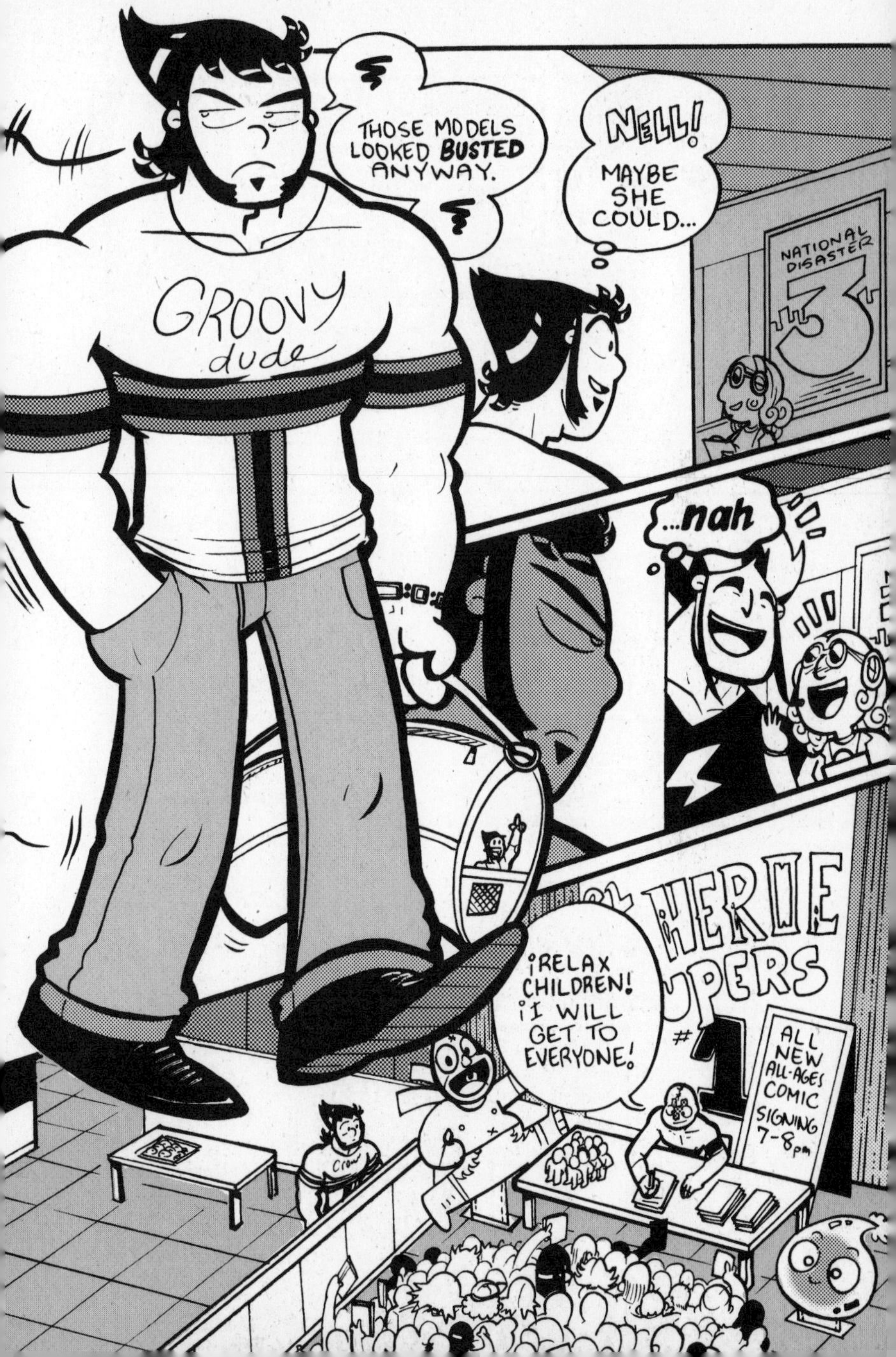
THOSE MODELS LOOKED BUSTED ANYWAY.
NELL! MAYBE SHE COULD...
NATIONAL DISASTER 3
GROOVY dude
...nah
HEROE UPERS #1
¡RELAX CHILDREN! ¡I WILL GET TO EVERYONE!
ALL NEW ALL-AGES COMIC SIGNING 7-8pm

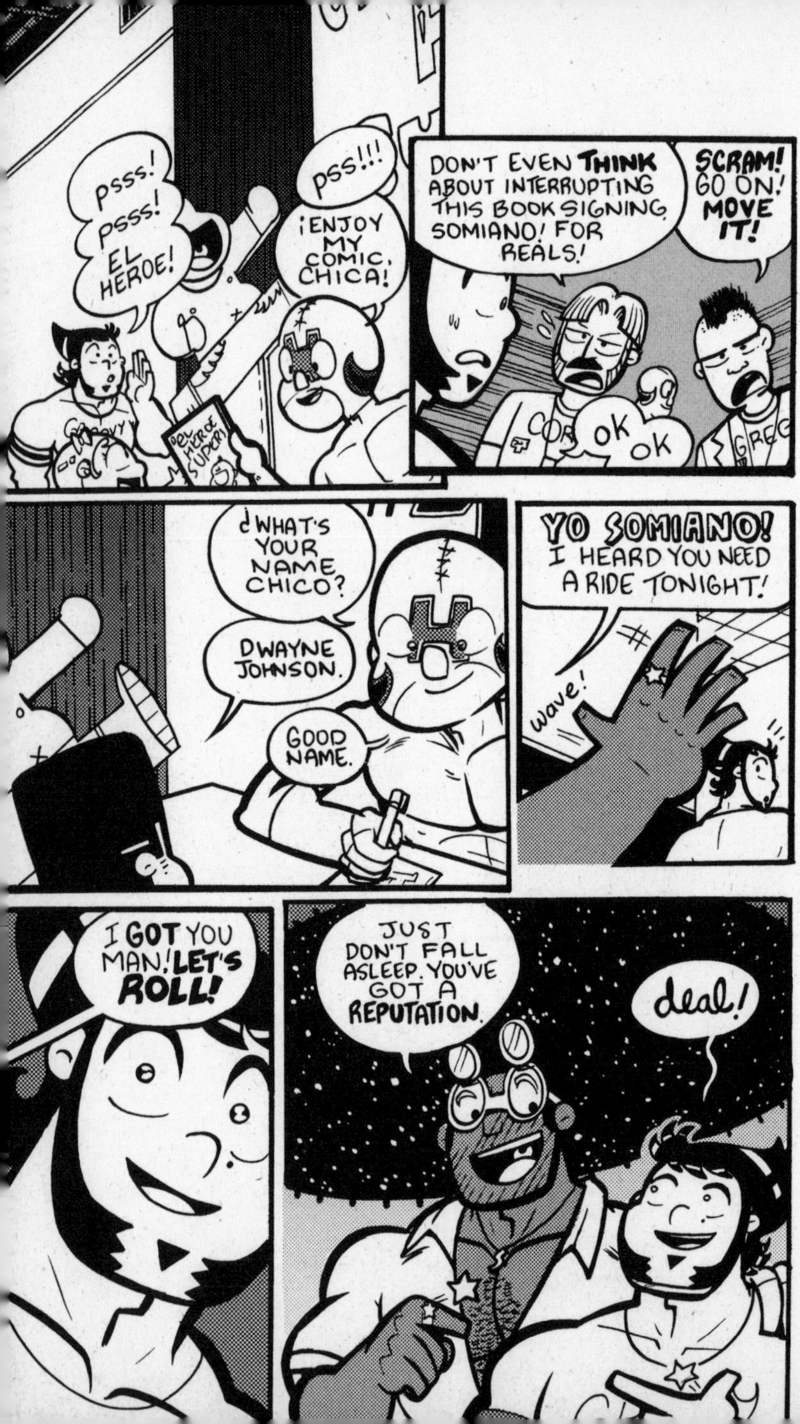
psss! psss! EL HEROE!
pss!!!
¡ENJOY MY COMIC, CHICA!
GROOVY
EL HEROE SUPER!
DON'T EVEN THINK ABOUT INTERRUPTING THIS BOOK SIGNING SOMIANO! FOR REALS!
SCRAM! GO ON! MOVE IT!
COR
OK OK
GREG
¿WHAT'S YOUR NAME CHICO?
DWAYNE JOHNSON.
GOOD NAME.
YO SOMIANO! I HEARD YOU NEED A RIDE TONIGHT!
wave!
I GOT YOU MAN! LET'S ROLL!
JUST DON'T FALL ASLEEP. YOU'VE GOT A REPUTATION.
deal!

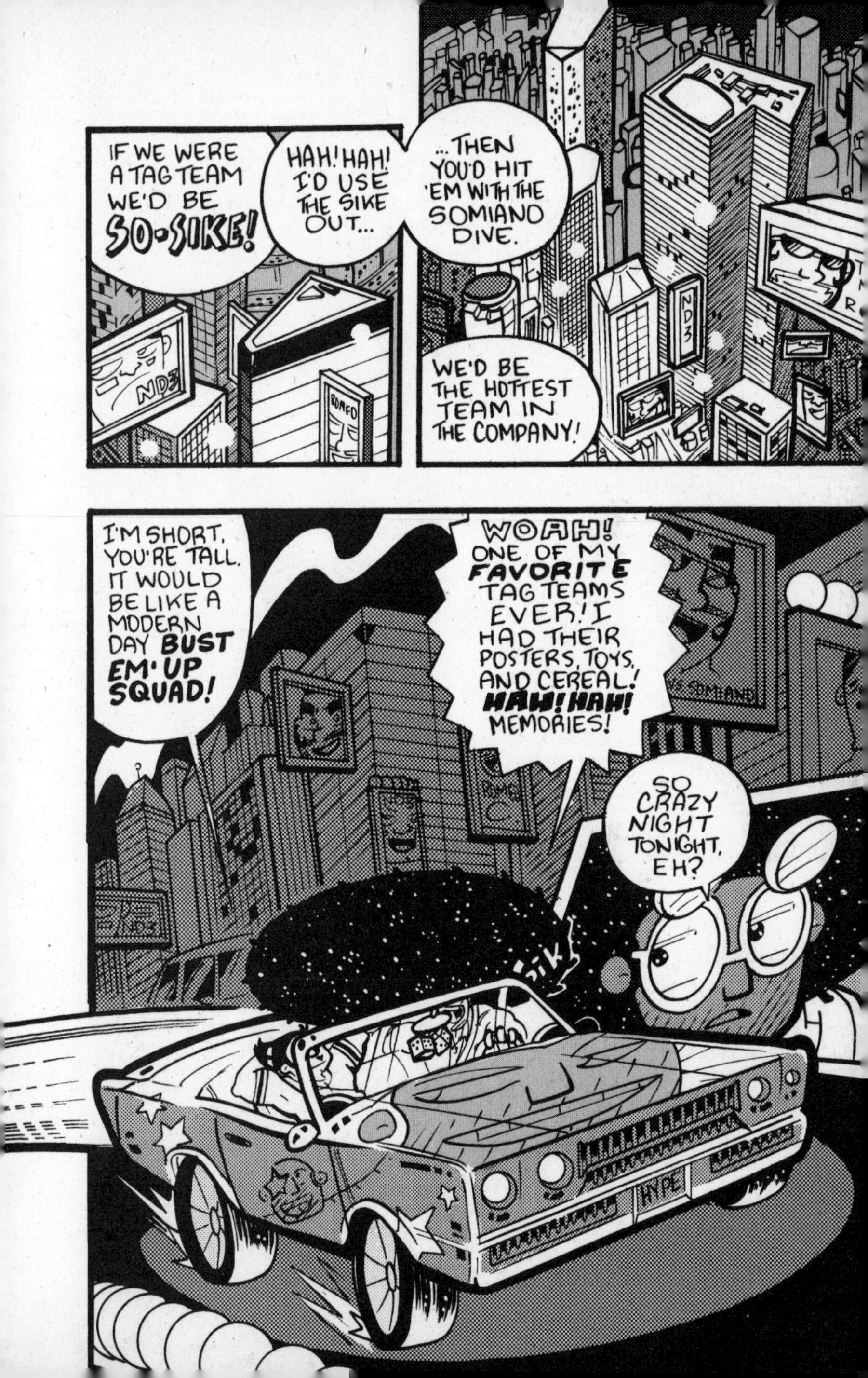
IF WE WERE A TAG TEAM WE'D BE SO-SIKE!
HAH! HAH! I'D USE THE SIKE OUT...
...THEN YOU'D HIT 'EM WITH THE SOMIANO DIVE.
WE'D BE THE HOTTEST TEAM IN THE COMPANY!
I'M SHORT. YOU'RE TALL. IT WOULD BE LIKE A MODERN DAY BUST EM' UP SQUAD!
WOAH! ONE OF MY FAVORITE TAG TEAMS EVER! I HAD THEIR POSTERS, TOYS, AND CEREAL! HAH! HAH! MEMORIES!
SO CRAZY NIGHT TONIGHT, EH?
ND3
ROMEO
VS SOMIANO
HYPE

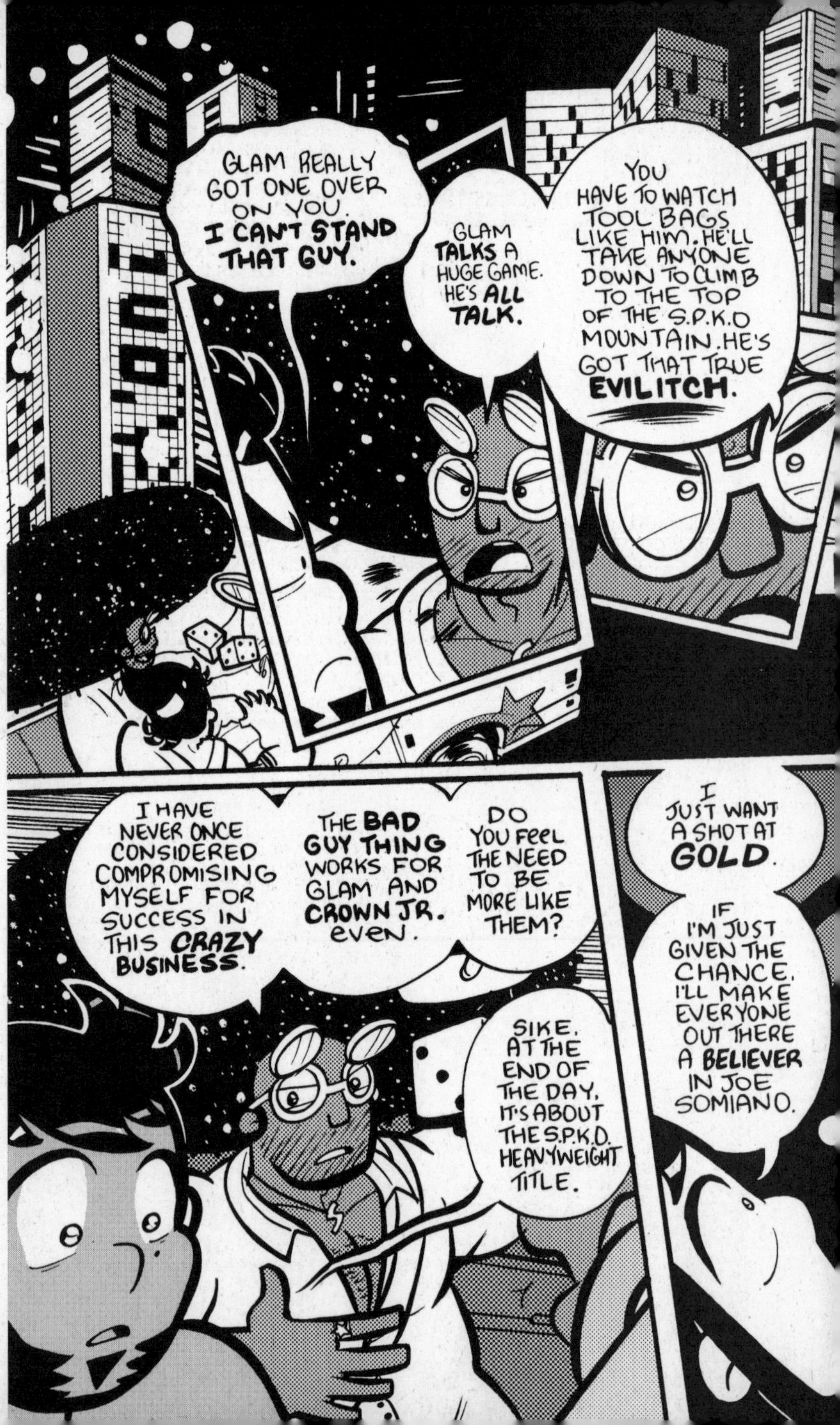
GLAM REALLY GOT ONE OVER ON YOU. I CAN'T STAND THAT GUY.
GLAM TALKS A HUGE GAME. HE'S ALL TALK.
YOU HAVE TO WATCH TOOL BAGS LIKE HIM. HE'LL TAKE ANYONE DOWN TO CLIMB TO THE TOP OF THE S.P.K.D MOUNTAIN. HE'S GOT THAT TRUE EVIL ITCH.
THE BAD GUY THING WORKS FOR GLAM AND CROWN JR. EVEN.
DO YOU FEEL THE NEED TO BE MORE LIKE THEM?
I HAVE NEVER ONCE CONSIDERED COMPROMISING MYSELF FOR SUCCESS IN THIS CRAZY BUSINESS.
SIKE. AT THE END OF THE DAY, IT'S ABOUT THE S.P.K.D. HEAVYWEIGHT TITLE.
I JUST WANT A SHOT AT GOLD.
IF I'M JUST GIVEN THE CHANCE, I'LL MAKE EVERYONE OUT THERE A BELIEVER IN JOE SOMIANO.

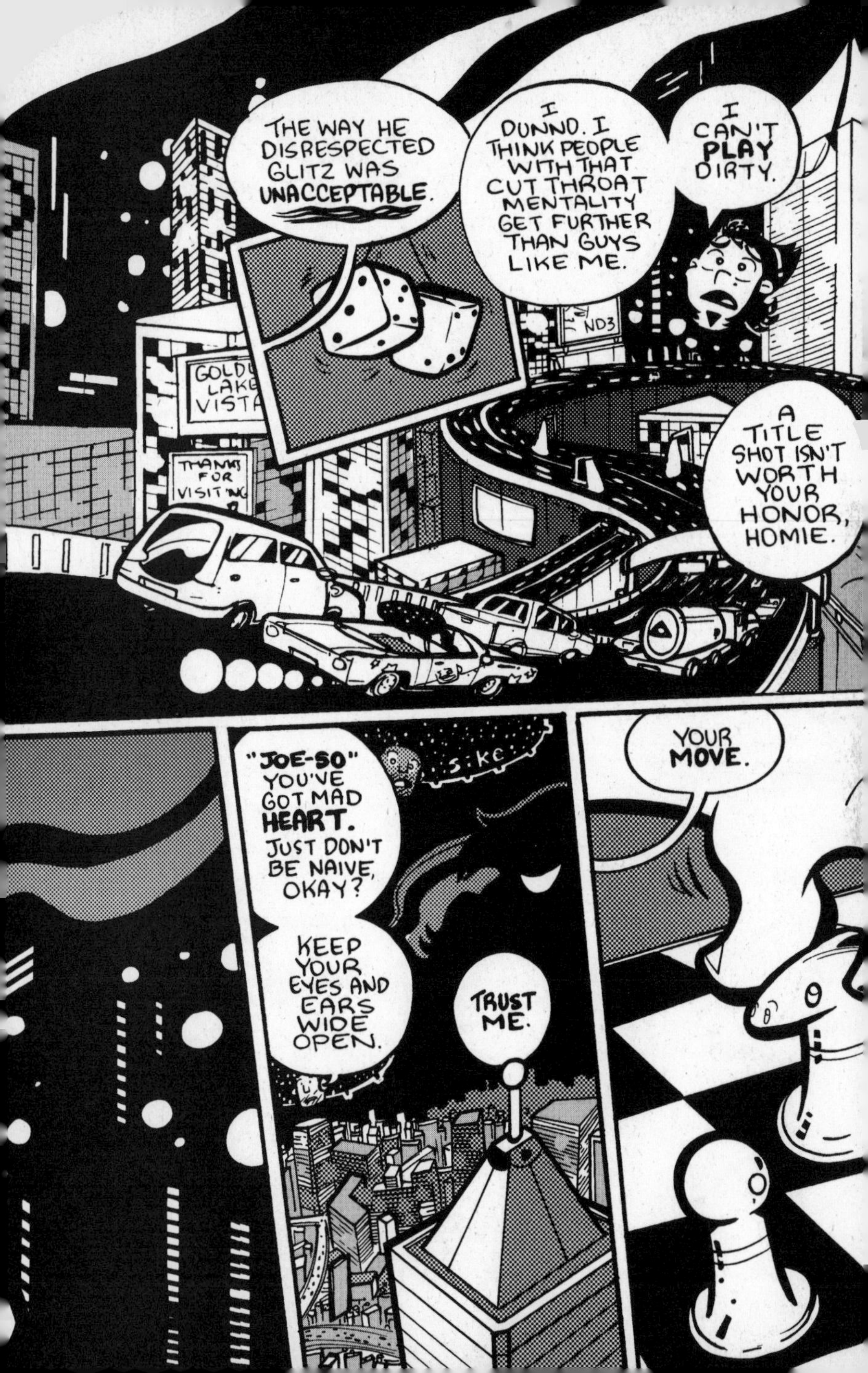
THE WAY HE DISRESPECTED GLITZ WAS UNACCEPTABLE.
I DUNNO. I THINK PEOPLE WITH THAT CUT THROAT MENTALITY GET FURTHER THAN GUYS LIKE ME.
I CAN'T PLAY DIRTY.
A TITLE SHOT ISN'T WORTH YOUR HONOR, HOMIE.
"JOE-SO" YOU'VE GOT MAD HEART. JUST DON'T BE NAIVE, OKAY?
KEEP YOUR EYES AND EARS WIDE OPEN.
TRUST ME.
YOUR MOVE.

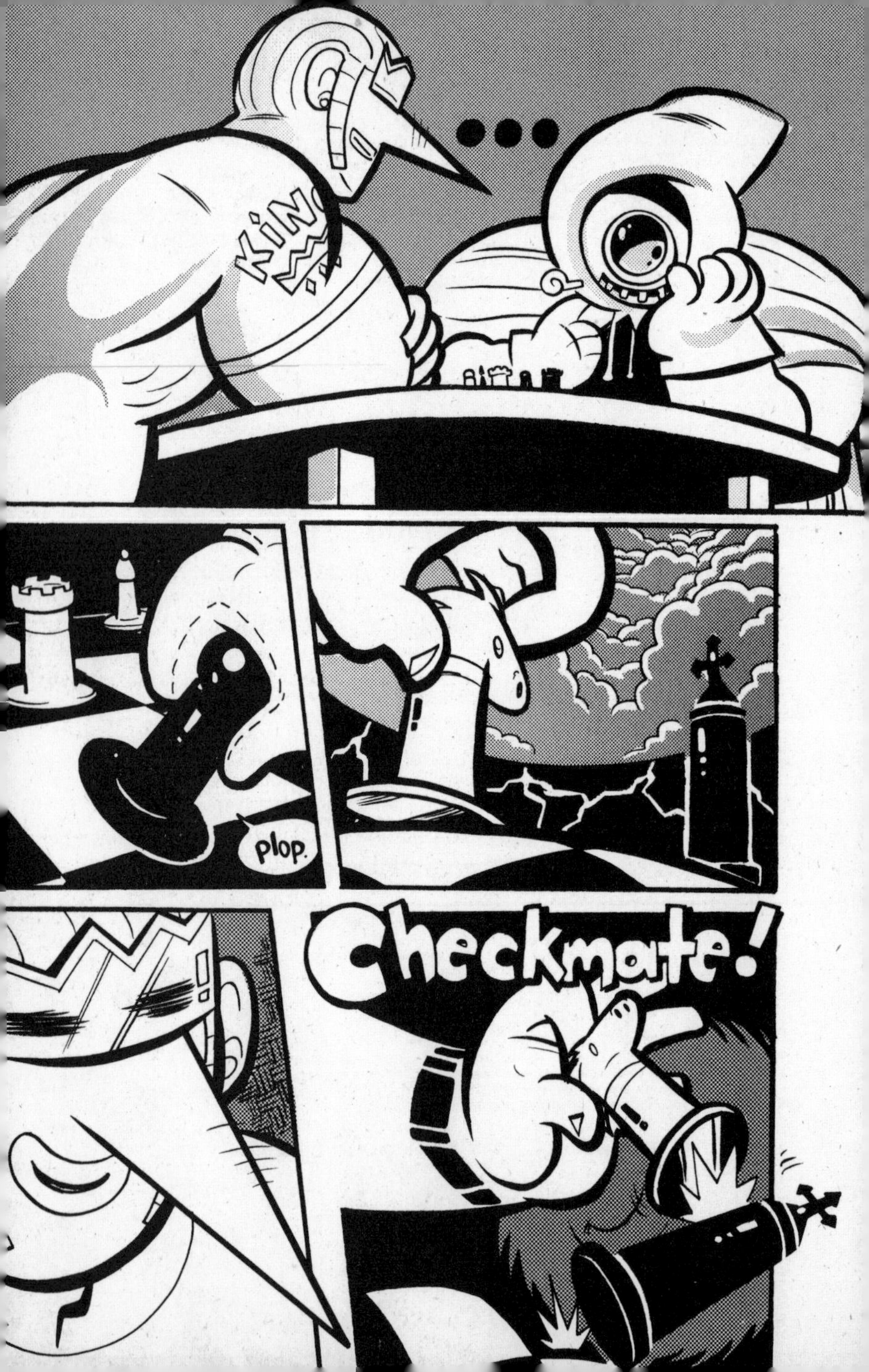
KING
...
plop.
Checkmate!

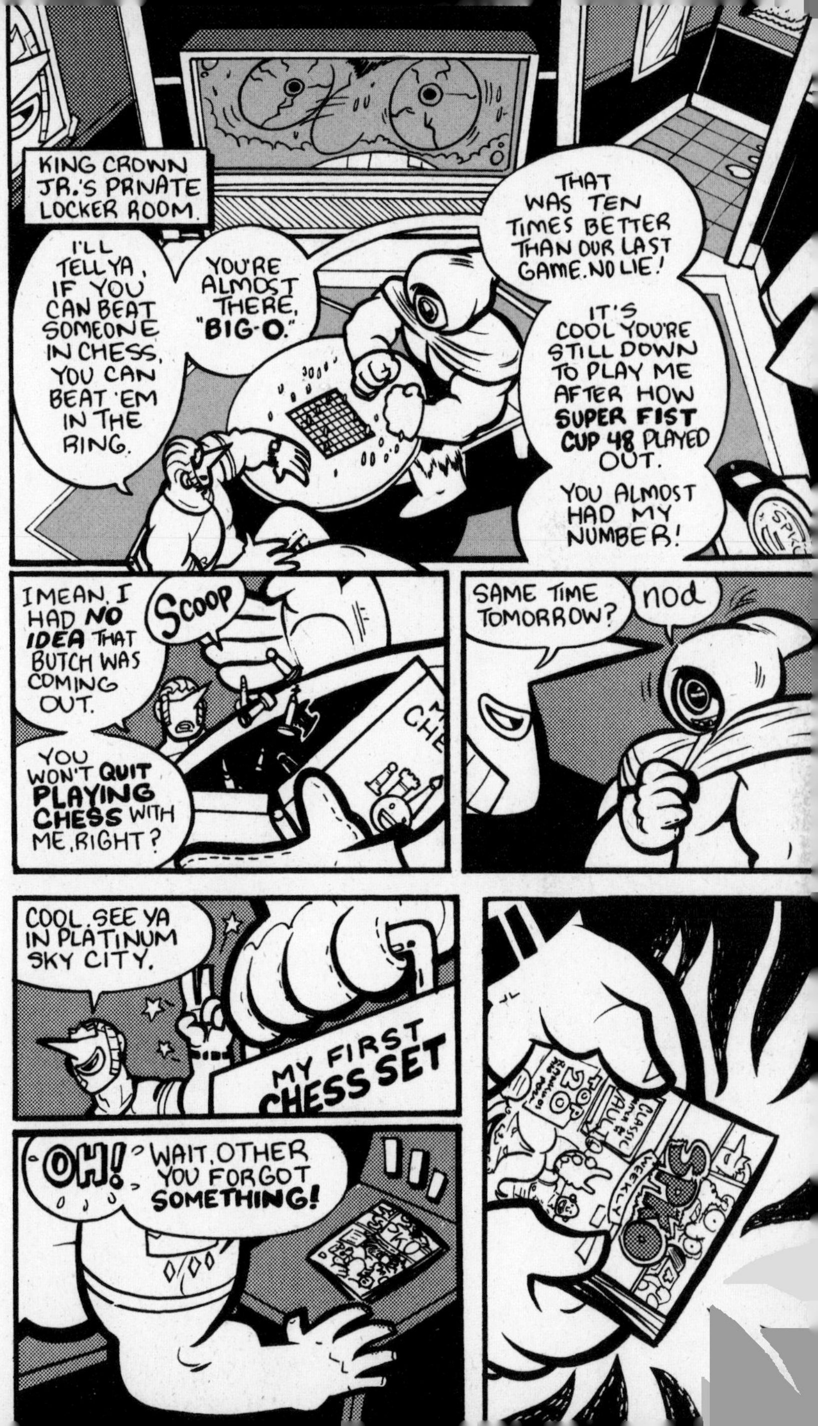
KING CROWN JR.'S PRIVATE LOCKER ROOM.
I'LL TELLYA, IF YOU CAN BEAT SOMEONE IN CHESS, YOU CAN BEAT 'EM IN THE RING.
YOU'RE ALMOST THERE, "BIG-O."
THAT WAS TEN TIMES BETTER THAN OUR LAST GAME. NO LIE!
IT'S COOL YOU'RE STILL DOWN TO PLAY ME AFTER HOW SUPER FIST CUP 48 PLAYED OUT.
YOU ALMOST HAD MY NUMBER!
I MEAN, I HAD NO IDEA THAT BUTCH WAS COMING OUT.
SCOOP
YOU WON'T QUIT PLAYING CHESS WITH ME, RIGHT?
SAME TIME TOMORROW?
nod
COOL. SEE YA IN PLATINUM SKY CITY.
MY FIRST CHESS SET
OH!
WAIT, OTHER YOU FORGOT SOMETHING!
WEEKLY

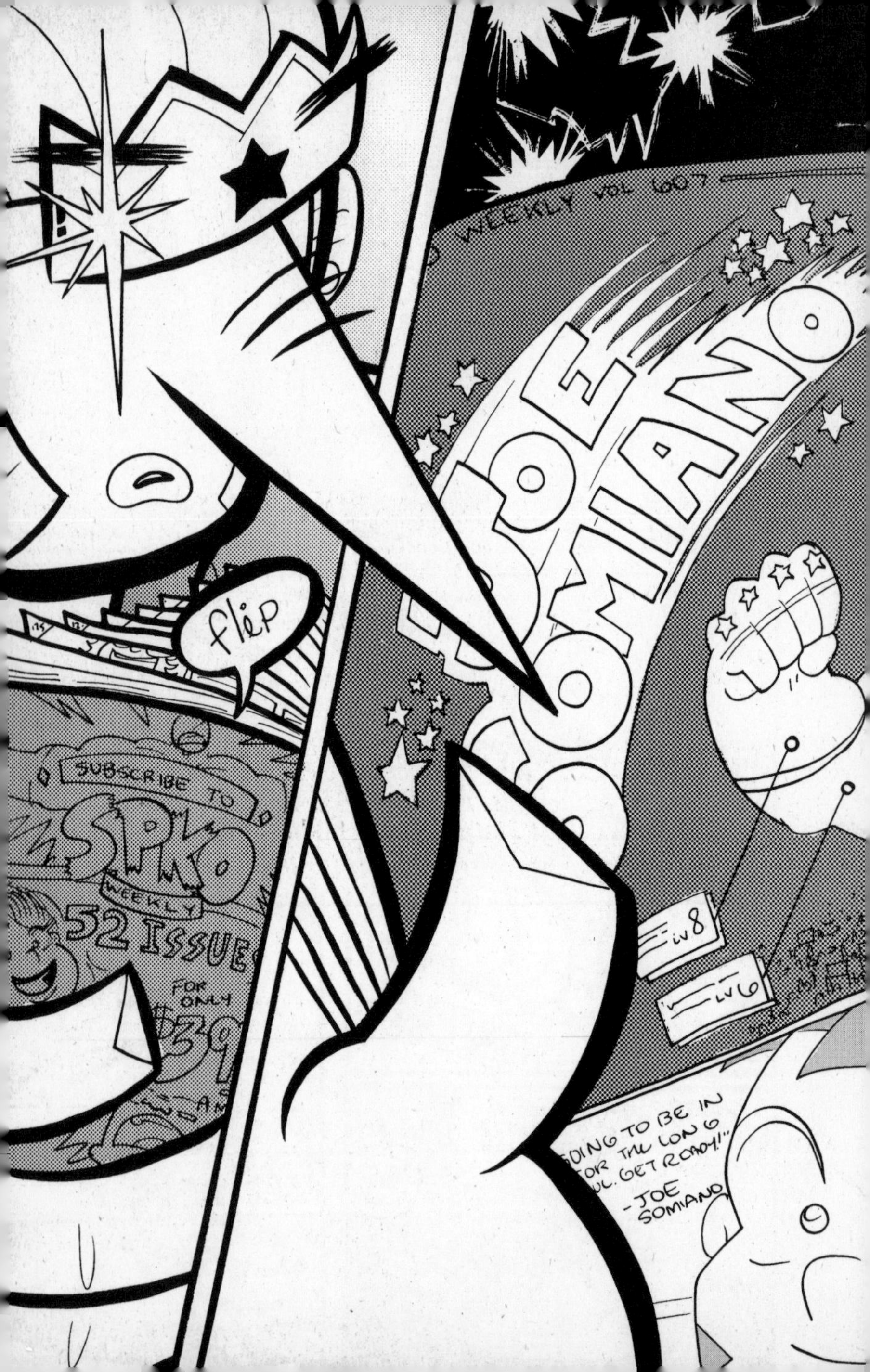

flip
WEEKLY VOL 607
JOE SOMIANO
SUBSCRIBE TO
SPKO
WEEKLY
52 ISSUES
FOR ONLY
LV 8
LV 6
GOING TO BE IN
FOR THE LONG
HAUL. GET READY!!
-JOE SOMIANO

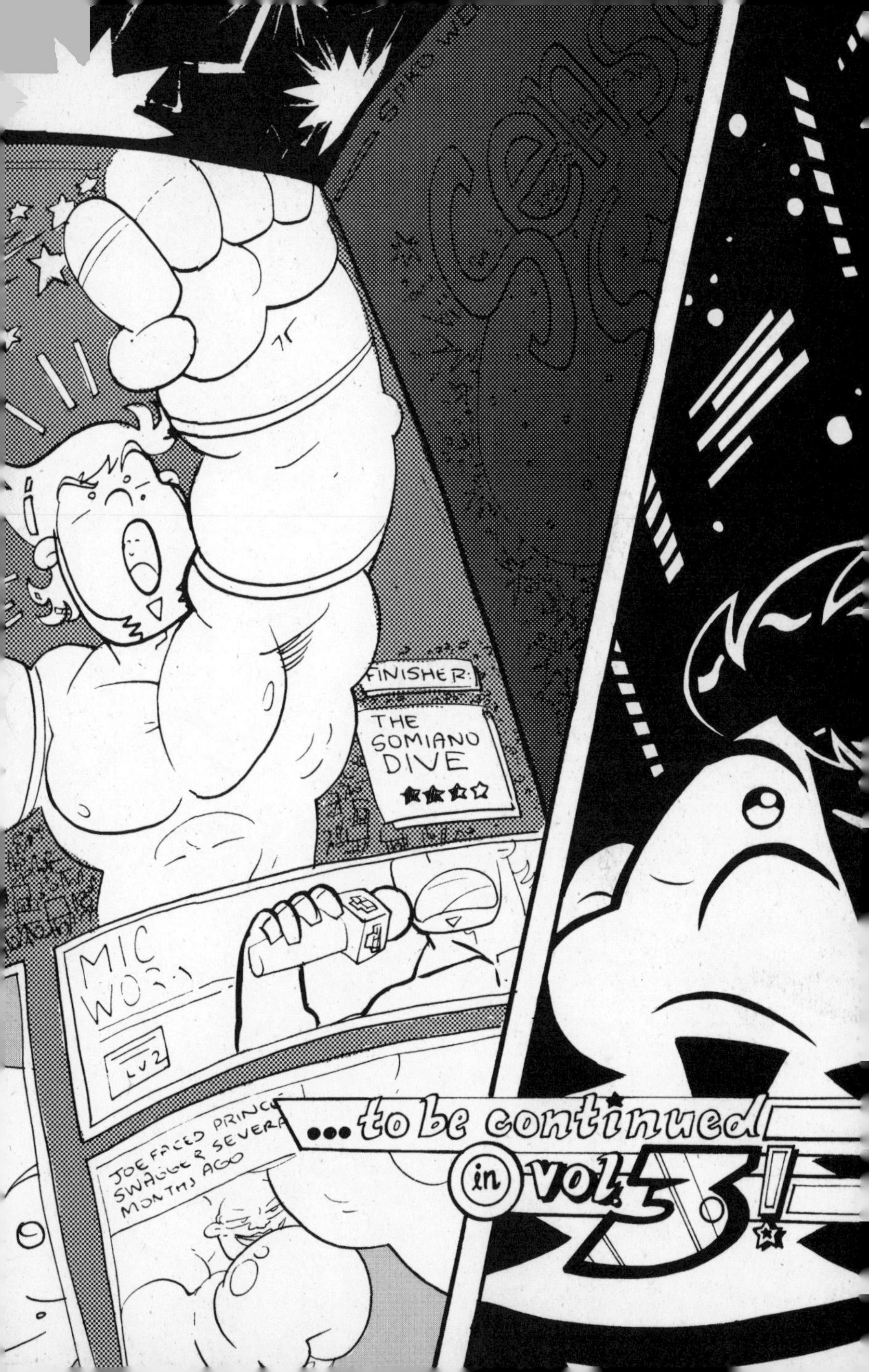
FINISHER:
THE SOMIANO DIVE
LV2
MONTHS AGO
...to be continued in vol. 3!

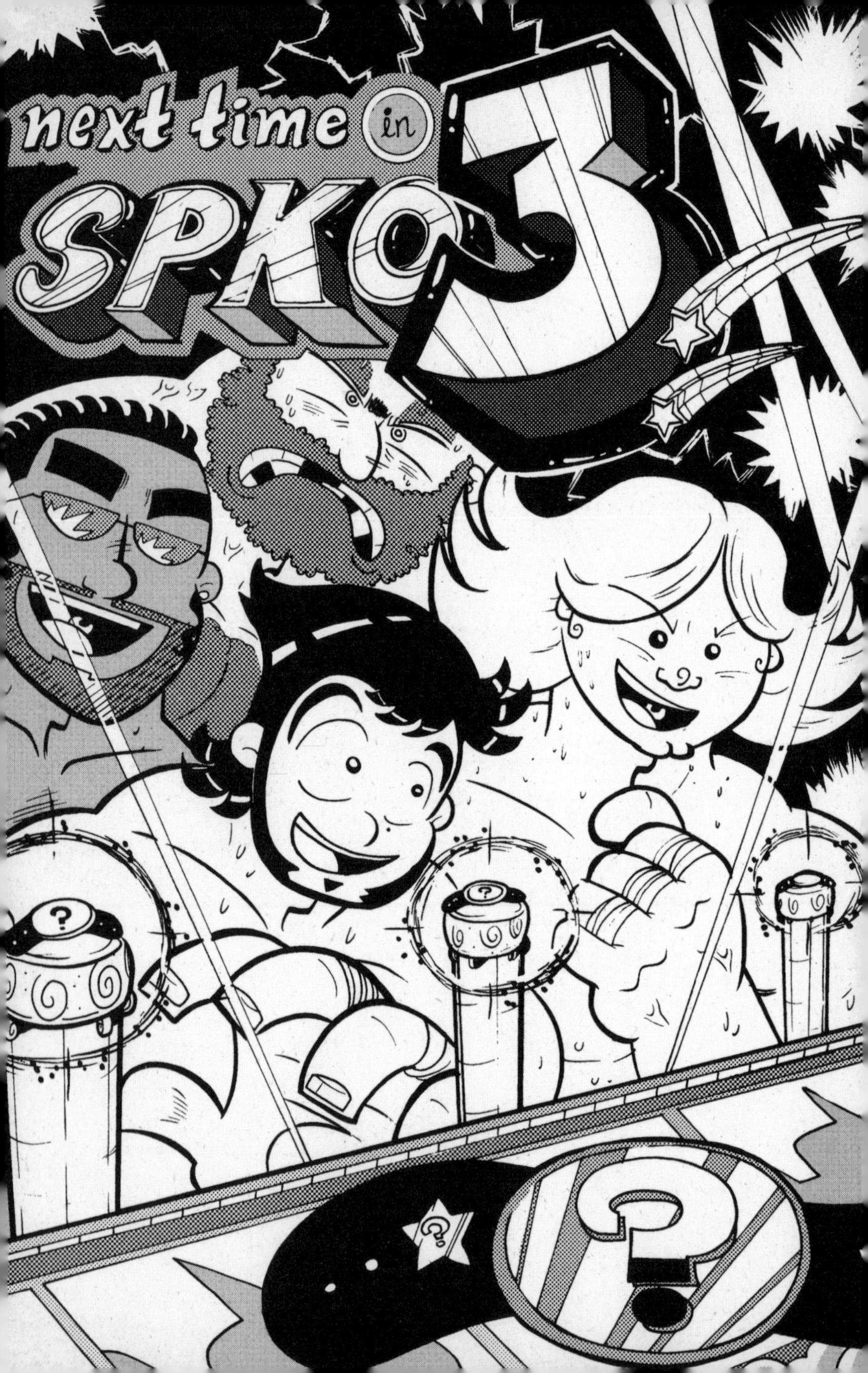
next time in
SPKO 3

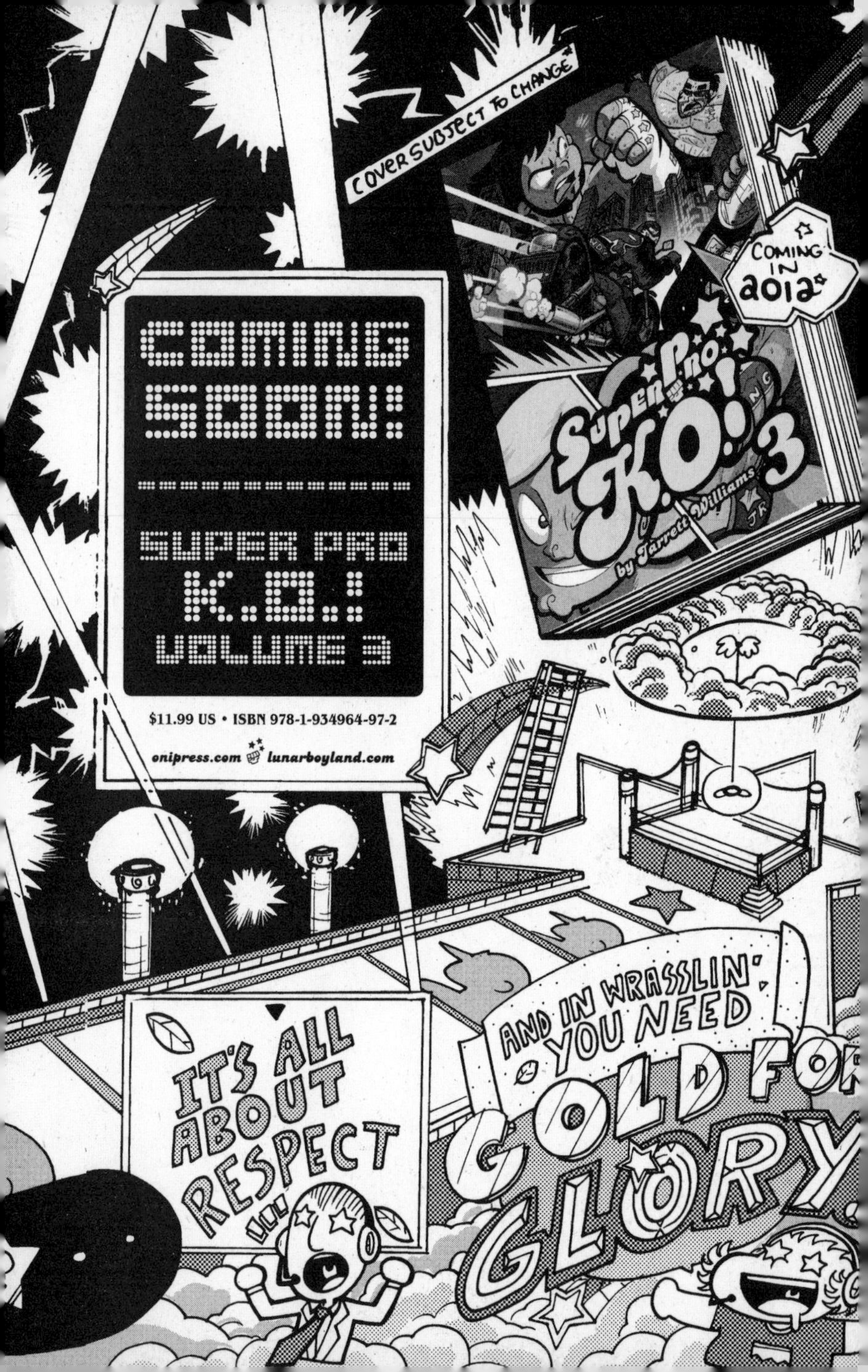
COVER SUBJECT TO CHANGE*
COMING IN 2012*
Super Pro K.O.! 3
by Jarrett Williams
COMING SOON!
SUPER PRO K.O.! VOLUME 3
$11.99 US • ISBN 978-1-934964-97-2
onipress.com lunarboyland.com
IT'S ALL ABOUT RESPECT
AND IN WRASSLIN', YOU NEED
GOLD FOR GLORY

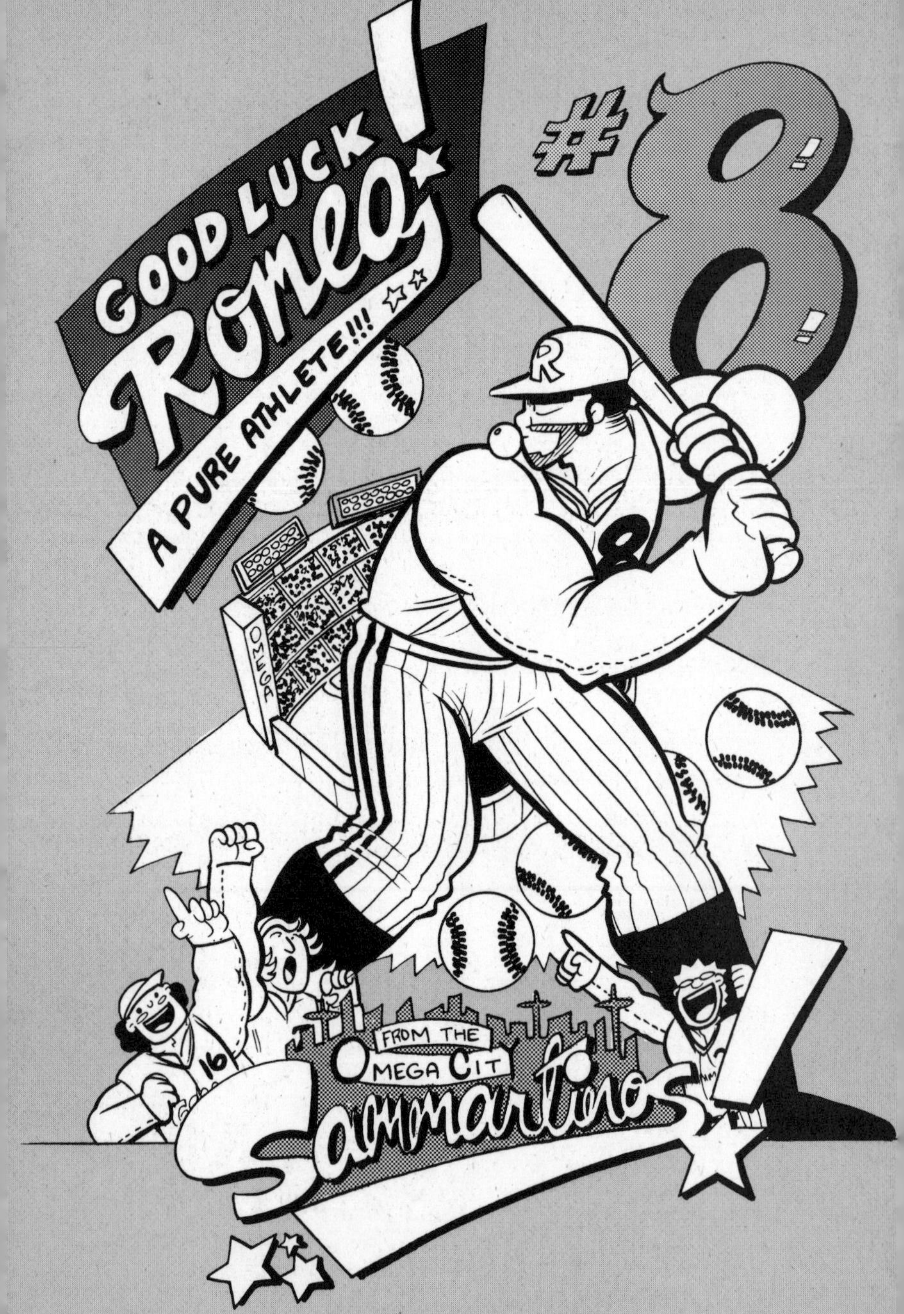
GOOD LUCK Romeo!
A PURE ATHLETE!!!
#8!!
OMEGA
FROM THE
OMEGA CIT
Sanmartinos!

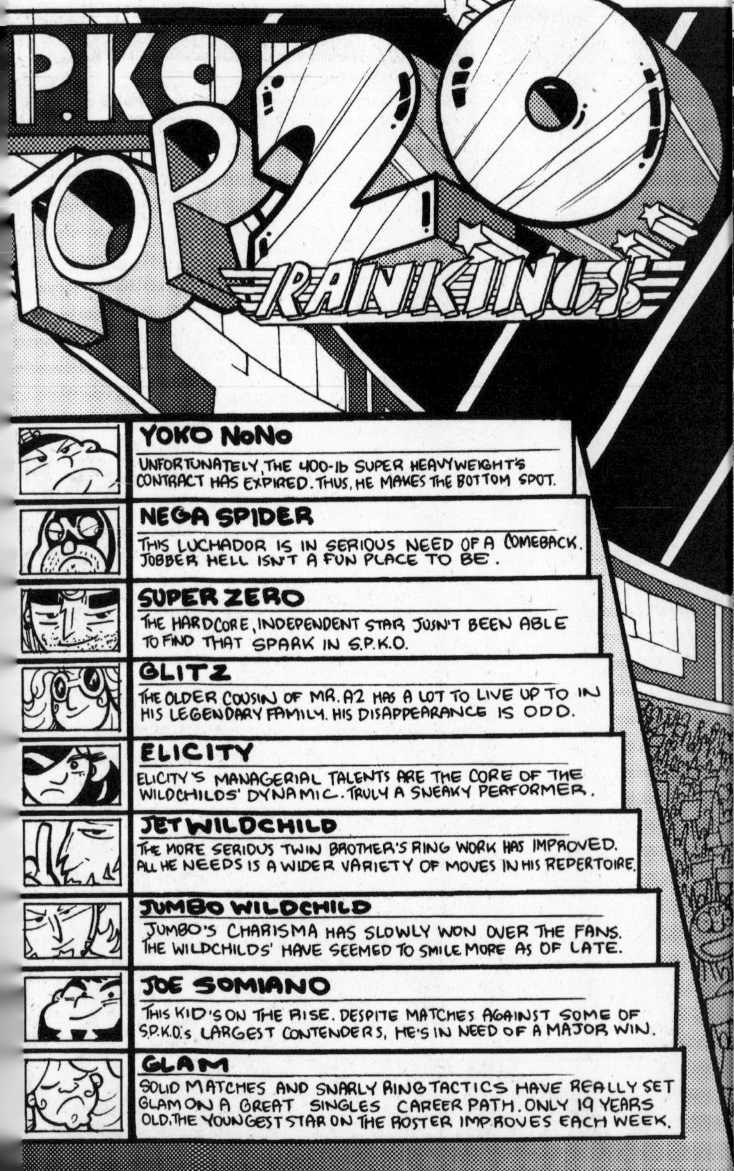

S.P.K.O. TOP 20 RANKINGS
YOKO NONO
UNFORTUNATELY, THE 400-lb SUPER HEAVYWEIGHT'S CONTRACT HAS EXPIRED. THUS, HE MAKES THE BOTTOM SPOT.
NEGA SPIDER
THIS LUCHADOR IS IN SERIOUS NEED OF A COMEBACK. JOBBER HELL ISN'T A FUN PLACE TO BE.
SUPER ZERO
THE HARDCORE, INDEPENDENT STAR JUSN'T BEEN ABLE TO FIND THAT SPARK IN S.P.K.O.
GLITZ
THE OLDER COUSIN OF MR. A2 HAS A LOT TO LIVE UP TO IN HIS LEGENDARY FAMILY. HIS DISAPPEARANCE IS ODD.
ELICITY
ELICITY'S MANAGERIAL TALENTS ARE THE CORE OF THE WILDCHILDS' DYNAMIC. TRULY A SNEAKY PERFORMER.
JET WILDCHILD
THE MORE SERIOUS TWIN BROTHER'S RING WORK HAS IMPROVED. ALL HE NEEDS IS A WIDER VARIETY OF MOVES IN HIS REPERTOIRE.
JUMBO WILDCHILD
JUMBO'S CHARISMA HAS SLOWLY WON OVER THE FANS. THE WILDCHILDS' HAVE SEEMED TO SMILE MORE AS OF LATE.
JOE SOMIANO
THIS KID'S ON THE RISE. DESPITE MATCHES AGAINST SOME OF S.P.K.O.'S LARGEST CONTENDERS, HE'S IN NEED OF A MAJOR WIN.
GLAM
SOLID MATCHES AND SNARLY RING TACTICS HAVE REALLY SET GLAM ON A GREAT SINGLES CAREER PATH. ONLY 19 YEARS OLD, THE YOUNGEST STAR ON THE ROSTER IMPROVES EACH WEEK.

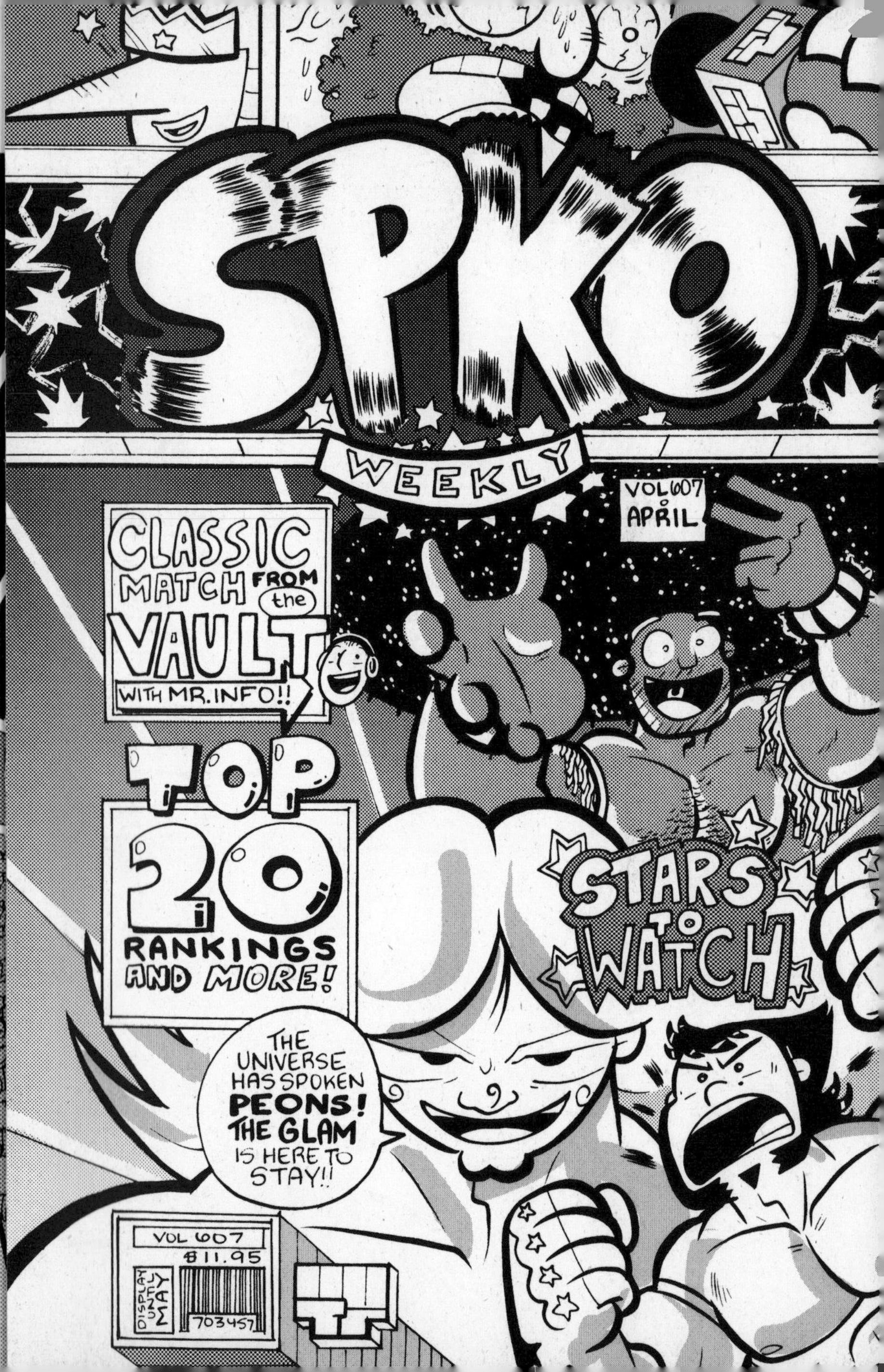

SPKO
WEEKLY
VOL 607
APRIL
CLASSIC MATCH FROM the VAULT
WITH MR. INFO!!
TOP 20 RANKINGS AND MORE!
STARS TO WATCH
THE UNIVERSE HAS SPOKEN PEONS! THE GLAM IS HERE TO STAY!!
VOL 607
$11.95
DISPLAY UNTIL MAY
703457

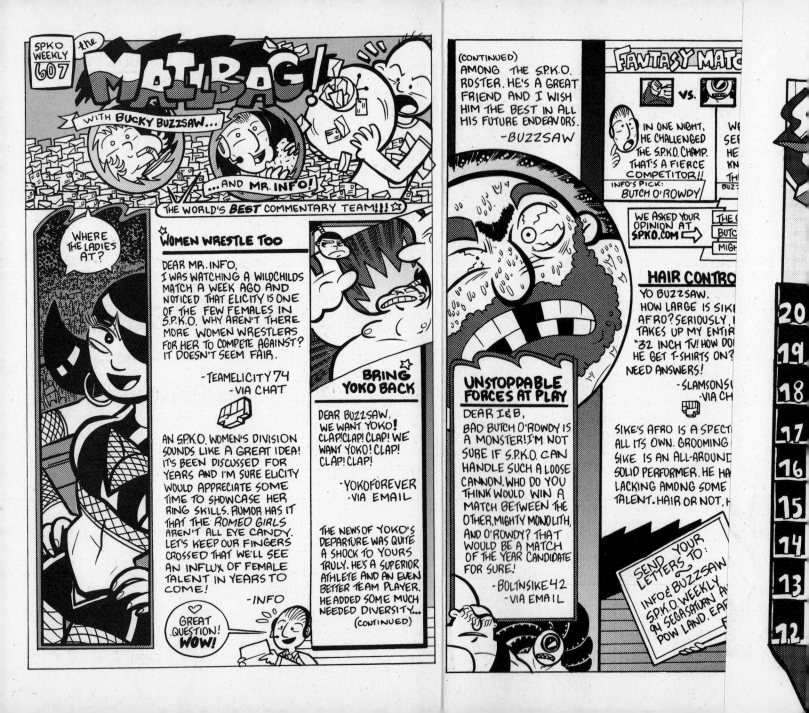

SPKO WEEKLY 607 — the MAILBAG!

WITH BUCKY BUZZSAW... ...AND MR. INFO!

THE WORLD'S BEST COMMENTARY TEAM!!!

Where the ladies at?

☆ WOMEN WRESTLE TOO

DEAR MR. INFO,
I WAS WATCHING A WILDCHILDS MATCH A WEEK AGO AND NOTICED THAT ELICITY IS ONE OF THE FEW FEMALES IN S.P.K.O. WHY AREN'T THERE MORE WOMEN WRESTLERS FOR HER TO COMPETE AGAINST? IT DOESN'T SEEM FAIR.

- TEAMELICITY 74
- VIA CHAT

AN S.P.K.O. WOMEN'S DIVISION SOUNDS LIKE A GREAT IDEA! IT'S BEEN DISCUSSED FOR YEARS AND I'M SURE ELICITY WOULD APPRECIATE SOME TIME TO SHOWCASE HER RING SKILLS. RUMOR HAS IT THAT THE ROMEO GIRLS AREN'T ALL EYE CANDY. LET'S KEEP OUR FINGERS CROSSED THAT WE'LL SEE AN INFLUX OF FEMALE TALENT IN YEARS TO COME!

- INFO

GREAT QUESTION! WOW!

☆ BRING YOKO BACK

DEAR BUZZSAW,
WE WANT YOKO! CLAP! CLAP! CLAP! WE WANT YOKO! CLAP! CLAP! CLAP!

- YOKOFOREVER
- VIA EMAIL

THE NEWS OF YOKO'S DEPARTURE WAS QUITE A SHOCK TO YOURS TRULY. HE'S A SUPERIOR ATHLETE AND AN EVEN BETTER TEAM PLAYER. HE ADDED SOME MUCH NEEDED DIVERSITY...
(CONTINUED)

(CONTINUED)
AMONG THE S.P.K.O. ROSTER. HE'S A GREAT FRIEND AND I WISH HIM THE BEST IN ALL HIS FUTURE ENDEAVORS.
-BUZZSAW

FANTASY MAT[CH]

VS.

IN ONE NIGHT, HE CHALLENGED THE S.P.K.O. CHAMP. THAT'S A FIERCE COMPETITOR!!
INFO'S PICK: BUTCH O'ROWDY

W[E] SE[...] HE [...] KN[...] TH[...] BUZZ[...]

WE ASKED YOUR OPINION AT SPKO.COM →

THE [...]
BUTC[...]
MIGH[...]

HAIR CONTRO[...]

YO BUZZSAW,
HOW LARGE IS SIK[E'S] AFRO? SERIOUSLY, [IT] TAKES UP MY ENTIR[E] "32 INCH TV! HOW DO[ES] HE GET T-SHIRTS ON? NEED ANSWERS!

- SLAMSONS[...]
- VIA CH[...]

SIKE'S AFRO IS A SPECT[...] ALL ITS OWN. GROOMING [...] SIKE IS AN ALL-AROUND SOLID PERFORMER. HE HA[S...] LACKING AMONG SOME [...] TALENT. HAIR OR NOT, H[...]

UNSTOPPABLE FORCES AT PLAY

DEAR I & B,
BAD BUTCH O'ROWDY IS A MONSTER! I'M NOT SURE IF S.P.K.O. CAN HANDLE SUCH A LOOSE CANNON. WHO DO YOU THINK WOULD WIN A MATCH BETWEEN THE OTHER MIGHTY MONOLITH, AND O'ROWDY? THAT WOULD BE A MATCH OF THE YEAR CANDIDATE FOR SURE!

- BOLTNSIKE 42
- VIA EMAIL

SEND YOUR LETTERS TO:
INFO & BUZZSAW
S.P.K.O. WEEKLY
94 SEGASATURN A[...]
POW LAND, EAR[...]

20
19
18
17
16
15
14
13
12

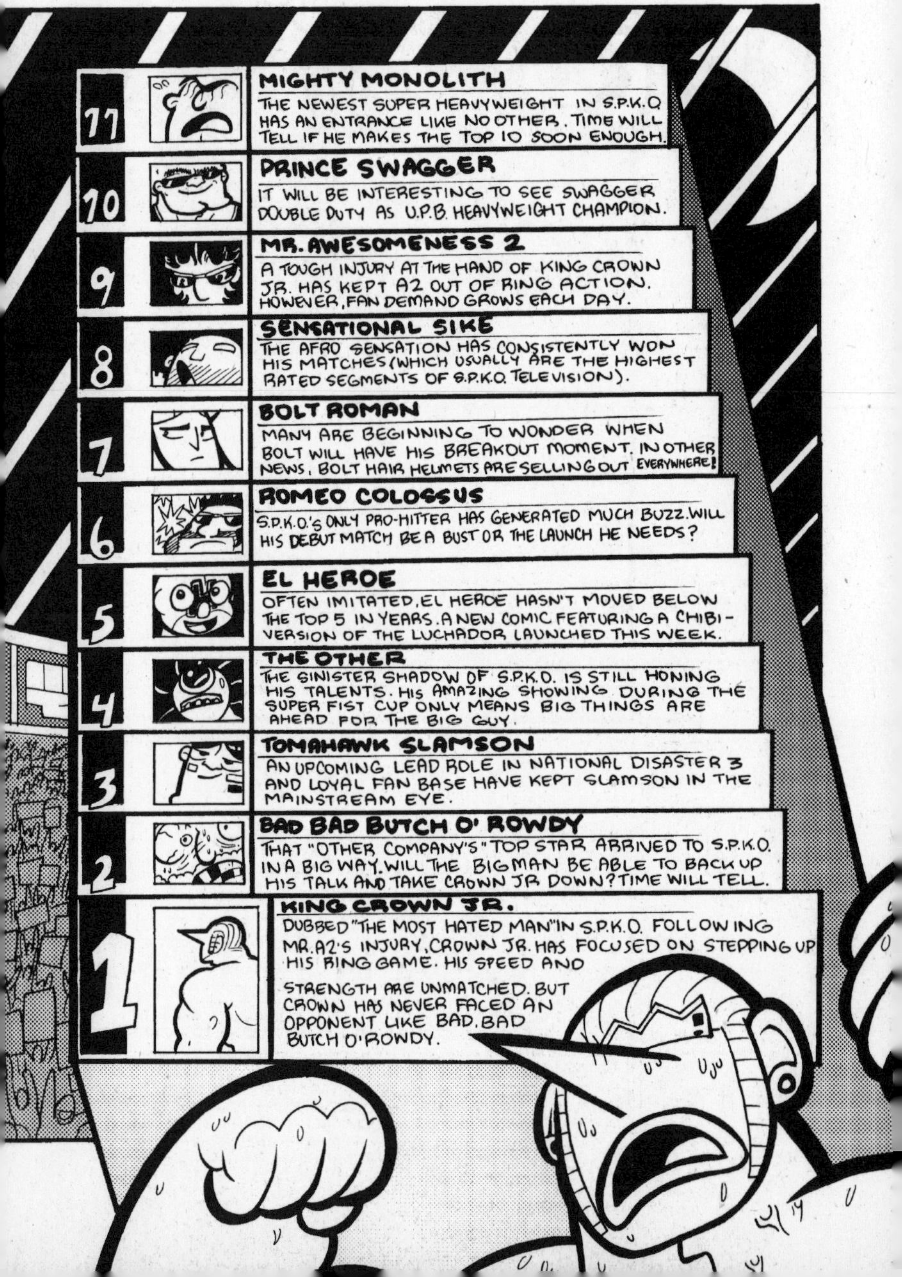
11
MIGHTY MONOLITH
THE NEWEST SUPER HEAVYWEIGHT IN S.P.K.O HAS AN ENTRANCE LIKE NO OTHER. TIME WILL TELL IF HE MAKES THE TOP 10 SOON ENOUGH.
10
PRINCE SWAGGER
IT WILL BE INTERESTING TO SEE SWAGGER DOUBLE DUTY AS U.P.B. HEAVYWEIGHT CHAMPION.
9
MR. AWESOMENESS 2
A TOUGH INJURY AT THE HAND OF KING CROWN JR. HAS KEPT A2 OUT OF RING ACTION. HOWEVER, FAN DEMAND GROWS EACH DAY.
8
SENSATIONAL SIKE
THE AFRO SENSATION HAS CONSISTENTLY WON HIS MATCHES (WHICH USUALLY ARE THE HIGHEST RATED SEGMENTS OF S.P.K.O. TELEVISION).
7
BOLT ROMAN
MANY ARE BEGINNING TO WONDER WHEN BOLT WILL HAVE HIS BREAKOUT MOMENT. IN OTHER NEWS, BOLT HAIR HELMETS ARE SELLING OUT EVERYWHERE!
6
ROMEO COLOSSUS
S.P.K.O.'S ONLY PRO-HITTER HAS GENERATED MUCH BUZZ. WILL HIS DEBUT MATCH BE A BUST OR THE LAUNCH HE NEEDS?
5
EL HEROE
OFTEN IMITATED, EL HEROE HASN'T MOVED BELOW THE TOP 5 IN YEARS. A NEW COMIC FEATURING A CHIBI-VERSION OF THE LUCHADOR LAUNCHED THIS WEEK.
4
THE OTHER
THE SINISTER SHADOW OF S.P.K.O. IS STILL HONING HIS TALENTS. HIS AMAZING SHOWING DURING THE SUPER FIST CUP ONLY MEANS BIG THINGS ARE AHEAD FOR THE BIG GUY.
3
TOMAHAWK SLAMSON
AN UPCOMING LEAD ROLE IN NATIONAL DISASTER 3 AND LOYAL FAN BASE HAVE KEPT SLAMSON IN THE MAINSTREAM EYE.
2
BAD BAD BUTCH O' ROWDY
THAT "OTHER COMPANY'S" TOP STAR ARRIVED TO S.P.K.O. IN A BIG WAY. WILL THE BIG MAN BE ABLE TO BACK UP HIS TALK AND TAKE CROWN JR DOWN? TIME WILL TELL.
1
KING CROWN JR.
DUBBED "THE MOST HATED MAN" IN S.P.K.O. FOLLOWING MR. A2'S INJURY, CROWN JR. HAS FOCUSED ON STEPPING UP HIS RING GAME. HIS SPEED AND
STRENGTH ARE UNMATCHED. BUT CROWN HAS NEVER FACED AN OPPONENT LIKE BAD, BAD BUTCH O'ROWDY.

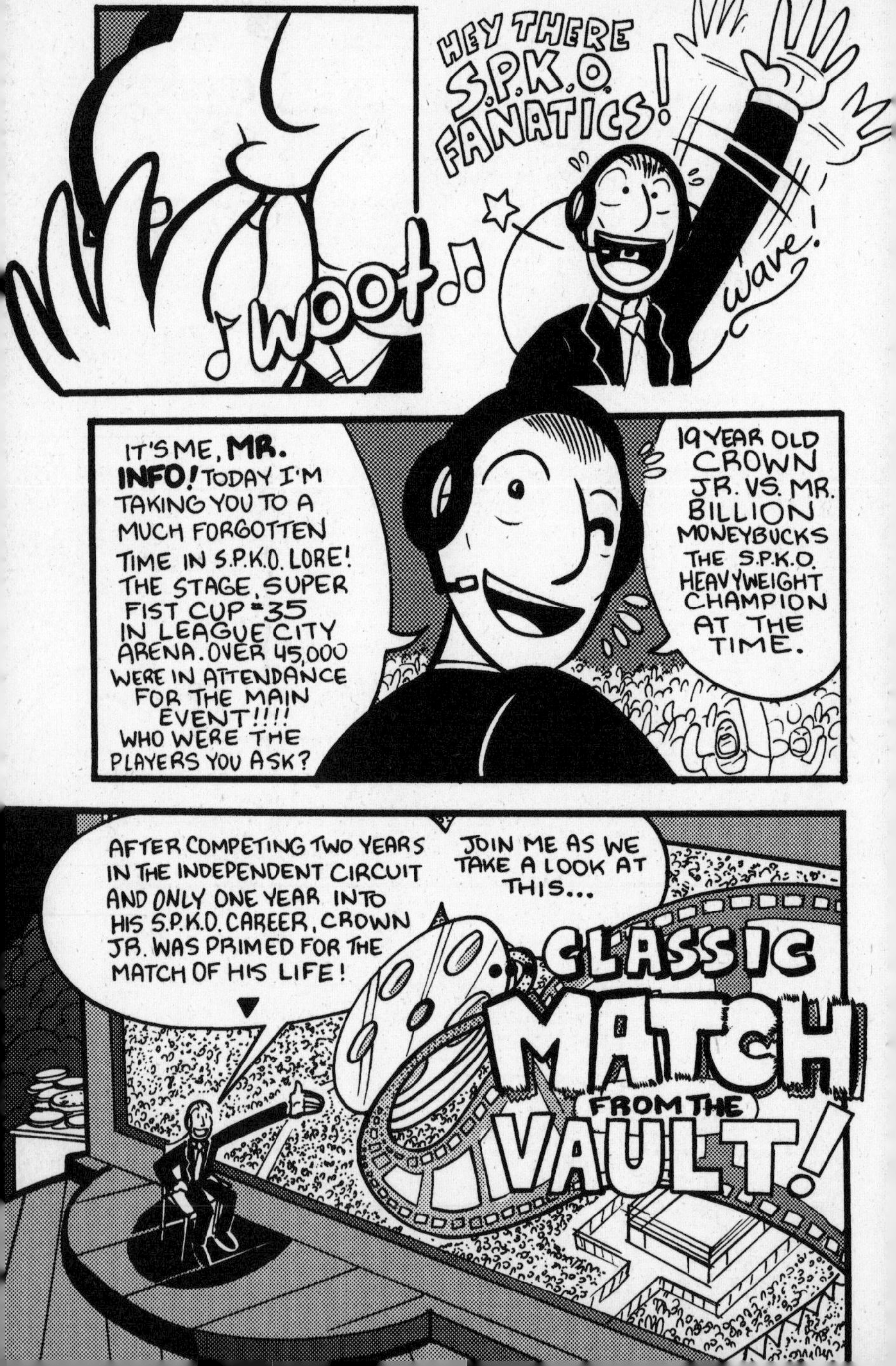
woot
HEY THERE S.P.K.O. FANATICS!
wave!
IT'S ME, MR. INFO! TODAY I'M TAKING YOU TO A MUCH FORGOTTEN TIME IN S.P.K.O. LORE! THE STAGE, SUPER FIST CUP #35 IN LEAGUE CITY ARENA. OVER 45,000 WERE IN ATTENDANCE FOR THE MAIN EVENT!!!! WHO WERE THE PLAYERS YOU ASK?
19 YEAR OLD CROWN JR. VS. MR. BILLION MONEYBUCKS THE S.P.K.O. HEAVYWEIGHT CHAMPION AT THE TIME.
AFTER COMPETING TWO YEARS IN THE INDEPENDENT CIRCUIT AND ONLY ONE YEAR INTO HIS S.P.K.O. CAREER, CROWN JR. WAS PRIMED FOR THE MATCH OF HIS LIFE!
JOIN ME AS WE TAKE A LOOK AT THIS...
CLASSIC MATCH FROM THE VAULT!

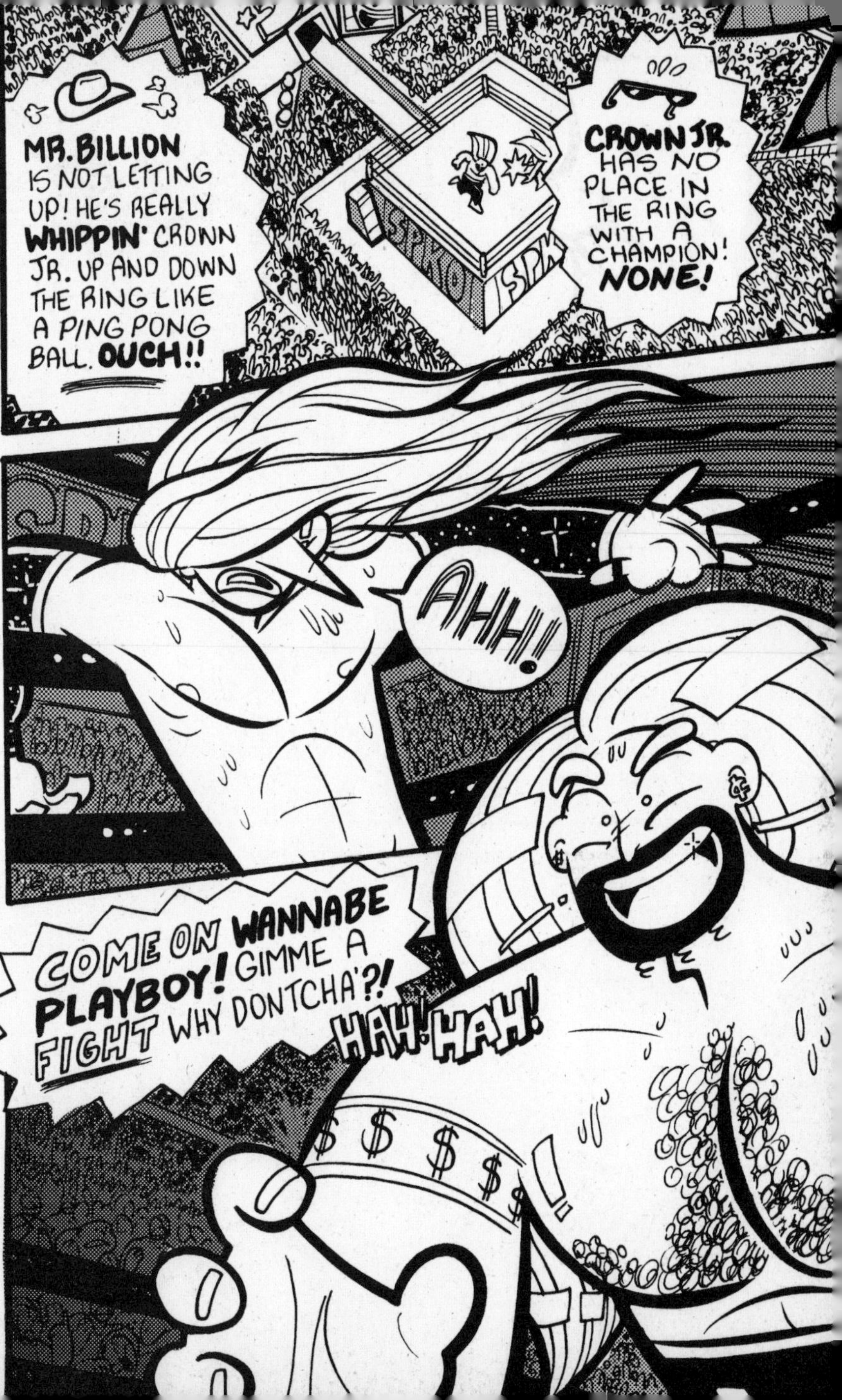
MR. BILLION IS NOT LETTING UP! HE'S REALLY WHIPPIN' CROWN JR. UP AND DOWN THE RING LIKE A PING PONG BALL. OUCH!!
CROWN JR. HAS NO PLACE IN THE RING WITH A CHAMPION! NONE!
AHH!
COME ON WANNABE PLAYBOY! GIMME A FIGHT WHY DONTCHA'?!
HAH! HAH!

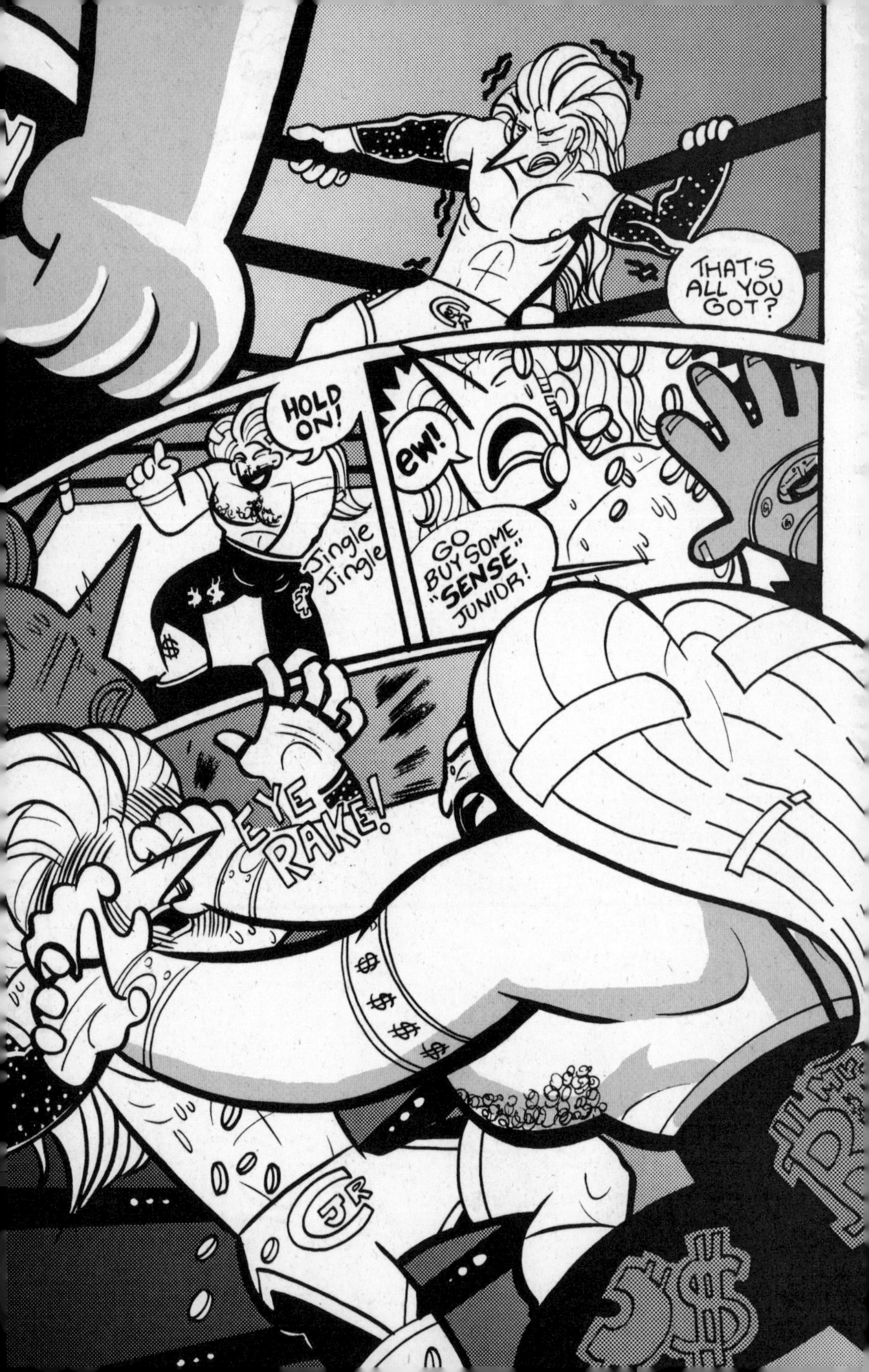
THAT'S ALL YOU GOT?
HOLD ON!
Jingle Jingle
ew!
GO BUY SOME "SENSE" JUNIOR!
EYE RAKE!

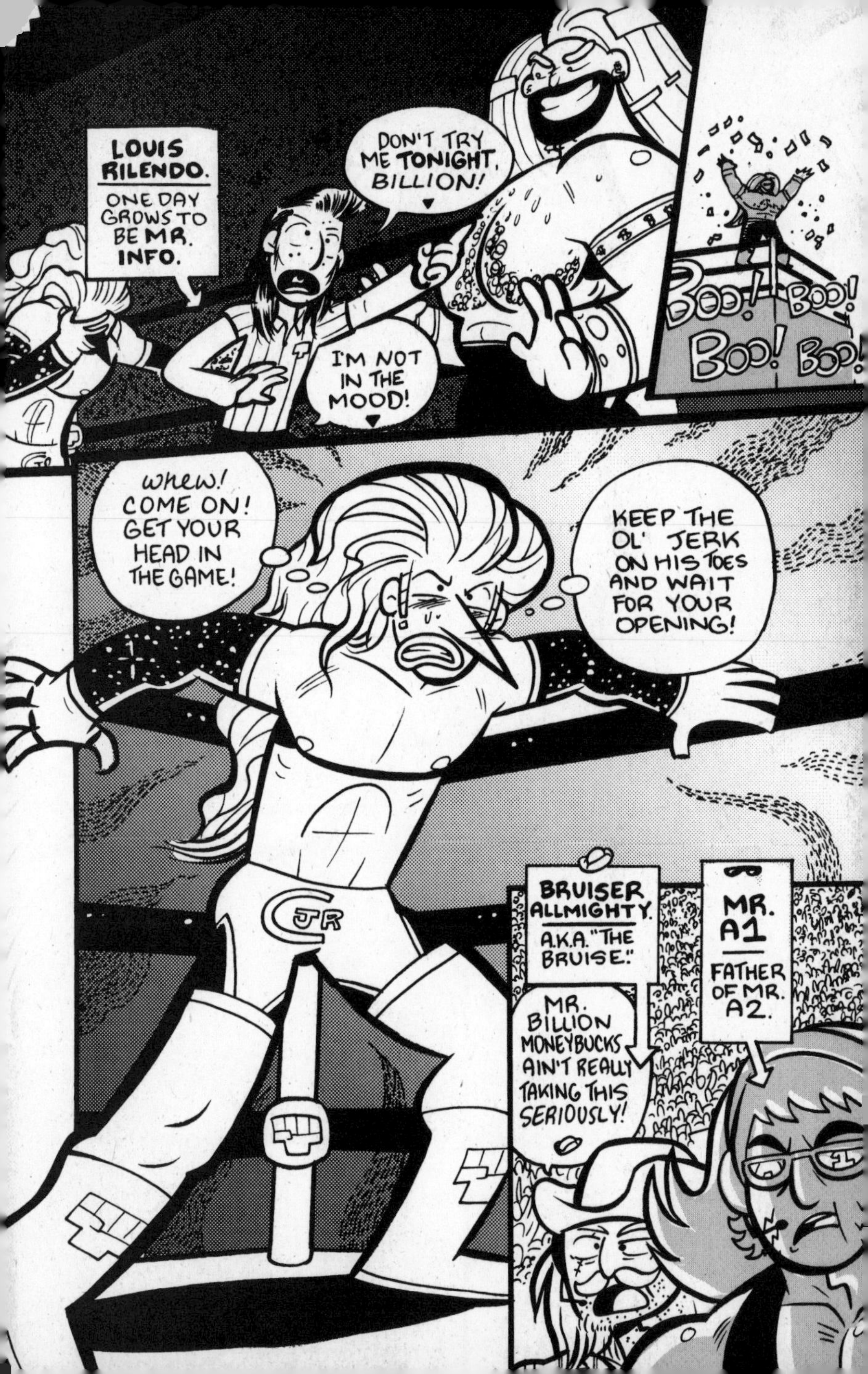
LOUIS RILENDO.
ONE DAY GROWS TO BE MR. INFO.
DON'T TRY ME TONIGHT, BILLION!
I'M NOT IN THE MOOD!
BOO! BOO! BOO! BOO!
whew! COME ON! GET YOUR HEAD IN THE GAME!
KEEP THE OL' JERK ON HIS TOES AND WAIT FOR YOUR OPENING!
JR
BRUISER ALLMIGHTY.
A.K.A. "THE BRUISE."
MR. A1
FATHER OF MR. A2.
MR. BILLION MONEYBUCKS AIN'T REALLY TAKING THIS SERIOUSLY!

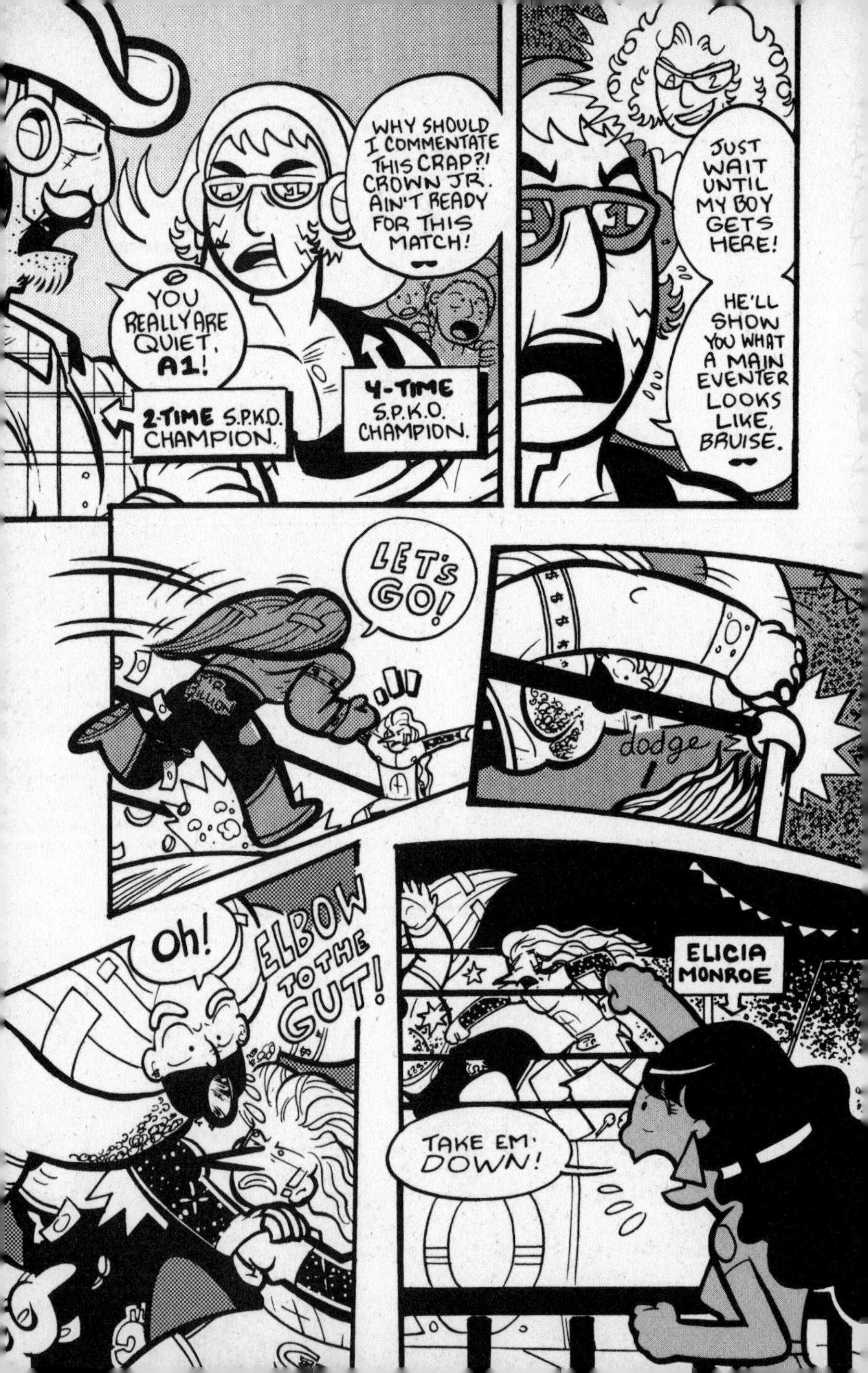
WHY SHOULD I COMMENTATE THIS CRAP?! CROWN JR. AIN'T READY FOR THIS MATCH!
YOU REALLY ARE QUIET, A1!
2-TIME S.P.K.O. CHAMPION.
4-TIME S.P.K.O. CHAMPION.
JUST WAIT UNTIL MY BOY GETS HERE!
HE'LL SHOW YOU WHAT A MAIN EVENTER LOOKS LIKE, BRUISE.
LET'S GO!
dodge
Oh!
ELBOW TO THE GUT!
ELICIA MONROE
TAKE EM DOWN!

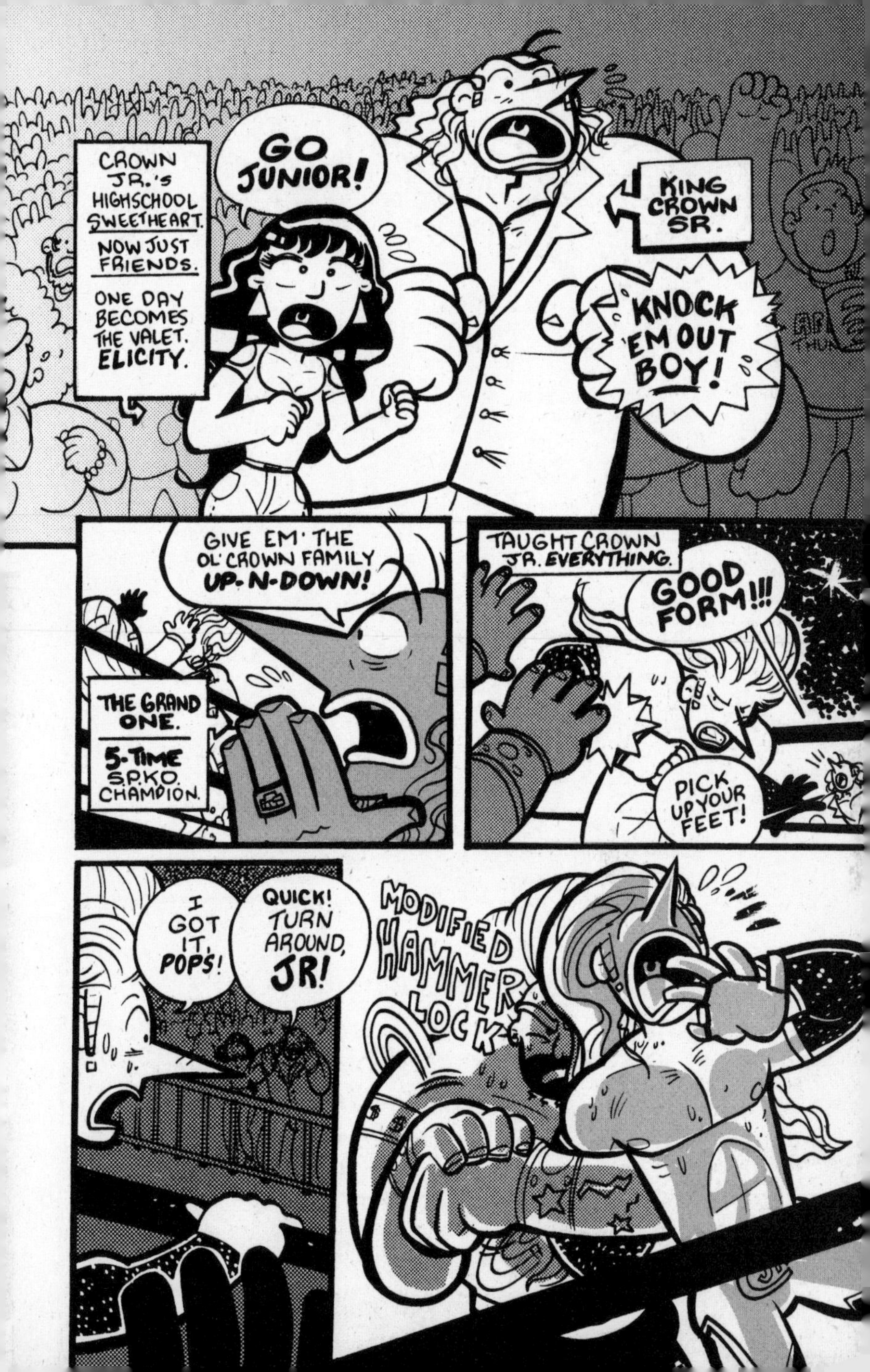

CROWN JR.'s HIGHSCHOOL SWEETHEART. NOW JUST FRIENDS. ONE DAY BECOMES THE VALET. ELICITY.
GO JUNIOR!
KING CROWN SR.
KNOCK EM OUT BOY!
GIVE EM' THE OL' CROWN FAMILY UP-N-DOWN!
THE GRAND ONE. 5-TIME S.P.K.O. CHAMPION.
TAUGHT CROWN JR. EVERYTHING.
GOOD FORM!!!
PICK UP YOUR FEET!
QUICK! TURN AROUND, JR!
I GOT IT, POPS!
MODIFIED HAMMER LOCK

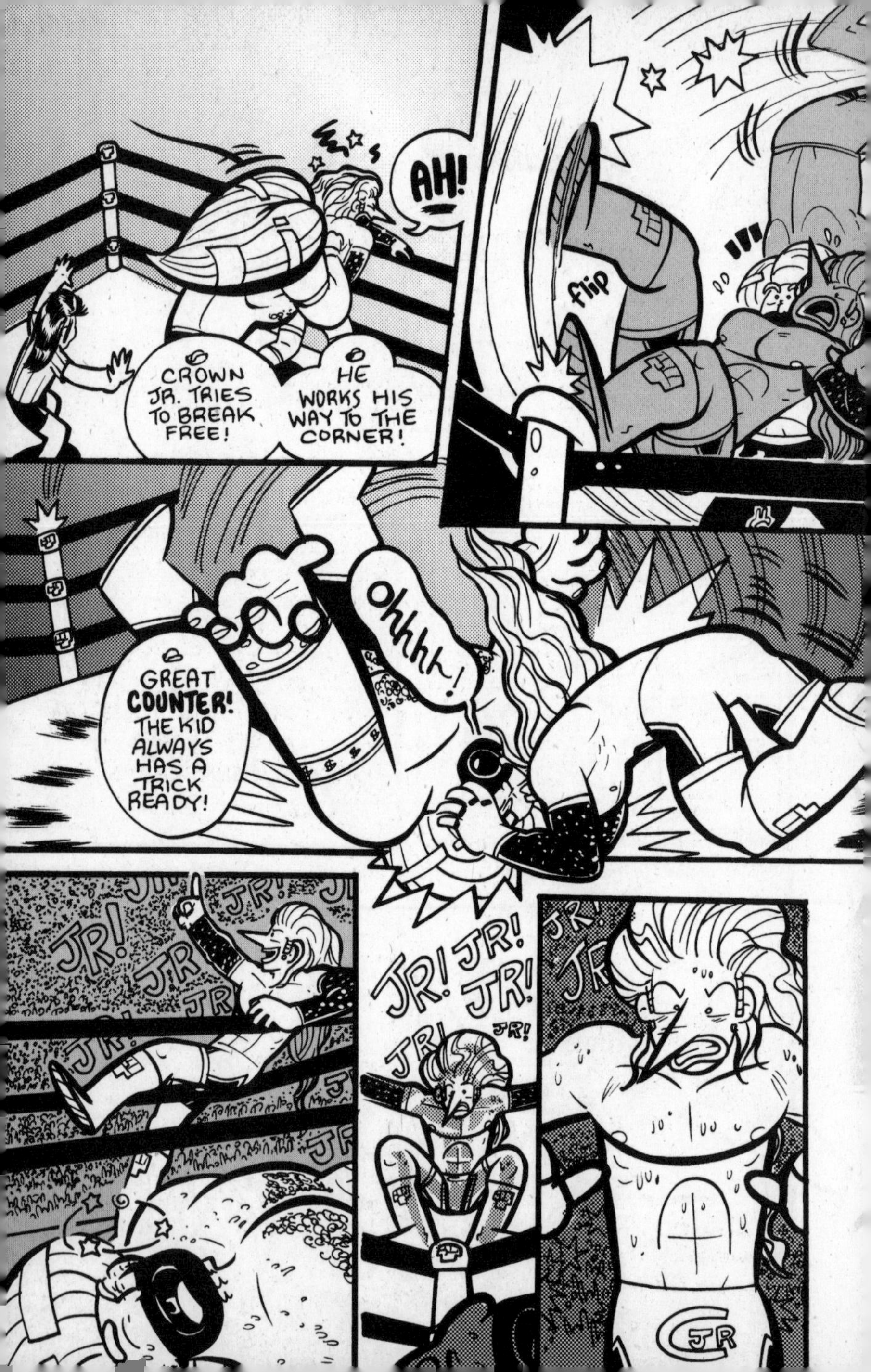
AH!
CROWN JR. TRIES TO BREAK FREE!
HE WORKS HIS WAY TO THE CORNER!
flip
GREAT COUNTER! THE KID ALWAYS HAS A TRICK READY!
ohhhh!
JR!
JR
JR
JR!
JR! JR! JR!
JR!
JR!
JR!
JR
CJR

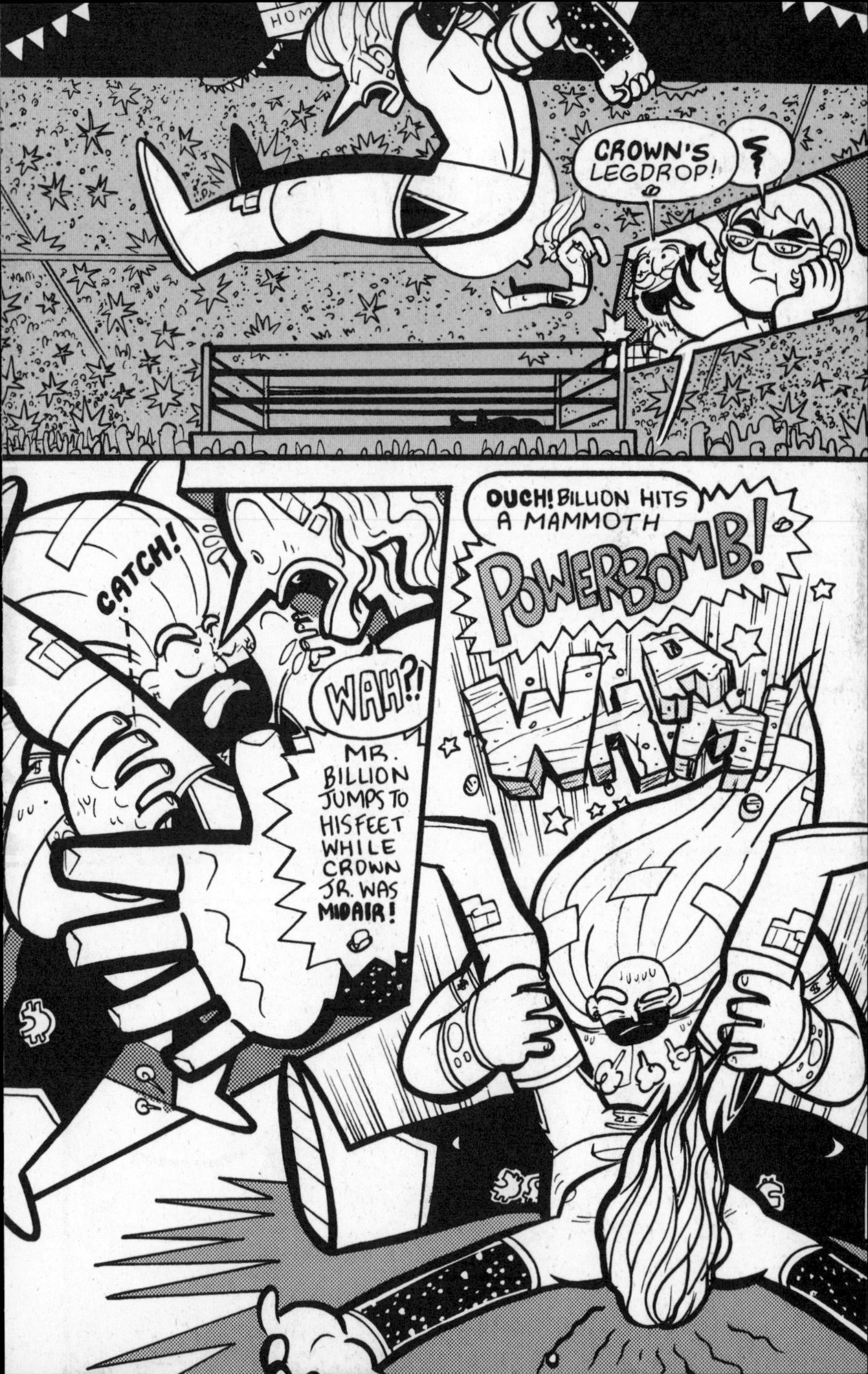

HOM
CROWN'S LEGDROP!
CATCH!
WAH?!
MR. BILLION JUMPS TO HIS FEET WHILE CROWN JR. WAS MIDAIR!
OUCH! BILLION HITS A MAMMOTH POWERBOMB!
WHAM!

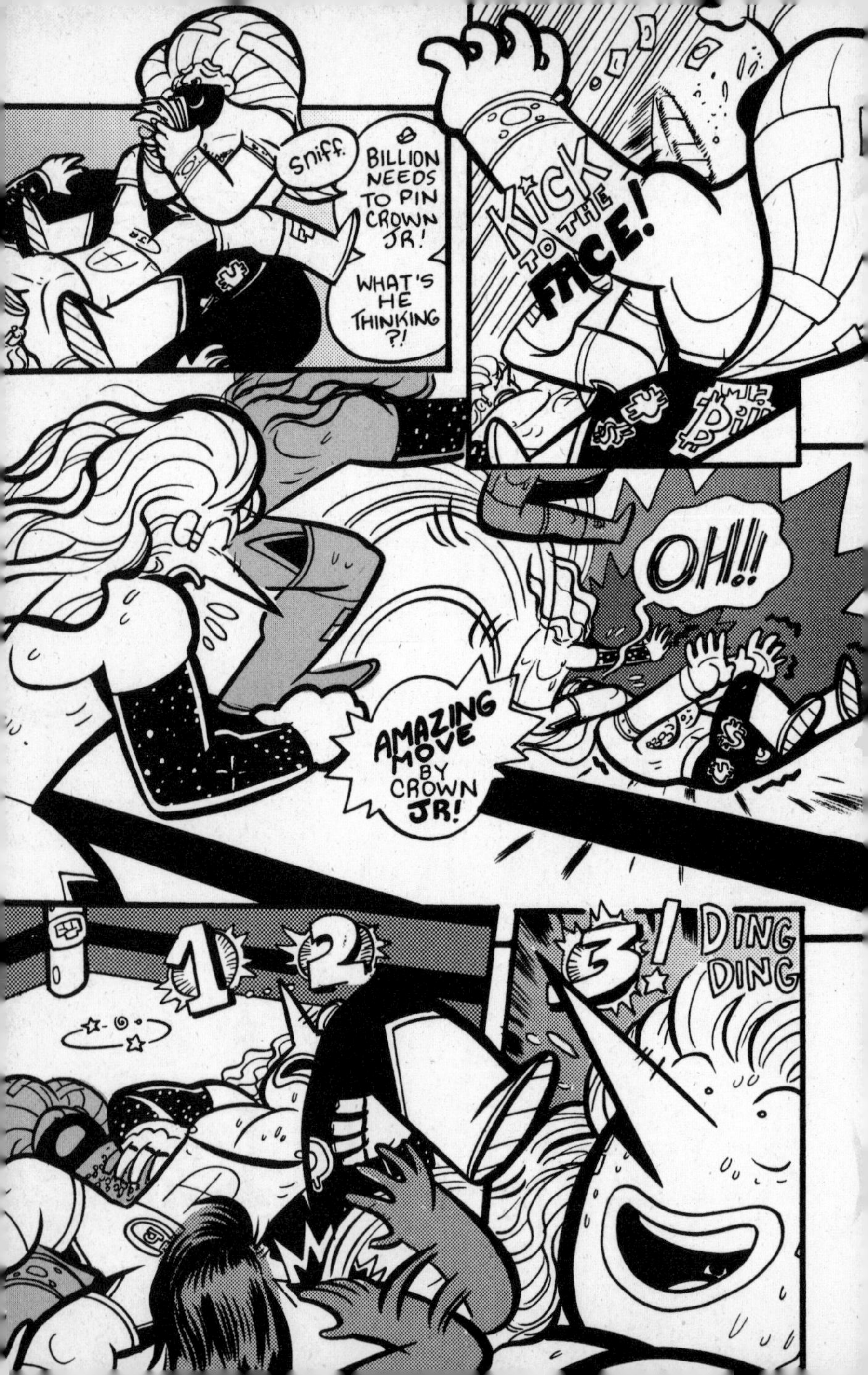

Sniff.
BILLION NEEDS TO PIN CROWN JR!
WHAT'S HE THINKING?!
KICK TO THE FACE!
OH!!
AMAZING MOVE BY CROWN JR!
1
2
3!
DING DING

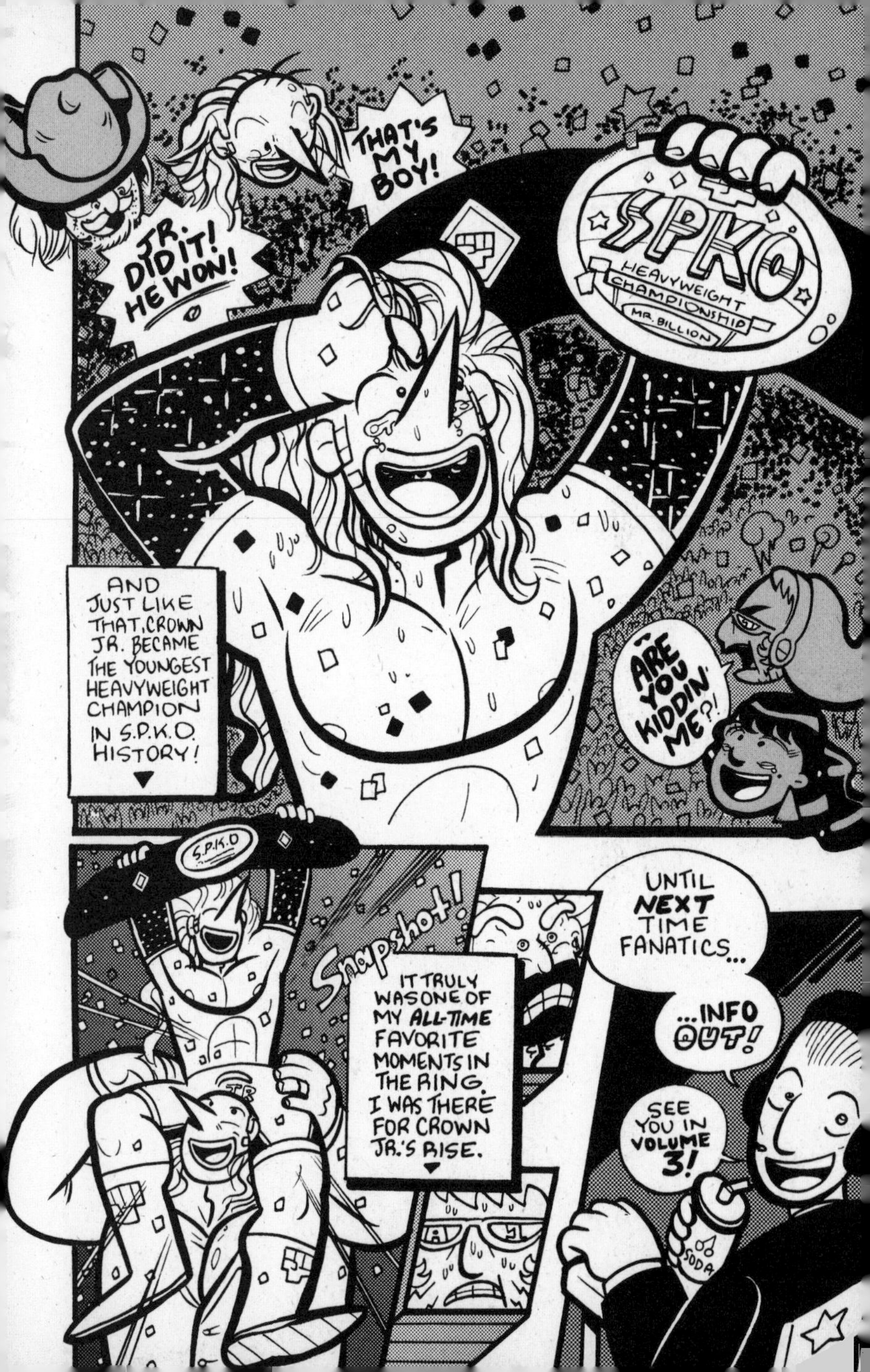
JR. DID IT! HE WON!
THAT'S MY BOY!
SPKO HEAVYWEIGHT CHAMPIONSHIP MR. BILLION
AND JUST LIKE THAT, CROWN JR. BECAME THE YOUNGEST HEAVYWEIGHT CHAMPION IN S.P.K.O. HISTORY!
ARE YOU KIDDIN' ME?!
S.P.K.O
Snapshot!
IT TRULY WAS ONE OF MY ALL-TIME FAVORITE MOMENTS IN THE RING. I WAS THERE FOR CROWN JR.'S RISE.
UNTIL NEXT TIME FANATICS...
...INFO OUT!
SEE YOU IN VOLUME 3!
SODA

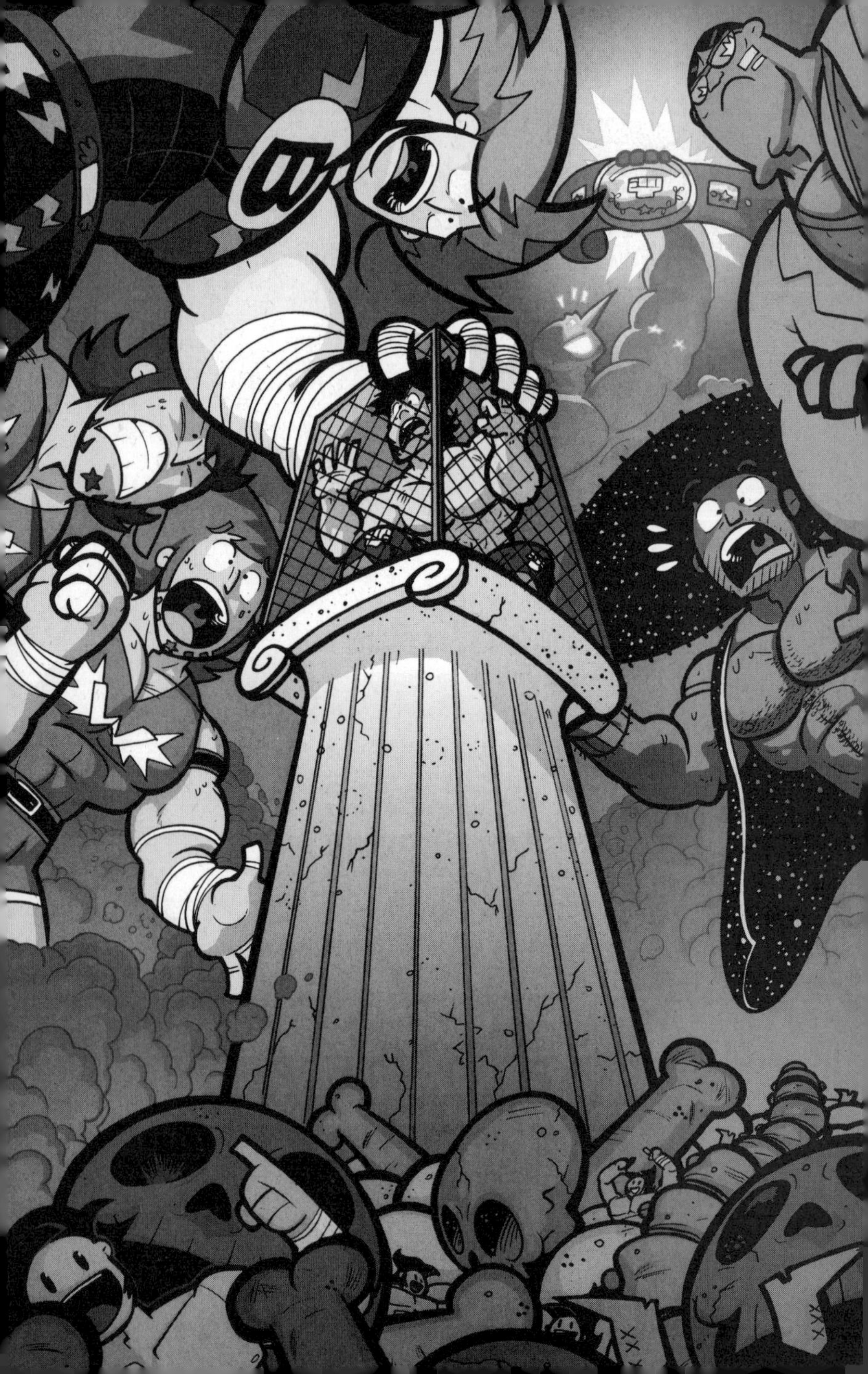

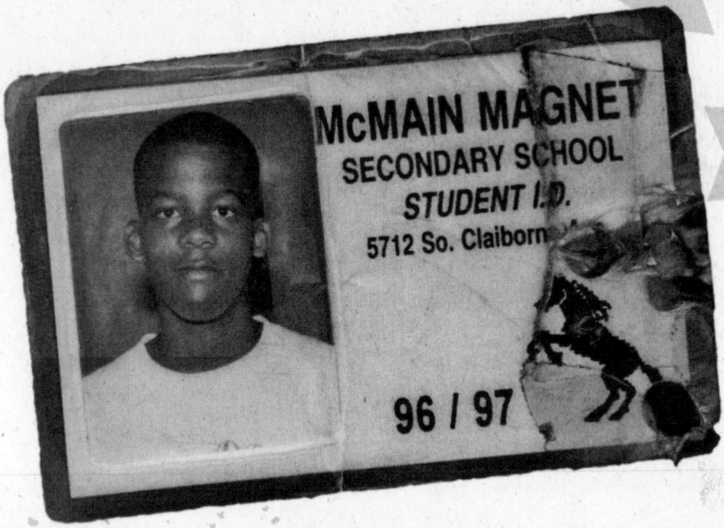
McMAIN MAGNET
SECONDARY SCHOOL
STUDENT I.D.
96 / 97

Jarrett Williams

was born in 1984 in New Orleans, Louisiana where he was cornfed comics and all sorts of retro vibes. He spends his nights drawing and dancing all over the place. He currently resides in Savannah, Georgia where he feels pretty good about life and what's up ahead. You can read more of his adventures at *www.lunarboyland.com*.

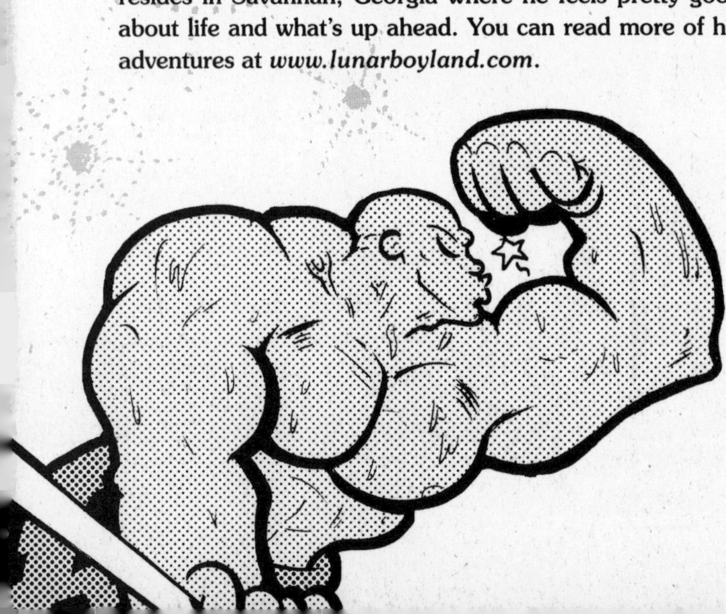

Available Now!

Super Pro K.O.! 1
by Jarrett Williams

RICK SPEARS
CHUCK BB
BLACK METAL
BOOK ONE

CROGANS
VENGEANCE
by Chris Schweizer

1
Vasilis Lolos
THE LAST CALL

NORTH WORLD

Polly and the Pirates
by Ted Naifeh

SCOTT PILGRIM'S
PRECIOUS LITTLE LIFE
VOL. 1
BRYAN LEE O'MALLEY

SIDESCROLLERS
MATTHEW LOUX

JAMES STOKOE

SUPER PRO K.O., VOLUME 1
By Jarrett Williams
264 pages, digest, B&W
$11.99 US • ISBN 978-1-934964-41-5

BLACK METAL
By Rick Spears & Chuck BB
160 pages, digest, B&W
$11.95 US • ISBN 978-1-932664-72-0

CROGAN'S VENGEANCE
By Chris Schweizer
192 pages, hardcover, B&W
$14.99 US • ISBN 978-1-934964-06-4

LAST CALL, VOLUME 1
By Vasilis Lolos
136 pages, digest, B&W
$11.95 US • ISBN 978-1-932664-69-0

NORTH WORLD, VOLUME 1: THE EPIC OF CONRAD
By Lars Brown
152 pages, digest, B&W
$11.95 US • ISBN 978-1-932664-91-1

POLLY AND THE PIRATES, VOLUME 1
By Ted Naifeh
176 pages, digest, B&W
$11.95 US • ISBN 978-1-932664-46-1

SCOTT PILGRIM, VOLUME 1: SCOTT PILGRIM'S PRECIOUS LITTLE LIFE
By Bryan Lee O'Malley
168 pages, digest, B&W
$11.99 US • ISBN 978-1-932664-08-9

SIDESCROLLERS
By Matthew Loux
216 pages, digest, B&W
$11.99 US • ISBN 978-1-932664-50-8

WONTON SOUP, VOLUME 1
By James Stokoe
200 pages, digest, B&W
$11.95 US • ISBN 978-1-932664-60-7

COMING IN 2012!

SUPER PRO K.O., Volume 3
By Jarrett Williams
264 pages, digest, B&W
$11.99 US • ISBN 978-1-934964-51-4

ONI PRESS

For more information on these and other fine Oni Press comic books and graphic novels, visit www.onipress.com. To find a comic specialty store in your area, call 1-888-COMICBOOK or visit www.comicshops.us.

www.onipress.com www.lunarboyland.com